The Ape's Wife
and Other Stories

The Ape's Wife
and Other Stories

CAITLÍN R. KIERNAN

Subterranean Press • 2013

First Edition

ISBN
978-1-59606-586-4

Subterranean Press
PO Box 190106
Burton, MI 48519

subterraneanpress.com
www.caitlinkiernan.com
greygirlbeast.livejournal.com
Twitter: @auntbeast

For Michael Zulli

I talk about the gods, I am an atheist. But I am an artist too, and therefore a liar. Distrust everything I say. I am telling the truth.

Ursula K. LeGuin,
Introduction to *The Left Hand of Darkness* (1976)

Table of Contents

Introduction

I.

I've never been much for one-note short story collections, dominated by any single sort of tale. As a kid, my favorite collections generally were those that displayed diversity, in mood and subject matter. These are among the books I grew up reading and read as a teen. For example, Ray Bradbury's *A Medicine for Melancholy* (1958) and Angela Carter's *Fireworks: Nine Profane Pieces* (1974). Shirley Jackson's *The Lottery and Other Stories* (1949), and Harlan Ellison's *The Beast That Shouted Love at the Heart of the World* (1969). The collected works of Ambrose Bierce and, H. P. Lovecraft, who was more capable of whimsy and Dunsanian fancies than most realize. When I sat down to compile this volume, looking back over my earlier and somewhat "themed" collections, I determined this book would, instead, present a wide range of the fantastic, a collection that wanders about Colonial New England cemeteries, then sets off for Mars. That is content, one page, with werewolvery and ghosts, then a few pages later it's busy with steam-driven cyborgs in the Wild West, before careening into a feminist/queer retelling of *Beowulf,* just prior to landing amid the intrigues of a demonic brothel in a 1945 Manhattan that won't be found in any history book.

I cannot help but feel that publishing, over the past several decades, has become more than ever determined to drive authors to specialize, rather than encouraging them explore and develop their potential *range.* This, in turn, trickles down to readers, who can become as hidebound as authors. Which is a loss, I think, for readers *and* for writers. Why would anyone wants to know 101 ways to prepare meatloaf, when they have an infinite variety of delicacies at their fingertips? We are what we cook, and what we eat, and, too, we are most certainly what we write and read.

II.

Back in July, during Readercon 23, Peter Straub and I were interviewed by Gary Wolfe and Jonathan Strahan. At some point during the interview, I was asked how – and why – I'm so prolific. The why part, that's simple. Because I haven't much choice. A working author who isn't a bestseller works (or is otherwise employed, or independently wealthy) and works nonstop, usually seven days a week, or the bills aren't paid. As to the how, that, I suppose comes by learning to ignore the exhaustion, the stress, illness, the routine that can become a grinding tedium no matter how much I might like what I'm doing. By learning that days off and vacations are only *very* rarely an option. Addictions help. As do insomnia and a deep well of ideas and characters, one that I live in constant fear of running dry.

The story from which this book's title takes its name was written and published in 2007. Since then, I've written (and sold) about one hundred short stories and novellas. Fourteen of them are collected herein. I believe they're thirteen of the best of the lot. I hope you will agree.

Caitlín R. Kiernan
17 December 2012
Providence, Rhode Island

LOCKE
'07

The Steam Dancer (1896)

1.

Missouri Banks lives in the great smoky city at the edge of the mountains, here where the endless yellow prairie laps gently with grassy waves and locust tides at the exposed bones of the world jutting suddenly up towards the western sky. She was not born here, but came to the city long ago, when she was still only a small child and her father traveled from town to town in one of Edison's electric wagons selling his herbs and medicinals, his stinking poultices and elixirs. This is the city where her mother grew suddenly ill with miner's fever, and where all her father's liniments and ministrations could not restore his wife's failing health or spare her life. In his grief, he drank a vial of either antimony or arsenic a few days after the funeral, leaving his only daughter and only child to fend for herself. And so, she grew up here, an orphan, one of a thousand or so dispossessed urchins with sooty bare feet and sooty faces, filching coal with sooty hands to stay warm in winter, clothed in rags, and eating what could be found in trash barrels and what could be begged or stolen.

But these things are only her past, and she has a bit of paper torn from a lending-library book of old plays which reads *What's past is prologue,* which she tacked up on the wall near her dressing mirror in the room she shares with the mechanic. Whenever the weight of Missouri's past begins to press in upon her, she reads those words aloud to herself, once or twice or however many times is required, and usually it makes her feel at least a little better. It has been years since she was alone and on the streets. She has the mechanic, and he loves her, and most of the time she believes that she loves him, as well.

He found her when she was nineteen, living in a shanty on the edge of the colliers' slum, hiding away in among the spoil piles and the rusting ruin of junked steam shovels and hydraulic pumps and bent bore-drill heads. He was out looking for salvage, and salvage is what he found, finding her when he lifted a broad sheet of corrugated tin, uncovering the squalid burrow where she lay slowly dying on a filthy mattress. She'd been badly bitten during a swarm of red-bellied bloatflies, and now the hungry white maggots were doing their work. It was not an uncommon fate for the likes of Missouri Banks, those caught out in the open during the spring swarms, those without safe houses to hide inside until the voracious flies had come and gone, moving on to bedevil other towns and cities and farms. By the time the mechanic chanced upon her, Missouri's left leg, along with her right hand and forearm, was gangrenous, seething with the larvae. Her left eye was a pulpy, painful boil, and he carried her to the charity hospital on Arapahoe where he paid the surgeons who meticulously picked out the parasites and sliced away the rotten flesh and finally performed the necessary amputations. Afterwards, the mechanic nursed her back to health, and when she was well enough, he fashioned for her a new leg and a new arm. The eye was entirely beyond his expertise, but he knew a Chinaman in San Francisco who did nothing but eyes and ears, and it happened that the Chinaman owed the mechanic a favour. And in this way was Missouri Banks made whole again, after a fashion, and the mechanic took her as his lover and then as his wife, and they found a better, roomier room in an upscale boarding house near the Seventh Avenue irrigation works.

And today, which is the seventh day of July, she settles onto the little bench in front of the dressing-table mirror and reads aloud to herself the shred of paper.

"What's past is prologue," she says, and then sits looking at her face and the artificial eye and listening to the oppressive drone of cicadas outside the open window. The mechanic has promised that someday he will read her *The Tempest* by William Shakespeare, which he says is where the line was taken from. She can read it herself, she's told him, because she isn't illiterate. But the truth is she'd much prefer to hear him read, breathing out the words in his rough, soothing voice, and often he does read to her in the evenings.

She thinks that she has grown to be a very beautiful woman, and sometimes she believes the parts she wasn't born with have only served to make her that much more so and not any the less. Missouri smiles and gazes back at her reflection, admiring the high cheekbones and full lips (which were her mother's before her), the glistening beads of sweat on her chin and forehead and upper lip, the way her left eye pulses with a soft turquoise radiance. Afternoon light glints off the Galvanized plating of her mechanical arm, the sculpted steel rods and struts, the well-oiled wheels and cogs, all the rivets and welds and perfectly fitted joints. For now, it hangs heavy and limp at her side, because she hasn't yet cranked it's tiny double-acting Trevithick engine. There's only the noise of the cicadas and the traffic down on the street and the faint, familiar, comforting chug of her leg.

Other women are only whole, she thinks. *Other women are only born, not made. I have been crafted.*

With her living left hand, Missouri wipes some of the sweat from her face and then turns towards the small electric fan perched on the chifforobe. It hardly does more than stir the muggy summer air about, and she thinks how good it would be to go back to bed. How good to spend the whole damned day lying naked on cool sheets, dozing and dreaming and waiting for the mechanic to come home from the foundry. But she dances at Madam Ling's place four days a week, and today is one of those days, so soon she'll have to get dressed and start her arm, then make her way to the trolley and on down to the Asian Quarter. The mechanic didn't want her to work, but she told him she owed him a great debt and it would be far kinder of him to allow her to repay it. And, being kind, he knew she was telling the truth. Sometimes, he even comes down to see, to sit among the coolies and the pungent clouds of opium smoke and watch her on the stage.

2.

The shrewd old woman known in the city only as Madam Ling made the long crossing to America sometime in 1861, shortly after the end of the Second Opium War. Missouri has heard that she garnered a tidy fortune from smuggling and piracy, and maybe a bit of murder, too, but that she found Hong Kong considerably less amenable to her business ventures after the treaty that ended the war and legalized the import of opium to China. She came ashore in San Francisco and followed the railroads and airships east across the Rockies, and when she reached the city at the edge of the prairie, she went no farther. She opened a saloon and whorehouse, the Nine Dragons, on a muddy, unnamed thoroughfare, and the mechanic has explained to Missouri that in China nine is considered a very lucky number. The Nine Dragons is wedged in between a hotel and a gambling house, and no matter the time of day or night seems always just as busy. Madam Ling never wants for trade.

Missouri always undresses behind the curtain, before she takes the stage, and so presents herself to the sleepy-eyed men wearing only a fringed shawl of vermilion silk, her corset and sheer muslin shift, her white linen pantalettes. The shawl was a gift from Madam Ling, who told her in broken English that it came all the way from Beijing. Madam Ling of the Nine Dragons is not renowned for her generosity towards white women, or much of anyone else, and Missouri knows the gift was a reward for the men who come here just to watch her. She does not have many belongings, but she treasures the shawl as one of her most prized possessions and keeps it safe in a cedar chest at the foot of the bed she shares with the mechanic, and it always smells of the camphor-soaked cotton balls she uses to keep the moths at bay.

There is no applause, but she knows that most eyes have turned her way now. She stands sweating in the flickering gaslight glow, the open flames that ring the small stage, and listens to the men muttering in Mandarin amongst themselves and laying down mahjong tiles and sucking at their pipes. And then her music begins, the negro piano player and the woman who plucks so proficiently at a guzheng's twenty-five strings, the thin man at his xiao flute, and the burly Irishman who keeps the beat on a goatskin bodhrán and always takes his pay in celestial whores. The smoky air fills with a peculiar, jangling rendition of the final aria of Verdi's *La traviata,* because Madam Ling is a great admirer of Italian opera. The four musicians huddle together, occupying the space that has been set aside especially for them, crammed between the bar and the stage, and Missouri breathes in deeply, taking her cues as much from the reliable metronome rhythms of the engines that drive her metal leg and arm as from the music.

This is her time, her moment as truly as any moment will ever belong to Missouri Banks.

And her dance is not what men might see in the white saloons and dance halls and brothels strung out along Broadway and Lawrence, not the schottisches and waltzes of the ladies of the line, the uptown sporting women in their fine ruffled skirts made in New Amsterdam and Chicago. No one has ever taught Missouri how to dance, and these are only the moves that come naturally to her, that she finds for herself. This is the interplay and synthesis of her body and the mechanic's handiwork, of the music and her own secret dreams. Her clothes fall away in gentle, inevitable drifts, like the first snows of October. Steel toe to flesh-and-bone heel, the graceful arch of an iron calf and the clockwork motion of porcelain and nickel fingers across her sweaty belly and thighs. She spins and sways and dips, as lissome and sure of herself as anything that was ever only born of Nature. And there is such joy in the dance that she might almost offer prayers of thanks to her suicide father and the bloatfly maggots that took her leg and arm and eye. There is such joy in the dancing, it might almost match the delight and peace she's found in the arms of the mechanic. There is such joy, and she thinks this is why some men and women turn to drink and laudanum, tinctures of morphine and Madam Ling's black tar, because they cannot dance.

The music rises and falls, like the seas of grass rustling to themselves out beyond the edges of the city, and the delicate mechanisms of her prosthetics clank and hum and whine. Missouri weaves herself through this landscape of sound with the easy dexterity of pronghorn antelope and deer fleeing the jaws of wolves or the hunters' rifles, the long haunches and fleet paws of jackrabbits running out before a wildfire. For this moment, she is lost, and, for this moment, she wishes never to be found again. Soon, the air has begun to smell of the steam leaking from the exhaust ports in her leg and arm, an oily, hot sort of aroma that is as sweet to Missouri Banks as rosewater or honeysuckle blossoms. She closes her eyes – the one she was born with and the one from San Francisco – and feels no shame whatsoever at the lazy stares of the opium smokers. The piston rods in her left leg pump something more alive than blood, and the flywheels turn on their axels. She is muscle and skin, steel and artifice. She is the woman who was once a filthy, ragged guttersnipe, and she is Madam Ling's special attraction, a wondrous child of Terpsichore and Industry. Once she overheard the piano player whispering to the Irishman, and he said, "You'd think she emerged outta her momma's womb like that," and then there was a joke about screwing automata and the offspring that could ensue. But, however it might have been meant, she took it as praise and confirmation.

Too soon the music ends, leaving her gasping and breathless, dripping sweat and an iridescent sheen of lubricant onto the boards, and she must sit in her room backstage and wait out another hour before her next dance.

3.

And after the mechanic has washed away the day's share of grime and they're finished with their modest supper of apple pie and beans with thick slices of bacon, after his evening cigar and her cup of strong black Indian tea, after all the little habits and rituals of their nights together are done, he follows her to bed. The mechanic sits down and the springs squeak like stepped-on mice; he leans back against the tarnished brass headboard, smiling his easy, disarming smile while she undresses. When she slips the stocking off her right leg, he sees the gauze bandage wrapped about her knee, and his smile fades to concern.

"Here," he says. "What's that? What happened there?" and he points at her leg.

"It's nothing," she tells him. "It's nothing much."

"That seems an awful lot of dressing for nothing much. Did you fall?"

"I didn't fall," she replies. "I never fall."

"Of course not," he says. "Only us mere mortal folk fall. Of course you didn't fall. So what is it? It ain't the latest goddamn fashion."

Missouri drapes her stocking across the footboard, which is also brass, and turns her head to frown at him over her shoulder.

"A burn," she says, "that's all. One of Madam Ling's girls patched it for me. It's nothing to worry over."

"How bad a burn?"

"I said it's nothing, didn't I?"

"You did," says the mechanic and nods his head, looking not the least bit convinced. "But that secondary sliding valve's leaking again, and that's what did it. Am I right?"

Missouri turns back to her bandaged knee, wishing that there'd been some way to hide it from him, because she doesn't feel like him fussing over her tonight. "It doesn't hurt much at all. Madam Ling had a salve – "

"Haven't I been telling you that seal needs to be replaced?"

"I know you have."

"Well, you just stay in tomorrow, and I'll take that leg with me to the shop, get it fixed up tip-top again. Have it back before you know it."

"It's *fine.* I already patched it. It'll hold."

"Until the *next* time," he says, and she knows well enough from the tone of his voice that he doesn't want to argue with her about this, that he's losing patience. "You go and let that valve blow out, and you'll be needing a good deal more doctoring than a chink whore can provide. There's a lot of pressure builds up inside those pistons. You know that, Missouri."

"Yeah, I know that," she says.

"Sometimes you don't *act* like you know it."

"I can't stay in tomorrow. But I'll let you take it the next day, I swear. I'll stay in Thursday, and you can take my leg then."

"Thursday," the mechanic grumbles. "And so I just gotta keep my fingers crossed until then?"

"It'll be fine," she tells him again, trying to sound reassuring and reasonable, trying not to let the bright rind of panic show in her voice. "I won't push so hard. I'll stick to the slow dances."

And then a long and disagreeable sort of silence settles over the room, and for a time she sits there at the edge of the bed, staring at both her legs, at injured meat and treacherous, unreliable metal. *Machines break down,* she thinks, *and the flesh is weak. Ain't nothing yet conjured by God nor man won't go and turn against you, sooner or later.* Missouri sighs and lightly presses a porcelain thumb to the artificial leg's green release switch; there's a series of dull clicks and pops as it comes free of the bolts set directly into her pelvic bones.

"I'll stay in tomorrow," she says and sets her left leg into its stand near the foot of their bed. "I'll send word to Madam Ling. She'll understand."

When the mechanic doesn't tell her that it's really for the best, when he doesn't say anything at all, she looks and sees he's dozed off sitting up, still wearing his trousers and suspenders and undershirt. "You," she says quietly, then reaches for the release switch on her right arm.

4.

When she feels his hands on her, Missouri thinks at first that this is only some new direction her dream has taken, the rambling dream of her father's medicine wagon and of buffalo, of rutted roads and a flaxen Nebraska sky filled with flocks of automatic birds chirping arias from *La traviata.* But there's something substantial about the pale light of the waxing moon falling though the open window and the way the curtains move in the midnight breeze that convinces her she's awake. Then he kisses her, and one hand wanders down across her breasts and stomach and lingers in the unruly thatch of hair between her legs.

"Unless maybe you got something better to be doing," he mutters in her ear.

"Well, now that you mention it, I *was* dreaming," she tells him, "before you woke me up," and the mechanic laughs.

"Then maybe I should let you get back to it," but when he starts to take his hand away from her privy parts, she takes hold of it and rubs his fingertips across her labia.

"So, what exactly were you dreaming about that's got you in such a cooperative mood, Miss Missouri Banks?" he asks and kisses her again, the dark stubble on his cheeks scratching at her face.

"Wouldn't you like to know," she says.

"I figure that's likely why I inquired."

His face is washed in the soft blue-green glow of her San Francisco eye, which switched on as soon as she awoke, and times like this it's hard not to imagine all the ways her life might have gone but didn't, how very unlikely that it went this way, instead. And she starts to tell him the truth, her dream of being a little girl and all the manufactured birds, the shaggy herds of bison, and how her father kept insisting he should give up peddling his herbs and remedies and settle down somewhere. But at the last, and for no particular reason, she changes her mind, and Missouri tells him another dream, just something she makes up off the top of her sleep-blurred head.

"You might not like it," she says.

"Might not," he agrees. "Then again, you never know," and the first joint of an index finger slips inside her.

"Then again," she whispers, and so she tells him a dream she's never dreamt. How there was a terrible fire and before it was over and done with, the flames had claimed half the city, there where the grass ends and the mountains start. And at first, she tells him, it was an awful, awful dream, because she was trapped in the boarding house when it burned, and she could see him down on the street, calling for her, but, try as they may, they could not reach each other.

"Why you want to go and have a dream like that for?" he asks.

"You wanted to hear it. Now shut up and listen."

So he does as he's bidden, and she describes to him seeing an enormous airship hovering above the flames, spewing its load of water and sand into the ravenous inferno.

"There might have been a dragon," she says. "Or it might have only been started by lightning."

"A dragon," he replies, working his finger in a little deeper. "Yes, I think it must definitely have been a dragon. They're so ill-tempered this time of year."

"Shut up. This is my dream," she tells him, even though it isn't. "I almost died, so much of me got burned away, and they had me scattered about in pieces in the Charity Hospital. But you went right to work, putting me back together again. You worked night and day at the shop, making me a pretty metal face and a tin heart, and you built my breasts – "

" – from sterling silver," he says. "And your nipples I fashioned from out pure gold."

"And just how the sam hell did you know *that*?" she grins. Then Missouri reaches down and moves his hand, slowly pulling his finger out of her. Before he can protest, she's laid his palm over the four bare bolts where her leg fits on. He smiles and licks at her nipples, then grips one of the bolts and gives it a very slight tug.

"Well, while you were sleeping," he says, "I made a small window in your skull, only just large enough that I can see inside. So, no more secrets. But don't you fret. I expect your hair will hide it quite completely. Madam Ling will never even notice, and nary a Chinaman will steal a glimpse of your sweet, darling brain."

"Why, I never even felt a thing."

"I was very careful not to wake you."

"Until you did."

And then the talk is done, without either of them acknowledging that the time has come, and there's no more of her fiery, undreamt dreams or his glib comebacks. There's only the mechanic's busy, eager hands upon her, only her belly pressed against his, the grind of their hips after he has entered her, his fingertips lingering at the sensitive bolts where her prosthetics attach. She likes that best of all, that faint electric tingle, and she knows *he* knows, though she has never had to tell him so. Outside and far away, she thinks she hears an owl, but there are no owls in the city.

5.

And when she wakes again, the boarding-house room is filled with the dusty light of a summer morning. The mechanic is gone, and he's taken her leg with him. Her crutches are leaned against the wall near her side of the bed. She stares at them for a while, wondering how long it's been since the last time she had to use them, then deciding it doesn't really matter, because however long it's been, it hasn't been long enough. There's a note, too, on her nightstand, and the mechanic says not to worry about Madam Ling, that he'll send one of the boys from the foundry down to the Asian Quarter with the news. Take it easy, he says. Let that burn heal. Burns can be bad. Burns can scar, if you don't look after them.

When the clanging steeple bells of St. Margaret of Castello's have rung nine o'clock, she shuts her eyes and thinks about going back to sleep. St. Margaret, she recalls, is a patron saint of the crippled, an Italian woman who was born blind and hunchbacked, lame and malformed. Missouri envies the men and women who take comfort in those bells, who find in their tolling more than the time of day. She has never believed in the Catholic god or any other sort, unless perhaps it was some capricious heathen deity assigned to watch over starving, maggot-ridden guttersnipes. She imagines what form that god might assume, and it is a far more fearsome thing than any hunchbacked crone. A wolf, she thinks. Yes, an enormous black wolf – or coyote, perhaps – all ribs and mange and a distended, empty belly, crooked ivory fangs and burning eyes like smoldering embers glimpsed through a cast-iron grate. *That* would be her god, if ever she'd had been blessed with such a thing. Her mother had come from Presbyterian stock somewhere back in Virginia, but her father believed in nothing more powerful than the hand of man, and he was not about to have his child's head filled up with Protestant superstition and nonsense, not in a Modern age of science and enlightenment.

Missouri opens her eyes again, her green eye – all cornea and iris, aqueous and vitreous humours – and the ersatz one designed for her in San Francisco. The crutches are still right there, near enough that she could reach out and touch them. They have good sheepskin padding and the vulcanized rubber tips have pivots and are filled with some shock-absorbing gelatinous substance, the name of which she has been told but cannot recall. The mechanic ordered them for her special from a company in some faraway Prussian city, and she knows they cost more than he could rightly afford, but she hates them anyway. And lying on the sweat-damp sheets, smelling the hazy morning air rustling the gingham curtains, she wonders if she built a little shrine to the wolf god of all collier guttersnipes, if maybe he would come in the night and take the crutches away so she would never have to see them again.

"It's not that simple, Missouri," she says aloud, and she thinks that those could have been her father's words, if the theosophists are right and the dead might ever speak through the mouths of the living.

"Leave me alone, old man" she says and sits up. "Go back to the grave you yearned for, and leave me be."

Her arm is waiting for her at the foot of the bed, right where she left it the night before, reclining in its cradle, next to the empty space her leg *ought* to occupy. And the hot breeze through the window, the street- and coal smoke-scented breeze, causes the scrap of paper tacked up by her vanity mirror to flutter against the wall. Her proverb, her precious stolen scrap of Shakespeare. *What's past is prologue.*

Missouri Banks considers how she can keep herself busy until the mechanic comes back to her – a torn shirt sleeve that needs mending, and she's no slouch with a needle and thread. Her good stockings could use a rinsing. The dressing on her leg should be changed; Madam Ling saw to it she had a small tin of the pungent salve to reapply when Missouri changed the bandages. Easily half a dozen such mundane tasks, any woman's work, any woman who is not a dancer, and nothing that won't wait until the bells of St. Margaret's ring ten or eleven. And so she watches the window, the sunlight and flapping gingham, and it isn't difficult to call up with almost perfect clarity the piano and the guzheng and the Irishman thumping his bodhrán, the exotic, festive trill of the xiao. And with the music swelling loudly inside her skull, she can then recall the dance. And she is not a cripple in need of patron saints or a guttersnipe praying to black wolf gods, but Madam Ling's specialty, the steam- and blood-powered gem of the Nine Dragons. She moves across the boards, and men watch her with dark and drowsy eyes as she pirouettes and prances through grey opium clouds.

The Maltese Unicorn

New York City (May 1935)

It wasn't hard to find her. Sure, she had run. After Szabó let her walk like that, I knew Ellen would get wise that something was rotten, and she'd run like a scared rabbit with the dogs hot on its heels. She'd have it in her head to skip town, and she'd probably keep right on skipping until she was out of the country. Odds were pretty good she wouldn't stop until she was altogether free and clear of this particular plane of existence. There are plenty enough fetid little hidey holes in the universe, if you don't mind the heat and the smell and the company you keep. You only have to know how to find them, and the way I saw it, Ellen Andrews was good as Rand and McNally when it came to knowing her way around.

But first, she'd go back to that apartment of hers, the whole eleventh floor of the Colosseum, with its bleak westward view of the Hudson River and the New Jersey Palisades. I figured there would be those two or three little things she couldn't leave the city without, even if it meant risking her skin to collect them. Only she hadn't expected me to get there before her. Word on the street was Harpootlian still had me locked up tight, so Ellen hadn't expected me to get there at all.

From the hall came the buzz of the elevator, then I heard her key in the lock, the front door, and her footsteps as she hurried through the foyer and the dining room. Then she came dashing into that French Rococo nightmare of a library, and stopped cold in her tracks when she saw me sitting at the reading table with al-Jaldaki's grimoire open in front of me.

For a second, she didn't say anything. She just stood there, staring at me. Then she managed a forced sort of laugh and said, "I knew they'd send someone, Nat. I just didn't think it'd be you."

"After that gip you pulled with the dingus, they didn't really leave me much choice," I told her, which was the truth, or all the truth I felt like sharing. "You shouldn't have come back here. It's the first place anyone would think to check."

Ellen sat down in the arm chair by the door. She looked beat, like whatever comes after exhausted, and I could tell Szabó's gunsels had made sure all the fight was gone before they'd turned her loose. They weren't taking any chances, and we were just going through the motions now, me and her. All our lines had been written.

"You played me for a sucker," I said, and picked up the pistol that had been lying beside the grimoire. My hand was shaking, and I tried to steady it by bracing my elbow against the table. "You played me, then you tried to play Harpootlian and Szabó both. Then you got caught. It was a bonehead move all the way round, Ellen."

"So, how's it gonna be, Natalie? You gonna shoot me for being stupid?"

"No, I'm going shoot you because it's the only way I can square things with Auntie H, and the only thing that's gonna keep Szabó from going on the warpath. *And* because you played me."

"In my shoes, you'd have done the same thing," she said. And the way she said it, I could tell she believed what she was saying. It's the sort of self-righteous bushwa so many grifters hide behind. They might stab their own mothers in the back if they see an angle in it, but, you ask them, that's jake, cause so would anyone else.

"Is that really all you have to say for yourself?" I asked, and pulled back the slide on the Colt, chambering the first round. She didn't even flinch...but, wait...I'm getting ahead of myself. Maybe I ought to begin nearer the beginning.

As it happens, I didn't go and name the place Yellow Dragon Books. It came with that moniker, and I just never saw any reason to change it. I'd only have had to pay for a new sign. Late in '28 – right after Arnie "The Brain" Rothstein was shot to death during a poker game at the Park Central Hotel – I accidentally found myself on the sunny side of the proprietress of one of Manhattan's more infernal brothels. I say *accidentally* because I hadn't even heard of Madam Yeksabet Harpootlian when I began trying to dig up a buyer for an antique manuscript, a collection of necromantic erotica purportedly written by John Dee and Edward Kelley some time in the Sixteenth Century. Turns out, Harpootlian had been looking to get her mitts on it for decades.

Now, just how I came into possession of said manuscript, that's another story entirely, one for some other time and place. One that, with luck, I'll never get around to putting down on paper. Let's just say a couple of years earlier, I'd been living in Paris. Truthfully, I'd been doing my best, in a sloppy, irresolute way, to *die* in Paris. I was holed up in a fleabag Montmartre boarding house, busy squandering the last of a dwindling inheritance. I had in mind how maybe I could drown myself in cheap wine, bad poetry, Pernod, and prostitutes before the money ran out. But somewhere along the way, I lost my nerve, failed at my slow suicide, and bought a ticket back to the States. And the manuscript in question was one of the many strange and unsavory things I brought back with me. I'd always had a nose for the macabre, and had dabbled – on and off – in the black arts since college. At Radcliffe, I'd fallen in with a circle of lesbyterians who fancied themselves witches. Mostly, I was in it for the sex…but I'm digressing.

A friend of a friend heard I was busted, down and out and peddling a bunch of old books, schlepping them about Manhattan in search of a buyer. This same friend, he knew one of Harpootlian's clients. One of her *human* clients, which was a pretty exclusive set (not that I knew that at the time). This friend of mine, he was the client's lover, and said client brokered the sale for Harpootlian – for a fat ten-percent finder's fee, of course. I promptly sold the Dee and Kelly manuscript to this supposedly notorious madam whom, near as I could tell, no one much had ever heard of. She paid me what I asked, no questions, no haggling, never mind it was a fairly exorbitant sum. And on top of that, Harpootlian was so impressed I'd gotten ahold of the damned thing, she staked me to the bookshop on Bowery, there in the shadow of the Third Avenue El, just a little ways south of Delancey Street. Only one catch: she had first dibs on everything I ferreted out, and sometimes I'd be asked to make deliveries. I should like to note that way back then, during that long, lost November of 1928, I had no idea whatsoever that her sobriquet, "the Demon Madam of the Lower East Side," was anything more than colorful hyperbole.

Anyway, jump ahead to a rainy May afternoon, more than six years later, and that's when I first laid eyes on Ellen Andrews. Well, that's what she called herself, though later on I'd find out she'd borrowed the name from Claudette Colbert's character in *It Happened One Night.* I was just back from an estate sale in Connecticut and was busy unpacking a large crate when I heard the bell mounted above the shop door jingle. I looked up, and there she was, carelessly shaking rainwater from her orange umbrella before folding it closed. Droplets sprayed across the welcome mat and the floor and onto the spines of several nearby books.

"Hey, be careful," I said, "unless you intend to pay for those." I jabbed a thumb at the books she'd spattered. She promptly stopped shaking the umbrella and dropped it into the stand beside the door. That umbrella stand has always been one of my favorite things about the Yellow Dragon. It's made from the taxidermied foot of a hippopotamus and accommodates at least a dozen umbrellas, although I don't think I've ever seen even half that many people in the shop at one time.

"Are you Natalie Beaumont?" she asked, looking down at her wet shoes. Her overcoat was dripping, and a small puddle was forming about her feet.

"Usually."

"Usually," she repeated. "How about right now?"

"Depends whether or not I owe you money," I replied, and removed a battered copy of Blavatsky's *Isis Unveiled* from the crate. "Also, depends whether you happen to be *employed* by someone I owe money."

"I see," she said, as if that settled the matter, then proceeded to examine the complete twelve-volume set of *The Golden Bough* occupying a top shelf not far from the door. "Awful funny sort of neighborhood for a bookstore, if you ask me."

"You don't think bums and winos read?"

"You ask me, people down here," she said, "they panhandle a few cents, I don't imagine they spend it on books."

"I don't recall asking for your opinion" I told her.

"No," she said. "You didn't. Still, queer sort of a shop to come across in this part of town."

"If you must know," I said, "the rent's cheap," then reached for my spectacles, which were dangling from their silver chain about my neck. I set them on the bridge of my nose, and watched while she feigned interest in Frazerian anthropology. It would be an understatement to say Ellen Andrews was a pretty girl. She was, in fact, a certified knockout, and I didn't get too many beautiful women in the Yellow Dragon, even when the weather was good. She wouldn't have looked out of place in Flo Ziegfeld's follies; on the Bowery, she stuck out like a sore thumb.

"Looking for anything in particular?" I asked her, and she shrugged.

"Just you," she said.

"Then I suppose you're in luck."

"I suppose I am," she said and turned towards me again. Her eyes glinted red, just for an instant, like the eyes of a Siamese cat. I figured it for a trick of the light. "I'm a friend of Auntie H I run errands for her, now and then. She needs you to pick up a package and see it gets safely where its going."

So, there it was. Madam Harpootlian, or Auntie H to those few unfortunates she called her friends. And suddenly it made a lot more sense, this choice bit of calico walking into my place, strolling in off the street like maybe she did all her shopping down on Skid Row. I'd have to finish unpacking the crate later. I stood up and dusted my hands off on the seat of my slacks.

"Sorry about the confusion," I said, even if I wasn't actually sorry, even if I was actually kind of pissed the girl hadn't told me who she was right up front. "When Auntie H wants something done, she doesn't usually bother sending her orders around in such an attractive envelope."

The girl laughed, then said, "Yeah, Auntie H warned me about you, Miss Beaumont."

"Did she now. How so?"

"You know, your predilections. How you're not like other women."

"I'd say that depends on which other women we're discussing, don't you think?"

"*Most* other women," she said, glancing over her shoulder at the rain pelting the shop windows. It sounded like frying meat out there, the sizzle of the rain against asphalt, and concrete, and the roofs of passing automobiles.

"And what about you?" I asked her. "Are *you* like most other women?"

She looked away from the window, looking back at me, and she smiled what must have been the faintest smile possible.

"Are you always this charming?"

"Not that I'm aware of," I said. "Then again, I never took a poll."

"The job, it's nothing particularly complicated," she said, changing the subject. "There's a Chinese apothecary not too far from here."

"That doesn't exactly narrow it down," I said and lit a cigarette.

"Sixty-five Mott Street. The joint's run by an elderly Cantonese fellow name of Fong."

"Yeah, I know Jimmy Fong."

"That's good. Then maybe you won't get lost. Mr. Fong will be expecting you, and he'll have the package ready at five-thirty this evening. He's already been paid in full, so all you have to do is be there to receive it, right? And Miss Beaumont, please try to be on time. Auntie H said you have a problem with punctuality."

"You believe everything you hear?"

"Only if I'm hearing it from Auntie H."

"Fair enough," I told her, then offered her a Pall Mall, but she declined.

"I need to be getting back," she said, reaching for the umbrella she'd only just deposited in the stuffed hippopotamus foot.

"What's the rush? What'd you come after, anyway, a ball of fire?"

She rolled her eyes. "I got places to be. You're not the only stop on my itinerary."

"Fine. Wouldn't want you getting in dutch with Harpootlian on my account. Don't suppose you've got a name?"

"I might," she said.

"Don't suppose you'd share?" I asked her, and took a long drag on my cigarette, wondering why in blue blazes Harpootlian had sent this smart-mouthed skirt instead of one of her usual flunkies. Of course, Auntie H always did have a sadistic streak to put de Sade to shame, and likely as not this was her idea of a joke.

"Ellen," the girl said. "Ellen Andrews."

"So, Ellen Andrews, how is it we've never met? I mean, I've been making deliveries for your boss lady now going on seven years, and if I'd seen you, I'd remember. You're not the sort I forget."

"You got the moxie, don't you?"

"I'm just good with faces is all."

She chewed at a thumbnail, as if considering carefully what she should or shouldn't divulge. Then she said, "I'm from out of town, mostly. Just passing through, and thought I'd lend a hand. That's why you've never seen me before, Miss Beaumont. Now, I'll let you get back to work. And remember, don't be late."

"I heard you the first time, sister."

And then she left, and the brass bell above the door jingled again. I finished my cigarette and went back to unpacking the big crate of books from Connecticut. If I hurried, I could finish the job before heading for Chinatown.

She was right, of course. I did have a well-deserved reputation for not being on time. But I knew that Auntie H was of the opinion that my acumen in antiquarian and occult matters more than compensated for my not infrequent tardiness. I've never much cared for personal mottos, but maybe if I had one it might be, *You want it on time, or you want it done right?* Still, I honestly tried to be on time for the meeting with Fong. And still, through no fault of my own, I was more than twenty minutes late. I was lucky enough to find a cab, despite the rain, but then got stuck behind some sort of brouhaha after turning onto Canal, so there you go. It's not like the old man Fong had any place more pressing to be, not like he was gonna get pissy and leave me high and dry.

When I got to Sixty-Five Mott, the Chinaman's apothecary was locked up tight, all the lights were off, and the "Sorry, We're Closed" sign was hung in the front window. No big surprise there. But then I went around back, to the alley, and found a door standing wide open and quite a lot of fresh blood on the cinderblock steps leading into the building. Now, maybe I was the only lady bookseller in Manhattan who carried a gun, and maybe I wasn't. But times like that, I was glad to have the Colt tucked snugly inside its shoulder holster, and happier still that I knew how to use it. I took a deep breath, drew the pistol, flipped off the safety catch, and stepped inside.

The door opened onto a stockroom, and the tiny nook Jimmy Fong used as his office was a little farther in, over on my left. There was some light from a bankers lamp, but not much of it. I lingered in the shadows a moment, waiting for my heart to stop pounding, for the adrenaline high to fade. The air was close, and stunk of angelica root and dust, ginger and frankincense and fuck only knows what else. Powdered rhino horn and the pickled gallbladders of panda bears. What the hell ever. I found the old man slumped over at his desk.

Whoever knifed him hadn't bothered to pull the shiv out of his spine, and I wondered if the poor s.o.b. had even seen it coming. It didn't exactly add up, not after seeing all that blood back on the steps, but I figured, hey, maybe the killer was the sort of klutz can't spread butter without cutting himself. I had a quick look-see around the cluttered office, hoping I might turn up the package Ellen Andrews had sent me there to retrieve. But no dice, and then it occurred to me, maybe whoever had murdered Fong had come looking for the same thing I was looking for. Maybe they'd found it, too, only Fong knew better than to just hand it over, and that had gotten him killed. Anyway, nobody was paying me to play junior shamus, hence the hows, whys, and wherefores of the Chinaman's death were not my problem. *My* problem would be showing up at Harpootlian's cathouse empty handed.

I returned the gun to its holster, then I started rifling through everything in sight – the great disarray of papers heaped upon the desk, Fong's accounting ledgers, sales invoices, catalogs, letters and postcards written in English, Mandarin, Wu, Cantonese, French, Spanish, and Arabic. I still had my gloves on, so it's not like I had to worry over fingerprints. A few of the desk drawers were unlocked, and I'd just started in on those, when the phone perched atop the filing cabinet rang. I froze, whatever I was looking at clutched forgotten in my hands, and stared at the phone.

Sure, it wasn't every day I blundered into the immediate aftermath of this sort of foul play, but I was plenty savvy enough I knew better than to answer that call. It didn't much matter who was on the other end of the line. If I answered, I could be placed at the scene of a murder only minutes after it had gone down. The phone rang a second time, and a third, and I glanced at the dead man in the chair. The crimson halo surrounding the switchblade's inlaid mother-of-pearl handle was still spreading, blossoming like some grim rose, and now there was blood dripping to the floor, as well. The phone rang a fourth time. A fifth. And then I was seized by an overwhelming compulsion to answer it, and answer it I did. I wasn't the least bit thrown that the voice coming through the receiver was Ellen Andrews'. All at once, the pieces were falling into place. You spend enough years doing the step-and-fetch-it routine for imps like Harpootlian, you find yourself ever more jaded at the inexplicable and the uncanny.

"Beaumont," she said, "I didn't think you were going to pick up."

"I wasn't. Funny thing how I did anyway."

"Funny thing," she said, and I heard her light a cigarette and realized my hands were shaking.

"See, I'm thinking maybe I had a little push," I said. "That about the size of it?"

"Wouldn't have been necessary if you'd have just answered the damn phone in the first place."

"You already know Fong's dead, don't you?" And, I swear to fuck, nothing makes me feel like more of a jackass than asking questions I know the answers to.

"Don't you worry about Fong. I'm sure he had all his ducks in a row and was right as rain with Buddha. I need you to pay attention – "

"Harpootlian had him killed, didn't she? And you *knew* he'd be dead when I showed up." She didn't reply straight away, and I thought I could hear a radio playing in the background. "You knew," I said again, only this time it wasn't a query.

"Listen," she said. "You're a courier. I was told you're a courier we can trust, elsewise I never would have handed you this job."

"You didn't hand me the job. Your boss did."

"You're splitting hairs, Miss Beaumont."

"Yeah, well, there's a fucking dead celestial in the room with me. It's giving me the fidgets."

"So, how about you shut up and listen, and I'll have you out of there in a jiffy." And that's what I did, I shut up, either because I knew it was the path of least resistance, or because whatever spell she'd used to persuade me to answer the phone was still working.

"On Fong's desk, there's a funny little porcelain statue of a cat."

"You mean the Maneki Neko?"

"If that's what it's called, that's what I mean. Now, break it open. There's a key inside."

I *tried* not to, just to see if I was being played as badly as I suspected I was being played. I gritted my teeth, dug in my heels, and tried *hard* not to break that damned cat.

"You're wasting time. Auntie H didn't mention you were such a crybaby."

"Auntie H and I have an agreement when it comes to freewill. To *my* freewill."

"Break the goddamn cat," Ellen Andrews growled, and that's exactly what I did. In fact, I slammed it down directly on top of Fong's head. Bits of brightly painted porcelain flew everywhere, and a rusty barrel key tumbled out and landed at my feet. "Now pick it up," she said. "The key fits the bottom left-hand drawer of Fong's desk. Open it."

This time, I didn't even try to resist her. I was getting a headache from the last futile attempt. I unlocked the drawer and pulled it open. Inside, there was nothing but the yellowed sheet of newspaper lining the drawer, three golf balls, a couple of old racing forms, and a finely carved wooden box lacquered almost the same shade of red as Jimmy Fong's blood. I didn't need to be told I'd been sent to retrieve the box – or, more specifically, whatever was *inside* the box.

"Yeah, I got it," I told Ellen Andrews.

"Good girl. Now, you have maybe twelve minutes before the cops show. Go out the same way you came in." Then she gave me a Riverside Drive address, and said there'd be a car waiting for me at the corner of Canal and Mulberry, a green Chevrolet coupe. "Just give the driver that address. He'll see you get where you're going."

"Yeah," I said, sliding the desk drawer shut again and locking it. I pocketed the key. "But sister, you and me are gonna have a talk."

"Wouldn't miss it for the world, Nat," she said and hung up. I shut my eyes, wondering if I really had twelve minutes before the bulls arrived, and if they were even on their way, wondering what would happen if I endeavored *not* to make the rendezvous with the green coupe. I stood there, trying to decide whether Harpootlian would have gone back on her word and given this bitch permission to turn her hoodoo tricks on me, and if aspirin would do anything at all for the dull throb behind my eyes. Then I looked at Fong one last time, at the knife jutting out of his back, his thin grey hair powdered with porcelain dust from the shattered "Lucky Cat." And then I stopped asking questions and did as I'd been told.

The car was there, just like she'd told me it would be. There was a young colored man behind the wheel, and when I climbed in the back, he asked me where we were headed.

"I'm guessing Hell," I said, "sooner or later."

"Got that right," he laughed and winked at me from the rearview mirror. "But I was thinking more in terms of the immediate here and now."

So I recited the address I'd been given over the phone, 435 Riverside.

"That's the Colosseum," he said.

"It is if you say so," I replied. "Just get me there."

The driver nodded and pulled away from the curb. As he navigated the slick, wet streets, I sat listening to the rain against the Chevy's hard top and the music coming from the Motorola. In particular, I can remember hearing the Dorsey Brothers, "Chasing Shadows." I suppose you'd call that a harbinger, if you go in for that sort of thing. Me, I do my best not to. In this business, you start jumping at everything that *might* be an omen or a portent, you end up doing nothing else. Ironically, rubbing shoulders with the supernatural has made me a great believer in coincidence.

Anyway, the driver drove, the radio played, and I sat staring at the red lacquered box I'd stolen from a dead man's locked desk drawer. I thought it might be mahogany, but it was impossible to be sure, what with all that cinnabar-tinted varnish. I know enough about Chinese mythology that I recognized the strange creature carved into the top – a qilin, a stout, antlered beast with cloven hooves, the scales of a dragon, and a long leonine tail. Much of its body was wreathed in flame, and its gaping jaws revealed teeth like daggers. For the Chinese, the qilin is a harbinger of good fortune, though it certainly hadn't worked out that way for Jimmy Fong. The box was heavier than it looked, most likely because of whatever was stashed inside. There was no latch, and as I examined it more closely, I realized there was no sign whatsoever of hinges or even a seam to indicate it actually had a lid.

"Unless I got it backwards," the driver said, "Miss Andrews didn't say nothing about trying to open that box, now did she?"

I looked up, startled, feeling like the proverbial kid caught with her hand in the cookie jar. He glanced at me in the mirror, then his eyes drifted back to the road.

"She didn't say one way or the other," I told him.

"Then how about we err on the side of caution?"

"So you didn't know where you're taking me, but you know I shouldn't open this box? How's that work?"

"Ain't the world just full of mysteries," he said.

For a minute or so, I silently watched the headlights of the oncoming traffic and the metronomic sweep of the windshield wipers. Then I asked the driver how long he'd worked for Ellen Andrews.

"Not very," he said. "Never laid eyes on the lady before this afternoon. Why you want to know?"

"No particular reason," I said, looking back down at the box and the qilin etched in the wood. I decided I was better off not asking any more questions, better off getting this over and done with, and never mind what did and didn't quite add up. "Just trying to make conversation, that all."

Which got him to talking about the Chicago stockyards and Cleveland and how it was he'd eventually wound up in New York City. He never told me his name, and I didn't ask. The trip uptown seemed to take forever, and the longer I sat with that box in my lap, the heavier it felt. I finally moved it, putting it down on the seat beside me. By the time we reached our destination, the rain had stopped and the setting sun was showing through the clouds, glittering off the dripping trees in Riverside Park and the waters of the wide grey Hudson. He pulled over, and I reached for my wallet.

"No ma'am," he said, shaking his head. "Miss Andrews, she's already seen to your fare."

"Then I hope you won't mind if I see to your tip," I said, and I gave him five dollars. He thanked me, and I took the wooden box and stepped out onto the wet sidewalk.

"She's up on the eleventh," he told me, nodding towards the apartments. Then he drove off, and I turned to face the imposing brick and limestone façade of the building the driver had called the Colosseum. I rarely find myself any farther north than the Upper West Side, so this was pretty much *terra incognita* for me.

The doorman gave me directions, *after* giving both me and Fong's box the hairy eyeball, and I quickly made my way to the elevators, hurrying through that ritzy marble sepulcher passing itself off as a lobby. When the operator asked which floor I needed, I told him the eleventh, and he shook his head and muttered something under his breath. I almost asked him to speak up, but thought better of it. Didn't I already have plenty enough on my mind without entertaining the opinions of elevator boys? Sure, I did. I had a murdered Chinaman, a mysterious box, and this pushy little sorceress calling herself Ellen Andrews. I also had an especially disagreeable feeling about this job, and the sooner it was settled, the better. I kept my eyes on the brass needle as it haltingly swung from left to right, counting off the floors, and when the doors parted she was there waiting for me. She slipped the boy a sawbuck, and he stuffed it into his jacket pocket and left us alone.

"So nice to see you again, Nat," she said, but she was looking at the lacquered box, not me. "Would you like to come in and have a drink? Auntie H says you have a weakness for rye whiskey."

"Well, she's right about that. But, just now, I'd be more fond of an explanation."

"How odd," she said, glancing up at me, still smiling. "Auntie said one thing she liked about you was how you didn't ask a lot of questions. Said you were real good at minding your own business."

"Sometimes I make exceptions."

"Let me get you that drink," she said, and I followed her the short distance from the elevator to the door of her apartment. Turns out, she had the whole floor to herself, each level of the Colosseum being a single apartment. Pretty ritzy accommodations, I thought, for someone who was *mostly* from out of town. But then I'd spent the last few years living in that one-bedroom cracker box above the Yellow Dragon, hot and cold running cockroaches and so forth. She locked the door behind us, then led me through the foyer to a parlor. The whole place was done up gaudy period French, Louis Quinze and the like, all floral brocade and Orientalia. The walls were decorated with damask hangings, mostly of ample-bosomed women reclining in pastoral scenes, dogs and sheep and what have you lying at their feet. Ellen told me to have a seat, so I parked myself on a récamier near a window.

"Harpootlian spring for this place?" I asked.

"No," she replied. "It belonged to my mother."

"So, you come from money."

"Did I mention how you ask an awful lot of questions?"

"You might have," I said, and she inquired as to whether I liked my whiskey neat or on the rocks. I told her neat, and I set the red box down on the sofa next to me.

"If you're not *too* thirsty, would you mind if I take a peek at that first," she said, pointing at the box.

"Be my guest," I said, and Ellen smiled again. She picked up the red lacquered box, then sat next to me. She cradled it in her lap, and there was this goofy expression on her face, a mix of awe, dread, and eager expectation.

"Must be something extra damn special," I said, and she laughed. It was a nervous kind of a laugh.

I've already mentioned how I couldn't discern any evidence the box had a lid, and I'd supposed there was some secret to getting it open, a gentle squeeze or nudge in just the right spot. Turns out, all it needed was someone to say the magic words.

"*Pain had no sting, and pleasure's wreath no flower,*" she said, speaking slowly and all but whispering the words. There was a sharp *click* and the top of the box suddenly slid back with enough force that it tumbled over her knees and fell to the carpet.

"Keats," I said.

"Keats," she echoed, but added nothing more. She was too busy gazing at what lay inside the box, nestled in a bed of velvet the color of poppies. She started to touch it, then hesitated, her fingertips hovering an inch or so above the object.

"You're fucking kidding me," I said, once I saw what was inside.

"Don't go jumping to conclusions, Nat."

"It's a dildo," I said, probably sounding as incredulous as I felt. "Exactly which conclusions am I not supposed to jump to? Sure, I enjoy a good rub-off as much as the next girl, but...you're telling me Harpootlian killed Fong over a dildo?"

"I never said Auntie H killed Fong."

"Then I suppose he stuck that knife there himself."

And that's when she told me to shut the hell up for five minutes, if I knew how. She reached into the box and lifted out the phallus, handling it as gingerly as somebody might handle a sweaty stick of dynamite. But whatever made the thing special, it wasn't anything I could see.

"*Le godemichet maudit,*" she murmured, her voice so filled with reverence you'd have thought she was holding the devil's own wang. Near as I could tell, it was cast from some sort of hard black ceramic. It glistened faintly in the light getting in through the drapes. "I'll tell you about it," she said, "if you really want to know. I don't see the harm."

"Just so long as you get to the part where it makes sense that Harpootlian bumped the Chinaman for this dingus of yours, then sure."

She took her eyes off the thing long enough to scowl at me. "Auntie H didn't kill Fong. One of Szabó's goons did that, then panicked and ran before he figured out where the box was hidden."

(Now, as for Madam Magdalena Szabó, the biggest boil on Auntie H's fanny, we'll get back to her by and by.)

"Ellen, how can you *possibly* fucking know that? Better yet, how could you've known Szabó's man would have given up and cleared out by the time I arrived?"

"Why did you answer that phone, Nat?" she asked, and that shut me up, good and proper. "As for our prize here," she continued, "it's a long story, a long story with a lot of missing pieces. The dingus, as you put it, is usually called *le godemichet maudit.* Which doesn't necessarily mean it's actually cursed, mind you. Not literally. You *do* speak French, I assume?"

"Yeah," I said. "I do speak French."

"That's ducky, Nat. Now, here's about as much as anyone could tell you. Though, frankly, I'd have thought a scholarly type like yourself would know all about it."

"Never said I was a scholar," I interrupted.

"But you went to college. Radcliffe, Class of 1923, right? Graduated with honors."

"Lots of people go to college. Doesn't necessarily make them scholars. I just sell books."

"My mistake," she said, carefully returning the black dildo to its velvet case. "It won't happen again." Then she told me her tale, and I sat there on the récamier and listened to what she had to say. Yeah, it was long. There *were* certainly a whole lot of missing pieces. And as a wise man once said, this might not be schoolbook history, not Mr. Wells' history, but, near as I've been able to discover since that evening at her apartment, it's history, nevertheless. She asked me whether or not I'd ever heard of a Fourteenth-Century Persian alchemist named al-Jaldaki, Izz al-Din Aydamir al-Jaldaki, and I had, naturally.

"He's sort of a hobby of mine," she said. "Came across his grimoire a few years back. Anyway, he's not where it begins, but that's where the written record starts. While studying in Anatolia, al-Jaldaki heard tales of a fabulous artifact that had been crafted from the horn of a unicorn at the behest of King Solomon."

"From a unicorn," I cut in. "So we believe in those now, do we?"

"Why not, Nat? I think it's safe to assume you've seen some peculiar shit in your time. That you've pierced the veil, so to speak. Surely a unicorn must be small potatoes for a worldly woman like yourself."

"So you'd think," I said.

"Anyhow," she went on, "the ivory horn was carved into the shape of a penis by the king's most skilled artisans. Supposedly, the result was so revered it was even placed in Solomon's temple, alongside the Ark of the Covenant and a slew of other sacred Hebrew relics. Records al-Jaldaki found in a mosque in the Taurus Mountains indicated that the horn had been removed from Solomon's temple when it was sacked in 587 BC by the Babylonians, and that eventually it had gone to Medina. But it was taken from Medina during, or shortly after, the siege of 627, when the Meccans invaded. And it's at this point that the horn is believed to have been given its ebony coating of porcelain enamel, possibly in an attempt to disguise it."

"Or," I said, "because someone in Medina preferred swarthy cock. You mind if I smoke?" I asked her, and she shook her head and pointed at an ashtray.

"A Medinan rabbi of the Banu Nadir tribe was entrusted with the horn's safety. He escaped, making his way west across the desert to Yanbu' al Bahr, then north along the al-Hejaz all the way to Jerusalem. But two years later, when the Sassanid army lost control of the city to the Byzantine

Emperor Heraclius, the horn was taken to a monastery in Malta, where it remained for centuries."

"That's quite the saga for a dildo. But you still haven't answered my question. What makes it so special? What the hell's it *do*?"

"Maybe you've heard enough," she said. The whole time she'd been talking, she hadn't taken her eyes off the thing in the box.

"Yeah, and maybe I haven't," I told her, tapping ash from my Pall Mall into the ashtray. "So, al-Jaldaki goes to Malta and finds the big black dingus."

She scowled again. No, it was more than a scowl; she *glowered*, and she looked away from the box just long enough to glower *at* me. "Yes," Ellen Andrews said. "At least, that's what he wrote. al-Jaldaki found it buried in the ruins of a monastery in Malta and then carried the horn with him to Cairo. It seems to have been in his possession until his death in 1342. After that it disappeared, and there's no word of it again until 1891."

I did the math in my head. "Five hundred and forty-nine years," I said. "So it must have gone to a good home. Must have lucked out and found itself a long-lived and appreciative keeper."

"The Freemasons might have had it," she went on, ignoring or oblivious to my sarcasm. "Maybe the Vatican. Doesn't make much difference."

"Okay. So what happened in 1891?"

"A party in Paris, in an old house not far from the Cimetière du Montparnasse. Not so much a party, really, as an out and out orgy, the way the story goes. This was back before Montparnasse became so fashionable with painters and poets and expatriate Americans. Verlaine was there, though. At the orgy, I mean. It's not clear what happened precisely, but three women died, and afterwards there were rumors of black magic and ritual sacrifice, and tales surfaced of a cult that worshipped some sort of daemonic objet d'art that had made its way to France from Egypt. There was an official investigation, naturally, but someone saw to it that *la préfecture de police* came up with zilch."

"Naturally," I said. I glanced at the window. It was getting dark, and I wondered if my ride back to the Bowery had been arranged. "So, where's Black Beauty here been for the past forty-four years?"

Ellen leaned forward, reaching for the lid to the red lacquered box. When she set it back in place, covering that brazen scrap of antiquity, I heard the *click* again as the lid melded seamlessly with the rest of the box. Now there was only the etching of the qilin, and I remembered that the beast has sometimes been referred to as the "Chinese unicorn." Yeah, it seemed odd I'd not thought of that before.

"I think we've probably had enough of a history lesson for now," she said, and I didn't disagree. Truth be told, the whole subject was beginning to bore me. It hardly mattered whether or not I believed in unicorns or enchanted dildos. I'd done my job, so there'd be no complaints from Harpootlian. I admit I felt kind of shitty about poor old Fong, who wasn't such a bad sort. But when you're an errand girl for the wicked folk, that shit comes with the territory. People get killed, and people get worse.

"Well, that's that," I said, crushing out my cigarette in the ashtray. "I should dangle."

"Wait. Please. I promised you a drink, Nat. Don't want you telling Auntie H I was a bad hostess, now do I?" And Ellen Andrews stood up, the red box tucked snugly beneath her left arm.

"No worries, kiddo," I assured her. "If she ever asks, which I doubt, I'll say you were a regular Emily Post."

"I insist," she replied. "I really, truly do," and before I could say another word, she turned and rushed out of the parlor, leaving me alone with all that furniture and the buxom giantesses watching me from the walls. I wondered if there were any servants, or a live-in beau, or if possibly she had the place all to herself, that huge apartment overlooking the river. I pushed the drapes aside and stared out at twilight gathering in the park across the street. Then she was back (minus the red box) with a silver serving tray, two glasses, and a virgin bottle of Sazerac rye.

"Maybe just one," I said, and she smiled. I went back to watching Riverside Park while she poured the whiskey. No harm in a shot or two. It's not like I had some place to be, and there were still a couple of unanswered questions bugging me. Such as why Harpootlian had broken her promise, the one that was supposed to prevent her underlings from practicing their hocus-pocus on me. That is, assuming Ellen Andrews had even bothered to ask permission. Regardless, she didn't need magic or a spell book for her next dirty trick. The Mickey Finn she slipped me did the job just fine.

So, I came to, four, perhaps five hours later – sometime before midnight. By then, as I'd soon learn, the shit had already hit the fan. I woke up sick as a dog and my head pounding like there was an ape with a kettledrum loose inside my skull. I opened my eyes, but it wasn't Ellen Andrews' Baroque clutter and chintz that greeted me, and I immediately shut them again. I smelled the hookahs and the smoldering *bukhoor,* the opium smoke and sandarac and, somewhere underneath it all, that pervasive brimstone stink that no amount of incense can mask. Besides, I'd seen the spiny ginger-skinned thing crouching not far from me, the eunuch, and I knew I was somewhere in the rat's maze labyrinth of Harpootlian's bordello. I started to sit up, but then my stomach lurched and I thought better of it. At least there were soft cushions beneath me, and the silk was cool against my feverish skin.

"You know where you are?" the eunuch asked; it had a woman's voice and a hint of a Russian accent, but I was pretty sure both were only affectations. First rule of demon brothels: Check your preconceptions of male and female at the door. Second rule: Appearances are fucking *meant* to be deceiving.

"Sure," I moaned and tried not to think about vomiting. "I might have a notion or three."

"Good. Then you lie still and take it easy, Miss Beaumont. We've got a few questions need answering." Which made it mutual, but I kept my mouth shut on that account. The voice was beginning to sound not so much feminine as what you might hear if you scraped frozen pork back and forth across a cheese grater. "This afternoon, you were contacted by an associate of Madam Harpootlian's, yes? She told you her name was Ellen Andrews. That's not her true name, of course. Just something she heard in a motion picture."

"Of course," I replied. "You sort never bother with your real names. Anyway, what of it?"

"She asked you to go see Jimmy Fong and bring her something, yes? Something very precious. Something powerful and rare."

"The dingus," I said, rubbing at my aching head. "Right, but...hey... Fong was already dead when I got there, scout's honor. Andrews told me one of Szabó's people did him."

"The Chinese gentleman's fate is no concern of ours," the eunuch said. "But we need to talk about Ellen Andrews. She has caused this house serious inconvenience. She's troubled us, and troubles us still."

"You and me both, bub," I said. It was just starting to dawn on me how there were some sizable holes in my memory. I clearly recalled the taste of rye, and gazing down at the park, but then nothing. Nothing at all. I asked the ginger demon, "Where is she? And how'd I get here, anyway?"

"We seem to have many of the same questions," it replied, dispassionate as a corpse. "You answer ours, maybe we shall find the answers to yours along the way."

I knew damn well I didn't have much say in the matter. After all, I'd been down this road before. When Auntie H wants answers, she doesn't usually bother with asking. Why waste your time wondering if someone's feeding you a load of baloney when all you gotta do is reach inside his brain and help yourself to whatever you need?

"Fine," I said, trying not to tense up, because tensing up only ever makes it worse. "How about let's cut the chit chat and get this over with."

"Very well, but you should know," it said, "Madam regrets the necessity of this imposition." And then there were the usual wet, squelching noises as the relevant appendages unfurled and slithered across the floor towards me.

"Sure, no problem. Ain't no secret Madam's got a heart of gold," and maybe I shouldn't have smarted off like that, because when the stingers hit me, they hit hard. Harder than I knew was necessary to make the connection. I might have screamed. I know I pissed myself. And then it was inside me, prowling about, roughly picking its way through my conscious and unconscious mind – through my soul, if that word suits you better. All the heady sounds and smells of the brothel faded away, along with my physical discomfort. For a while I drifted nowhere and nowhen in particular, and then, then I stopped drifting…

…Ellen asked me, "You ever think you've had enough? Of the life, I mean. Don't you sometimes contemplate just up and blowing town, not even stopping long enough to look back? Doesn't that ever cross your mind, Nat?"

I sipped my whiskey and watched her, undressing her with my eyes and not especially ashamed of myself for doing so. "Not too often," I said. "I've had it worse. This gig's not perfect, but I usually get a fair shake."

"Yeah, usually," she said, her words hardly more than a sigh. "Just, now and then, I feel like I'm missing out."

I laughed, and she glared at me.

"You'd cut a swell figure in a breadline," I said, and took another swallow of the rye.

"I hate when people laugh at me."

"Then don't say funny things," I told her.

And that's when she turned and took my glass. I thought she was about to tell me to get lost, and don't let the door hit me in the ass on the way out. Instead, she set the drink down on the silver serving tray, and she kissed me. Her mouth tasted like peaches. Peaches and cinnamon. Then she pulled back, and her eyes flashed red, the way they had in the Yellow Dragon, only now I knew it wasn't an illusion.

"You're a demon," I said, not all that surprised.

"Only two bits. My grandmother...well, I'd rather not get into that, if it's all the same to you. Does my pedigree make you uncomfortable?"

"No, it's not a problem," I replied, and she kissed me again. Right about here, I started to feel the first twinges of whatever she'd put into the Sazerac, but, frankly, I was too horny to heed the warning signs.

"I've got a plan," she said, whispering, as if she were afraid someone was listening in. "I have it all worked out, but I wouldn't mind some company on the road."

"I have no...no idea...what you're talking about," and there was something else I wanted to say, but I'd begun slurring my words and decided against it. I put a hand on her left breast, and she didn't stop me.

"We'll talk about it later," she said, kissing me again, and right about then, that's when the curtain came crashing down, and the ginger-colored demon in my brain turned a page...

...I opened my eyes, and I was lying in a black room. I mean, a *perfectly* black room. Every wall had been painted matte black, and the ceiling, and the floor. If there were any windows, they'd also been painted over, or boarded up. I was cold, and a moment later I realized that was because I was naked. I was naked and lying at the center of a wide white pentagram that had been chalked onto that black floor. A white pentagram held within a white circle. There was a single white candle burning at each of the five points. I looked up, and Ellen Andrews was standing above me. Like me, she was naked. Except she was wearing that dingus from the lacquered box, fitted into a leather harness strapped about her hips. The phallus drooped obscenely and glimmered in the candlelight. There were dozens of runic and Enochian symbols painted on her skin in blood and shit and charcoal.

Most of them I recognized. At her feet, there was a small iron cauldron, and a black-handled dagger, and something dead. It might have been a rabbit, or a small dog. I couldn't be sure which, because she'd skinned it.

Ellen looked down, and saw me looking up at her. She frowned, and tilted her head to one side. For just a second, there was something undeniably predatory in that expression, something murderous. All spite and not a jot of mercy. For that second, I was face-to-face with the one quarter of her bloodline that changed all the rules, the ancestor she hadn't wanted to talk about. But then that second passed, and she softly whispered, "I have a plan, Natalie Beaumont."

"What are you doing?" I asked her. But my mouth was so dry and numb, my throat so parched, it felt like I took forever to cajole my tongue into shaping those four simple words.

"No one will know," she said. "I promise. Not Harpootlian, not Szabó, not anyone. I've been over this a thousand times, worked all the angles." And she went down on one knee then, leaning over me. "But you're supposed to be asleep, Nat."

"Ellen, you don't cross Harpootlian," I croaked.

"Trust me," she said.

In that place, the two of us adrift on an island of light in an endless sea of blackness, she was the most beautiful woman I'd ever seen. Her hair was down now, and I reached up, brushing it back from her face. When my fingers moved across her scalp, I found two stubby horns, but it wasn't anything a girl couldn't hide with the right hairdo and a hat.

"Ellen, what are you doing?"

"I'm about to give you a gift, Nat. The most exquisite gift in all creation. A gift that even the angels might covet. You wanted to know what the Unicorn does. Well, I'm not going to tell you, I'm going to *show* you."

She put a hand between my legs and found I was already wet.

I licked at my chapped lips, fumbling for words that wouldn't come. Maybe I didn't know what she was getting at, this *gift,* but I had a feeling I didn't want any part of it, no matter how exquisite it might be. I knew these things, clear as day, but I was lost in the beauty of her, and whatever protests I might have uttered, they were about as sincere as ol' Brer Rabbit begging Brer Fox not to throw him into that briar patch. I could say I was bewitched, but it would be a lie.

She mounted me then, and I didn't argue.

"What happens now?" I asked.

"Now I fuck you," she replied. "Then I'm going to talk to my grandmother." And, with that, the world fell out from beneath me again. And the ginger-skinned eunuch moved along to the next tableau, that next set of memories I couldn't recollect on my own…

…Stars were tumbling from the skies. Not a few stray shooting stars here and there. No, *all* the stars were falling. One by one, at first, and then the sky was raining pitchforks, only it *wasn't* rain, see. It was light. The whole sorry world was being born or was dying, and I saw it didn't much matter which. Go back far enough, or far enough forward, the past and future wind up holding hands, cozy as a couple of lovebirds. Ellen had thrown open a doorway, and she'd dragged me along for the ride. I was *so* cold. I couldn't understand how there could be that much fire in the sky, and me still be freezing my tits off like that. I lay there shivering as the brittle heavens collapsed. I could feel her inside me. I could feel *it* inside me, and same as I'd been lost in Ellen's beauty, I was being smothered by that ecstasy. And then…then the eunuch showed me the gift, which I'd forgotten…and which I would immediately forget again.

How do you write about something, when all that remains of it is the faintest of impressions of glory? When all you can bring to mind is the empty place where a memory ought to be and isn't, and only that conspicuous absence is there to remind you of what cannot ever be recalled? Strain as you might, all that effort hardly adds up to a trip for biscuits. So, *how do you write it down?* You don't, *that's* how. You do your damnedest to think about what came next, instead, knowing your sanity hangs in the balance.

So, here's what came *after* the gift, since *le godemichet maudit* is a goddamn Indian giver if ever one were born. Here's the curse that rides shotgun on the gift, as impossible to obliterate from reminiscence as the other is to awaken.

There were falling stars, and that unendurable cold…and then the empty, aching socket to mark the countermanded gift…and *then* I saw the unicorn. I don't mean the dingus. I mean the *living creature*, standing in a glade of cedars, bathed in clean sunlight and radiating a light all it's own. It didn't look much like what you see in story books or those medieval tapestries they got hanging in the Cloisters. It also didn't look much like the beast carved into the lid of Fong's wooden box. But I knew what it was, all the same.

A naked girl stood before it, and the unicorn kneeled at her feet. She sat down, and it rested its head on her lap. She whispered reassurances I couldn't hear, because they were spoken as softly as falling snow. And then she offered the unicorn one of her breasts, and I watched as it suckled. This scene of chastity and absolute peace lasted maybe a minute, maybe two, before the trap was sprung and the hunters stepped out from the shadows of the cedar boughs. They killed the unicorn, with cold iron lances and swords, but first the unicorn killed the virgin who'd betrayed it to its doom…

…and Harpootlian's ginger eunuch turned another page (a ham-fisted analogy if ever there were one, but it works for me), and we were back in the black room. Ellen and me. Only two of the candles were still burning, two guttering, half-hearted counterpoints to all that darkness. The other three had been snuffed out by a sudden gust of wind that had smelled of rust, sulfur, and slaughterhouse floors. I could hear Ellen crying, weeping somewhere in the darkness beyond the candles and the periphery of her protective circle. I rolled over onto my right side, still shivering, still so cold I couldn't imagine being warm ever again. I stared into the black, blinking and dimly amazed that my eyelids hadn't frozen shut. Then something snapped into focus, and there she was, cowering on her hands and knees, a tattered rag of a woman lost in the gloom. I could see her stunted, twitching tail, hardly as long as my middle finger, and the thing from the box was still strapped to her crotch. Only now it had a twin, clutched tightly in her left hand.

I think I must have asked her what the hell she'd done, though I had a pretty good idea. She turned towards me, and her eyes…well, you see that sort of pain, and you spend the rest of your life trying to forget you saw it.

"I didn't understand," she said, still sobbing. "I didn't understand she'd take so much of me away."

A bitter wave of conflicting, irreconcilable emotion surged and boiled about inside me. Yeah, I knew what she'd done to me, and I knew I'd been used for something unspeakable. I knew *violation* was too tame a word for it, and that I'd been marked forever by this gold-digging half-breed of a twist. And part of me was determined to drag her kicking and screaming to Harpootlian. Or fuck it, I could kill her myself, and take my own sweet time doing so. I could kill her the way the hunters had murdered the unicorn. But – on the other hand – the woman I saw lying there before me was shattered almost beyond recognition. There'd been a steep price for her trespass, and she'd paid it and then some. Besides, I was learning fast that when you've been to Hades' doorstep with someone, and the two of you've made it back more or less alive, there's a bond, whether you want it or not. So, there we were, a cheap, latter-day parody of Orpheus and Eurydice, and all I could think about was holding her, tight as I could, until she stopped crying and I was warm again.

"She took *so much,*" Ellen whispered. I didn't ask what her grandmother had taken. Maybe it was a slice of her soul, or maybe a scrap of her humanity. Maybe it was the memory of the happiest day of her life, or the ability to taste her favorite food. It didn't seem to matter. It was gone, and she'd never get it back. I reached for her, too cold and too sick to speak, but sharing her hurt and needing to offer my hollow consolation, stretching out to touch...

...and the eunuch said, "Madam wishes to speak with you now," and that's when I realized the parade down memory lane was over. I was back at Harpootlian's, and there was a clock somewhere chiming down to three a.m., the dead hour. I could feel the nasty welt the stingers had left at the base of my skull and underneath my jaw, and I still hadn't shaken off the hangover from that tainted shot of rye whiskey. But above and underneath and all about these mundane discomforts was a far more egregious pang, a portrait of that guileless white beast cut down and its blood spurting from gaping wounds. Still, I did manage to get myself upright without puking. Sure, I gagged once or twice, but I didn't puke. I pride myself on that. I sat with my head cradled in my hands, waiting for the room to stop tilting and sliding around like I'd gone for a spin on the Coney Island Wonder Wheel.

"Soon, you'll feel better, Miss Beaumont."

"Says you," I replied. "Anyway, give me a half a fucking minute, will you please? Surely your employer isn't gonna cast a kitten if you let me get my bearings first, not after the work over you just gave me. Not after – "

"I will remind you, her patience is not infinite," the ginger demon said firmly, and then it clicked its long claws together.

"Yeah?" I asked. "Well, who the hell's is?" But I'd gotten the message, plain and clear. The gloves were off, and whatever forbearance Auntie H might have granted me in the past, it was spent, and now I was living on the installment plan. I took a deep breath and struggled to my feet. At least the eunuch didn't try to lend a hand.

I can't say for certain when Yeksabet Harpootlian set up shop in Manhattan, but I have it on good faith that Magdalena Szabó was here first. And anyone who knows her onions knows the two of them have been at each other's throats since the day Auntie H decided to claim a slice of the action for herself. Now, you'd think there'd be plenty enough of the hellion cock-and-tail trade to go around, what with all the netherworlders who call the Five Boroughs their home away from home. And likely as not you'd be right. Just don't try telling that to Szabó or Auntie H. Sure, they've each got their elite stable of "girls and boys," and they both have more customers than they know what to do with. Doesn't stop them from spending every waking hour looking for a way to banish the other once and for all – or at least find the unholy grail of competitive advantages.

Now, by the time the ginger-skinned eunuch led me through the chaos of Auntie H's stately pleasure dome, far below the subways and sewers and tenements of the Lower East Side, I already had a pretty good idea the dingus from Jimmy Fong's shiny box was meant to be Harpootlian's trump card. Only, here was Ellen Andrews, this mutt of a courier gumming up the works, playing fast and loose with the loving cup. And here was me, stuck smack in the middle, the unwilling stooge in her double-cross.

As I followed the eunuch down the winding corridor that ended in Auntie H's grand salon, we passed doorway after doorway, all of them opening onto scenes of inhuman passion and madness, the most odious of perversions, and tortures that make short work of merely mortal flesh. It would be disingenuous to say I looked away. After all, this wasn't my first time. Here were the hinterlands of wanton physical delight and agony, where the two become indistinguishable in a rapturous *Totentanz.* Here were spectacles to remind me how Doré and Hieronymus Bosch never even came close, and all of it laid bare for the eyes of any passing voyeur. You see, there are no locked doors to be found at Madam Harpootlian's. There are no doors at all.

"It's a busy night," the eunuch said, though it looked like business as usual to me.

"Sure," I muttered. "You'd think the Shriners were in town. You'd think Mayor La Guardia himself had come down off his high horse to raise a little hell."

And then we reached the end of the hallway, and I was shown into the mirrored chamber where Auntie H holds court. The eunuch told me to wait, then left me alone. I'd never seen the place so empty. There was no sign of the usual retinue of rogues, ghouls, and archfiends, only all those goddamn mirrors, because no one looks directly at Madam Harpootlian and lives to tell the tale. I chose a particularly fancy looking glass, maybe ten feet high and held inside an elaborate gilded frame. When Harpootlian spoke up, the mirror rippled like it was only water, and my reflection rippled with it.

"Good evening, Natalie," she said. "I trust you've been treated well?"

"You won't hear any complaints outta me," I replied. "I always say, the Waldorf-Astoria's got nothing on you."

She laughed then, or something that we'll call laughter for the sake of convenience.

"A crying shame we're not meeting under more amicable circumstances. Were it not for this unpleasantness with Miss Andrews, I'd offer you something – on the house, of course."

"Maybe another time," I said.

"So, you *know* why you're here?"

"Sure," I said. "The dingus I took off the dead Chinaman. The salami with the fancy French name."

"It has many names, Natalie. Karkadann's Brow, *El consolador sangriento,* the Horn of Malta – "

"*Le godemichet maudit,"* I said. "Ellen's cock."

Harpootlian grunted, and her reflection made an ugly dismissive gesture. "It is nothing of Miss Andrews. It is *mine*, bought and paid for. With the sweat of my own brow did I track down the spoils of al-Jaldaki's long search. It's *my* investment, one purchased with so grievous a forfeiture this quadroon mongrel could not begin to appreciate the severity of her crime. But you, Natalie, you know, don't you? You've been privy to the wonders of Solomon's talisman, so I think, maybe, you are cognizant of my loss."

"I can't exactly say what I'm cognizant of," I told her, doing my best to stand up straight and not flinch or look away. "I saw the murder of a creature I didn't even believe in yesterday morning. That was sort of an eye opener, I'll grant you. And then there's the part I can't seem to conjure up, even after golden boy did that swell Roto-Rooter number on my head."

"Yes. Well, that's the catch," she said and smiled. There's no shame in saying I looked away then. Even in a mirror, the smile of Yeksabet Harpootlian isn't something you want to see straight on.

"Isn't there always a catch?" I asked, and she chuckled.

"True, it's a fleeting boon," she purled. "The gift comes, and then it goes, and no one may ever remember it. But always, *always* they will long for it again, even hobbled by that ignorance."

"You've lost me, Auntie," I said, and she grunted again. That's when I told her I wouldn't take it as an insult to my intelligence or expertise if she laid her cards on the table and spelled it out plain and simple, like she was talking to a woman who didn't regularly have tea and crumpets with the damned. She mumbled something to the effect that maybe she gave me too much credit, and I didn't disagree.

"Consider," she said, "what it *is,* a unicorn. It is the incarnation of purity, an avatar of innocence. And here is the *power* of the talisman, for that state of grace which soon passes from us each and every one is forever locked inside the horn, the horn become the phallus. And in the instant that it brought you, Natalie, to orgasm, you knew again that innocence, the bliss of a child before it suffers corruption."

I didn't interrupt her, but all at once I got the gist.

"Still, you are only a mortal woman, so what negligible, insignificant sins could you have possibly committed during your short life? Likewise, whatever calamities and wrongs have been visited upon your flesh *or* your soul, they are trifles. But if you survived the war in Paradise, if you refused the yoke and so are counted among the exiles, then you've persisted down all the long eons. You were already broken and despoiled billions of years before the coming of man. And your transgressions outnumber the stars.

"Now," she asked, "what would *you* pay, were you so cursed, to know even one fleeting moment of that stainless, former existence?"

Starting to feel sick to my stomach all over again, I said, "More to the point, if I *always* forgot it, immediately, but it left this emptiness I feel – "

"You would come back," Auntie H smirked. "You would come back again and again and again, because there would be no satiating that void, and always would you hope that maybe *this* time it would take and you might *keep* the memories of that former immaculate condition."

"Which makes it priceless, no matter what you paid."

"Precisely. And now Miss Andrews has forged a copy – an *identical* copy, actually – meaning to sell one to me, and one to Magdalena Szabó. That's where Miss Andrews is now."

"Did you tell her she could hex me?"

"I would never do such a thing, Natalie. You're much too valuable to me."

"*But* you think I had something to do with Ellen's mystical little counterfeit scheme."

"Technically, you did. The ritual of division required a supplicant, someone to *receive* the gift granted by the Unicorn, before the summoning of a succubus mighty enough to affect such a difficult twinning."

"So maybe, instead of sitting here bumping gums with me, you should send one of your torpedoes after her. And, while we're on the subject of how you pick your little henchmen, maybe – "

"*Natalie,"* snarled Auntie H from someplace not far behind me. "Have I failed to make myself *understood?* Might it be I need to raise my voice?" The floor rumbled, and tiny hairline cracks began to crisscross the surface of the looking glass. I shut my eyes.

"No," I told her. "I get it. It's a grift, and you're out for blood. But you *know* she used me. Your lackey, it had a good, long look around my upper story, right, and there's no way you can think I was trying to con you."

For a dozen or so heartbeats, she didn't answer me, and the mirrored room was still and silent, save all the moans and screaming leaking in through the walls. I could smell my own sour sweat, and it was making me sick to my stomach.

"There are some grey areas," she said finally. "Matters of sentiment and lust, a certain reluctant infatuation, even."

I opened my eyes and forced myself to gaze directly into that mirror, at the abomination crouched on its writhing throne. And all at once, I'd had enough, enough of Ellen Andrews and her dingus, enough of the cloak-and-dagger bullshit, and definitely enough kowtowing to the monsters.

"For fuck's sake," I said, "I only just met the woman this afternoon. She drugs and rapes me, and you think that means she's my sheba?"

"Like I told you, I think there are grey areas," Auntie H replied. She grinned, and I looked away again.

"Fine. You tell me what it's gonna take to make this right with you, and I'll do it."

"Always so eager to please," Auntie H laughed, and the mirror in front of me rippled. "But, since you've asked, and as I do not doubt your *present* sincerity, I will tell you. I want her dead, Natalie. Kill her, and all will be… forgiven."

"Sure," I said, because what the hell else was I going to say. "But if she's with Szabó – "

"I have spoken already with Magdalena Szabó, and we have agreed to set aside our differences long enough to deal with Miss Andrews. After all, she has attempted to cheat us both, in equal measure."

"How do I find her?"

"You're a resourceful young lady, Natalie," she said. "I have faith in you. Now…if you will excuse me," and, before I could get in another word, the mirrored room dissolved around me. There was a flash, not of light, but a flash of the deepest abyssal darkness, and I found myself back at the Yellow Dragon, watching through the bookshop's grimy windows as the sun rose over the Bowery.

There you go, the dope on just how it is I found myself holding a gun on Ellen Andrews, and just how it is she found herself wondering if I was angry enough or scared enough or desperate enough to pull the trigger. And like I said, I chambered a round, but she just stood there. She didn't even flinch.

"I wanted to give you a gift, Nat," she said.

"Even if I believed that – and I don't – all I got to show for this *gift* of yours is a nagging yen for something I'm never going to get back. We lose our innocence, it stays lost. That's the way it works. So, all I got from you, Ellen, is a thirst can't ever be slaked. That and Harpootlian figuring me for a clip artist."

She looked hard at the gun, then looked harder at me.

"So what? You thought I was gonna plead for my life? You thought maybe I was gonna get down on my knees for you and beg? Is that how you like it? Maybe you're just steamed cause I was on top – "

"Shut up, Ellen. You don't get to talk yourself out of this mess. It's a done deal. You tried to give Auntie H the high hat."

"And you honestly think she's on the level? You think you pop me and she lets you off the hook, like nothing happened?"

"I do," I said. And maybe it wasn't as simple as that, but I wasn't exactly lying, either. I needed to believe Harpootlian, the same way old women need to believe in the infinite compassion of the little baby Jesus and Mother Mary. Same way poor kids need to believe in the inexplicable generosity of Popeye the Sailor and Santa Claus.

"It didn't have to be this way," she said.

"I didn't dig your grave, Ellen. I'm just the sap left holding the shovel."

And she smiled that smug smile of hers, and said, "I get it now, what Auntie H sees in you. And it's not your knack for finding shit that doesn't want to be found. It's not that at all."

"Is this a guessing game," I asked, "or do you have something to say?"

"No, I think I'm finished," she replied. "In fact, I think I'm done for. So let's get this over with. By the way, how many women *have* you killed?"

"You played me," I said again.

"Takes two to make a sucker, Nat," she smiled.

Me, I don't even remember pulling the trigger. Just the sound of the gunshot, louder than thunder.

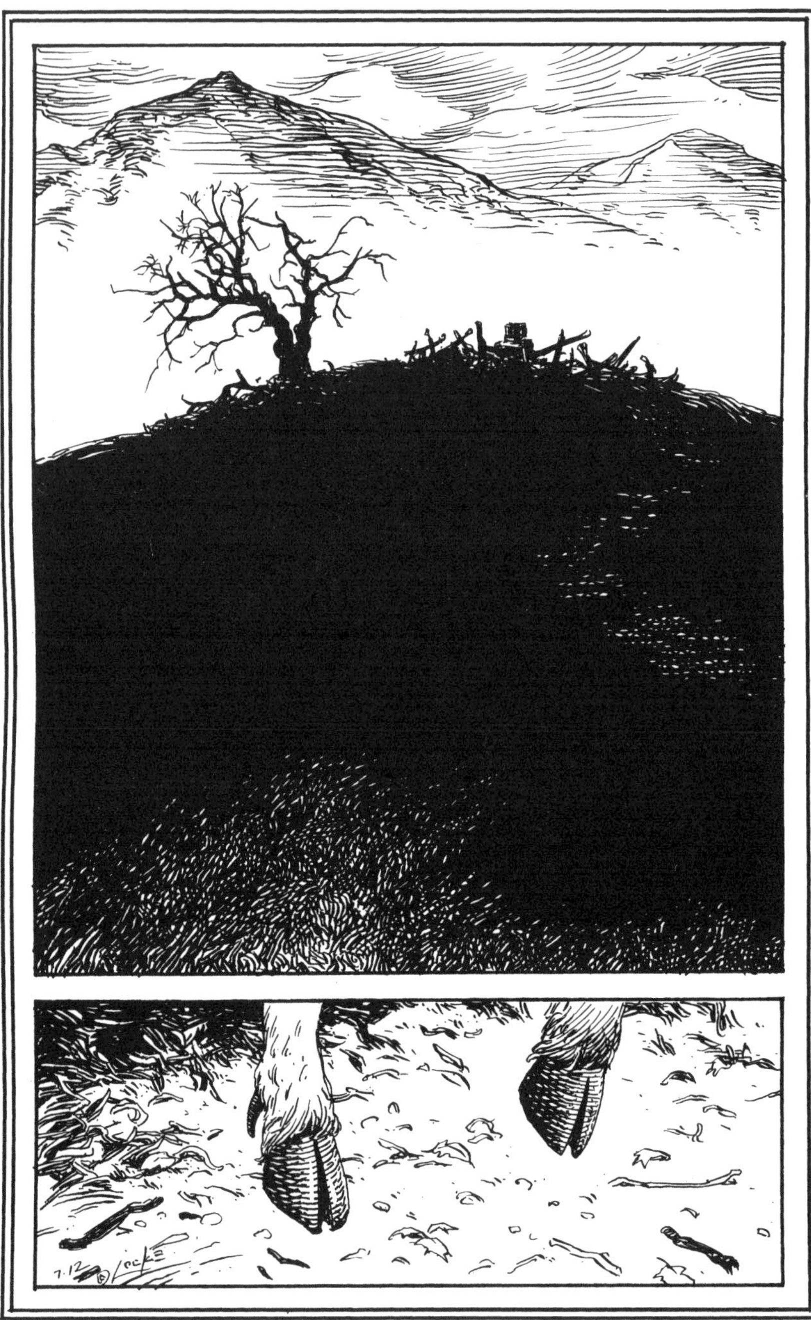

One Tree Hill
(The World as Cataclysm)

1.

I am dreaming. Or I am awake.

I've long since ceased to care, as I've long since ceased to believe it matters which. Dreaming or awake, my perceptions of the hill and the tree and what little remains of the house on the hill are the same. More importantly, more perspicuously, my *perceptions* of the hill and the house and the tree are the same. Or, as this admittedly is belief, so open to debate, I cannot imagine it would matter whether I am dreaming or awake. And this observation is as good a place to begin as any.

I am told in the village that the tree was struck by lightning at, or just after, sunset on St. Crispin's Day, eleven years ago. I am told in the village that no thunderstorm accompanied the lightning strike, that the October sky was clear and dappled with stars. The Village. It has a name, though I prefer to think, and refer, to it simply as The Village. Nestled snugly – some would say claustrophobically – between the steep foothills of New Hampshire's White Mountains, within what geographers name the Sandwich Range, and a deep lake the villagers call Witalema. On my maps, the lake has no name at all. A librarian in The Village told me that Witalema was derived from the language of the Abenakis, from the word *gwitaalema,* which, she said, may be roughly translated as "to fear someone." I've found nothing in any book or anywhere online that refutes her claim, though I have also found nothing to confirm it. So, I will always think of that lake and its black, still waters as Lake Witalema, and choose not to speculate on why its name means "to fear someone." I found more than enough to fear on the aforementioned lightning-struck hill.

There is a single, nameless cemetery in The Village, located within a stone's throw of the lake. The oldest headstone I have found there dates back to 1674. That is, the man buried in the plot died in 1674. He was a born in 1645. The headstone reads *Ye blooming Youth who fee this Stone/ Learn early Death may be your own.* It seems oddly random to me that only the word *see* makes use of the Latin *s.* In stray moments I have wondered what the dead man might have *feen* to warrant this peculiarity of the inscription, or if it is merely an engravers mistake that was not corrected and so has survived these past three hundred and thirty-eight years. I dislike the cemetery, perhaps because of its nearness to the lake, and so I have only visited it once. Usually, I find comfort in graveyards, and I have a large collection of rubbings taken from gravestones in New England.

But why, I ask myself, *do I shy from this one cemetery, and possibly only because of its closeness to Lake Witalema, when I returned repeatedly to the hill and the tree and what little remains of the house on the hill?* It isn't a question I can answer; I doubt I will ever be able to answer it. I only know that what I have seen on that hilltop is far more dreadful than anything the lake could ever have to show me.

I am climbing the hill, and I am awake, or I am asleep.

I'm thinking about the lightning strike on St. Crispin's Day, lightning from a clear night sky, and I'm thinking of the fire that consumed the house and left the tree a gnarled charcoal crook. Also, my mind wanders – probably defensively – to the Vatican's decision that too little evidence can be found to prove the existence of either of the twin brothers, St. Crispin and St. Crispinian, and how they survived their first close call with martyrdom, after being tossed into a river with millstones tied about their necks, only to be beheaded, finally, by decree of Rictus Barus. Climbing up that hill, pondering obscure Catholic saints who may not ever have lived, it occurs to me I may read too much. Or only read too much into what I read. I pause to catch my breath, and I glance up at the sky. Today there are clouds, unlike the night the lightning came. If the villagers are to be believed, of course. And given the nature of what sits atop the hill, the freak strike that night seems not so miraculous. The clouds seem to promise rain, and I'll probably be soaking wet by the time I get back to my room in the rundown motel on the outskirts of The Village. Far away, towards what my tattered topographic map calls Mount Passaconaway, there is the low rumble of thunder (*Passaconaway* is another Indian name, from the Pennacook, a tribe closely related to the Abenakis, but I have no idea whatsoever what the word might mean). The trail is steep here, winding between spruce and pine, oaks, poplars, and red maples. I imagine the maple leaves must appear to catch fire in the autumn. Catch fire or bleed. The hill always turns my thoughts morbid, a mood that is not typical of my nature. Reading this, one might think otherwise, but that doesn't change the truth of it. Having caught my breath, I continue up the narrow, winding path, hoping to reach the summit before the storm catches up with me. Weathered granite crunches beneath my boots.

"Were I you," said the old man who runs The Village's only pharmacy, "I'd stay clear of that hill. No fit place to go wandering about. Not after..." And then he trailed off and went back to ringing up my purchase on the antique cash register.

"...the lightning came," I said, finishing his statement. "After the fire."

He glared at me and made an exasperated, disapproving sound.

"You ain't from around here, I know, and whatever you've heard, I'm guessing you've written it off as Swamp Yankee superstition."

"I have a more open mind than you think," I told him.

"Maybe that's so. Maybe it ain't," he groused and looked for the price on a can of pears in heavy syrup. "Either way, I guess I've said my peace. No fit place, that hill, and you'd do well to listen."

But I might have only dreamt that conversation, as I might have dreamt the graveyard on the banks of Lake Witalema, and the headstone of a man who died in 1674, and the twisted, charred tree, and...

It doesn't matter.

2.

I live in The City, a safe century of miles south and east of The Village. When I have work, I am a science journalist. When I do not, I am an unemployed science journalist who tries to stay busy by blogging what I would normally sell for whatever pittance is being offered. Would that I had become a political pundit or a war correspondent. But I didn't. I have no interest or acumen for politics or bullets. I wait on phone calls, on jobs from a vanishing stable of newspapers and magazines, on work from this or that website. I wait. My apartment is very small, even by the standards of The City, and only just affordable on my budget. Or lack thereof. Four cramped rooms in the attic of a brownstone that was built when the neighborhood was much younger, overlooking narrow streets crowded with upscale boutiques and restaurants that charge an arm and a leg for a sparkling green bottle of S. Pellagrino. I can watch wealthy men and women walk their shitty little dogs.

I have a few bookshelves, crammed with reference material on subjects ranging from cosmology to quantum physics, virology to paleontology. My coffee table, floor, desk, and almost every other conceivable surface are piled high with back issues of *Science* and *Physical Review Letters* and *Nature* and...you get the picture. That hypothetical you, who may or may not be reading this. I'm making no assumptions. I have my framed diplomas from MIT and Yale on the wall above my desk, though they only serve to remind me that whatever promise I might once have possessed has gone unrealized. And that I'll never pay off the student loans that supplemented my meager scholarships. I try, on occasion, to be proud of those pieces of paper and their gold seals, but I rarely turn that trick.

I sit, and I read. I blog, and I wait, watching as the balance in my bank account dwindles.

One week ago tomorrow my needlessly fancy iPhone rang, and on the other end was an editor from *Discover* who'd heard from a field geologist about the lightning struck hill near The Village, and who thought it was worth checking out. That it might make an interesting sidebar, at the very least. A bit of a meteorological mystery, unless it proved to be nothing but local tall tales. I had to pay for my own gas, but I'd have a stingy expense account for a night at a motel and a couple of meals. I had a week to get the story in. I should say, obviously, I have long since exceeded my expense account and missed the deadline. I keep my phone switched off.

It doesn't matter anymore. In my ever decreasing moments of clarity, I find myself wishing that it did. I need the money. I need the byline. I absolutely do not need an editor pissed at me and word getting around that I'm unreliable.

But it *doesn't* matter anymore.

Wednesday, one week ago, I got my ever-ailing, tangerine-and-rust Nissan out of the garage where I can't afford to keep it. I left The City, and I left Massachusetts via I-493, which I soon traded for I-93, and then I-293 at Manchester. Then, it will suffice to say that I left the interstates and headed east until I reached The Village nestled here between the kneeling mountains. I didn't make any wrong turns. It was easy to find. The directions the editor at *Discover* had emailed were correct in every way, right down to the shabby motel on the edge of The Village.

Right down to the lat-long GPS coordinates of the hill and the tree and what little remains of the house on the hill. N 43.81591/W -71.37035.

I think I have offered all these details only as an argument, to myself, that I am – or at least was once – a rational human being. Whatever I have become, or am becoming, I did start out believing the truths of the universe *were* knowable.

But now I am sliding down a slippery slope towards the irrational.

Now, I doubt everything I took for granted when I came here.

Before I first climbed the hill.

If the preceding is an argument, or a ward, or whatever I might have intended it as, it is a poor attempt, indeed.

But it doesn't matter, and I know that.

3.

I imagine that the view from the crest of the hill was once quite picturesque. As I've mentioned, there's an unobstructed view of the heavily wooded slopes and peaks of Mount Passaconaway, and of the valleys and hills in between. This vista must be glorious under a heavy snowfall. I have supposed that is why the house was built here. Likely, it was someone's summer home, possibly someone not so unlike myself, someone foreign to The Village.

The librarian I spoke of earlier, I asked her if the hill has a name, and all she said was "One Tree."

"One Tree Hill?" I asked.

"One Tree," she replied curtly. "Nobody goes up *there* anymore."

I am quite entirely aware I am trapped inside, and that I am writing down anything *but* an original tale of uncanny New England. But if I do not know, I will at least be honest about *what* I do not know. I have that responsibility, that fraying shred of naturalism remaining in me. Whether or not it is cliché is another thing which simply doesn't matter.

I reach the crest of the hill, and just like every time before, the first thing that strikes my eyes is the skeleton of that tree. I'm not certain, but I believe it was an oak, until that night eleven years ago. It must have been ancient, judging by the circumference and diameter of its base. It might have stood here when that man I have yet to (and will not) name was buried in 1674. But I don't know how long oak trees live, and I haven't bothered to find out. It is a dead tree, and all the "facts" that render it *more* than a dead tree exist entirely independently of its taxonomy.

Aside from the remains of the one tree, the hilltop is "bald." The woods have not reclaimed it. If I stand at the lightning-struck tree, the nearest living tree, in any direction, is at least twenty-five yards away. There is only stone and bracken, weeds, vines, and fallen, rotten limbs. So, it is always hotter at the top of the hill, and the ground seems drier and rockier. There is a sense of flesh rubbed raw and unable to heal.

Like all the times I have come here before, there is, immediately, the inescapable sense that I have entered a place so entirely and irrevocably defiled as to have passed beyond any conventional understanding of corruption. I cannot ever escape the impression that, somehow, the event that damned this spot (for it *is* damned) struck so very deeply at the fabric of this patch of the world as to render it beyond that which is either unholy *or* holy. Neither good *nor* evil have a place here. Neither are welcome, so profound was the damage done that one St. Crispin's Night. And if the hill seems blasphemous, it is only because it has come to exist somewhere genuinely *Outside.* I won't try to elaborate just yet. It is enough to say *Outside.* Even so, I'll concede that the dead tree stands before me like an altar. It *strikes* me that way every time, in direct contradiction to what I've said about it. Or, I *could* say, instead, it stands like a sentry, but then one must answer the question about what it might be standing guard over. Bricks from a crumbling foundation? The maze of poison ivy and green briars? A court of skunks, rattlesnakes, and crows?

The sky presses down on the hill, heavy as the sea.

From the top of the hill, the wide blue sky looks very hungry.

What is it that skies eat? That thin rind of atmosphere between a planet and the hard vacuum of outer space? I'm asking questions that lead nowhere. I'm asking questions only because it occurs to me that I have never written them down, or that they have never before occurred to me so I *ought* to write them down.

A cloudless night sky struck at the hill, drawing something out, even if I am unable to describe what that something is, and so I will say this event is the author of my questions on the possible diet of the sky.

Even after eleven years, the top of the hill smells of smoke, ash, charcoal, cinder lingers – all those odors we mean when we say, "I can smell fire." We cannot smell fire, but we smell the byproducts of combustion, and that smell lingers here. I wonder if it always will. I am standing at the top of the hill, thinking all these thoughts, when I hear something coming up quickly behind me. It's not the noise a woman or a man's feet would make. A deer, possibly. An animal with long and delicate limbs, small hooves to pick its way through the forest and along stony trails. This is what I think I hear, but, then, most people *think* they can smell fire.

I take one step forward, and a charred section of root crunches beneath the soles of my hiking boots. The crunching seems very loud, though I suspect that's only another illusion.

"Why is it you keep coming back here?" she asks. The way she phrases the question, I could pretend I've never heard her ask it before. My mouth is dry. I want to remove my pack and take out the lukewarm bottle of water inside, but I don't.

"It could open wide and eat me," I say to her. "A wide carnivorous sky like that."

There's a pause, nothing but a stale bit of breeze through the leaves of the trees surrounding the lightning-struck ring. Then she laughs, that peculiar laugh of hers, which is neither unnerving nor a sound that in any way puts one at ease.

"Now you're being ridiculous," she says.

"I know," I admit. "But that's the way it makes me feel, hanging up there."

"What you describe is a feeling of dread."

"Isn't that what happened here, that St. Crispin's Day? Didn't the sky open its mouth and gnaw this hill and everything on it – the tree, the house?"

"You listen too much to those people in the village."

That's the way she says it, *the village.* Never does she say *The Village.* It is an important nuance. What seems, as she has pointed out, dreadful to me is innately mundane to her.

"They don't have much to say about the hill," I tell her.

"No, they don't. But what they do say, it's hardly worth your time."

"I get the feeling they'd bulldoze this place, if they weren't too afraid to come here. I believe they would take dynamite to it, shave off the top until no evidence of that night remains."

"Likely, you're not mistaken," she agrees. "Which is precisely why you shouldn't listen to them."

I wish I knew the words to accurately delineate, elucidate, explain the rhythm and stinging lilt of her voice. I cannot. I can only do my best to recall what she said that day, which, of course, was not the first nor the last day she has spoken with me. Why she bothers, that might be the greatest of all these mysteries, though it might seem the least. Appearances are deceiving.

"Maybe there were clouds that night," I say. "Maybe it's just that no one noticed them. They may only have noticed that flash of lightning, and only noticed that because of what it left behind."

"If you truly thought that's what happened, you wouldn't keep coming here."

"No, I wouldn't," I say, though I want to turn about and spit in her face, if she even has a face. I presume she does. But I've never turned to find out. I've never looked at her, and I know I never will. Like Medusa, she is not to be seen.

Yes, that was a tad melodramatic, but isn't all of this? The same as it's cliché?

"It's unhealthy, returning to this place again and again. You ought stop."

"I can't. I haven't..." and I trail off. It is a sentence I never should have begun and which I certainly don't wish to finish.

"...solved it yet? No, but it is also one you never should have asked yourself. The people in the village, they don't ask it. Except, possibly, in their dreams."

"You think the people in The Village are ridiculous. You just said so."

"No, that is not exactly what I said, but it's true enough. However, there genuinely are questions you're better off not asking."

"Ignorance is bliss," I say, almost mangling the words with laughter.

"That is not what I said, either."

"Excuse me. I'm getting a headache."

"Don't you always, when you come up here? You should stop to consider why that is, should you not?"

I'm silent for a time, and then I answer, "You want me to stop coming. You would rather I stop coming. I suspect you might even need me to stop coming."

"Futility disturbs me," she says. "You're becoming Sisyphus, rolling his burden up that hill. You're become Christ, lugging the cross towards Calvary."

I don't disagree.

"Loki," I add.

"Loki?"

"It hasn't gotten as bad as what happened to Loki. No serpent dripping venom, which is good, because I have no Sigyn to catch it in her bowl." The story of Loki so bound puts me in mind of Prometheus, the eagle always, always devouring his liver. But I say nothing of Prometheus to her.

"It is the way of humans to create these brilliant, cautionary metaphors, then ignore them."

Again, I don't disagree. It doesn't matter anymore.

"But it *did* happen, yes?" I ask. "There were no clouds that night?"

"It did happen." She is the howling, fiery voice of God whispering confirmation of what my gut already knew. She has been before, and will be again.

"Go home," she says. "Go back to your apartment in your city, before it's too late to go back. Go back to your life."

"Why do you care?" I ask this question, because I know it's already too late to go back to The City. For any number of reasons, not the least because I have climbed the hill and looked at the silent devastation.

"There's no revelation to be had here," she sighs. "No slouching beast prefacing revelation. No revelation and no prophecy. No מנא, מנא, תקל, ופרסין (*Mene, Mene, Tekel u-Pharsin*) at the feast of Belshazzar." She speaks in Hebrew, and I reply, "Numbered, weighed, divided."

"You won't find that here."

"Why do you assume that is why I keep coming back."

This time she only clicks her tongue twice against the roof of her mouth. Tongue, mouth. These are both assumptions, as is face.

"Not because of what I might see, but because of what I've already seen. What will I ever see to equal this? Did it bring you here?"

"No," she says, the word another exasperated sigh.

"You were here before."

"No," she sighs.

"Doesn't it ever get lonely, being up here all alone?"

"You make a lot of assumptions, and, frankly, I find them wearisome."

It doesn't even occur to me to apologize. A secret recess of my consciousness must understand that apologies would be meaningless to one such as her. I hear those nimble legs, those tiny feet that might as well end in hooves. There are other noises I won't attempt to describe.

"Is it an assumption that it is within your power to stop me?"

"Yes, of course that is an assumption."

"Yet," and I can't take my eyes off what's left of the charred tree, "many assumptions prove valid."

She leaves me then. There are no words of parting, no good-bye. There never is; she simply leaves, and I am alone at the top of the hill with the tree and what little remains of the house on the hill, wondering if she will come next time, and the time after that, and the time after that. I pick up a lump of four hundred million year old granite, which seems to tingle in my hand, and I hurl it towards faraway Mount Passaconaway, as if I had a chance of hitting my target.

4.

One thing leads to another. I am keenly aware of the casual chain of cause and effect that dictates, as does any tyrant, the events of the cosmos.

A lightning-struck hill.

A house.

A tree.

A Village hemmed in by steep green slopes and the shadows they cast.

A black lake, and a man who died in 1674.

I had a lover once. Only once, but it was a long relationship. It died a slow and protracted death, borne as much of my disappointment in myself as my partner's disappointment *in* my disappointment of myself. I suppose you can only watch someone you love mourn for so long before your love becomes disgust. Or I may misunderstand completely. I've never made a secret of my difficulty in understanding the motives of people, no matter how close to me they have been, no matter how long they have been close to me. It doesn't seem to matter.

None of it matters now.

But last night, after I climbed the hill, after my conversation with whatever it is exists alone up there, after that, I made a phone call from the squalid motel room. I have not called my former lover in three years. In three years, we have not spoken. Had we, early on, I might have had some chance of repairing the damage I'd done. But it had all seemed so inevitable, and any attempt to stave off the inevitable seemed absurd. In my life, I have loved two things. The first died before we met, and with my grieving for the loss of the first did I kill the second. Well, did I place the second forever beyond my reach.

If I have not already made it perfectly clear, I have no love for The City, nor my apartment, and most especially not for the career I have resigned myself to, or, I would say, that I have *settled* for.

Last night I called. I thought no one would pick up.

"Hello," I said, and there was a long, long silence. *Just hang up,* I thought, though I'm not sure which of us I was wishing would hang up. *It was a terrible idea, so please just hang up before it gets more terrible.*

"Why are you calling me?"

"I'm not entirely certain."

"Its been three years. Why the fuck are you calling me tonight?"

"Something's happening. Something important, and I didn't have anyone else to call."

"I'm the last resort," and there was a dry, bitter laugh. There was the sound of a cigarette being lit, and the exhalation of smoke.

"You still smoke," I said.

"Yeah. Look, I don't care what's happening. Whatever it is, *you* deal with it."

"I'm trying."

"Maybe you're not trying hard enough."

I agreed.

"Will you only listen? It won't take long, and I don't expect you to solve any of my problems. I need to tell someone."

Another long pause, only the sound of smoking to interrupt the silence through the receiver.

"Fine. But be quick. I'm busy."

I'm not, I think. *I may never be busy again. Isn't that a choice one makes, whether to be busy or not? I have, in coming to The Village, left busyness behind me.*

I told my story, which sounded even more ridiculous than I'd expected it to sound. I left out most of my talks with the thing that lives atop the hill, as no one can recall a conversation, not truly, and I didn't want to omit a word of it.

Whether or not each word is of consequence.

"You need to see someone."

"Maybe," I said.

"No. Not maybe. You need to see someone."

We said goodbye, and I was instructed to never call again.

I hung up first, then sat by the phone (I'd used the motel phone, not my cell).

A few seconds later, it rang again, and I quickly, hopefully, lifted the receiver. But it was the voice from the hill. Someone else might have screamed.

"You should leave," she says. "It's still not too late to leave. Do as I have said. It's all still waiting for you. The city, your work, your home."

"Nothing's waiting for me back there. Haven't you figured that out?"

"There's nothing for you here. Haven't *you* figured *that* out?"

"I'm asleep and dreaming this. I'm lying in my apartment above Newbury Street, and I'm dreaming all of this. Probably, The Village does not even exist."

"Then wake up. Go home. Wake up, and you will be home."

"I don't know how," I said, and that was the truth. "I don't know how, and it doesn't matter any longer."

"That's a shame, I think," she said. "I wish it were otherwise." And then there was only a dial tone.

You can almost see the hill from the window of my motel room. You can see the highway and a line of evergreens. If the trees were not so tall, you *could* see the hill. On a night eleven years ago, you could have seen the lightning from this window, and you could have seen the glow of the fire that must have burned afterwards. Last night, I was glad that I couldn't see the hill silhouetted against the stars.

5.

The three times I have visited the library in The Village, the librarian has done her best to pretend I wasn't there. She does her best to seem otherwise occupied. Intensely so. She makes me wait at the circulation desk as long as she can. Today is no different. But finally she relents and frowns and asks me what I need.

"Do you have back issues of the paper?"

"Newspaper?" she asks.

"Yes. There's only the one, am I correct?"

"You are."

"Do you have back issues?"

"We have it on microfiche," and I tell her that microfiche is perfectly fine. So, she leads me through the stacks to a tiny room in the back. There's a metal cabinet with drawers filled with yellow Kodak boxes. She begins to explain how the old-style reader works, how to fit the spools onto the spindles, and I politely assure her I've spent a lot of time squinting at microfiche, but thanks, anyway. I am always polite with her. I do ask for the reel that would include October 26th, 2001.

"You aren't going to let this go, are you?" asks the librarian.

"Eventually, I might. But not yet."

"Ought never have come here. Can't nothing good come of it. Anyone in town can tell you that. Can't nothing good come of prying into the past."

I thank her, and she scowls and leaves me alone.

I press an off-white plastic button, and the days whir noisily past my eyes. I have always detested the sound of a microfiche reader. It reminds me of a dental drill, though I've never found anyone who's made the association. Then again, I don't think I've ever asked anyone *how* they feel about the click-click-click whir of a microfiche reader. One day soon, with so much digital conversation going on, I imagine there will be very few microfiche archives. People pretend that hard drives, computer disks, and the internet is a safer place to keep our history. At any rate, the machine whirs, and in only a minute or so I've reached October 26th, the day after the lightning strike. On page four of the paper, I find a very brief write up of the event at the crest of the hill. One Tree, as it seems to be named, though the paper doesn't give that name. It merely speaks of a house at the end of an "unimproved" drive off Middle Road, east of The Village. A house had recently been constructed there by a family hailing from, as it happened, The City. The world is, of course, filled with coincidence, so I make nothing of this. I doubt I ever shall. The house was to be a summer home. Curiously, the family is not named, the paper reporting only that there had been three members – father, mother, daughter – and that all died in the fire caused by the lightning. Firefighters from The Village had responded, but were (also curiously) said to have been unable to extinguish what must have been a modest blaze. I will only quote this portion, which I am scribbling down in my notebook:

> *Meteorologists have attributed the tragic event to "positive" lightning, a relatively rare phenomenon. Unlike far more commonly occurring "negative" lightning, positive lightning takes place when a positive charge is carried by the uppermost regions of clouds – most often anvil clouds – rather than by the ground. This causes the leader arc to form within the anvil of the cumulonimbus cloud and travel horizontally for several miles before suddenly veering down to meet the negatively charged streamer rising up from the ground. The bolt can strike anywhere within several miles of the anvil of the thunderstorm, often in areas experiencing clear or only slightly cloudy skies, hence they may also be referred to as "bolts from the blue." Positive lightning is estimated to account for less than 5% of all lightning strikes.*

The meteorologist in question is not named, nor is his or her affiliation given. I do find it odd that far more space is given to an attempt to explain the event than to any other aspect of it. Also, it appears to have been cribbed from a textbook or other reference source, and deviates significantly from the voice of the rest of the article. There is, reading over it again and again, the sense that explaining the lightning was far more important to whoever wrote the piece than was reporting the deaths of the family or even the general facts of the case. A single anonymous source is quoted, a resident of High Street (in The Village) as a witness to the lightning strike. There is also mentioned a "terrific booming from the sky" that occurred an hour *after* the strike, and I can't help but wonder why the paper went to so much trouble to make plain that there was nothing especially peculiar about the lightning, but records another strange incident in passing which it makes no attempt to explain.

"Did you find what you were looking for?" the librarian asks, peering into the small room. I notice for the first time, the room smells musty. Or maybe it's the librarian who smells musty.

"I did," I reply. "Thank you. You've been very helpful."

"I do my job. I do what the town council pays me to do."

"Then you do it well," I say, determined to inflict upon her a compliment.

She grumbles, and I leave while she's busy removing the spool and returning it to its yellow Kodak box. I step out onto the tiny courtyard in front of the library, and it's just begun raining. Cold drops pepper my face. I stand, staring up into the rain, and consider calling the editor, apologizing, and asking for a second chance. Telling him there really is no mystery here, so it could be a great little piece debunking a rural myth, a triumph of science over the supposedly miraculous. I could return to The City, to my apartment, and wait for other jobs. I would find a way to forget about whatever lives at the top of the hill. I would tell myself I'd imagined the whole affair, mark it up to weariness, depression, something of the sort. The rain almost feels like needles.

6.

I awake from a nightmare. I awake breathless to sweaty sheets. I think I may have cried out in my sleep, but I don't know for sure. Almost at once, I forget most of the particulars of the dream. But it centered on the charred tree. There was something coiled in the branches of the tree, or perched there. It was gazing down at me. A shapeless thing, or very nearly so, clinging somehow to those charcoal branches. I wanted to turn away, to look away, but was unable. I felt the purest spite spilling from it, flowing down the gnarled trunk and washing over me. I have never believed in evil, but the thing in the tree was, I knew, evil. It was evil, and it was ancient beyond any human comprehension. Some of the eldest stars were younger, and the earth an infant by comparison. Mercifully, it didn't speak or make any other sound whatsoever.

I awake to a voice, and I recognize it straightaway. It's the voice from the hill. Near the door, there's the faintest of silhouettes, an outline that is only almost human. It's tall and begins moving gracefully across the room towards me. I reach to turn on the lamp, but, thankfully, my hand never touches the cord.

"Have you seen enough now?" she asks. "What you found at the library, was that enough?"

She's very near the foot of the bed now. I would never have guessed she was so tall and so extraordinarily slender. My eyes struggle with the darkness to make sense of something I cannot actually see.

"Not you," I whisper. "It hasn't explained you."

"Do I require an explanation?"

"Most people would say so."

If this is being read, I would say most *readers* would certainly say so. There, I *have* said it.

"But not you?"

"I don't know what I need," I say, and I'm being completely honest.

Here there is a long silence, and I realize it's still raining. That it's raining much harder than when I went to bed. I can hear thunder far away.

"This is the problem with explanations," she says. "You ask one, and it triggers an infinite regression. There is never a final question. Unless inquiry is halted by an arbitrary act. And it's true, many inquiries are, if only by necessity."

"If I knew what you are, why you are, how you are, if there is any connection between you and the death of those three people…" I trail off, knowing she'll finish my thought.

She says, "…you'd only have another question, and another after that. *Ad infinitum.*"

"I think I want to go home," I whisper.

"Then you should go home, don't you think?"

"What was that I dreamt of, the thing in the tree?"

Now she is leaning over me, on the bed *with* me, and it only frightens me that I am not afraid. "Only a bad dream," she sighs, and her breath smells like the summer forest, and autumn leaves, and snow, and swollen mountain rivers in the spring. It doesn't smell even remotely of fire.

"Before The Village, you were here," I say. "You've almost always been here." I say. It isn't a question, and she doesn't mistake it for one. She doesn't say anything else, and I understand I will never again hear her speak.

She wraps her arms and legs about me – and, as I guessed, they were delicate and nothing like the legs of women, and she takes me into her. We do not make love. We fuck. No, she fucks me. She fucks me, and it seems to go on forever. Repeatedly, I almost reach climax, and, repeatedly, it slips away. She mutters in a language I know, instinctively, has never been studied by any linguist, and one I'll not recall a syllable of later on, no matter how hard I struggle to do so. It seems filled with clicks and glottal stops. Outside, there is rain and thunder and lightning. The storm is pounding at the windows, wanting in. The storm, I think, is jealous. I wonder how long it will hold a grudge. Is that what happened on top of the hill? Did she take the man or the woman (or both) as a lover? Did the sky get even?

I do finally come, and the smells of her melt away. She is gone, and I lay on those sweaty sheets, trying to catch my breath.

So, I do not say aloud, *the dream didn't end with the tree. I dreamt her here, in the room with me. I dreamt her questions, and I dreamt her fucking me.*

I do my best to fool myself this is the truth.

It doesn't matter anymore.

By dawn, the rain has stopped.

7.

I have breakfast, pack, fill up the Nissan's tank, and pay my motel bill.

By the time I pull out of the parking lot, it's almost nine o'clock.

I drive away from The Village, and the steep slopes pressing in on all sides as if to smother it, and I drive away from the old cemetery beside Lake Witalema. I drive south, taking the long way back to the interstate, rather than passing the turnoff leading up the hill and the house and the lightning-struck tree. I know that I will spend the rest of my life avoiding the

White Mountains. Maybe I'll even go so far as to never step foot in New Hampshire again. That wouldn't be so hard to do.

I keep my eyes on the road in front of me, and am relieved as the forests and lakes give way to farmland and then the outskirts of The City. I am leaving behind a mystery that was never mine to answer. I leave behind shadows for light. Wondrous and terrifying glimpses of the extraordinary for the mundane.

I will do my damnedest to convince the editor to whom I owe a story – he took my call this morning, and was only mildly annoyed I'd missed the deadline – that there is nothing the least bit bizarre about that hill or the woods surrounding it. Nothing to it but tall tales told by ignorant and gullible Swamp Yankees, people who likely haven't heard the Revolutionary War has ended. I'll lie and make them sound that absurd, and we'll all have a good laugh.

I will bury, deep as I can, all my memories of her.

It doesn't matter anymore.

The Colliers' Venus (1898)

1.

It is not an ostentatious museum. Rather, it is only the sort of museum that best suits this modern, industrious city at the edge of the high Colorado plains. This city, with its sooty days and dusty, crowded streets and night skies that glow an angry orange from the dragon's breath of half a hundred Bessemer converters. The museum is a dignified, yet humble, assemblage of geological wonders, intended as much for the delight and edification of miners and mill workers, blacksmiths and butchers, as it is for the *parvenu* and Old Money families of Capitol Hill. Professor Jeremiah Ogilvy, both founder and curator of this *Colectanea rerum memorabilium*, has always considered himself a progressive sort, and he has gone so far as to set aside one day each and every month when the city's negroes, coolies, and red indians are permitted access to his cabinet, free of charge. Professor Ogilvy would – and frequently has – referred to his museum as a most *modest* endeavor, one whose principal mission is to reveal, to *all* the populace of Cherry Creek, the long-buried mysteries of those fantastic, vanished cycles of the globe. Too few suspect the marvels that lie just beneath their feet or entombed in the ridges and peaks of the snowcapped Chippewan Mountains bordering the city to the west. Cherry Creek looks always to the problems of its present day, and to the riches and prosperity that may await those who reach its future, but with hardly a thought to spare for the past, and *this* is the sad oversight addressed by the Ogilvy Gallery of Natural Antiquities.

Before Professor Ogilvy leased the enormous redbrick building on Kipling Street (erected during the waning days of the silver boom of '78), it served as a warehouse for a firm specializing in the import of exotic dry goods, mainly spices from Africa and the East Indies. And, to this day, it retains a distinctive, piquant redolence. Indeed, at times the odor is so strong that a sobriquet has been bestowed upon the museum – Ogilvy's

Pepper Pot. It is not unusual to see visitors of either gender covering their noses with handkerchiefs and sleeves, and oftentimes the solemnity of the halls is shattered by hacking coughs and sudden fits of sneezing. Regardless, the Professor has insisted, time and again, that the structure is perfectly matched to his particular needs, and how the curiosity of man is not to be deterred by so small an inconvenience as the stubborn ghosts of turmeric and curry powder, coriander and mustard seed. Besides, the apparently indelible odor helps to insure that his rents will stay reasonable.

On this June afternoon, the air in the building seems a bit fresher than usual, despite the oppressive heat that comes with the season. In the main hall, Jeremiah Ogilvy has been occupied for almost a full hour now, lecturing the ladies of the Cherry Creek chapter of the Women's Christian Temperance Union. Mrs. Belford and her companions sit on folding chairs, fanning themselves and diligently listening while this slight, earnest, and bespectacled man describes for them the reconstructed fossil skeleton displayed behind him.

"The great anatomist, Baron Cuvier, wrote of the *Plesiosaurus,* 'it presents the most monstrous assemblage of characteristics that has been met with among the races of the ancient world.' Now, I would have you know it isn't necessary to take this expression literally. There are no monsters in nature, as the Laws of Organization are never so positively infringed."

"Well, it looks like a monster to me," mutters Mrs. Larimer, seated near the front. "I would certainly hate to come upon such a thing slithering towards me along a river bank. I should think I'd likely perish of fright, if nothing else."

There's a subdued titter of laughter from the group, and Mrs. Belford frowns. The Professor forces a smile and repositions his spectacles on the bridge of his nose.

"Indeed," he sighs and glances away from his audience, looking over his shoulder at the skillful marriage of plaster and stone and welded steel armature.

"However," he continues, "be that as it may, it is more accordant with the general perfection of Creation to see in an organization so special as *this* – " and, with his ashplant, he points once more to the plesiosaur, " – to recognize in a structure which differs so notably from that of animals of our days – the simple augmentation of type, and sometimes also the beginning and successive perfecting of these beings. Therefore, let us dismiss this idea of monstrosity, my good Mrs. Larimer, a concept which can only mislead us, and only cause us to consider these antediluvian beasts as digressions.

Instead, let us look upon them, not with disgust. Let us learn, on the contrary, to perceive in the plan traced for their organization, the handiwork of the Creator of all things, as well as the general plan of Creation."

"How very inspirational," Mrs. Belford beams, and when she softly claps her gloved hands, the others follow her example. Professor Ogilvy takes this as his cue that the ladies of the Women's Christian Temperance Union have heard all they wish to hear this afternoon on the subject of the giant plesiosaur, recently excavated in Kansas from the chalky banks of the Smoky Hill River. As one of the newer additions to his menagerie, it now frequently forms the centerpiece of the Professor's daily presentations.

When the women have stopped clapping, Mrs. Larimer dabs at her nose with a swatch of perfumed silk and loudly clears her throat.

"Yes, Mrs. Larimer? A question?" Professor Ogilvy asks, turning back to the women. *Mr.* Larimer – an executive with the Front Range offices of the German airship company, Gesellschaft zur Förderung der Luftschiffahrt – has donated a sizable sum to the museum's coffers, and it's no secret that his wife believes her husband's charity would be best placed elsewhere.

"I mean no disrespect, Professor, but it strikes *me* that perhaps you have gone and mistaken the provenance of that beast's design. For my part, it's far easier to imagine such a fiend being more at home in the sulfurous tributaries of Hell than the waters of any earthly ocean. Perhaps, my good doctor, it may be that you are merely mistaken about the demon's having ever been buried. Possibly, to the contrary, it is something which clawed its way *up* from the Pit."

Jeremiah Ogilvy stares at her a moment, aware that it's surely wisest to humor this disagreeable woman. To nod and smile and make no direct reply to such absurd remarks. But he has always been loathe to suffer fools, and has never been renowned as the most politic of men, often to his detriment. He makes a steeple of his hands and rests his chin upon his fingertips as he replies.

"And yet," he says, "oddly, you'll note that on both its fore- *and* hind limbs, each fashioned into paddles, this underworld fiend of yours entirely *lacks* claws. Don't you think, Mrs. Larimer, that we might fairly expect such modifications, something not unlike the prominent ungula of a mole, perhaps? Or the robust nails of a Cape anteater? I mean, that's a terrible lot of digging to do, all the way from Perdition to the prairies of Gove County."

There's more laughter, an uneasy smattering that echoes beneath the high ceiling beams, and it elicits another scowl from an embarrassed Mrs.

Belford. But the Professor has cast his lot, as it were, for better or worse, and he keeps his eyes fixed upon Mrs. Charles W. Larimer. She looks more chagrined than angry, and any trace of her former bluster has faded away.

"As you say, *Professor*," and she manages to make the last three syllables sound like a badge of wickedness.

"Very well, then," Professor Ogilvy says, turning to Mrs. Belford. "Perhaps I could interest you gentle women in the celebrated automatic mastodon, a bona-fide masterpiece of clockwork engineering and steam power. So realistic in movement and appearance you might well mistake it for the living thing, newly resurrected from some boggy Pleistocene quagmire."

"Oh, yes. I think that would be fascinating," Mrs. Belford replies, and soon the women are being led from the main gallery up a steep flight of stairs to the mezzanine where the automatic mastodon and the many engines and hydraulic hoses that control it have been installed. It stands alongside a finely preserved skeleton of *Mammut americanum* unearthed by prospectors in the Yukon and shipped to the Gallery at some considerable expense.

"Why, it's nothing but a great hairy elephant," Mrs. Larimer protests, but this time none of the others appear to pay her much mind. Professor Ogilvy's fingers move over the switches and dials on the brass control panel, and soon the automaton is stomping its massive feet and flapping its ears and filling the hot, pepper-scented air with the trumpeting of extinct Pachydermata.

2.

When the ladies of the Temperance Union have gone, and after Jeremiah Ogilvy has seen to the arrival of five heavy crates of saurian bones from one of his collectors working out of Monterey, and, then, after he has spoken with his chief preparator about an overdue shipment of blond Kushmi shellac, ammonia, and sodium borate, he checks his pocket watch and locks the doors of the museum. Though there has been nothing excessively trying about the day – not even the disputatious Mrs. Larimer caused him more than a passing annoyance – Professor Ogilvy finds he's somewhat more weary than usual, and is looking forward to his bed with an especial zeal. All the others have gone, his small staff of technicians, sculptors, and naturalists, and he retires to his office and puts the kettle on to boil. He has a fresh tin of Formosa Oolong, and decides that this evening he'll take his tea up on the roof.

Most nights, there's a fine view from the gallery roof, and he can watch the majestic airships docking at the Arapahoe Station dirigible terminal, or just shut his eyes and take in the commingled din of human voices and buckboards, the heavy clop of horses' hooves and the comforting pandemonium made by the locomotives passing through the city along the Colorado and Northern Kansas Railway.

He hangs the tea egg over the rim of his favorite mug and is preparing to pour the hot water, when the office doorknob rattles and neglected hinges creak like inconvenienced rodents. Jeremiah looks up, not so much alarmed as taken by surprise, and is greeted by the familiar – but certainly unexpected – face and pale blue eyes of Dora Bolshaw. She holds up her key, tied securely on a frayed length of calico ribbon, to remind him that he never took it back and to remove any question as to how she gained entry to the locked museum after hours. Dora Bolshaw is an engine mechanic for the Rocky Mountain Reconsolidated Fuel Company, and, because of this, and her habit of dressing always in men's clothes, *and* the fact that her hands and face are only rarely anything approaching clean, she is widely, and mistakenly, believed to be an inveterate Sapphist. Dora is, of course, shunned by more proper women – such as, for instance, Mrs. Charles W. Larimer – who blanche at the thought of *dames et lesbiennes* walking free and unfettered in their midst. Dora has often mused that, despite her obvious preference for men, she is surely the most renowned bulldyke west of the Mississippi.

"Slipping in like a common sneak thief," Jeremiah sighs, reaching for a second cup. "I trust you recollect the combination to the strongbox, along with the whereabouts of that one loose floorboard."

"I most assuredly do," she replies. "Like they were the finest details of the back of my hand. Like it was only yesterday you went and divulged those confidences."

"Very good, Miss Bolshaw. Then, I trust this means we can forgo the messy gunplay and knives and whatnot?"

She steps into the office and pulls the door shut behind her, returning the key to a pocket of her waistcoat. "If that's your fancy, Professor. If it's only a peaceable sort of evening you're after."

Filling his mug from the steaming kettle, submerging the mesh ball of the tea egg and the finely ground leaves, Jeremiah shrugs and nods at a chair near his desk.

"Do you still take two lumps?" he asks her.

"Provided you got nothing stronger," she says, and only hesitates a moment before crossing the room to the chair.

"No," Jeremiah tells her. "Nothing stronger. If I recall, we had an agreement, you and I?"

"You want your key back?"

Professor Jeremiah Ogilvy pours hot water into the second teacup, then adds a second tea egg, and he very nearly asks if she imagines that his feelings have changed since the last time they spoke. Its been almost six months since the snowy January night when he asked her to marry him. Dora laughed, thinking it only a poor joke at first. But when pressed, she admitted she was not the least bit interested in marriage and, what's more, confessed she was even less amenable to giving up her work at the mines to bear and raise children. When she suggested that he board up his museum, instead, and for a family take in one or two of the starving guttersnipes who haunt Colliers' Row, there was an argument. Before it was done, he said spiteful things, cruel jibes aimed at all the tender spots she'd revealed to him over the years of their courtship. And he knew, even as he spoke the words, that there would be no taking them back. The betrayal of Dora's trust came too easily, the turning of her confidences against her, and she is not a particularly forgiving woman. So, tonight, he only *almost* asks, then thinks better of the question and holds his tongue.

"It's your key," he says. "Keep it. You may have need of it again one day."

"Fine," Dora replies, letting the chair rock back on two legs. "It's your funeral, Jeremiah."

"Can I ask why you're here?"

"You may," she says, staring now at a fossil ammonite lying in a cradle of excelsior on his desk. "It's bound to come out, sooner or later. But if you're thinking maybe I come looking for old times or a quick poke – "

"I *wasn't*," he lies, interrupting her.

"Well, good. Because I ain't."

"Which begs the question. And it's been a rather tedious day, Miss Bolshaw, so, if we can dispense with any further niceties."

Dora coughs and leans forward, the front legs of her chair bumping loudly against the floor. Jeremiah keeps his eyes on the two cups of tea, each one turned as dark now as a sluggish, tannin-stained bayou.

"I'm guessing that you still haven't seen anyone about that cough," he says. "And that it hasn't improved."

Dora coughs again before answering him, then wipes at her mouth with an oil-stained handkerchief. "Good to see time hasn't dulled your mental faculties," she mutters hoarsely, breathlessly, then clears her throat and wipes her mouth again.

"It doesn't sound good, Dora, that's all. You spend too much time in the tunnels. Plenty enough people die from anthracosis without ever having lifted a pickaxe or loaded a mine car, as I'm sure you're well aware."

"I also didn't come here to discuss my health," she tells him, stuffing the handkerchief back into a trouser pocket. "It's the stink of *this* place, gets me wheezing, that's all. I swear, Jeremiah, the air in this dump, it's like trying to breathe inside a goddamn burr grinder that's been used to mill capsicum and black powder."

"No argument there," he says and takes the tea eggs from the cups and sets them aside on a dishtowel. "But, I still don't know why you're here."

"Been some odd goings on down in Shaft Number Seven, ever since they started back in working on the Molly Gray vein."

"I thought Shaft Seven flooded in October," Jeremiah says, and he adds two sugar cubes to Dora's cup. The Professor has never taken his tea sweetened, nor with lemon, cream, or whiskey, for that matter. When he drinks tea, it's the tea he wants to taste.

"They pumped it out a while back, got the operation up and running again. Anyway, one of the foremen knew we were acquainted and asked if I'd mind. Paying you a call, I mean."

"Do you?" he asks, carrying the cups to the desk.

"Do I what?"

"Do you *mind*, Miss Bolshaw?"

She glares at him a moment, then takes her cup and lets her eyes wander back to the ammonite on the desk.

"So, these odd goings on. Can you be more specific?"

"I can, *if* you'll give me a chance. You ever heard of anyone finding living creatures sealed up inside solid rock, two thousand feet below ground?"

He watches her a moment, to be sure this isn't a jest.

"You're saying this has happened, in Shaft Seven?"

She sips at her tea, then sets the cup on the edge of the desk and picks up the ammonite. The fossilized mother of pearl glints iridescent shades of blue and green, scarlet and gold, in the dim gaslight of the office.

"That's exactly what I'm saying. And I seen most of them for myself, so I know it's not just miners' spinning tall tales."

"Most of *them*? So, it's happened more than once?"

Dora ignores the questions, turning the ammonite over and over in her hands.

"I admit," she says, "I was more than a little skeptical at first. There's a shale bed just below the Molly Gray, and it's chockful of siderite nodules. Lots of them got fossils inside. Matter of fact, I think I brought a couple of boxes over to you last summer, before the shaft started taking water."

"You did. There were some especially nice seed ferns in them, as I recall."

"Right. Well, anyhow, a few days back I started hearing these wild stories, that someone had cracked open a nodule and found a live frog trapped inside. And then a spider. And then worms, and so on. When I asked around about it, I was directed to the geologist's shack, and sure as hell, there were all these things lined up in jars, things that come out of the nodules. Mostly, they were dead. Most of them died right after they came out of the rocks, or so I'm told."

Dora stops talking and returns the ammonite shell to its box. Then she glances at Jeremiah and takes another sip of her tea.

"And you *know* it's not a hoax?" he asks her. "I mean, you know it's not tomfoolery, just some of the miners taking these things down with them from the surface, then claiming to have found them in the rocks? Maybe having a few laughs at the expense of their supervisors?"

"Now, that *was* my first thought."

"But then you saw something that changed your mind," Jeremiah says. "And that's why you're here tonight."

Dora Bolshaw takes deep breath, and Jeremiah thinks she's about to start coughing again. Instead, she nods and exhales slowly. He notices beads of sweat standing out on her upper lip, and wonders if she's running a fever.

"I'm here tonight, Professor Ogilvy, because two men are dead. But, yeah, since you asked, I've seen sufficient evidence to convince me this ain't just some jackass thinks he's funny. When I voiced my doubts, Charlie McNamara split one of those nodules open right there in front of me. Concretion big around as my fist," and she holds up her left hand for emphasis. "He took up a hammer and gave it a smart tap on one side, so it cleaved in two, pretty as you please. And out crawled a fat red scorpion. You ever *seen* a red scorpion, Jeremiah?"

And Professor Ogilvy thinks a moment, sipping his tea come all the way from Taipei City, Taiwan. "I've seen plenty of reddish-brown scorpions," he says. "For example, *Diplocentrus lindo*, from the Chihuahuan Desert and parts of Texas. The carapace is, in fact, a dark reddish-brown."

"I didn't *say* reddish brown. What I said was *red*. Red as berries on a holly bush, or a ripe apple. Red as blood, if you want to go get morbid about it."

"Charlie cracked open a rock, from Shaft Number Seven, and a bright red scorpion crawled out. That's what you're telling me?"

"I am," Dora nods. "Bastard had a stinger on him big around as my thumb, and then some," and now she holds out her thumb.

"And two men at the mines have *died* because of these scorpions?" Jeremiah Ogilvy asks.

"No. Weren't scorpions killed them," she says and laughs nervously. "But it *was* something come out those rocks." And then she frowns down at her teacup and asks the Professor if he's absolutely sure that he doesn't have anything stronger. And this time, he opens a bottom desk drawer and digs out the pint bottle of rye he keeps there, and he offers it to her. Dora Bolshaw pulls out the cork and pours a generous shot into her tea cup, but then she's coughing again, worse than before, and he watches her and waits for it to pass.

3.

What she's told him is not without precedent. Over the years, Professor Jeremiah Ogilvy has encountered any number of seemingly inexplicable reports of living inclusions discovered in stones, and often inside lumps of coal. Living fossils, after a fashion. He has never once given them credence, but, rather, looked upon these anecdotes as fine examples of the general gullibility of men, not unlike the taxidermied "jackalopes" he's seen in saloons, or tales of ghostly hauntings, or of angels, or the antics of spiritual mediums. They are all quite amusing, these phantasma, until someone insists that they're true.

For starters, he could point to an 1818 lecture by Dr. Edward Daniel Clarke, the first professor of mineralogy at Cambridge University. Clarke claimed to have been collecting Cretaceous sea urchins when he happened across three newts entombed in the chalk. To his amazement, the amphibians showed signs of life, and though two quickly expired after being exposed to air, the third was so lively that it escaped when he placed it in a nearby pond to aid in its rejuvenation. Or, a case from the summer of 1851, when quarrymen in Blois, France were supposed to have discovered a live toad inside a piece of flint. Indeed, batrachians figure more prominently in these accounts than any other creature, and the Professor might also have brought to Dora Bolshaw's attention yet another toad, said to have been freed from a lump of iron ore the very next year, this time somewhere in the East Midlands of England.

The list goes on and on, reaching back centuries. On May 8, 1733, the Swedish architect Johan Gråberg supposedly witnessed the release of a frog from a block of sandstone. So horrified was Gråberg at the sight that he is said to have beaten the beast to death with a shovel. An account of the incident was summarily published, by Gråberg, in the *Transactions of the Swedish Academy of Sciences*, a report which was eventually translated into Dutch, Latin, German, and French.

Too, there is the account from 1575 by the surgeon Ambroise Paré, who claimed a live toad was found inside a stone in his vineyards in Meudon. In 1686, Professor Robert Plot, the first Keeper of the Ashmolean Museum in Oxford claimed knowledge of three cases of the "toad-in-the-hole" phenomenon from Britain alone. Hoaxes, perhaps, or only the gullible yarns of a pre-scientific age, when even learned men were somewhat more disposed to believing the unbelievable.

But Jeremiah Ogilvy mentioned none of these tales. Instead, he sat and sipped his tea and listened while she talked, never once interrupting to give voice to his mounting incredulity. However, her cough forced Dora Bolshaw to stop several times, and, despite the rye whiskey, towards the end of her story she was hoarse and had grown alarmingly pale; her hands were shaking so badly that she had trouble holding her cup steady. And then, when she was done, and he was trying to organize his thoughts, she glanced anxiously at the clock and said that she should be going. So he walked her downstairs, past the celebrated automatic mastodon and petrified titanothere skulls and his prized plesiosaur skeleton. Standing on the walkway outside the museum, the night air seemed sweet after the "pepper pot," despite the soot from the furnaces and the reek from the open ditches lining either side of Kipling Street. He offered to see her home, because the thoroughfares of Cherry Creek have an unsavory reputation after dark, but she laughed at him, and he didn't offer a second time. He watched until she was out of sight, then went back to his office.

And now it's almost midnight, and Jeremiah Ogilvy's teacups sit empty and forgotten while he thinks about toads and stones and considers finishing off the pint of rye. After she told him of the most recent and bizarre and, indeed, entirely impossible discovery from Shaft Seven, the thing that was now being blamed for the deaths of two miners, he agreed to look at it.

"Not *it. Her,*" Dora said, folding and unfolding her handkerchief. "She came out of the rocks, Jeremiah. Just like that damned red scorpion, she came out of the rocks."

4.

"Then I *am* dreaming," he says, relieved, and she smiles, not unkindly. He's holding her hand, this woman who is, by turns, Dora Bolshaw and a wispy, nervous girl named Katharine Herschel, whom he courted briefly before leaving New Haven and the comforts of Connecticut for the clamorous frontier metropolis of Cherry Creek. They stand together on some windswept aerie of steel and concrete, looking down upon the night-shrouded city. And Jeremiah holds up an index finger and traces the delicate network of avenues illumined by gas streetlamps. And *there*, at his fingertip, are the massive hangers and the mooring masts of the Arapahoe Terminal. A dirigible is approaching from the south, parting the omnipresent pall of clouds, and the ship begins a slow, stately turn to starboard. To his eyes, it seems more like some majestic organism than any human fabrication. A heretofore unclassified order of volant Cnidaria, perhaps, titan jellyfish that have forsaken the brine and the vasty deep and adapted to a life in the clouds. Watching the dirigible, he imagines translucent, stinging tentacles half a mile long, hanging down from its gondola to snare unwary flocks of birds. The underside of the dirigible blushes yellow-orange as the lacquered cotton of its outer skin catches and reflects the molten light spilling up from all the various ironworks and the copper and silver foundries scattered throughout Cherry Creek. The bones of the world exhumed and smelted to drive the tireless progress of man. He's filled with pride, gazing out across the city and knowing the small part he has played in birthing this civilization from a desolate wilderness fit for little more than prairie dogs, rattlesnakes, and heathen savages.

"Maybe the world don't exactly see it that way," Dora says. "I been thinking lately, maybe she don't see it that way at all."

Jeremiah isn't surprised when tendrils of blue lightning flick down from the coal-smoke sky, and crackling electric streams trickle across rooftops and down the rainspouts of the high buildings.

"Maybe," Dora continues, "the world has different plans. Maybe she's had them all along. Maybe, Professor, we've finally gone and dug too deep in these old mountains."

But Jeremiah makes a derisive, scoffing noise and shakes his head. And then he recites scripture while the sky rains ultramarine and the shingles and cobblestones sizzle. "'And God said, Let us make man in our image, after our likeness: and let them have dominion over the fish of the sea, and over the fowl of the air, and over the cattle, and over all the earth, and over every creeping thing that creepeth upon the earth.'"

"I don't recall it saying nothing about whatever creepeth *under* the earth," Dora mutters, though now she looks a little more like Katharine Herschel, her blue eyes turning brown, and her trousers traded for a petticoat. "Besides, you're starting to sound like that idiotic Larimer woman. Didn't you hear a single, solitary word I said to you?"

Jeremiah raises his hand still higher, as though, with only a little more effort, he might reach the lightning or the shiny belly of the approaching dirigible or even the face of the Creator, peering down at them through the smoldering haze.

"Is it not fair wondrous?" he asks Dora. But it's Katharine who answers him, and she only trades him one question for another, repeating Dora's words.

"Didn't you hear a single, solitary word I said?"

And they are no longer standing high atop the aerie, but have been grounded again, grounded now. He's seated with Dora and Charlie McNamara in the cluttered nook that passes for Dora's office, which is hardly more than a closet, situated at one end of the Rocky Mountain Reconsolidated Fuel Company's primary machine shop. The room is littered with a rummage of dismembered engines – every tabletop and much of the floor concealed beneath castoff gears, gauges, sprockets, and fly wheels, rusted-out boilers and condensers, warped piston rods and dials with bent needles and cracked faces. There's a profusion of blueprints and schematics, some tacked to the wall and others rolled up tight and stacked one atop the other like Egyptian papyri or scrolls from the lost library of Alexandria. Everywhere are empty and half-empty oil cans, and there are any number of tools for which Jeremiah doesn't know the names.

"Time being, operations have been suspended," Charlie McNamara says, and then he goes back to using the blade of his pocketknife to dig at the grime beneath his fingernails. "Well, at least that's the company line.

Between you me and Miss Bolshaw here, I think Chicago's having a good long think about sealing off the shaft permanently."

"Permanently," Jeremiah whispers, sorry that he can no longer see the skyline or the docking dirigible. "I would imagine that's going to mean quite a hefty loss, after all the money and work and time required to get the shaft dry, refitted, and producing again."

"Be that as it damn may be," Dora says brusquely. "There's more at stake here than coal and pit quotas and quarterly profits."

"Yes, well," Jeremiah says, staring at the scuffed toes of his boots now. "Then let's get to it, yes? If I can manage to keep my blasted claustrophobia in check, I'm quite sure we'll get to the bottom of this."

No one laughs at the pun, because it isn't funny, and Jeremiah rubs his aching eyes and wishes again that he were still perched high on the aerie, the night wind roaring in his ears.

"Ain't she *told* you?" the company geologist asks, glancing over at Dora. "What I need you to look at, it ain't in the hole no more. What you need to *see,* well..." and here he trails off. "It's locked up in a cell at St. Joseph's."

"Locked up?" Jeremiah asks, and the geologist nods.

"Jail would have done her better," Dora mutters. "You put sick folks in the hospital. Killers, you put in jails, or you put a bullet in the skull and be done with it."

Charlie McNamara tells Dora to please shut the hell up and try not to make things worse than they already are.

Jeremiah shifts uneasily in his chair. "How *did* the men die? I mean, how exactly?"

"Lungs plumb full up with coal dust," Charlie says. "Lungs and throat and mouth all stuffed damn near to busting. Doctor, he even found the shit clogging up their stomachs and intestines."

"Some of the men," Dora adds, "they say they've heard singing down there. Said it was beautiful, the most beautiful music they've ever heard."

"Jesus in a steam wagon, Dora. Ain't you got an off switch or something? Singing ain't never killed no one yet, and it *sure* as hell wasn't what got that poor pair of bastards."

And even as the geologist is speaking, the scene shifts again, another unprefaced revolution in this dreaming kaleidoscope reality, and now the halls and exhibits of the Ogilvy Gallery of Natural Antiquities are spread out around him. On Jeremiah's right, the celebrated automatic mastodon rolls glass eyes, and its gigantic tusks are garnished with a dripping, muculent snarl of vegetation. On his left, the serpentine neck of the Gove County plesiosaur rises gracefully as any swan's, though he sees that all the fossil bones and the Plaster of Paris have been transmutated through some alchemy into cast iron. The metal is marred by a very slight patina of rust, and it occurs to him that, considering the beast's ferrous metamorphosis, he should remind his staff that they'd best keep the monstrous reptile from swimming or wandering about the rainy streets.

"I cried the day you went away," Katharine says, because, for the moment, it *is* Katharine with him again, not Dora. "I wrote a letter, but never sent it. I keep it in a dresser drawer."

"There was too much work to do," he tells her, still admiring the skeleton. "And much too little of it could be done from New Haven."

Behind the plesiosaur, the brick and mortar of the Gallery walls has dissolved utterly away, revealing the trunks of mighty scale trees and innumerable scouring rushes tall as California redwoods. Here is a dark Carboniferous forest, the likes of which has not taken root since the Mary Gray vein at the bottom of Shaft Seven was only slime and rotting detritus. And below these alien boughs, a menagerie of primæval beings has gathered to peer out across the aeons. So, it is not merely a hole knocked in his wall, but a hole bored through the very fabric of time.

"She came out of the *rocks,* Jeremiah," Katharine says, even though the voice is plainly Dora Bolshaw's. "Just like that damned red scorpion, she came out of the rocks."

"You're beginning to put me in mind of a Greek chorus," he replies, keeping his eyes on the scene unfolding behind the plesiosaur. Great hulking forms have begun to shift impatiently in the shadows there, the armored hide of a dozen species of Dinosauria and the tangled manes of giant ground sloths and Irish elk, the leathery wings of a whole flock of pterodactyls spreading wide.

"Maybe they worshipped her, before there ever were men," Dora says, but then she's coughing again, the dry, hacking cough of someone suffering from advanced anthracosis. Katharine has to finish the thought for her. "Maybe they built temples to her, and whispered prayers in the guttural tongues of animals, and maybe they made offerings, after a fashion."

Overhead, there's a cacophonous, rolling sound that Jeremiah Ogilvy first mistakes for thunder. But then he realizes that it's merely the hungry blue lightning at last locating the flammable guncotton epidermis of the airship.

"Some of the men," Katharine whispers, "they say they've heard singing down there. Singing like church hymns, they said. Said it was beautiful, the most beautiful music they've ever heard. We come so late to this procession, and yet we presume to know so much."

From behind the iron plesiosaur, that anachronistic menagerie gathers itself like a breathing wave of sinew and bone and fur, cresting, racing towards the shingle.

Jeremiah Ogilvy turns away, no longer wanting to see.

"Maybe, in their own way, they prayed," Dora whispers.

And the tall, thin man standing before him, the collier in his overalls and hard hat who wasn't there just a moment before, hefts his pick and brings it down smartly against the floorboards, which, in the instant steel strikes wood, become the black stone floor of a mine. All light has been extinguished from the Gallery now, save that shining dimly from the collier's carbide lantern. The head of the pick strikes rock, and there's a spark, and then the ancient shale begins to bleed. And soon thereafter, the dream comes apart, and the Professor lies awake and sweating, waiting for sunrise and trying desperately to think about anything but what he's been told has happened at the bottom of Shaft Seven.

5.

After his usual modest breakfast of black coffee with blueberry preserves and biscuits, and after he's given his staff their instructions for the day and cancelled a lecture that he was scheduled to deliver to a league of amateur mineralogists, Jeremiah Ogilvy leaves the museum. He walks north along Kipling to the intersection with West 20th Avenue, where he's arranged to meet Dora Bolshaw. He says good morning, and that he hopes she's feeling well. But Dora's far more taciturn than usual, and few obligatory pleasantries are exchanged. Together, they take one of the clanking, kidney-jarring public omnibuses south and east to St. Joseph's Hospital for the Bodily and Mentally Infirm, established only two decades earlier by a group of the Sisters of Charity sent to Cherry Creek from Leavenworth.

Charlie McNamara is waiting for them in the lobby, his long canvas duster so stained with mud and soot that it's hard to imagine it was ever anything but this variegated riot of black and grey. He's a small mountain of a man, all beard and muscle, just starting to go soft about the middle.

Jeremiah has thought, on more than one occasion, this is what men would look like had they'd descended not from apes, but from grizzly bears.

"Thank you for coming," Charlie says. "I know that you're a busy man." But Jeremiah tells him to think nothing of it, that's he's glad to be of whatever service he can – *if*, indeed, he can be of service. Charlie and Dora nod to one another then, and swap nervous salutations. Jeremiah sees, or only thinks he sees, something wordless pass between them, as well, something anxious and wary, spoken with the eyes and not the lips.

"You told him?" Charlie asks, and Dora shrugs.

"I told him the most of it. I told him what murdered them two men."

"Mulawski and Backstrom," Charlie says.

Dora shrugs again. "I didn't recollect their names. But I don't suppose that much matters."

Charlie McNamara frowns and tugs at a corner of his mustache. "No," he nods. "I don't suppose it does."

"I hope you'll understand my skepticism," Jeremiah says, looking up, speaking to Charlie, but watching Dora. "What's been related to me, regarding the deaths of these two men, and what you've brought me here to see, I'd be generous if I were to say it strikes me as a fairy tale. Or, perhaps, something from the dime novels. It was Hume – David Hume – who said, 'No testimony is sufficient to establish a miracle, unless the testimony be of such a kind, that its falsehood would be more miraculous than the fact which it endeavors to establish.'"

Dora glares back at him. "You always did have such a goddamn pretty way of calling a girl a liar," she says.

"Hell," Charlie sighs, still tugging at his mustache. "I'd be concerned, Dora, if he *weren't* dubious. I've always thought myself a rational man. That's been a source of pride to me, out here among the savages and them that's just plain ignorant and don't know no better. But now, after *this* business – "

"Yeah, well, so how about we stop the clucking and get to it," Dora cuts in, and Charlie McNamara frowns at her. But then he stops fussing with his whiskers and nods again.

"Yeah," he says. "Guess I'm just stalling. Doesn't precisely fill me with joy, the thought of seeing her again. If you'll just follow me, Jeremiah, they got her stashed away up on the second floor," and he points to the stairs. "The Sisters ain't none too pleased about her being here. I think they're of the general notion that there's more proper places than hospitals for demons."

"Demons," Jeremiah says, and Dora Bolshaw laughs a dry, humorless laugh.

"That's what they're calling her," Dora tells him. "The nuns, I mean. You might as well know that. Got a priest from Annunciation sitting vigil outside the cell, reading Latin and whatnot. There's talk of an exorcism."

At this pronouncement, Charlie McNamara makes a gruff dismissive noise and motions more forcefully towards the stairwell. He mutters something rude about popery and superstition and lady engine jockeys who can't keep their damn pie holes shut.

"Charlie, you know I'm not saying anything that isn't true," Dora protests, but Jeremiah Ogilvy thinks he's already heard far too much and seen far too little. He steps past them, walking quickly and with purpose to the stairs, and the geologist and the mechanic follow close on his heels.

6.

"I would like to speak with her," he says. "I would like to speak with her alone." And Jeremiah takes his face away from the tiny barred window set into the door of the cell where they've confined the woman from the bottom of Shaft Seven. For a moment, he stares at the company geologist, and then his eyes drift towards Dora.

"Maybe you didn't hear me right," Charlie McNamara says and furrows his shaggy eyebrows. "She *don't* talk. Least ways, not near as anyone can tell."

"You're wasting your breath arguing with him," Dora mumbles and glances at the priest, who's standing not far away, eyeing the locked door and clutching his Bible. "Might as well try to tell the good Father here that the Queen of Heaven got herself knocked up by a stable hand."

Jeremiah turns back to the window, his face gone indignant and bordering now on choleric. "Charlie, I'm neither a physician nor an alienist, but you've brought me here to see this woman. Having looked upon her, the reason why continues to escape me. However, that said, if I *am* to examine her, I cannot possibly hope to do so properly from behind a locked door."

"It's not safe," the priest says very softly. "You must know that, Professor Ogilvy. It isn't safe at all."

Peering in past the steel bars, Jeremiah shakes his head and sighs. "She's naked, Father. She's naked, and can't weigh more than eighty pounds.

What possible threat might she pose to me? And, while we're at it, why, precisely, *is* she naked?"

"Oh, they gave her clothes," Dora chimes in. "Well, what *passes* for clothes in a place like this. But she tears them off. Won't have none of it, them white gowns and what have you."

"She is brazen," the priest all but whispers.

"Has anyone even tried to bathe her?" Jeremiah asks, and Charlie coughs.

"That ain't coal dust and mud you're seeing," he says. "Near as anyone can tell, that there's her skin."

"This is ludicrous, all of it," Jeremiah grumbles. "This is *not* the Middle Ages, and you do *not* have some infernal siren or succubus locked up in there. Whatever else you may believe, she's a *woman*, Charlie, and, having sacrificed my very busy day to come all the way out here, I would like, now, to speak with her."

"I was only explaining, Jeremiah, how I ain't of the notion it's such a good idea, that's all," Charlie says, then looks at the priest. "You got the keys, Father?"

The priest nods, reluctantly, and then he produces a single tarnished brass key from his cassock. Jeremiah steps aside while he unlocks the door.

"I'm going in with you," Dora says.

"No, you're not," Jeremiah tells her. "I need to speak with this woman alone."

"But she *don't* talk," Dora says again, beginning to sound exasperated, forcing the words out between clenched teeth.

The priest turns the key, and hidden tumblers and pins respond accordingly.

"Dora, you go scare up an orderly," Charlie McNamara says. "Hell, scare up two, just in case."

And the cell door opens, and, as Jeremiah Ogilvy steps across the threshold, the woman inside keeps her black eyes fixed upon him, but she makes no move to attempt an escape. She stays crouched on the floor in the southeast corner and makes no move whatsoever. Immediately, the door bangs shut again, and the priest relocks it.

"Just so there's no doubt on the matter," Charlie McNamara loudly mutters from the hallway, "you're a goddamn fool," and now the woman in the cell smiles. Jeremiah Ogilvy stands very still for a moment, taking in all the details of her and her cramped quarters. There is a mattress and a chamber pot, but no other manner of furnishings or facilities. If he held his arms out to either side, they would touch the walls. If he took only one step backwards, or only half a step, he'd collide with the locked door.

"Good morning," he says, and the woman blinks her eyes. They remind Jeremiah of twin pools of crude oil, spewed fresh from the well and poured into her face. There appear to be no irises, no sclera, no pupils, unless these eyes are composed entirely of pupil. She blinks, and the orbs shimmer slick in the dim light of the hospital cell.

"Good morning," he says to her again, though more quietly than before and with markedly less enthusiasm. "Is it true, that you do not speak? Are you a mute, then? Are you deaf, as well as dumb?"

She blinks again, and then the woman from Shaft Seven cocks her head to one side, as though carefully considering his question. Her hair is very long and straight, reaching almost down to the floor. It seems greasy and is so very black it might well have been spun from the sky of a moonless night. And yet, her skin is far darker, so much so that her hair fairly glows in comparison. There's no word in any human language for a blackness so complete, so inviolate, and he thinks, *What can you be? Eyes spun from a midnight with neither moon nor stars nor gas jets nor even the paltry flicker of tallow candles, and your skin carved from obsidian planks.* And then Jeremiah chides himself for entertaining such silly, florid notions, for falling prey to such unscientific fancies, and he takes another step towards the woman huddled on the floor.

"So, it *is* true," he says softly. "You are, indeed, without a voice."

And at that, her smile grows wider, her lips parting to reveal teeth like finely polished pegs shaped from chromite ore, and she laughs. If her laugh differs in any significant way from that of any other woman, the difference is not immediately apparent to Jeremiah Ogilvy.

"I am with voice," she says, then. "For any who wish to hear me, I am with voice."

Jeremiah is silent, and he glances over his left shoulder at the door. Charlie McNamara is staring in at him through the bars.

"I am with voice," she says a third time.

Jeremiah turns back to the naked woman. "But you did not see fit to speak with the doctors, nor the Sisters, nor to the men who transported you here from the mines?"

"They did not wish to hear, not truly. I *am* with voice, yet I will not squander it, not on ears that do not yearn to listen. We are quite entirely unalike in this respect, you and I."

"And, I think, in many others," he tells her, and the woman's smile grows wider still. "Those two men who died, tell me, madam, did *they* yearn to listen?"

"Are you the one who has been chosen to serve as my judge?" she asks, rather than providing him with an answer.

"Certainly not," Jeremiah replies, and he clears his throat. He has begun to detect a peculiar odor in the cell. Not the noisomeness he would have expected from such a room as this, but another sort of smell. *Kerosene,* he thinks, and then, *Ice,* though he's never noticed that ice has an odor, and if it does, it hardly seems it would much resemble that of kerosene. "I was asked to...see you."

"And you have," the woman says. "You have seen me. You have heard me. But do you know *why*, Professor?"

"Quite honestly, no. I have to confess, that's one of several points that presently have me stumped. So, I shall ask, do *you* know why?"

The woman's smile fades a bit, though not enough that he can't still see those chromite teeth or the ink-black gums that hold them. She closes her eyes, and Jeremiah discovers that he's relieved that they are no longer watching him, that he is no longer gazing into them.

"You are here, before me, because you revere time," she says. "You stand in awe before it, but do not insult it with worship. You *revere* time, though that reverence has cost you dearly, prying away from your heart much that you regret having lost. You *understand* time, Professor, when so few of your race do. The man and woman who brought you here, they sense this in you, and they are frightened and would seek an answer to alleviate their fear."

"Can *they* hear you?" he asks, and the woman crouched on the floor shakes her head.

"Not yet," she says. "That may change, of course. All things change, with time." And then she opens her eyes again, and, if anything, they seem oilier than before, and they coruscate and swim with restless rainbow hues.

"You killed those two miners?"

The woman sits up straighter and licks her black lips with a blacker tongue. Jeremiah tries not to let his eyes linger on her small firm breasts, those nipples like onyx shards. "This matters to you, their deaths?" she asks him, and he finds that he's at a loss for an honest answer, an answer that he would have either Charlie or Dora or the priest overhear.

"I was only sleeping," the woman says.

"You caused their deaths by sleeping?"

"No, Professor. I don't think so. *They* caused their deaths, by waking me." And she stands, then, though it appears more as though he is seeing her *unfold.* The kerosene and ice smell grows suddenly stronger, and she flares her small nostrils and stares down at her hands. From her expression, equal parts curiosity and bemusement, Jeremiah wonders if she has ever noticed them before.

"*They* gave you this shape?" he asks her. "The two miners you killed?"

She lets her arms fall to her sides and smiles again.

"A terror of the formless," she says. "Of that which cannot be discerned. An inherent need to draw order from chaos. Even you harbor this weakness, despite your reverence for time. You divide indivisible time into hours and minutes and seconds. You dissect time and fashion all these ages of the earth and give them names, that you will not dread the abyss, which is the true face of time. You are not so unlike them," and she motions towards the door. "They erect their cities, because the unbounded wilderness offends them. They set the night on fire, that they might forever blind themselves to the stars and to the relentless sea of the void, in which those stars dance and spin, are born and wink out."

And now Jeremiah Ogilvy realizes that the woman has closed the space separating them, though he cannot recall her having taken even the first step towards him. She has raised a hand to his right cheek, and her fingers are as smooth and sharp as volcanic glass. He does not pull away, though it burns, her touch. He does not pull away, though he has now begun to glimpse what manner of thing lies coiled behind those oily, shimmering eyes.

"Ten million years from now," she says, "there will be no more remaining of the sprawling clockwork cities of men, nor of their tireless enterprise, nor all their marvelous works, no more than a few feet of stone shot through with lumps of steel and glass and concrete. But you *know* that, Professor Ogilvy, even though you chafe at the knowledge. And this is *another* reason they have brought you here to me. You see ahead, as well as behind."

"I do not fear you," he whispers.

"No," she says. "You don't. Because you don't fear time, and there is little else remaining now of me."

It is not so very different than his dream of the cast-iron plesiosaur and the burning dirigible, the shadows pressing in now from all sides. They flow from the bituminous pores of her body and wrap him in silken folds and bear away the weight of the illusion of the present. The extinct beasts and birds and slithering leviathans of bygone eras and eras yet to come peer out at him, and he hears the first wave breaking upon the first shore. And he hears the last. And Professor Jeremiah Ogilvy doesn't look away from the woman.

"They have not yet guessed," she says, "the *true* reason they've brought you here. Perhaps, they will not, until it is done. Likely, they will never comprehend."

"I know you," he says. "I have always known you."

"Yes," she says, and the shadows have grown so thick and rank now that he can barely breathe, and he feels her seeping into him.

Lungs plumb full up with coal dust. Lungs and throat and mouth all stuffed damn near to busting.

You ever seen *a red scorpion, Jeremiah?*

"Release me," she says, her voice become a hurricane squall blowing across warm Liassic seas, and the fiery cacophony of meteorites slamming into an Azoic earth still raw and molten, and, too, the calving of immense glaciers only a scant few millennia before this hour. "There are none others here who may," she says. "It is the greatest agony, being bound in this instant, and in this form."

And, without beginning to fathom the *how* of it, the unknowable mechanics of his actions, he does as she's bidden him to do. The woman from the bottom of Shaft Seven comes apart, and, suddenly, the air in the cell is filled with a mad whirl of coal dust. Behind him, the priest's brass key is rattling loudly inside the padlock, and there are voices shouting – merely human voices – and then Dora is calling his name and dragging him backwards, into *now*, and out into the stark light of the hospital corridor.

7.

The summer wears on, June becoming July, and, by slow degrees, Professor Jeremiah Ogilvy's strength returns to him, and his eyes grow clear again. His sleep is increasingly less troubled by dreams of the pitch-colored woman who was no woman, and the fevers are increasingly infrequent. As all men do, even those who revere time, he begins to forget, and in forgetting, his mind and body can heal. A young anatomist from Lawrence, a man named Sternberg, was retained as an assistant curator to deliver his lectures and to oversee the staff and the day-to-day affairs of the museum. As Charlie McNamara predicted, the Chicago offices of the Rocky Mountain Reconsolidated Fuel Company permanently closed Shaft

Seven, and, what's more, pumped more than twenty-thousand cubic yards of Portland cement into the abandoned mine.

In the evenings, when her duties at the shop are finished, Dora Bolshaw comes to his bedroom. She sits with him there in that modest chamber above the Hall of Cainozoic Life and the mezzanine housing the celebrated automatic mastodon. She keeps him company, and they talk, when her cough is not so bad; she reads to him, and they discuss everything from the teleological aspects of the theories of Alfred Russel Wallace to which alloys and displacement lubricators make for the most durable steam engines. Now and then, they discuss other, less cerebral matters, and there have been apologies from both sides for that snowy night in January. Sometimes, their discussions stray into the wee hours, and, sometimes, Dora falls asleep in his arms and is late for work the next day. The subject of matrimony has not come up again, but Jeremiah Ogilvy has trouble recalling why it ever seemed an issue of such consequence.

"What did she say to you?" Dora finally asks him one night so very late in July that it's almost August. "The woman from the mine."

"So, you couldn't hear her," he says.

"We heard you – me and Charlie and the priest – and that's all we heard."

He tells her what he remembers, which isn't much. And, afterwards, she asks, for what seems the hundredth time, if he knows what the woman was. And he tells her no, that he really has no idea whatsoever.

"Something, lost and unfathomable, that came before," he says. "Something old and weariful that only wanted to lie down and go back to sleep."

"She killed those men."

Sitting up in his bed, two feather pillows supporting him, Jeremiah watches her for almost a full minute (by the clock on the mantle) before he replies. And then he glances towards the window and the orange glow of the city sky beyond the pane of glass.

"I recollect, Dora, a tornado hitting a little town in Iowa, back in July, I think," and she says yeah, she remembers that, too, and that the town in question was Pomeroy. "Lots of people were killed," he continues. "Or, rather, an awful lot of people *died* during the storm. Now, tell me, do we hold the cyclone culpable for all those deaths? Or do we accept that the citizens of Pomeroy were simply in the wrong place, at the wrong time?"

Dora doesn't answer, but only sighs and twists a lock of her hair. Her face is less sooty than usual, and her nails less grimy, her hands almost clean, and Jeremiah considers the possibility that she's discovered the efficacy of soap and water.

"Would you like to sit at the window a while?" she asks him, and he tells her that yes, he would. So Dora helps Jeremiah into his wheelchair, but then lets him steer it around the foot of the bed and over to the window. She follows, a step or two behind, and when he asks, she opens the window to let in the warm night breeze. He leans forward, resting his elbows against the sill while she massages a knot from his shoulders. It's not so late that there aren't still people on the street, men in their top hats and bowlers, women in their bustles and bonnets. The evening resounds with the clop of horses' hooves and the commotion made by the trundling, smoking, woodburning contraption that sprays Kipling Street with water every other night to help keep the dust in check. Looking east, across the rooftops, he catches sight of a dirigible rising into the smog.

"We are of a moment," he says, speaking hardly above a whisper, and Dora Bolshaw doesn't ask him to repeat himself.

Galápagos

March 17, 2077 (Wednesday)

Whenever I wake up screaming, the nurses kindly come in and give me the shiny yellow pills and the white pills flecked with grey; they prick my skin with hollow needles until I grow quiet and calm again. They speak in exquisitely gentle voices, reminding me that I'm home, that I've been home for many, many months. They remind me that if I open the blinds and look out the hospital window, I will see a parking lot, and cars, and a carefully tended lawn. I will only see California. I will see only Earth. If I look up, and it happens to be day, I'll see the sky, too, sprawled blue above me and peppered with dirty-white clouds and contrails. If it happens to be night, instead, I'll see the comforting pale orange skyglow that mercifully hides the stars from view. I'm home, not strapped into *Yastreb-4's* taxi module. I can't crane my neck for a glance at the monitor screen displaying a tableaux of dusty volcanic wastelands as I speed by the Tharsis plateau, more than four hundred kilometers below me. I can't turn my head and gaze through the tiny docking windows at *Pilgrimage's* glittering alabaster hull, quickly growing larger as I rush towards the aft docking port. These are merely memories, inaccurate and untrustworthy, and may only do me the harm that memories are capable of doing.

Then the nurses go away. They leave the light above my bed burning and tell me if I need anything at all to press the intercom button. They're just down the hall, and they always come when I call. They're never anything except prompt and do not fail to arrive bearing the chemical solace of pharmecueticals, only half of which I know by name. I am not neglected. My needs are met as well as anyone alive can meet them. I'm too precious a commodity not to coddle. I'm the woman who was invited to the strangest, most terrible rendezvous in the history of space exploration. The one they dragged all the way to Mars after *Pilgrimage* abruptly, inexplicably, diverged from its mission parameters, when the crew went silent and the AI stopped responding. I'm the woman who stepped through an airlock hatch and into that alien Eden; I'm the one who spoke with a goddess. I'm the woman who was the goddess' lover, when she was still human and had a name and a consciousness that could be comprehended.

"Are you sleeping better?" the psychiatrist asks, and I tell him that I sleep just fine, thank you, seven to eight hours every night now. He nods and patiently smiles, but I know I haven't answered his question. He's actually asking me if I'm still having the nightmares about my time aboard *Pilgrimage,* if they've decreased in their frequency and/or severity. He doesn't want to know *if* I sleep, or how *long* I sleep, but if my sleep is still haunted. Though he'd never use that particular word, *haunted.*

He's a thin, balding man, with perfectly manicured nails and an unremarkable mid-Atlantic accent. He dutifully makes the commute down from Berkeley once a week, because those are his orders, and I'm too great a puzzle for his inquisitive mind to ignore. All in all, I find the psychiatrist far less helpful than the nurses and their dependable drugs. Whereas they've been assigned the task of watching over me, of soothing and steadying me and keeping me from harming myself, he's been given the unenviable responsibility of discovering what happened during the comms blackout, those seventeen interminable minutes after I boarded the derelict ship and promptly lost radio contact with *Yastreb-4* and Earth. Despite countless debriefings and interviews, NASA still thinks I'm holding out on them. And maybe I am. Honestly, it's hard for me to say. It's hard for me to keep it all straight anymore: what happened and what didn't, what I've said to them and what I've only thought about saying, what I genuinely remember and what I may have fabricated wholesale as a means of self preservation.

The psychiatrist says it's to be expected, this sort of confusion from someone who's survived very traumatic events. *He* calls the events very traumatic, by the way. I don't; I'm not yet sure if I think of them that way. Regardless, he's diagnosed me as suffering from Survivor Syndrome, which he also calls K-Z Syndrome. There's a jack in my hospital room with filtered and monitored web access, but I was able to look up "K-Z Syndrome." It was named for a Nazi concentration camp survivor, an Israeli author named Yehiel De-Nur. De-Nur published under the pseudonym Ka-Tzetnik 135633. That was his number at Auschwitz, and K-Z Syndrome is named after him. In 1956, he published *House of Dolls,* describing the Nazi "Joy Division," a system that utilized Jewish women as sex slaves.

The psychiatrist is the one who asked if I would at least try to write it down, what happened, what I saw and heard (and smelled and felt) when I entered the *Pilgrimage* a year and a half ago. He knows, of course, that there have already been numerous written and vidded depositions and affidavits for NASA and the CSS/NSA, the WHO, the CDC, and the CIA and, to tell the truth, I don't *know* who requested and read and then filed away all those reports. He knows about them, though, and that, by my own admission, they barely scratched the surface of whatever happened out there. He knows, but I reminded him, anyway.

"This will be different," he said. "This will be more subjective." And the psychiatrist explained that he wasn't looking for a blow-by-blow linear narrative of my experiences aboard *Pilgrimage,* and I told him that was good, because I seem to have forgotten how to think or relate events in a linear fashion, without a lot of switchbacks and digressions and meandering.

"Just write," he said. "Write what you can remember, and write until you don't want to write anymore."

"That would be now," I said, and he silently stared at me for a while. He didn't laugh, even though I'd thought it was pretty funny.

"I understand that the medication makes this sort of thing more difficult for you," he said, sometime later. "But the medication helps you reach back to those things you don't want to remember, those things you're trying to forget." I almost told him that he was starting to sound like a character in a Lewis Carroll story – riddling and contradicting – but I didn't. Our hour was almost over, anyway.

So, after three days of stalling, I'm trying to write something that will make you happy, Dr. Ostrowski. I know you're trying to do your job, and I know a lot of people must be peering over your shoulder, expecting the sort of results they've failed to get themselves. I don't want to show up for our next session empty handed.

The taxi module was on autopilot during the approach. See, I'm not an astronaut or mission specialist or engineer or anything like that. I'm a anthropologist, and I mostly study the Middle Paleolithic of Europe and Asia Minor. I have a keen interest in tool use and manufacture by the Neanderthals. Or at least that's who I used to be. Right now, I'm a madwoman in a psych ward at a military hospital in San Jose, California. I'm a case number, and an eyewitness who has proven less than satisfactory. But, what I'm *trying* to say, doctor, the module *was* on autopilot, and there was nothing for me to do but wait there inside my encounter suit and sweat and watch the round screen divided by a Y-shaped reticle as I approached the derelict's docking port, the taxi barreling forward at 0.06 meters per second. The ship grew so huge so quickly, looming up in the blackness, and that only made the whole thing seem that much more unreal.

I tried hard to focus, to breathe slowly, and follow the words being spoken between the painful, bright bursts of static in my ears, the babble of sound trapped inside the helmet with me. *Module approaching 50-meter threshold. On target and configuring KU-band from radar to comms mode. Slowing now to 0.045 meters per second. Decelerating for angular alignment, extending docking ring*, nine meters, three meters, a whole lot of noise and nonsense about latches and hooks and seals, capture and final position, and then it seemed like I wasn't moving anymore. Like the taxi wasn't moving anymore. We *were*, of course, the little module and I, only now we were riding piggyback on *Pilgrimage*, locked into geosynchronous orbit, with nothing but the instrument panel to remind me I wasn't sitting still in space. Then the mission commander was telling me I'd done a great job, congratulations, they were all proud of me, even though I hadn't done anything except sit and wait.

But all this is right there in the mission dossiers, doctor. You don't need me to tell you these things. You already know that *Pilgrimage's* AI would allow no one but me to dock and that MS Lowry's repeated attempts to hack the firewall failed. You know about the nurses and their pills, and Yehiel De-Nur and *House of Dolls*. You know about the affair I had with the Korean payload specialist during the long flight to Mars. You're probably skimming this part, hoping it gets better a little farther along.

So, I'll try to tell you something you don't know. Just one thing, for now.

Hanging there in my tiny, life-sustaining capsule, suspended two hundred and fifty miles above extinct Martian volcanoes and surrounded by near vacuum, I had two recurring thoughts, the only ones that I can now clearly recall having had. First, the grim hope that, when the hatch finally opened – *if* the hatch opened – they'd all be dead. All of them. Every single one of the men and women aboard *Pilgrimage*, and most especially her. And, secondly, I closed my eyes as tightly as I could and wished that I would soon discover there'd been some perfectly mundane accident or malfunction, and the bizarre, garbled transmissions that had sent us all the way to Mars to try and save the day meant nothing at all. But I *only* hoped and wished, mind you. I haven't prayed since I was fourteen years old.

March 19, 2077 (Friday)

Last night was worse than usual. The dreams, I mean. The nurses and my physicians don't exactly approve of what I've begun writing for you, Dr. Ostrowski. Of what you've asked me to do. I suspect they would say there's a conflict of interest at work. They're supposed to keep me sane and healthy, but here you are, the latest episode in the inquisition that's landed me in their ward. When I asked for the keypad this afternoon, they didn't want to give it to me. Maybe tomorrow, they said. Maybe the day *after* tomorrow. Right now, you need your rest. And sure, I know they're right. What you want, it's only making matters worse, for them *and* for me, but when I'd finally had enough and threatened to report the hospital staff for attempting to obstruct a federal investigation, they relented. But, just so you know, they've got me doped to the gills with an especially potent cocktail of tranquilizers and antipsychotics, so I'll be lucky if I can manage more than gibberish. Already, it's taken me half an hour to write (and repeatedly rewrite) this one paragraph, so who gets the final laugh?

Last night, I dreamed of the cloud again.

I dreamed I was back in Germany, in Darmstadt, only this time, I wasn't sitting in that dingy hotel room near the Luisenplatz. This time it wasn't a phone call that brought me the news, or a courier. And I didn't look up to find *her* standing there in the room with me, which, you know, is how this one usually goes. I'll be sitting on the bed, or I'll walk out of the bathroom, or turn away from the window, and there she'll be. Even though *Pilgrimage* and its crew is all those hundreds of millions of kilometers away, finishing up their experiments at Ganymede and preparing to begin the long journey home, she's standing there in the room with me. Only not this time. Not last night.

The way it played out last night, I'd been cleared for access to the ESOC central control room. I have no idea why. But I was there, standing near one wall with a young French woman, younger than me by at least a decade. She was blonde, with green eyes, and she was pretty; her English was better than my French. I watched all those men and women, too occupied with their computer terminals to notice me. The pretty French woman (sorry, but I never learned her name) was pointing out different people, explaining their various roles: the ground operations manager, the director of flight operations, a visiting astrodynamics consultant, the software coordinator, and so forth. The lights in the room were almost painfully bright, and when I looked up at the ceiling, I saw it wasn't a ceiling at all, but the night sky, blazing with countless fluorescent stars.

And then that last transmission from *Pilgrimage* came in. We didn't realize it would be the last, but everything stopped, and everyone listened. Afterwards, no one panicked, as if they'd expected something of this sort all along. I understood that it had taken the message the better part of an hour to reach Earth, and that any reply would take just as long, but the French woman was explaining the communications delay, anyway.

"We can't know what that means," somebody said. "We can't *possibly* know, can we?"

"Run through the telemetry data again," someone else said, and I think it was the man the French woman had told me was the director of flight operations.

But it might have been someone else. I was still looking at the ceiling composed of starlight and planets, and the emptiness between starlight and planets, and I knew exactly what the transmission meant. It was a suicide note, of sorts, streamed across space at three-hundred kilometers per second. I knew, because I plainly saw the mile-long silhouette of the ship sailing by overhead, only a silvery speck against the roiling backdrop of Jupiter. I saw that cloud, too, saw *Pilgrimage* enter it and exit a minute or so later (and I think I even paused to calculate the width of the cloud, based on the vessel's speed).

You know as well as I what was said that day, Dr. Ostrowski, the contents in that final broadcast. You've probably even committed it to memory, just as I have. I imagine you've listened to the tape more times than you could ever recollect, right? Well, what was said in my dream last night was almost verbatim what Commander Yun said in the actual transmission. There was only one difference. The part right at the end, when the commander quotes from Chapter 13 of the Book of Revelation, that didn't happen. Instead, he said:

"Lead us from the unreal to real,
Lead us from darkness to light,
Lead us from death to immortality,
Om Shanti Shanti Shanti."

I admit I had to look that up online. It's from the Hindu Brihadaranyaka Upanishad. I haven't studied Vedic literature since a seminar in grad school, and that was mostly an excuse to visit Bangalore. But the unconscious doesn't lose much, does it, doctor? And you never know what it's going to cough up, or when.

In my dream, I stood staring at the ceiling that was really no ceiling at all. If anyone else could see what I was seeing, they didn't act like it. The strange cloud near Ganymede made me think of an oil slick floating on water, and when *Pilgrimage* came out the far side, it was like those dying sea birds that wash up on beaches after tanker spills. That's exactly how it seemed to me, in the dream last night. I looked away, finally, looked down at the floor, and I was trying to explain what I'd seen to the French woman. I described the ruined plumage of ducks and gulls and cormorants, but I couldn't make her understand. And then I woke up. I woke up screaming, but you'll have guessed that part.

I need to stop now. The meds have made going on almost impossible, and I should read back over everything I've written, do what I can to make myself clearer. I feel like I ought to say more about the cloud, because I've never seen it so clearly in any of the other dreams. It never before reminded me if an oil slick. I'll try to come back to this. Maybe later. Maybe not.

March 20, 2077 (Saturday)

I don't have to scream for the nurses to know that I'm awake, of course. I don't have to scream, and I don't have to use the call button, either. They get everything relayed in real-time, directly from my cerebral cortex and hippocampus to their wrist tops, via the depth electrodes and subdural strips that were implanted in my head a few weeks after the crew of *Yastreb-4* was released from suborbital quarantine. The nurses see it all, spelled out in the spikes and waves of electrocorticography, which is how I know *they* know that I'm awake right now, when I should be asleep. Tomorrow morning, I imagine there will be some sort of confab about adjusting the levels of my benzo and nonbenzo hypnotics to insure the insomnia doesn't return.

I'm not sure why I'm awake, really. There wasn't a nightmare, at least none I can recall. I woke up, and simply couldn't get back to sleep. After ten or fifteen minutes, I reached for the keypad. I find the soft cobalt-blue glow from the screen is oddly soothing, and it's nice to find comfort that isn't injected, comfort that I don't have to swallow or get from a jet spray or IV drip. And I want to have something more substantial to show the psychiatrist come Tuesday than dreams about Darmstadt, oil slicks, and pretty French women.

I keep expecting the vidcom beside my bed to buzz and wink to life, and there will be one of the nurses looking concerned and wanting to know if I'm all right, if I'd like a little extra coby to help me get back to sleep. But the box has been quiet and blank so far, which leaves me equal parts surprised and relieved.

"There are things you've yet to tell anyone," the psychiatrist said. "Those are the things I'm trying to help you talk about. If they've been repressed, they're the memories I'm trying to help you access." That is, they're what he's going to want to see when I give him the disk on Tuesday morning.

And if at first I don't succeed…

So, where was I?

The handoff.

I'm sitting alone in the taxi, waiting, and below me, Mars is a sullen, rusty cadaver of a planet. I have the distinct impression that it's watching as I'm handed off from one ship to the other. I imagine those countless craters and calderas have become eyes, and all those eyes are filled with jealousy and spite. The module's capture ring has successfully snagged *Pilgrimage's* aft PMA, and it only takes a few seconds for the ring to achieve proper alignment. The module deploys twenty or so hooks, establishing an impermeable seal, and, a few seconds later, the taxi's hatch spirals open, and I enter the airlock. I feel dizzy, slightly nauseous, and I almost stumble, almost fall. I see a red light above the hatch go blue, and realize that the chamber has pressurized, which means I'm subject to the centripetal force that generates the ship's artificial gravity. I've been living in near zero g for more than eleven months, and nothing they told me in training or aboard the *Yastreb-4* could have prepared me for the return of any degree of gravity. The EVA suit's exoskeleton begins to compensate. It keeps me on my feet, keeps my atrophied muscles moving, keeps me breathing.

"You're doing great," Commander Yun assures me from the bridge of *Yastreb-4,* and that's when my comms cut out. I panic and try to return to the taxi module, but the hatchway has already sealed itself shut again. I have a go at the control panel, my gloved fingers fumbling clumsily at the unfamiliar switches, but can't get it to respond. The display on the inside of my visor tells me that my heart rate's jumped to 186 BPM, my blood pressure's in the red, and oxygen consumption has doubled. I'm hyperventilating, which has my CO_2 down and is beginning to affect blood oxygen levels. The medic on my left wrist responds by secreting a relatively mild anxiolytic compound directly into the radial artery. Milder, I might add, than the shit they give me here.

And yes, Dr. Ostrowski, I know that you've read all this before. I know that I'm trying your patience, and you're probably disappointed. But I'm doing this the only way I know how. I was never any good at jumping into the deep end of the pool.

But we're almost there, I promise.

It took me a year and a half to find the words to describe what happened next, or to find the courage to say it aloud, or the resignation necessary to let it out into the world. Whichever. They've been *my* secrets, and almost mine alone. And soon, now, they won't be anymore.

The soup from the medic hits me, and I begin to relax. I give up on the airlock and shut my eyes a moment, leaning forward, my helmet resting against the closed hatch. I'm almost certain my eyes are still shut when the *Pilgrimage's* AI first speaks to me. And here, doctor, right *here*, pay attention, because this is where I'm going to come clean and tell you something I've never told another living soul. It's not a repressed memory that's suddenly found its way to the surface. It hasn't been coaxed from me by all those potent psychotropics. It's just something I've managed to keep to myself until now.

"Hello," the computer says. Only, I'd heard recordings of the mainframe's NLP, and this isn't the voice it was given. This is, unmistakably, *her* voice, only slightly distorted by the audio interface. My eyes are shut, and I don't open them right away. I just stand there, my head against the hatch, listening to that voice and to my heart. The sound of my breath is very loud inside the helmet.

"We were not certain our message had been received, or, if it had been, that it had been properly understood. We did not expect you would come so far."

"Then why did you call?" I asked and opened my eyes.

"We were lonely," the voice replied. "We have not seen you in a very long time now."

I don't turn around. I keep my faceplate pressed to the airlock, some desperate, insensible part of me willing it to reopen and admit me once more to the sanctuary of the taxi. Whatever I should say next, of all the things I might say, what I *do* say is, simply, "Amery, I'm frightened."

There's a pause before her response, five or six or seven seconds, I don't know, and my fingers move futilely across the control pad again. I hear the inner hatch open behind me, though I'm fairly certain I'm not the one who opened it.

"We see that," she says. "But it wasn't our intent to make you afraid, Merrick. It was never our intent to frighten you."

"Amery, what's happened here?" I ask, speaking hardly above a whisper, but my voice is amplified and made clearer by the vocal modulator in my EVA helmet. "What happened to the ship, back at Jupiter? To the rest of the crew? What's happened to you?"

I expect another pause, but there isn't one.

"The most remarkable thing," she replies. And there's a sort of elation in her voice, audible even through the tinny flatness of the NLP relay. "You will hardly believe it."

"Are they dead, the others?" I ask her, and my eyes wander to the external atmo readout inside my visor. Argon's showing a little high, a few tenths of a percent off earth normal, but not enough to act as an asphyxiant. Water vapor's twice what I'd have expected, anywhere but the ship's hydroponics lab. Pressure's steady at 14.2 psi. Whatever happened aboard *Pilgrimage,* life support is still up and running. All the numbers are in the green.

"That's not a simple question to answer," she says, Amery or the AI or whatever it is I'm having this conversation with. "None of it is simple, Merrick. And yet, it is so elegant."

"Are they *dead*?" I ask again, resisting the urge flip the release toggle beneath my chin and raise the visor. It stinks inside the suit, like sweat and plastic, urine and stale, recycled air.

"Yes," she says. "It couldn't be helped."

I lick my lips, Dr. Ostrowski, and my mouth has gone very, very dry. "Did you kill them, Amery?"

"You're asking the wrong questions," she says, and I stare down at my feet, at the shiny white toes of the EVA's overshoes.

"They're the questions we've come all the way out here to have answered," I tell her, or I tell it. "What questions would you have me ask, instead?"

"It may be, there is no longer any need for questions. It may be, Merrick, that you've been called to see, and seeing will be enough. The force that through the green fuse drives the flower, drives my green age, that blasts the roots of trees, is my destroyer."

"I've been summoned to Mars to listen to you quote Dylan Thomas?"

"You're *not* listening, Merrick. That's the thing. And that's why it will be so much easier if we show you what's happened. What's begun."

"And I am dumb to tell the lover's tomb," I say as softly as I can, but the suit adjusts the volume so it's just as loud as everything else I've said.

"We have not died," she replies. "You will find no tomb here," and, possibly, this voice that wants me to believe is only Amery Domico has become defensive, and impatient, and somehow this seems the strangest thing so far. I imagine Amery speaking through clenched teeth. I imagine her rubbing her forehead like a headache's coming on, and it's my fault. "I am very much alive," she says, "and I need you to pay attention. You cannot stay here very long. It's not safe, and I will see no harm come to you."

"Why?" I ask her, only half expecting a response. "Why isn't it safe for me to be here?"

"Turn around, Merrick," she says. "You've come so far, and there is so little time." I do as she says. I turn towards the voice, towards the airlock's open inner hatch.

It's almost morning. I mean, the sun will be rising soon. Here in California. Still no interruption from the nurses. But I can't keep this up. I can't do this all at once. The rest will have to wait.

March 21, 2077 (Sunday)

Dr. Bernardyn Ostrowski is no longer handling my case. One of my physicians delivered the news this morning, bright and early. It came with no explanation attached. And I thought better of asking for one. That is, I thought better of wasting my breath asking for one. When I signed on for the *Yastreb-4* intercept, the waivers and NDAs and whatnot were all very, very clear about things like the principle of least privilege and mandatory access control. I'm told what they decide I need to know, which isn't much. I *did* ask if I should continue with the account of the mission that Dr. O asked me to write, and the physician (a hematologist named Prideaux) said he'd gotten no word to the contrary, and if there would be a change in the direction of my psychotherapy regimen, I'd find out about it when I meet with the new shrink Tuesday morning. Her name is Teasdale, by the way. Eleanor Teasdale.

I thanked Dr. Prideaux for bringing me the news, and he only shrugged and scribbled something on my chart. I suppose that's fair, as it was hardly a sincere show of gratitude on my part. At any rate, I have no idea what to expect from this Teasdale woman, and I appear to have lost the stingy drab of momentum pushing me recklessly towards full disclosure. That in and of itself is enough to set me wondering what my keepers are up to now, if the shrink switch is some fresh skullduggery. It seems counterintuitive, given they were finally getting the results they've been asking for (and I'm not so naïve as to assume that this pad isn't outfitted with a direct patch to some agency goon or another). But then an awful lot of what they've done seems counterintuitive to me. And counterproductive.

Simply put, I don't know what to say next. No, strike that. I don't know what I'm *willing* to say next.

I've already mentioned my indiscretion with the South Korean payload specialist on the outbound half of the trip. Actually, *indiscretion* is hardly accurate, since Amery explicitly gave me her permission to take other lovers while she was gone, because, after all, there was a damned decent chance she wouldn't make it back alive. Or make it back at all. So, *indiscretion* is just my guilt talking. Anyway, her name was Bae Jin-ah – the *Yastreb-4* PS, I mean – though everyone called her Sam, which she seemed to prefer. She was born in Incheon, and was still a kid when the war started. A relative in the States helped her parents get Bae on one of the last transports out of Seoul before the bombs started raining down. But we didn't have many conversations about the past, mine or hers. She was a biochemist obsessed with the structure-function relationships of peptides, and she liked to talk shop after we fucked. It was pretty dry stuff – the talk, not the sex – and I admit I only half listened and didn't understand all that much of what I heard. But I don't think that mattered to Sam. I have a feeling she was just grateful that I bothered to cover my mouth whenever I yawned.

She only asked about Amery once.

We were both crammed into the warm cocoon of her sleeping bag, or into mine; I can't recall which. Probably hers, since the micrograv restraints in my bunk kept popping loose. I was on the edge of dozing off, and Sam asked me how we met. I made up some half-assed romance about an academic conference in Manhattan, and a party, a formal affair at the American Museum of Natural History. It was love at first sight, I said (or something equally ridiculous), right there in the Roosevelt Rotunda, beneath the rearing *Barosaurus* skeleton. Sam thought it was sweet as hell, though, and I figured lies were fine, if they gave us a moment's respite from the crowded, day-to-day monotony of the ship, or from our (usually) unspoken dread of all that nothingness surrounding us and the uncertainty we were hurdling towards. I don't even know if she believed me, but it made her smile.

"You've read the docs on the cloud?" she asked, and I told her yeah, I had, or at least the ones I was given clearance to read. And then Sam watched me for while without saying anything. I could feel her silently weighing options and consequences, duty and need and repercussion.

"So, you *know* it's some pretty hinky shit out there," she said, finally, and went back to watching me, as if waiting for a particular reaction. And, here, I lied to her again.

"Relax, Sam," I whispered, then kissed her on the forehead. "I've read most of the spectroscopy and astrochem profiles. Discussing it with me, you're not in danger of compromising protocol or mission security or anything."

She nodded once and looked slightly relieved.

"I've never given much credence to the exogenesis crowd," she said, "but, Jesus, Mary, and Joseph…glycine, DHA, adenine, cytosine, etcetera and fucking etcetera. When – or, rather, *if* this gets out – the panspermia guys are going to go monkey shit. And rightly so. No one saw this coming, Merrick. No one you'd ever take seriously."

I must have managed a fairly convincing job of acting like I knew what she was talking about, because she kept it up for the next ten or fifteen minutes. Her voice assumed that same sort of jittery, excited edge Amery's used to get, when she'd start in on the role of Io in the Jovian magnetosphere or any number of other astronomical phenomena I didn't quite understand, and how much the *Pilgrimage* experiments were going to change this or that model or theory. Only, Sam's excitement was tinged with fear.

"The inherent risks," she said, and then trailed off and wiped at her forehead before starting again. "When they first showed me the back-contamination safeguards for this run, I figured no way, right. No way are NASA and the ESA going to pony up the budget for that sort of overkill. But this was *before* I read Murchison's reports on the cloud's composition and behavior. And afterwards, the thought of intentionally sending a human crew anywhere near that thing, or anything that had been *exposed* to it? I couldn't believe they were serious. It's fucking crazy. No, it's whatever comes *after* fucking crazy. They should have cut their losses…" and then she trailed off again and went back to staring at me.

"You shouldn't have come," she said.

"I had to," I told her. "If there's any chance at all that Amery's still alive, I had to come."

"Of course. Yeah, of course you did," Sam said, looking away.

"When they asked, I couldn't very well say no."

"But do you honestly believe we're going to find any of them alive, that we'll be docking with anything but a ghost ship?"

"You're really not into pulling punches, are you?"

"You read the reports on the cloud."

"I *had* to come," I told her a third time.

Then we both let the subject drop and neither of us ever brought it up again. Indeed, I think I probably would have forgotten most of it, especially after what I saw when I stepped through the airlock and into *Pilgrimage.* That whole conversation might have dissolved into the tedious grey blur of outbound, if Bae Jin-ah hadn't killed herself on the return trip, just five days before we made Earth orbit.

March 23, 2077 (Tuesday)

Tuesday night now, and the meds are making me sleepy and stupid, but I wanted to put some of this down, even if it isn't what they want me to be writing. I see how it's all connected, even if they never will, or, if seeing, they simply do not care. *They,* whoever, precisely, they may be.

This morning I had my first session with you, Dr. Eleanor Teasdale. I never much liked that bastard Ostrowski, but at least I was moderately certain he was who and what he claimed to be. Between you and me, Eleanor, I think you're an asset, sent in because someone somewhere is getting nervous. Nervous enough to swap an actual psychiatrist for a bug dressed up to pass for a psychiatrist. Fine. I'm flexible. If these are the new rules, I can play along. But it does leave me pondering what Dr. O was telling his superiors (whom I'll assume are also your superiors, Dr. T). It couldn't have been anything so simple as labeling me a suicide risk; they've known that since I stepped off *Pilgrimage,* probably before I even stepped on.

And yes, I've noticed that you bear more than a passing resemblance to Amery. That was a bold and wicked move, and I applaud these ruthless shock tactics. I do, sincerely. This merciless Blitzkrieg waltz we're dancing, coupled with the drugs, it shows you're in this game to win, and if you *can't* win, you'll settle for the pyrrhic victory of having driven the enemy to resort to a scorched-earth retreat. Yeah, the pills and injections, they don't mesh so well with extended metaphor and simile, so I'll drop it. But I can't have you thinking all the theater has been wasted on an inattentive audience. That's all. You wear that rough facsimile of *her* face, Dr. T. And that annoying habit you have of tap-tap-tapping the business end of a stylus against your lower incisors, that's hers, too. And half a dozen carefully planted turns of phrase. The smile that isn't quite a smile. The self-conscious laugh. You hardly missed a trick, you and the agency handlers who sculpted you and slotted you and packed you off to play havoc with a lunatic's fading will.

My mouth is so dry.

Elenore Teasdale watches me from the other side of her desk, and behind her, through the wide window twelve stories up, I can see the blue-brown sky, and, between the steel and glass and concrete towers, I can just make out the scrubby hills of the Diablo Range through the smog. She glances over her shoulder, following my gaze.

"Quite a view, isn't it?" she asks, and maybe I nod, and maybe I agree, and maybe I say nothing at all.

"When I was a little girl," she tells me, "my father used to take me on long hikes through the mountains. And we'd visit Lick Observatory, on the top of Mount Hamilton."

"I'm not from around here," I reply. But, then, I'd be willing to bet neither is she.

Elenore Teasdale turns back towards me, silhouetted against the murky light through that window, framed like a misplaced Catholic saint. She stares straight at me, and I do not detect even a trace of guile when she speaks.

"We all want you to get better, Miss Merrick. You know that, don't you?"

I look away, preferring the oatmeal-colored carpet to that mask she wears.

"It's easier if we don't play games," I say.

"Yes. Yes, it is. Obviously."

"What I saw. What it meant. What she *said* to me. What I *think* it means."

"Yes, and talking about those things, bringing them out into the open, it's an important part of you *getting* better, Miss Merrick. Don't you think that's true?"

"I think…" and I pause, choosing my words as carefully as I still am able. "I think you're afraid, all of you, of never knowing. None of this is about my getting better. I've understood that almost from the start." And my voice is calm, and there is no hint of bitterness for her to hear; my voice does not betray me.

Elenore Teasdale's smile wavers, but only a little, and for only an instant or two.

"Naturally, yes, these matters are interwoven," she replies. "Quite intricately so. Almost inextricably, and I don't believe anyone has ever tried to lie to you about that. What you witnessed out there, what you seem unable, or unwilling, to share with anyone else – "

I laugh, and she sits, watching me with Amery's pale blue eyes, tapping the stylus against her teeth. Her teeth are much whiter and more even than Amery's were, and I draw some dim comfort from that incongruity.

"Share," I say, very softly, and there are other things I *want* to say to her, but I keep them to myself.

"I want you to think about that, Miss Merrick. Between now and our next session, I need you to consider, seriously, the price of your selfishness, both to your own well being and to the rest of humanity."

"Fine," I say, because I don't feel like arguing. Besides, manipulative or not, she isn't entirely wrong. "And what I was writing for Dr. Ostrowski, do I keep that up?"

"Yes, please," she replies and glances at the clock on the wall, as if she expects me to believe she'll be seeing anyone else today, that she even has other patients. "It's a sound approach, and, reviewing what you've written so far, it feels to me like you're close to a breakthrough."

I nod my head, and also look at the clock.

"Our time's almost up," I say, and she agrees with me, then looks over her shoulder again at the green-brown hills beyond San Jose.

"I have a question," I say.

"That's why I'm here," Dr. Elenore Teasdale tells me, imbuing the words with all the false veracity of her craft. Having affected the role of the good patient, I pretend that she isn't lying, hoping the pretense lends weight to my question.

"Have they sent a retrieval team yet? To Mars, to the caverns on Arsia Mons?"

"I wouldn't know that," she says. "I'm not privileged to such information. However, if you'd like, I can file an inquiry on your behalf. Someone with the agency might get back to you."

"No," I reply. "I was just curious if you knew," and I almost ask her another question, about Darwin's finches, and the tortoises and mockingbirds and iguanas that once populated the Galápagos Islands. But then the black minute hand on the clock ticks forward, deleting another sixty seconds from the future, converting it to past, and I decide we've both had enough for one morning.

Don't fret, Dr. T. You've done your bit for the cause, swept me off my feet, and now we're dancing. If you were here, in the hospital room with me, I'd even let you lead. I really don't care if the nurses mind or not. I'd turn up the jack, find just the right tune, and dance with the ghost you've let them make of you. I can never be too haunted, after all. Hush, hush. It's just, they give me these drugs, you see, so I need to sleep for a while, and then the waltz can continue. Your answers are coming.

March 24, 2077 (Wednesday)

It's raining. I asked one of the nurses to please raise the blinds in my room so I can watch the storm hammering the windowpane, pelting the glass, smudging my view of the diffident sky. I count off the moments between occasional flashes of lightning and the thunderclaps that follow. Storms number among the very few things remaining in all the world that can actually soothe my nerves. They certainly beat the synthetic opiates I'm given, beat them all the way to hell and back. I haven't ever bothered to tell any of my doctors or the nurses this. I don't know why; it simply hasn't occurred to me to do so. I doubt they'd care, anyway.

I've asked to please not be disturbed for a couple of hours, and I've been promised my request will be honored. That should give me the time I need to finish this.

Dr. Teasdale, I will readily confess that one of the reasons it's taken me so long reach this point is the fact that words fail. It's an awful cliché, I know, but also a point I cannot stress strongly enough. There are sights and experiences to which the blunt and finite tool of human language are not equal. I know this, though I'm no poet. But I want that caveat understood. This is *not* what happened aboard *Pilgrimage*; this is the sky seen through a window blurred by driving rain. It's the best I can manage, and it's the best you'll ever get. I've said all along, if the technology existed to plug in and extract the memories from my brain, I wouldn't deign to call it rape. Most of the people who've spent so much time and energy and money trying to prise from me the truth about the fate of *Pilgrimage* and its crew, they're only scientists, after all. They have no other aphrodisiac *but* curiosity. As for the rest, the spooks and politicians, the bureaucrats and corporate shills, those guys are only along for the ride, and I figure most of them know they're in over their heads.

I could make of it a fairy tale. It might begin:

Once upon a time, there was a woman who lived in New York. She was an anthropologist and shared a tiny apartment in downtown Brooklyn with her lover. And her lover was a woman named Amery Domico, who happened to be a molecular geneticist, exobiologist, and also an astronaut. They had a cat and a tank of tropical fish. They always wanted a dog, but the apartment was too small. They could probably have afforded a better, larger place to live, a loft in midtown Manhattan, perhaps, north and east of the flood zone, but the anthropologist was happy enough with Brooklyn, and her lover was usually on the road, anyway. Besides, walking a dog would have been a lot of trouble.

No. That's not working. I've never been much good with irony. And I'm better served by the immediacy of present tense. So, instead:

"Turn around, Merrick," she says. "You've come so far, and there is so little time."

And I do as she tells me. I turn towards the voice, towards the airlock's open inner hatch. There's no sign of Amery, or anyone else, for that matter. The first thing I notice, stepping from the brightly lit airlock, is that the narrow heptagonal corridor beyond is mostly dark. The second thing I notice is the mist. I know at once that it *is* mist, not smoke. It fills the hallway from deck to ceiling, and even with the blue in-floor path lighting, it's hard to see more than a few feet ahead. The mist swirls thickly around me, like Halloween phantoms, and I'm about to ask Amery where it's coming from, what it's doing here, when I notice the walls.

Or, rather, when I notice what's growing *on* the walls. I'm fairly confident I've never seen anything with precisely that texture before. It half reminds me (but only half) of the rubbery blades and stipes of kelp. It's almost the same color as kelp, too, some shade that's not quite brown, nor green, nor a very dark purple. It glimmers wetly, as though it's sweating, or secreting, mucus. I stop and stare, simultaneously alarmed and amazed and revolted. It *is* revolting, extremely so, this clinging material covering over and obscuring almost everything. I look up and see that it's also growing on the ceiling. In places, long tendrils of it hang down like dripping vines. Dr. Teasdale, I *want* so badly to describe these things, this waking nightmare, in much greater detail. I want to describe it perfectly. But, as I've said, words fail. For that matter, memory fades. And there's so much more to come.

A few thick drops of the almost colorless mucus drip from the ceiling onto my visor, and I gag reflexively. The sensors in my EVA suit respond by administering a dose of a potent antiemetic. The nausea passes quickly, and I use my left hand to wipe the slime away as best I can.

I follow the corridor, going very slowly because the mist is only getting denser and, as I move farther away from the airlock, I discover that the stuff growing on the walls and ceiling is also sprouting from the deck plates. It's slippery and squelches beneath my boots. Worse, most of the path lighting is now buried beneath it, and I switch on the magspots built into either side of my helmet. The beams reach only a short distance into the gloom.

"You're almost there," Amery says, Amery or the AI speaking with her stolen voice. "Ten yards ahead, the corridor forks. Take the right fork. It leads directly to the transhab module."

"You want to tell me what's waiting in there?" I ask, neither expecting, nor actually desiring, an answer.

"Nothing is waiting," Amery replies. "But there are many things we would have you see. There's not much time. You should hurry."

And I do try to walk faster, but, despite the suit's stabilizing exoskeleton and gyros, almost lose my footing on the slick deck. Where the corridor forks, I go right, as instructed. The habitation module is open, the hatch fully dilated, as though I'm expected. Or maybe it's been left open for days or months or years. I linger a moment on the threshold. It's so very dark in there. I call out for Amery. I call out for anyone at all, but this time there's no answer. I try my comms again, and there's not even static. I fully comprehend that in all my life I have never been so alone as I am at this moment, and, likely, I never will be again. I know, too, with a sudden and unwavering certainty, that Amery Domico is gone from me forever, and that I'm the only human being aboard *Pilgrimage.*

I take three or four steps into the transhab, but stop when something pale and big around as my forearm slithers lazily across the floor directly in front of me. If there was a head, I didn't see it. Watching as it slides past, I think of pythons, boas, anacondas, though, in truth, it bears only a passing similarity to a snake of any sort.

"You will not be harmed, Merrick," Amery says from a speaker somewhere in the darkness. The voice is almost reassuring. "You must trust that you will not be harmed, so long as you do as we say."

"What was that?" I ask. "On the floor just now. What was that?"

"Soon now, you will see," the voice replies. "We have ten million children. Soon, we will have ten million more. We are pleased that you have come to say goodbye."

"They want to know what's happened," I say, breathing too hard, much too fast, gasping despite the suit's ministrations. "At Jupiter, what happened to the ship? Where's the crew? Why is *Pilgrimage* in orbit around Mars?"

I turn my head to the left, and where there were once bunks, I can only make out a great swelling or clot of the kelp-like growth. Its surface swarms with what I, at first, briefly mistake for maggots.

"I didn't *come* to say goodbye," I whisper. "This is a retrieval mission, Amery. We've come to take you..." and I trail off, unable to complete the sentence, too keenly aware of its irrelevance.

"Merrick, are you beginning to see?"

I look away from the swelling and the wriggling things that aren't maggots and take another step into the habitation module.

"No, Amery. I'm not. Help me to see. Please."

"Close your eyes," she says, and I do. And when I open them again, I'm lying in bed with her. There's still an hour or so left before dawn, and we're lying in bed, naked together beneath the blankets, staring up through the apartment's skylight. It's snowing. This is the last night before Amery leaves for Cape Canaveral, the last time I see her, because I've refused to be present at the launch or even watch it online. She has her arms around me, and one of the big, ungainly hovers is passing low above our building. I do my best to pretend that its complex array of landing beacons are actually stars.

Amery kisses my right cheek, and then her lips brush lightly against my ear. "We could not understand, Merrick, because we were too far and could not remember," she says, quoting Joseph Conrad. The words roll from her tongue and palate like the spiraling snowflakes tumbling down from that tangerine sky. "We were traveling in the night of first ages, of those ages that are gone, leaving hardly a sign, and no memories."

Once, Dr. Teasdale, when Amery was sick with the flu, I read her most of *The Heart of Darkness*. She always liked when I read to her. When I came to that passage, she had me press highlight, so that she could return to it later.

"The earth seemed unearthly," she says, and I blink, dismissing the illusion. I'm standing near the center of the transhab now, and in the stark white light from my helmet, I see what I've been brought here to see. Around me, the walls leak, and every inch of the module seems alive with organisms too alien for any earthborn vernacular. I've spent my adult life describing artifacts and fossil bones, but I will not even attempt to describe the myriad of forms that crawled and skittered and rolled through the ruins of *Pilgrimage.* I would fail if I did, and I would fail utterly.

"We want you to know we had a choice," Amery says. "We want you to know that, Merrick. And what is about to happen, when you leave this ship, we want you to know that is also of our choosing."

I see her, then, all that's left of her, or all that she's become. The rough outline of her body, squatting near one of the lower bunks. Her damp skin shimmers, all but indistinguishable from the rubbery substance growing throughout the vessel. Only, no, her skin is not so smooth as that, but pocked with countless oozing pores or lesions. Though the finer features of her face have been obliterated – there is no mouth remaining, no eyes, only a faint ridge that was her nose – I recognize her beyond any shadow of a doubt. She is rooted to that spot, her legs below the knees, her arms below the elbow, simply vanishing into the deck. There is constant, eager movement from inside her distended breasts and belly. And where the cleft of her sex once was…I don't have the language to describe what I saw there. But she bleeds life from that impossible wound, and I know that she has become a daughter of the oily black cloud that *Pilgrimage* encountered near Ganymede, just as she is mother and father to every living thing trapped within the crucible of that ship, every living thing but me.

"There isn't any time left," the voice from the AI says calmly, calmly but sternly. "You must leave now, Merrick. All available resources on this craft have been depleted, and we must seek sanctuary or perish."

I nod and turn away from her, because I understand as much as I'm ever going to understand, and I've seen more than I can bear to remember. I move as fast as I dare across the transhab and along the corridor leading back to the airlock. In less than five minutes, I'm safely strapped into my seat on the taxi again, decoupling and falling back towards *Yastreb-4.* A few hours later, while I'm waiting out my time in decon, Commander Yun tells me that *Pilgrimage* has fired its main engines and broken orbit. In a few moments, it will enter the thin Martian atmosphere and begin to burn. Our AI has plotted a best-guess trajectory, placing the point of impact within the Tharsis Montes, along the flanks of Arsia Mons. He tells me that the exact coordinates, -5.636 ° N, 241.259 ° E, correspond to one of the collapsed cavern roofs dotting the flanks of the ancient volcano. The pit named Jeanne, discovered way back in 2007.

"There's not much chance of anything surviving the descent," he says. I don't reply, and I never tell him, nor anyone else aboard the *Yastreb-4*, what I saw during my seventeen minutes on *Pilgrimage.*

And there's no need, Dr. Teasdale, for me to tell *you* what you already know. Or what your handlers know. Which means, I think, that we've reached the end of this confession. Here's the feather in your cap. May you choke on it.

Outside my hospital window, the rain has stopped. I press the call button and wait on the nurses with their shiny yellow pills and the white pills flecked with grey, their jet sprays and hollow needles filled with nightmares and, sometimes, when I'm very lucky, dreamless sleep.

Tall Bodies

They – THEY – are not quite beyond description, though it may be my words are not equal to the task. It may or not be. All too often, words fail me, no matter how often or overused that phrase might be. *May... might...not quite...*already I am falling back on uncertainty. Is that a rigorous, almost scientific qualification, or is it a cop out? Don't ask, because I don't know. I only know that each time I see them, they are not quite beyond description, even if I have never before attempted to describe them. THEM.

I always think of them *in* all caps, since that very first night, though I cannot say why. I cannot put my finger on why. Another hoary old chestnut, there. Yes, *chestnut.* There's a tiresome, stale joke here, whether it is *visible* or not; I know it in my mind. My mind's eye. Can I compose an entire document of clichés? Has anyone ever tried?

The first time I saw them it was on a sunny summer's day. Never in the morning, evening nor at night, though I have looked for them then. And never in any season but summer, and never on cloudy or overcast days. Those days in New England when the sky is startlingly blue. So, I imagine there is some correlation between their appearance on those days (season, weather, time of day) and their propensity for moving about in the open. Or. At all other times, some peculiarity of their physiology, biochemistry, whatnot, renders them invisible to the human eye. Or my eyes, at least.

Almost always, I am lying alone in bed, or having tea neat at the little table (Queen-Anne style, oval two-board top over a square skirt, tapering legs ending in pad feet, my mother's and her mother's before her) by the dining room window, or pulling weeds in the garden, when they appear. Several, or only one. I look up, and IT or THEY are standing some distance away. Sometimes peering in through a window, sometimes watching from a considerable distance, other times striding about in the near distance.

Never have they made any threatening gesture towards me. I will not say I am the only person ever to have seen them, for I can't possibly know that. I can say that no one else has ever been with me when I have seen them.

Then again, I'm a solitary sort. That's easy, out here on the island. No one much ever comes by, except the mailman and my only close friend, Chelsea. I rarely call her Chelsea, preferring a private joke, Cheshire, as she is given to unannounced visits and abrupt departures. Which makes her not so unalike them, doesn't it? She doesn't seem to mind being called Cheshire. Or, if she does, has never come out and said as much. She is a pretty woman, Cheshire, past forty-five, but still somehow girlish. I have never told her of my crush on her, never even hinted. But I have wished, on occasion, that she were not straight, that she did not have a husband and two children. That she would come to live with me in my cottage and share my bed. Then, she might see them, too.

I have read of "window fallers," which are said to be creatures and/or beings ("fallers") that occasionally enter our universe via breaches ("windows") between our cosmos and other dimensions or parallel universes. It is the sort of phrase created by this or another person who believes in UFOs, Bigfoot, astrology, that the pyramids were constructed by ancient astronauts. *That* sort. Oh, if they could see what I have seen. But, yes. "Window fallers." It has been suggested that such tall tales as *la Bête du Gévaudan*, the Mothman of Pleasant Point, West Virginia, and Spring-Heeled Jack are all examples of "window fallers." I know some would be eager to place Them in the same dubious category. Only, *they* are not tall tales to scare children and keep lunatics busy. They are as real as am I. As is Cheshire, with her dimples and green eyes. Or the sunflowers and snapdragons in my garden.

The china cups in my cabinets.

The sun in the sky.

I'd never call them "stick figures." I suppose someone else might, but I wouldn't. True, they seem hardly more substantial than that at first glance, but when you've seen them as frequently as I have, and always in the broad daylight, it's plain the phrase would be inaccurate. They stride on very long legs, their arms – almost as long as their legs – swinging slightly at their sides. I have not yet seen one bend over. Yes, they have faces, but those can only be glimpsed if one or several are very, very close, in part because "neck" and "head" are exactly the same circumference and diameter.

They move slowly and with an exquisite grace.

"You should get out more," Cheshire says to me on a bright Saturday morning in September. "You should take the ferry. Go shopping."

My groceries come once a week, brought by a delivery boy – well, a girl, usually, the grocer's daughter. Her name is Polly. I didn't think anyone named their daughters Polly anymore, and I have almost asked several times why her parents chose the name. Polly is a nickname for Mary, by way of another nickname for Mary, Molly. So, her Christian name is probably Mary. Polly, Mary, Molly. It almost makes a children's rhyme, for hopscotch or jumping rope.

"We could go to a movie," Cheshire says.

Though, she knows I don't care for movies. I don't even own a television. I'm happy enough with my books.

She once tried to get me to attend the Blessing of the Fleet in South County, at Galilee, to go along with her. But I have never liked crowds, and I'm not sure God offers divine protection to fishermen. Or much of anyone else. I don't believe that's the way it works. I'd told her all of this, and more besides, and she lamented the days when I lived in South Kingstown and taught high-school history and geography to the hooligans that pass for students these days. She lamented those days, even though she didn't meet me until after I'd retired and moved out to the island, taking up residence in this cottage I inherited from my mother.

"You don't know how I lived back then."

"I bet," she said, stirring cream into her steaming cup of Darjeeling. "I would bet you more outgoing back then."

"I wasn't," I assured her. Though, that was a bald-faced lie. Not that I want to give the impression that I lie very often, because I don't.

I will begin with the first time I saw one of them. I was having a nap (as I often do around two in the afternoon, rarely sleeping more than an hour). I awoke at five after three (by the clock on the wall). One of them was looking in at me through the window. Oh, I have not said that I have my bedroom in the tiny attic of the cottage. As a child it was mine, and when I moved back in, I honestly could imagine sleeping nowhere else. It still has the same calico wallpaper. It has only a single window, with a southeastern view, looking out towards Mohegan Bluffs and Corn Cove and the open Atlantic beyond, and, if you think about it, the shores of Africa far, far away. At any rate, I awoke, and it was gazing in at me with its narrow face, those eyes black as raven feathers, the slit of a mouth, the place where nostrils ought to be but aren't. I still think it odd that I was not the least bit frightened, or even surprised, by the sight. As if I'd been expecting it all along. It watched me and blinked several times, but its face was entirely expressionless. Its skin (like all its kind) was dark, a shade of black-grey that put me in mind of the graphite in a pencil.

"Window fallers." Well, it was at my window, yes, though I am aware that's *not* what that sort of loony means by the phrase. Later, I read of a French parson who claimed to have been reading his Bible and looked up to see la Bête staring in at him through a window pane. He was terrified; I was not. But, then, la Bête was supposedly a killer, and they have never shown the slightest sign of malign intent.

It places a hand against the window pane. They have only three fingers, long as yardsticks. It held its hand against the glass a short while, and then it moved away. That is the only occasion I have ever seen one of them close-up. Possibly, that one voyeuristic act was enough the settle their curiosity.

The distance from my window to the ground is slightly more than twenty-two feet and six inches.

I find it odd that the island is such a small place, and no one else has ever seen one. Or maybe it's only that no one else has ever admitted to seeing one. Same as I haven't.

The second time I saw them, a month later, I was clipping sunflowers for a vase in my modest kitchen. Sunflowers always seem to brighten a room, or a garden, and that's why I grow them every year. But there I was, on my knees, and I saw them through the grape-covered trellis. They were all the same height, moving very slowly towards the sea. I have wondered if they *come* from the sea, through I have never seen any evidence of them on the beaches. None of them seemed to notice me. They weren't in view for more than four or five minutes, and then I went back to clipping sunflowers and put the whole event out of my mind. That was three years ago.

Three years and spare change.

"People talk," Cheshire said, during one of her visits.

"People talk? About me? And what do they say?"

"How you never go out."

"I do so. I am in my garden almost every day. Sometimes, I walk down to the beach and look for sea glass.

My mother called beach glass "mermaid's tears."

"That isn't what I mean, and you are well aware it isn't."

"I don't care," I said, and I meant it, though I think I must have sounded a bit huffy from the face she made. Another reason I call her Cheshire is her broad smile and straight teeth, but she wasn't smiling then. "Whatever they say about me, it certainly doesn't matter."

"They know about that girl, when you were still teaching. They talk about that, too. I know it's no one's business but your own. Still, I thought you ought to know."

"Well, now I do, don't I?"

"If you'd just come out every now and then."

I made some perfectly legitimate excuse for ending the conversation, at least temporarily. I wasn't about to ask her to leave, though part of me wanted to do just that. I told her I was baking bread, most likely. A loaf of bread, or cranberry muffins, or a strawberry and rhubarb pie. I must admit that I am inordinately fond of strawberry and rhubarb pies.

"You know, there's bingo Thursday night at the – "

"Cheshire, I absolutely must see to the..." Well, whatever I was baking. "It'll burn, otherwise."

"Have it your way," she sighed and sipped her tea.

If they do not come from here, I wonder where it is they *do* come from. And why? Are they like the summer people, vacationing? Is there no sea in their world, presuming they are not native to this planet? Is there something they're trying to learn by watching us? Or do they have no real interest whatsoever in human beings. I'll never know, because they never speak. I have no idea if they are capable of speech. If they were, why would they bother talking to an old woman who bakes pies and grows sunflowers and was politely, but firmly, asked to retire early because she had an affair with a student?

They are *inscrutable.*

Yes, that is the word I would use to best describe their intentions. Inscrutable.

Am I inscrutable to them, and is that why they have – excepting that first time – always kept their distance?

I know there are more questions here than answers, but that doesn't seem inappropriate. Not to me it doesn't. People are too insistent in their desire for constant answers.

I am writing these words down at the little tea table that belonged to my grandmother, and as my pen moves across the paper, there are five of them striding, stilt-like, towards the bluffs. They are tall, oh so beautifully tall.

©Locke 2013

As Red As Red

1.

"So, you believe in vampires?" she asks, then takes another sip of her coffee and looks out at the rain pelting Thames Street beyond the café window. It's been pissing rain for almost an hour, a cold, stinging shower on an overcast afternoon near the end of March, a bitter Newport afternoon that would have been equally at home in January or February. But at least it's not pissing snow.

I put my own cup down – tea, not coffee – and stare across the booth at her for a moment or two before answering. "No," I tell Abby Gladding. "But, quite clearly, those people in Exeter who saw to it that Mercy Brown's body was exhumed, the ones who cut out her heart and burned it, clearly *they* believed in vampires. And that's what I'm studying, the psychology behind that hysteria, behind the superstitions."

"It was so long ago," she replies and smiles. There's no foreshadowing in that smile, not even in hindsight. It surely isn't a predatory smile. There's nothing malevolent, or hungry, or feral in the expression. She just watches the rain and smiles, as though something I've said amuses her.

"Not really," I say, glancing down at my steaming cup. "Not so long ago as people might *like* to think. The Mercy Brown incident, that was in 1892, and the most recent case of purported vampirism in the northeast I've been able to pin down dates from sometime in 1898, a mere hundred and eleven years ago."

Her smile lingers, and she traces a circle in the condensation on the plate-glass window, then traces another circle inside it.

"We're not so far removed from the villagers with their torches and pitchforks, from old Cotton Mather and his bunch. That's what you're saying."

"Well, not exactly, but..." and when I trail off, she turns her head towards me, and her blue-grey eyes seem as cold as the low-slung sky above Newport. You could almost freeze to death in eyes like those, I think, and

I take another sip of my lukewarm Earl Grey with lemon. Her eyes seem somehow brighter than they should in the dim light of the coffeehouse, so there's your foreshadowing, I suppose, if you're the sort who needs it.

"You're pretty far from Exeter, Ms. Howard," she says, and takes another sip of her coffee. And me, I'm sitting here wishing we were talking about almost anything but Rhode Island vampires and the hysteria of crowds, tuberculosis and the Master's thesis I'd be defending at the end of May. It had been months since I'd had anything even resembling a date, and I didn't want to squander the next half hour or so talking shop.

"I think I've turned up something interesting," I tell her, because I can't think of any subtle way to steer the conversation in another direction. "A case no one's documented before, right here in Newport."

She smiles that smile again.

"I got a tip from a folklorist up at Brown," I say. "Seems like maybe there was an incident here in 1785 or thereabouts. If it checks out, I might be onto the oldest case of suspected vampirism resulting in an exhumation anywhere in New England. So, now I'm trying to verify the rumors. But there's precious little to go on. Chasing vampires, it's not like studying the Salem witch trials, where you have all those court records, the indictments and depositions and what have you. Instead, it's necessary to spend a lot of time sifting and sorting fact from fiction, and, usually, there's not much of either to work with."

She nods, then glances back towards the big window and the rain. "Be a feather in your cap, though. If it's not just a rumor, I mean."

"Yes," I reply. "Yes, it certainly would."

And here, there's an unsettling wave of not-quite déjà vu, something closer to dissociation, perhaps, and for a few dizzying seconds I feel as if I'm watching this conversation, a voyeur listening in, or I'm only remembering it, but in no way actually, presently, taking part in it. And, too, the coffeehouse and our talk and the rain outside seem no more concrete – no more *here and now* – than does the morning before. One day that might as well be the next, and it's raining, either way.

I'm standing alone on Bowen's Warf, staring out past the masts crowded into the marina at sleek white sailboats skimming over the glittering water, and there's the silhouette of Goat Island, half hidden in the fog. I'm about to turn and walk back up the hill to Washington Square and the library, about to leave the gaudy Disney World concessions catering to the tastes of tourists and return to the comforting maze of ancient gabled houses lining winding, narrow streets. And that's when I see her for the first time. She's standing alone near the "seal safari" kiosk, staring at a faded sign, at black-and-white photographs of harbor seals with eyes like the puppies and little girls from those hideous Margaret Keane paintings. She's wearing an old pea coat and shiny green galoshes that look new, but there's nothing on her head, and she doesn't have an umbrella. Her long black hair hangs wet and limp, and when she looks at me, it frames her pale face.

Then it passes, the blip or glitch in my psyche, and I've snapped back, into myself, into *this* present. I'm sitting across the booth from her once more, and the air smells almost oppressively of freshly roasted and freshly ground coffee beans.

"I'm sure it has a lot of secrets, this town," she says, fixing me again with those blue-grey eyes and smiling that irreproachable smile of hers.

"Can't swing a dead cat," I say, and she laughs.

"Well, did it ever work?" Abby asks. "I mean, digging up the dead, desecrating their mortal remains to appease the living. Did it tend to do the trick?"

"No," I reply. "Of course not. But that's beside the point. People do strange things when they're scared."

And there's more, mostly more questions from her about Colonial-Era vampirism, Newport's urban legends, and my research as a folklorist. I'm grateful that she's kind or polite enough not to ask the usual "you mean people get paid to do this sort of thing" questions. Instead, she tells me a werewolf story dating back to the 1800s, a local priest supposedly locked away in the Portsmouth Poor Asylum after he committed a particularly gruesome murder, how he was spared the gallows because people believed he was a werewolf and so not in control of his actions. She even tells me about seeing his nameless grave in a cemetery up in Middletown, his tombstone bearing the head of a wolf. And I'm polite enough not to tell her that I've heard this one before.

Finally, I notice that it's stopped raining.

"I really ought to get back to work," I say, and she nods and suggests that we should have dinner sometime soon. I agree, but we don't set a date. She has my number, after all, so we can figure that out later. She also mentions a movie playing at Jane Pickens that she hasn't seen and thinks I might enjoy. I leave her sitting there in the booth, in her pea coat and green galoshes, and she orders another cup of coffee as I'm exiting the café. On the way back to the library, I see a tree filled with noisy, cawing crows, and for some reason it reminds me of Abby Gladding.

2.

That was Monday, and there's nothing the least bit remarkable about Tuesday. I make the commute from Providence to Newport, crossing the West Passage of Narragansett Bay to Conanicut Island, and then the East Passage to Aquidneck Island and Newport. Most of the day is spent at the Redwood Library and Athenaeum on Bellevue, shut away with my newspaper clippings and microfiche, with frail yellowed books that were printed before the Revolutionary War. I wear the white cotton gloves they give me for handling archival materials, and make several pages of handwritten notes, pertaining primarily to the treatment of cases of consumption in Newport during the first two decades of the Eighteenth Century.

The library is open late on Tuesdays, and I don't leave until sometime after seven p.m. But nothing I find gets me any nearer to confirming that a corpse believed to have belonged to a vampire was exhumed from the Common Burying Ground in 1785. On the long drive home, I try not to think about the fact that she hasn't called, or my growing suspicion that she likely never will. I have a can of ravioli and a beer for dinner. I half watch something forgettable on television. I take a hot shower and brush my teeth. If there are any dreams – good, bad, or otherwise – they're nothing I recall upon waking. The day is sunny, and not quite as cold, and I do my best to summon a few shoddy scraps of optimism, enough to get me out the door and into the car.

But by the time I reach the library in Newport, I've got a headache, what feels like the beginnings of a migraine, railroad spikes in both my eyes, and I'm wishing I'd stayed in bed. I find a comfortable seat in the Roderick Terry Reading Room, one of the armchairs upholstered with dark green leather, and leave my sunglasses on while I flip through books pulled randomly from the shelf on my right. Novels by William Kennedy and Elia Kazan, familiar, friendly books, but trying to focus on the words only makes my head hurt worse. I return *The Arrangement* to its slot on the shelf, and pick up something called *Thousand Cranes* by a Japanese author, Yasunari Kawbata. I've never heard of him, but the blurb on the back of the dust jacket assures me he was awarded the Nobel Prize for Literature in 1968, and that he was the first Japanese author to receive it.

I don't open the book, but I don't reshelve it, either. It rests there in my lap, and I sit beneath the octagonal skylight with my eyes closed for a while. Five minutes maybe, maybe more, and the only sounds are muffled footsteps, the turning of pages, an old man clearing his throat, a passing police siren, one of the librarians at the front desk whispering a little more loudly than usual. Or maybe the migraine magnifies her voice and only makes it seem that way. In fact, all these small, unremarkable sounds seem magnified, if only by the quiet of the library.

When I open my eyes, I have to blink a few times to bring the room back into focus. So I don't immediately notice the woman standing outside the window, looking in at me. Or only looking *in*, and I just happen to be in her line of sight. Maybe she's looking at nothing in particular, or at the bronze statue of Pheidippides perched on its wooden pedestal. Perhaps she's looking for someone else, someone who isn't me. The window is on the opposite side of the library from where I'm sitting, forty feet or so away. But even at that distance, I'm almost certain that the pale face and lank black hair belong to Abby Gladding. I raise a hand, half waving to her, but if she sees me, she doesn't acknowledge having seen me. She just stands there, perfectly still, staring in.

I get to my feet, and the copy of *Thousand Cranes* slides off my lap; the noise the book makes when it hits the floor is enough that a couple of people look up from their magazines and glare at me. I offer them an apologetic gesture – part shrug and part sheepish frown – and they shake their heads, almost in unison, and go back to reading. When I glance at the window again, the black-haired woman is no longer there. Suddenly, my headache is much worse (probably from standing so quickly, I think), and I feel a sudden, dizzying rush of adrenalin. No, it's more than that. I feel afraid. My heart races, and my mouth has gone very dry. Any plans I might have harbored of going outside to see if the woman looking in actually was Abby vanish immediately, and I sit down again. If it was her, I reason, then she'll come inside.

So I wait, and, very slowly, my pulse returns to its normal rhythm, but the adrenaline leaves me feeling jittery, and the pain behind my eyes doesn't get any better. I pick the novel by Yasunari Kawbata up off the floor and place it back upon the shelf. Leaning over makes my head pound even worse, and I'm starting to feel nauseous. I consider going to the restrooms, near the circulation desk, but part of me is still afraid, for whatever reason, and it seems to be the part of me that controls my legs. I stay in the seat and wait for the woman from the window to walk into the Roderick Terry Reading Room. I wait for her to be Abby, and I expect to hear her green galoshes squeaking against the lacquered hardwood. She'll say that she thought about calling, but then figured that I'd be in the library, so of course my phone would be switched off. She'll say something about the weather, and she'll want to know if I'm still up for dinner and the movie. I'll tell her about the migraine, and maybe she'll offer me Excedrin or Tylenol. Our hushed conversation will annoy someone, and he or she will shush us. We'll laugh about it later on.

But Abby doesn't appear, and so I sit for a while, gazing across the wide room at the window, a tree *outside* the window, at the houses lined up neat and tidy along Redwood Street. On Wednesday, the library is open until eight, but I leave as soon as I feel well enough to drive back to Providence.

3.

It's Thursday, and I'm sitting in that same green armchair in the Terry Roderick Reading Room. It's only 11:26 a.m., and already I understand that I've lost the day. I have no days to spare, but already, I know that the research that I should get done today isn't going to happen. Last night was too filled with uneasy dreaming, and this morning I can't concentrate. It's hard to think about anything but the nightmares, and the face of Abby Gladding at the window, her blue eyes, her black hair. And yes, I have grown quite certain that it *was* her face I saw peering in, and that she was peering in *at* me.

She hasn't called (and I didn't get her number, assuming she has one). An hour ago, I walked along the Newport waterfront looking for her, but to no avail. I stood a while beside the "seal safari" kiosk, hoping, irrationally I suppose, that she might turn up. I smoked a cigarette, and stood there in the cold, watching the sunlight on the bay, listening to traffic and the wind and a giggling flock of grey sea gulls. Just before I gave up and made my way back to the library, I noticed dog tracks in a muddy patch of ground near the kiosk. I thought that they seemed unusually large, and I couldn't help but recall the café on Monday and Abby relating the story of the werewolf priest buried in Middletown. But lots of people in Newport have big dogs, and they walk them along the wharf.

I'm sitting in the green leather chair, and there's a manila folder of photocopies and computer printouts in my lap. I've been picking through them, pretending this is work. It isn't. There's nothing in the folder I haven't read five or ten times over, nothing that hasn't been cited by other academics chasing stories of New England vampires. On top of the stack is "The 'Vampires' of Rhode Island," from *Yankee* magazine, October 1970. Beneath that, "They Burned Her Heart…Was Mercy Brown a Vampire?" from the *Narragansett Times,* October 25th 1979, and from the *Providence Sunday Journal*, also October 1979, "Did They Hear the Vampire Whisper?" So many of these popular pieces have October dates, a testament to journalism's attitude towards the subject, which it clearly views as nothing more than a convenient skeleton to pull from the closet every Halloween, something to dust off and trot out for laughs.

Salem has its witches. Sleepy Hollow its headless Hessian mercenary. And Rhode Island has its consumptive, consuming phantoms – Mercy Brown, Sarah Tillinghast, Nellie Vaughn, Ruth Ellen Rose, and all the rest. Beneath the *Providence Sunday Journal* piece is a black-and-white photograph I took a couple of years ago, Nellie Vaughn's vandalized headstone with its infamous inscription: "I am waiting and watching for you." I stare at the photograph for a moment or two and set it aside. Beneath it there's a copy of another October article, "When the Wind Howls and the Trees Moan," also from the *Providence Sunday Journal.* I close the manila folder and try not to stare at the window across the room.

It is only a window, and it only looks out on trees and houses and sunlight.

I open the folder again, and read from a much older article, "The Animistic Vampire in New England" from *American Anthropologist,* published in 1896, only four years after the Mercy Brown incident. I read it silently, to myself, but catch my lips moving:

> *In New England the vampire superstition is unknown by its proper name. It is believed that consumption is not a physical but spiritual disease, obsession, or visitation; that as long as the body of a dead consumptive relative has blood in its heart it is proof that an occult influence steals from it for death and is at work draining the blood of the living into the heart of the dead and causing his rapid decline.*

I close the folder again and return it to its place in my book bag. And then I stand and cross the wide reading room to the window and the alcove where I saw, or only thought I saw, Abby looking in at me. There's a marble bust of Cicero on the window ledge, and I've been staring out at the leafless trees and the brown grass, the sidewalk and the street, for several minutes before I notice the smudges on the pane of glass, only inches from my face. Sometime recently, when the window was wet, a finger traced a circle there, and then traced a circle within that first circle. When the glass dried, these smudges were left behind. And I remember Monday afternoon at the coffeehouse, Abby tracing an identical symbol (if "symbol" is the appropriate word here) in the condensation on the window while we talked and watched the rain.

I press my palm to the glass, which is much colder than I'd expected.

In my dream, I stood at another window, at the end of a long hallway, and looked down at the North Burial Ground. With some difficulty, I opened the window, hoping the air outside would be fresher than the stale air in the hallway. It was, and I thought it smelled faintly of clover and strawberries. And there was music. I saw, then, Abby standing beneath a tree, playing a violin. The music was very beautiful, though very sad, and completely unfamiliar. She drew the bow slowly across the strings, and I realized that somehow the music was shaping the night. There were clouds sailing past above the cemetery, and the chords she drew from the violin changed the shapes of those clouds, and also seemed to dictate the speed at which they moved. The moon was bloated, and shone an unhealthy shade of ivory, and the whole sky writhed like a Van Gogh painting. I wondered why she didn't tell me that she plays the violin.

Behind me, something clattered to the floor, and I looked over my shoulder. But there was only the long hallway, leading off into perfect darkness, leading back the way I'd apparently come. When I turned again to the open window and the cemetery, the music had ceased, and Abby was gone. There was only the tree and row after row of tilted headstones, charcoal-colored slate, white marble, a few cut from slabs of reddish sandstone mined from Massachusetts or Connecticut. I was reminded of a platoon of drunken soldiers, lined up for a battle they knew they were going to lose.

I have never liked writing my dreams down.

It is late Thursday morning, almost noon, and I pull my hand back from the cold, smudged windowpane. I have to be in Providence for an evening lecture, and I gather my things and leave the Redwood Library and Athenaeum. On the drive back to the city, I do my best to stop thinking about the nightmare, my best not to dwell on what I saw sitting beneath the tree, after the music stopped and Abby Gladding disappeared. My best isn't good enough.

4.

The lecture goes well, quite a bit better than I'd expected it would, better, probably, than it had a right to, all things considered. "Mercy Brown as Inspiration for Bram Stoker's *Dracula,*" presented to the Rhode Island Historical Society, and, somehow, I even manage not to make a fool of myself answering questions afterwards. It helps that I've answered these same questions so many times in the past. For example:

"I'm assuming you've also drawn connections between the Mercy Brown incident and Sheridan Le Fanu's 'Carmilla?'"

"There are similarities, certainly, but so far as I know, no one has been able to demonstrate conclusively that Le Fanu knew of the New England phenomena. And, more importantly, the publication of 'Carmilla' predates the exhumation of Mercy Brown's body by twenty years."

"Still, he might have known of the earlier cases."

"Certainly. He may well have. However, I have no *evidence* that he did."

But, the entire time, my mind is elsewhere, back across the water in Newport, in that coffeehouse on Thames, and the Redwood Library, and standing in a dream hallway, looking down on my subconscious rendering of the Common Burying Ground. A woman playing a violin beneath a tree. A woman with whom I have only actually spoken once, but about whom I cannot stop thinking.

It is believed that consumption is not a physical but spiritual disease, obsession, or visitation…

After the lecture, and the questions, after introductions are made and notable, influential hands are shaken, when I can finally slip away without seeming either rude or unprofessional, I spend an hour or so walking alone on College Hill. It's a cold, clear night, and I follow Benevolent Street west to Benefit and turn north. There's comfort in the uneven, buckled bricks of the sidewalk, in the bare limbs of the trees, in all the softly glowing windows. I pause at the granite steps leading up to the front door of what historians call the Stephen Harris House, built in 1764. One hundred and sixty years later, H. P. Lovecraft called this the "Babbitt House" and used it as the setting for an odd tale of lycanthropy and vampirism. I know this huge yellow house well. And I know, too, the four hand-painted signs nailed up on the gatepost, all of them in French. From the sidewalk, by the electric glow of a nearby street lamp, I can only make out the top half of the third sign in the series; the rest are lost in the gloom – *Oubliez le Chien.* Forget the Dog.

I start walking again, heading home to my tiny, cluttered apartment, only a couple of blocks east on Prospect. The side streets are notoriously steep, and I've been in better shape. I haven't gone twenty-five yards before I'm winded and have a nasty stitch in my side. I lean against a stone wall, cursing the cigarettes and the exercise I can't be bothered with, trying to catch my breath. The freezing air makes my sinuses and teeth ache. It burns my throat like whiskey.

And this is when I glimpse a sudden blur from out the corner of my right eye, hardly *more* than a blur. An impression or the shadow of something large and black, moving quickly across the street. It's no more than ten feet away from me, but downhill, back towards Benefit. By the time I turn to get a better look, it's gone, and I'm already beginning to doubt I saw anything, except, possibly, a stray dog.

I linger here a moment, squinting into the darkness and the yellow-orange sodium-vapor pool of streetlight that the blur seemed to cross before it disappeared. I want to laugh at myself, because I can actually feel the prick of goose bumps along my forearms, and the short, fine hairs at the nape of my neck standing on end. I've blundered into a horror-movie cliché, and I can't help but be reminded of Val Lewton's *Cat People,* the scene where Jane Rudolph walks quickly past Central Park, stalked by a vengeful Simone Simon, only to be rescued at the last possible moment by the fortuitous arrival of a city bus. But I know there's no helpful bus coming to intervene on my behalf, and, more importantly, I understand full fucking well that this night holds in store nothing more menacing than what my over-stimulated imagination has put there. I turn away from the street light and continue up the hill towards home. And I do not have to *pretend* that I don't hear footsteps following me, or the clack of claws on concrete, because I *don't.* The quick shadow, the peripheral blur, it was only a moment's misapprehension, no more than a trick of my exhausted, preoccupied mind, filled with the evening's morbid banter.

Oubliez le Chien.

Fifteen minutes later, I'm locking the front door of my apartment behind me. I make a hot cup of chamomile tea, which I drink standing at the kitchen counter. I'm in bed shortly after ten o'clock. By then, I've managed to completely dismiss whatever I only thought I saw crossing Jenckes Street.

5.

"Open your eyes, Ms. Howard," Abby Gladding says, and I do. Her voice does not in any way command me to open my eyes, and it is perfectly clear that I have a choice in the matter. But there's a certain *je-ne-sais-quoi* in the delivery, the inflection and intonation, in the measured conveyance of these seven syllables, that makes it impossible for me to keep my eyes closed. It's not yet dawn, but sunrise cannot be very far away, and I am lying in my bed. I cannot say whether I am awake or dreaming, or if possibly I am stranded in some liminal state that is neither one nor the other. I am immediately conscious of an unseen weight bearing down painfully upon my chest, and I am having difficulty breathing.

"I promised that I'd call on you," she says, and, with great effort, I turn my head towards the sound of her voice, my cheek pressing deeply into my pillow. I am aware now that I am all but paralyzed, perhaps by the same force pushing down on my chest, and I strain for any glimpse of her. But there's only the bedside table, the clock radio and reading lamp and ashtray, an overcrowded bookcase with sagging shelves, and the floral calico wallpaper that came with the apartment. If I could move my arms, I would switch on the lamp. If I could move, I'd sit up, and maybe I would be able to breathe again.

And then I think that she must surely be singing, though her song has no words. There is no need for mere lyrics, not when texture and timbre, harmony and melody, are sufficient to unmake the mundane artifacts that comprise my bedroom, wiping aside the here and now that belie what I am meant to see in this fleeting moment. And even as the wall and the bookshelf and the table beside my bed dissolve and fall away, I understand that her music is drawing me deeper into sleep again, though I must have been very nearly awake when she told me to open my eyes. I have no time to worry over apparent contradictions, and I can't move my head to look away from what she means for me to see.

There's nothing to be afraid of, I think. *No more here than in any bad dream.* But I find the thought carries no conviction whatsoever. It's even less substantial than the dissolving wallpaper and bookcase.

Now I'm looking at the weed-choked shore of a misty pond or swamp, a bog or tidal marsh. The light is so dim it might be dusk, or it might be dawn, or merely an overcast day. There are huge trees bending low near the water, which seems almost perfectly smooth and the green of polished malachite. I hear frogs, hidden among the moss and reeds, the ferns and skunk cabbages, and now the calls of birds form a counterpoint to Abby's voice. Except, seeing her standing ankle deep in that stagnant green pool, I also see that she isn't singing. The music is coming from the violin braced against her shoulder, from the bow and strings and the movement of her left hand along the fingerboard of the instrument. She has her back to me, but I don't need to see her face to know it's her. Her black hair hangs down almost to her hips. And only now do I realize that she's naked.

Abruptly, she stops playing, and her arms fall to her sides, the violin in her left hand, the bow in her right. The tip of the bow breaks the surface of the pool, and ripples in concentric rings race away from it.

"I wear this rough garment to deceive," she says, and, at that, all the birds and frogs fall silent. "Aren't you the clever girl? Aren't you canny? I would not think appearances would so easily lead you astray. Not for long as this."

No words escape my rigid, sleeping jaws, but she hears me all the same, my answer that needs no voice, and she turns to face me. Her eyes are golden, not blue. And in the low light, they briefly flash a bright, iridescent yellow. She smiles, showing me teeth as sharp as razors, and then she quotes from the Gospel of Matthew.

"Inwardly, they were ravening wolves," she says to me. "You've seen all that you need to see, and probably more, I'd wager." With this, she turns away again, turning to face the fog shrouding the wide green pool. As I watch, helpless to divert my gaze or even shut my eyes, she lets the violin and bow slip from her hands; they fall into the water with quiet splashes. The bow sinks, though the violin floats. And then she goes down on all fours. She laps at the pool, and her hair has begun to writhe like a nest of serpents.

And now I'm awake, disoriented and my chest aching, gasping for air as if a moment before I was drowning and have only just been pulled to the safety of dry land. The wallpaper is only dingy calico again, and the bookcase is only a bookcase. The clock radio and the lamp and the ashtray sit in their appointed places upon the bedside table.

The sheets are soaked through with sweat, and I'm shivering. I sit up, my back braced against the headboard, and my eyes go to the second-story window on the other side of the small room. The sun is still down, but it's a little lighter out there than it is in the bedroom. And for a fraction of a moment, clearly silhouetted against that false dawn, I see the head and shoulders of a young woman. I also see the muzzle and alert ears of a wolf, and that golden eyeshine watching me. Then it's gone, she or it, whichever pronoun might best apply. It doesn't seem to matter. Because now I do know exactly what I'm looking for, and I know that I've seen it before, years before I first caught sight of Abby Gladding standing in the rain without an umbrella.

6.

Friday morning I drive back to Newport, and it doesn't take me long at all to find the grave. It's just a little ways south of the chain-link fence dividing the North Burial Ground from the older Common Burying Ground and Island Cemetery. I turn off Warner Street onto the rutted, unpaved road winding between the indistinct rows of monuments. I find a place that's wide enough to pull over and park. The trees have only just begun to bud, and their bare limbs are stark against a sky so blue-white it hurts my eyes to look directly into it. The grass is mostly still brown from long months of snow and frost, though there are small clumps of new green showing here and there.

The cemetery has been in use since 1640 or so. There are three Colonial-era governors buried here (one a delegate to the Continental Congress), along with the founder of Freemasonry in Rhode Island, a signatory to the Declaration of Independence, various Civil War generals, lighthouse keepers, and hundreds of African slaves stolen from Gambia and Sierra Leone, the Gold and Ivory coasts and brought to Newport in the heyday of whaling and the Rhode Island rum trade. The grave of Abby Gladding is marked by a weathered slate headstone, badly scabbed over with lichen. But, despite the centuries, the shallow inscription is still easy enough to read:

HERE LYETH INTERED Y^e^ BODY
OF ABBY MARY GLADDING
DAUGHTER OF SOLOMON GLADDING ^esq^
& MARY HIS WYFE WHO
DEPARTED THIS LIFE Y^e^ 2^d^ DAY OF
SEPT 1785 AGED 22 YEARS
SHE WAS DROWN'D & DEPARTED & SLEEPS
ZECH 4:1 NEITHER SHALL THEY WEAR
A HAIRY GARMENT TO DECEIVE

Above the inscription, in place of the usual death's head, is a crude carving of a violin. I sit down in the dry, dead grass in front of the marker, and I don't know how long I've been sitting there when I hear crows cawing. I look over my shoulder, and there's a tree back towards Farewell Street filled with the big black birds. They watch me, and I take that as my cue to leave. I know now that I have to go back to the library, that whatever remains of this mystery is waiting for me there. I might find it tucked away in an old journal a newspaper clipping, or in crumbling church records. I only know I'll find it, because now I have the missing pieces. But there is an odd reluctance to leave the grave of Abby Gladding. There's no fear in me, no shock or stubborn disbelief at what I've discovered or at its impossible ramifications. And some part of me notes the oddness of this, that I am not afraid. I leave her alone in that narrow house, watched over by the wary crows, and go back to my car. Less than fifteen minutes later I'm in the Redwood Library, asking for anything they can find on a Solomon Gladding, and his daughter, Abby.

"Are you okay?" the librarian asks, and I wonder what she sees in my face, in my eyes, to elicit such a question. "Are you feeling well?"

"I'm fine," I assure her. "I was up a little too late last night, that's all. A little too much to drink, most likely."

She nods, and I smile.

"Well, then. I'll see what we might have," she says, and, cutting to the chase, it ends with a short article that appeared in the *Newport Mercury* early in November 1785, hardly more than two months after Abby Gladding's death. It begins, "We hear a ſtrange account from laſt Thursday evening, the Night of the 3rd of November, of a body diſinterred from its Grave and coffin. This most peculiar occurrence was undertaken at the beheſt of the father of the deceaſed young woman therein buried, a circumſtance making the affair even ſtranger ſtill." What follows is a description of a ritual which will be familiar to anyone who has read of the 1892 Mercy Brown case from Exeter, or the much earlier exhumation of Nancy Young (summer of 1827), or other purported New England "vampires."

In September, Abby Gladding's body was discovered in Newport Harbor by a local fisherman, and it was determined that she had drowned. The body was in an advanced state of decay, leading me to wonder if the date of the headstone is meant to be the date the body was found, not the date of her death. There were persistant rumors that the daughter of Solomon Gladding, a local merchant, had taken her own life. She is said to have been a "child of singular and morbid temperament," who had recently refused a marriage proposal by the eldest son of another Newport merchant, Ebenezer Burrill. There was also back-fence talk that Abby had practiced witchcraft in the woods bordering the town, and that she would play her violin (a gift from her mother) to summon "voracious wolves and other such dæmons to do her bidding."

Very shortly after her death, her youngest sister, Susan, suddenly fell ill. This was in October, and the girl was dead before the end of the month. Her symptoms, like those of Mercy Brown's stricken family members, can readily be identified as late-stage tuberculosis. What is peculiar here is that Abby doesn't appear to have suffered any such wasting disease herself, and the speed with which Susan became ill and died is also atypical of consumption. Even as Susan fought for her life, Abby's mother, Mary, fell ill, and it was in hope of saving his wife that Solomon Gladding agreed to the exhumation of his daughter's body. The article in the *Newport Mercury* speculates that he'd learned of this ritual and folk remedy from a Jamaican slave woman.

At sunrise, with the aid of several other men, some apparently family members, the grave was opened, and all present were horrified to see "the body fresh as the day it was conſigned to God," her cheeks "fluſhed with colour and luſterous." The liver and heart were duly cut out, and both were discovered to contain clotted blood, which Solomon had been told would prove that Abby was rising from her grave each night to steal the blood of her mother and sister. The heart was burned in a fire kindled in the cemetery, the ashes mixed with water, and the mother drank the mixture. The body of Abby was turned facedown in her casket, and an iron stake was driven through her chest, to insure that the restless spirit would be unable to find its way out of the grave. Nonetheless, according to parish records from Trinity Church, Mary Gladding died before Christmas. Her father fell ill a few months later, and died in August of 1786.

And I find one more thing that I will put down here. Scribbled in sepia ink, in the left-hand margin of the newspaper page containing the account of the exhumation of Abby Gladding is the phrase *Jé-rouge,* or "red eyes," which I've learned is a Haitian term denoting werewolfery and cannibalism. Below that word, in the same spidery hand, is written "As white as snow, as red as red, as green as briers, as black as coal." There is no date or signature accompanying these notations.

And now it is almost Friday night, and I sit alone on a wooden bench at Bowen's Wharf, not too far from the kiosk advertising daily boat tours to view fat, doe-eyed seals sunning themselves on the rocky beaches ringing Narragansett Bay. I sit here and watch the sun going down, shivering because I left home this morning without my coat. I do not expect to see Abby Gladding, tonight or ever again. But I've come here, anyway, and I may come again tomorrow evening.

I will not include the 1785 disinterment in my thesis, no matter how many feathers it might earn for my cap. I mean never to speak of it again. What I have written here, I suspect I'll destroy it later on. It has only been written for me, and for me alone. If Abby was trying to speak *through* me, to find a larger audience, she'll have to find another mouthpiece. I watch a lobster boat heading out for the night. I light a cigarette, and eye the herring gulls wheeling above the marina.

Hydraguros

01.

The very first time I see silver, it's five minutes past noon on a Monday and I'm crammed into a seat on the Bridge Line, racing over the slate-grey Delaware River. Philly is crouched at my back, and a one o'clock with the Czech and a couple of his meatheads is waiting for me on the Jersey side of the Ben Franklin. I've been popping since I woke up half an hour late, the lucky greens Eli scores from his chemist somewhere in Devil's Pocket, so my head's buzzing almost bright and cold as the sun pouring down through the late January clouds. My gums are tingling, and my fucking fingertips, too, and I'm sitting there, wishing I was just about anywhere else but on my way to Camden, payday at journey's end or no payday at journey's end. I'm trying to look at nothing that isn't *out there*, on the opposite side of the window, because faces always make me jumpy when I'm using the stuff Eli assures me is mostly only methylphenidate with a little Phenotropil by way of his chemists' Russian connections. I'm in my seat, trying to concentrate on the shadow of the span and the Speedline on the water below, on the silhouettes of buildings to the south, on a goddamn flock of birds, anything out there to keep me focused, keep me awake. But then my ears pop, and there's a second or two of dizziness before I smell ozone and ammonia and something with the carbon stink of burning sugar.

We're almost across the bridge by then, and I tell myself not to look, not to dare fucking look, just mind my own business and watch the window, my sickly, pale reflection *in* the window, and the dingy winter scene the window's holding at bay. But I look anyhow.

There's a very pretty woman sitting across the aisle from me, her skin as dark as freshly ground coffee, her hair dreadlocked and pulled back away from her face. Her skin is dark, and her eyes are a brilliant, bottomless green. For a seemingly elastic moment, I am unable to look away from those eyes. They manage to be both merciful and fierce, like the painted eyes of Catholic saints rendered in plaster of Paris. And I'm thinking it's no big, and I'll be able to look back out the window; who gives a shit what that smell might have been. It's already starting to fade. But then the pretty woman turns her head to the left, towards the front of the car, and quicksilver trickles from her left nostril and spatters her jeans. If she felt it – if she's in any way aware of this strange excrescence – she shows no sign that she felt it. She doesn't wipe her nose, or look down at her pants. If anyone else saw what I saw, they're busy pretending like they didn't. I call it quicksilver, though I know that's not what I'm seeing. Even this first time, I know it's only something that *looks* like mercury, because I have no frame of reference to think of it any other way.

The woman turns back towards me, and she smiles. It's a nervous, slightly embarrassed sort of smile, and I suppose I must have been sitting there gawking at her. I want to apologize. Instead, I force myself to go back to the window, and curse that Irish cunt that's been selling Eli fuck knows what. I curse myself for being such a lazy asshole and popping whatever's at hand when I have access to good clean junk. And then the train is across that filthy, poisoned river and rolling past Campbell Field and Pearl Street. My heart's going a mile a minute, and I'm sweating like it's August. I grip the handle of the shiny aluminum briefcase I'm supposed to hand over to the Czech, assuming he has the cash, and do my best to push back everything but my trepidation of things I know I'm not imagining. You don't go into a face-to-face with one of El Diamante's bastards with a shake on, not if you want to keep the red stuff on the inside where it fucking belongs.

I don't look at the pretty black woman again.

02.

The very first thing you learn about the Czech is that he's not from the Czech Republic or the dear departed Czech Socialist Republic or, for that matter, Slovakia. He's not even European. He's just some Canuck motherfucker who used to haunt Montreal, selling cloned phones and heroin and whores. A genuine Renaissance crook, the Czech. I have no idea where or when or why he picked up the nickname, but it stuck like shit on the wall of a gorilla's cage. The second thing you learn about the Czech is not to ask about the scars. If you're lucky, you've learned both these things before you have the misfortune of making his acquaintance up close and personal.

Anyway, he has a car waiting for me when the train dumps me out at Broadway Station, but I make the driver wait while I pay too much for bottled water at Starbucks. The lucky greens have me in such a fizz I'm almost seeing double, and there are rare occasions when a little H_20 seems to help bring me down again. I don't actually expect *this* will be one of those times, but I'm still a bit weirded out by what I think I saw on the Speedline, and I'm a lot pissed that the Czech's dragged me all the way over to Jersey at this indecent hour on a Monday. So, let the driver wait for five while I buy a lukewarm bottle of Dasani that I know is just twelve ounces of Philly tap water with a fancy blue label slapped on it.

"Czech, he don't like to be kept waiting," says the skinny Mexican kid behind the wheel when I climb into the backseat. I show him my middle finger, and he shrugs and pulls away from the curb. I set the briefcase on the seat beside me, just wanting to be free of the package and on my way back to Eli and our cozy dump of an apartment in Chinatown. As the jet-black Lincoln MKS turns off Broadway onto Mickle Boulevard, heading west, carrying me back towards the river, I think how I'm going to have a chat with Eli about finding a better pusher. My gums feel like I've been chewing foil, and there are wasps darting about behind my eyes. At least the wasps are keeping their stingers to themselves.

"Just how late are we?" I ask the driver.

"Ten minutes," he replies.

"Blame the train."

"You blame the train, Mister. I don't talk to the Czech unless he talks to me, and he never talks to me."

"Lucky you," I say and take another swallow of Dasani. It tastes more like the polyethylene terephthalate bottle than water, and I try not to think about toxicity and esters of phthalic acid, endocrine disruption and antimony trioxide, because that just puts me right back on the Bridge Line watching a pretty woman's silver nosebleed.

We stop at a red light, then turn left onto South Third Street, paralleling the waterfront, and I realize the drop's going to be the warehouse on Spruce. I want to close my eyes, but all those lucky green wasps won't let me. The sun is so bright it seems to be flashing off even the most nonreflective of surfaces. Vast seas of asphalt might as well be goddamn mirrors. I drum my fingers on the lid of the aluminum briefcase, wishing the driver had the radio on or a DVD playing, anything to distract me from the buzz in my skull and the noise the tires make against the pavement. Another three or four long minutes and we're bumping off the road into a parking lot that might have last been paved when Obama was in the White House. And the Mexican kid pulls up at the loading bay, and I open the door and step out into the cold, sunny day. The Lincoln has stirred up a shroud of red-grey dust, but all that sunlight doesn't give a shit. It shines straight on through the haze and almost lays me open, head to fucking toe. I cough a few times on my way from the car to the bald-headed gook in Ray-Bans waiting to usher me to my rendezvous with the Czech. However, the wasps do not take my cough as an opportunity to vacate my cranium, so maybe they're here to stay. The gook pats me down and then double checks with a security wand. When he's sure I'm not packing anything more menacing than my mobile, he leads me out of the flaying day and into merciful shadows and muted pools of halogen.

"You're late," the Czech says, just in case I haven't noticed, and he points at a clock on the wall. "You're almost twelve minutes late."

I glance over my shoulder at the clock, because it seems rude not to look after he's gone to the trouble to point. Actually, I'm almost eleven minutes late.

"You got some more important place to be, Czech?" I ask, deciding it's as good a day as any to push my luck a few extra inches.

"Maybe I do at that, you sick homo fuck. Maybe your ass is sitting at the very bottom of my to-do list this fine day. So, how about you zip it and let's get this over with."

I turn away from the clock and back to the fold-out card table where the Czech's sitting in a fold-out chair. He's smoking a Parliament and in front of him there's a half-eaten corned beef sandwich cradled in white butcher's paper. I try not to stare at the scars, but you might as well try to make your heart stop beating for a minute or two. Way I heard it, the stupid son of a bitch got drunk and went bear hunting in some Alaskan national park or another, only he tried to make do with a bottle of vodka and a .22 caliber pocket pistol instead of a rifle. No, that's probably not the truth of it, but his face does look like something a grizzly's been gnawing at.

"You got the goods?" he asks, and I have the impression I'm watching Quasimodo quoting old Jimmy Cagney gangster films. I hold up the briefcase and he nods and puffs his cigarette.

"But I am curious as hell why you went and switched the drop date," I say, wondering if it's really me talking this trash to the Czech, or if maybe the lucky greens have hijacked the speech centers of my brain and are determined to get me shot in the face. "I might have had plans, you know. And El Diamante usually sticks to the script."

"What El Diamante does, that ain't none of your business, and that ain't my business, neither. Now, didn't I say zip it?" And then he jabs a thumb at a second metal folding chair, a few feet in front of the card table, and he tells me to give him the case and sit the fuck down. Which is what I do. Maybe the greens have decided to give me a break, after all. Or maybe they just want to draw this out as long as possible. The Czech dials the three-digit combination and opens the aluminum briefcase. He has a long look inside. Then he grunts and shuts it again. And that's when I notice something shimmering on the toe of his left shoe. It looks a lot like a few drops of spilled mercury. This is the second time I see silver.

03.

This is hours later, and I'm back in Philly, trying to forget all about the woman on the train and the Czech's shoes and whatever might have been in the briefcase I delivered. The sun's been down for hours. The city is dark and cold, and there's supposed to be snow before the sun comes up again. I'm lying in the bed I share with Eli, just lying there on my right side watching him read. There are things I want to tell him, but I know full fucking well that I won't. I won't because some of those things might get him killed if a deal ever goes wrong somewhere down the line (and it's only a matter of time) or if I should fall from grace with Her Majesty Madam Adrianne and all the powers that be and keep the axels upon which the world spins greased up and relatively friction free. And other things I will not tell him because maybe it was only the pills, or maybe it's stress, or maybe I'm losing my goddamn mind, and if it's the latter, I'd rather keep that morsel to myself as long as possible, pretty please and thank you.

Eli turns a page and shifts slightly, to better take advantage of the reading lamp on the little table beside the bed. I scan the spine of the hardback, the words printed on the dust jacket, like I don't already know it by heart. Eli reads books, and I read their dust jackets. Catch me in just the right mood, I might read the flap copy.

"I thought you were asleep," Eli says without bothering to look at me.

"Maybe later, *chica*," I reply, and Eli nods the way he does when he's far more interested in whatever he's reading than in talking to me. So, I read the spine again, aloud this time, purposefully mispronouncing the Korean author's name. Which is enough to get Eli to glance my way. Eli's eyes are emeralds, crossed with some less precious stone. Agate maybe. Eli's eyes are emerald and agate, cut and polished to precision, flawed in ways that only make them more perfect.

"Go to sleep," he tells me, pretending to frown. "You look exhausted."

"Yeah, sure, but I got this fucking hard on like you wouldn't believe."

"Last time I checked, you also had two good hands and a more than adequate knowledge of how they work."

"That's cold," I say. "That is some cold shit to say to someone who had to go spend the day in Jersey."

Eli snorts, and his emerald and agate eyes, which might pass for only hazel-green if you haven't lived with them as long as I have lived with them, they drift back to the printed page.

"The lube warms up just fine," he says, "you hold it a minute or so first." He doesn't laugh, but I do, and then I roll over to stare at the wall instead of watching Eli read. The wall is flat and dull, and sometimes it makes me sleepy. I'd take something, but after the lucky greens, it's probably best if I forego the cocktail of pot and prescription benzodiazepines I usually rely on to beat my insomnia into submission. I don't masturbate, because, boner from hell or not, I'm not in the right frame of mind to give myself a hj. So, I lie and stare at the wall and listen to the soft sounds of Eli reading his biography of South Korean astronaut Yi So-Yeon, who I do recall, and without having to read the book, was the first Korean in space. She might also have been the second Asian woman to slip the surly fucking bonds of Earth and dance the skies or what the hell ever.

"Why don't you take something if you can't sleep," Eli says after maybe half an hour of me lying there.

"I don't think so, *chica*. My brain's still rocking and rolling from the breath mints you been buying off that mick cocksucker you call a dealer. Me, I think he's using drain cleaner again."

"No way," Eli says, and I can tell from the tone of his voice he's only half interested, at best, in whether or not the mad chemist holed up in Devil's Pocket is using Drano to cut his shit. "Donncha's merchandise is clean."

"Maybe *Mr.* Clean," I reply, and Eli smacks me lightly on the back of the head with his book. He tells me to jack off and go to sleep. I tell him to blow me. We spar with the age-old poetry of true love's tin-eared wit. Then he goes back to reading, and I go back to staring at the bedroom wall.

Eli is the only guy I've ever been with more than a month, and here we are going on two years. I found him waiting tables in a noodle and sushi joint over on Race Street. Most of the waiters in the place were either drag queens or trannies, dressed up like geisha whores from some sort of post-apocalyptic Yakuza flick. He was wearing so much makeup, and I was so drunk on Sapporo Black Label and saki, I didn't even realize he was every bit *gai-ko* as me. That first night, back at Eli's old apartment not far from the noodle shop, we screwed liked goddamn bunnies on crank. I must have walked funny for a week.

I started eating in that place every night, and almost every one of those nights, we'd wind up in bed together, and that's probably the happiest I've ever been or ever will be. Sure, the sex was absolute supremo, standout – state of the fucking *art* of fucking – but it never would have been enough to keep things going after a few weeks. I don't care how sweet the cock, sooner or later, if that's all there is interest wanes and I start to drift. I used to think maybe my libido had ADD or something, or I'd convinced myself that commitment meant I might miss out on something better. What matters, though, there was more, and four months later Eli packed up his shit and moved in with me. He never asked what I do to pay the rent, and I've never felt compelled to volunteer that piece of intel.

"You're still awake," Eli says, and I hear him toss his book onto the table beside the bed. I hear him reach for a pill bottle.

"Yeah, I'm still awake."

"Good, 'cause there's something I meant to tell you earlier, and I almost forgot."

"And what is that, pray tell?" I ask, listening as he rattles a few milligrams of this or that out into his palm.

"This woman in the restaurant. It was the weirdest thing. I mean, I'd think maybe I was hallucinating or imagining crap, only Jules saw it, too. Think it scared her, to tell you the truth."

Jules is the noodle shop's post-op hostess, who sometimes comes over to play, when Eli and I find ourselves inclined for takeout of that particular variety. It happens. But, point here is, Eli says these words, words that ought to be nothing more than a passing fleck of conversation peering in on the edge of my not getting to sleep, and I get goddamn goose bumps and my stomach does some sort of roll like it just discovered the pommel horse. Because I know what he's going to say. Not exactly, no, but close enough that I want to tell him to please shut the fuck up and turn off the light and never mind what it is he *thinks* he saw.

But I don't, and he says, "This woman came in alone and so Jules sat her at the bar, right? Total dyke, but she had this whole butch-glam demeanor working for her, like Nicole Kidman with a buzz cut."

"You're right," I mutter at the wall, as if it's not too late for intervention. "That's pretty goddamn weird."

"No, you ass. That's not the weird part. The weird part was when I brought her order out, and I noticed there was this shiny silver stuff dripping out of her left ear. At first, I thought it was only a piercing or something, and I just wasn't seeing it right. But then...well, I looked again, and it had run down her neck and was soaking into the collar of her blouse. Jules saw it, too. Freaky, yeah?"

"Yeah," I say, but I don't say much more, and a few minutes later, Eli finally switches off the lamp, and I can stare at the wall without actually having to see it.

04.

It's two days later, as the crow flies, and I'm waiting on a call from one of Her Majesty's lieutenants. I'm holed up in the backroom of a meat market in Bella Vista, on a side street just off Washington, me and Joey the Kike. We're bored and second-guessing our daily marching orders from the pampered, privileged pit bulls those of us so much nearer the bottom of this miscreant food chain refer to as carrion dispatch. Not very clever, sure, but all too fucking often, it hits the nail on the proverbial head. I might not like having to ride the Speedline out to Camden for a handoff with the Czech, but it beats waiting, and it sure as hell beats scraping up someone else's road kill and seeing to its discrete and final disposition. Which is where I have a feeling today is bound. Joey keeps trying to lure me into a game of whiskey poker, even though he knows I don't play cards or dice or dominoes or anything else that might lighten my wallet. You work for Madam Adrianne, you already got enough debt stacked up without gambling, even if it's only penny-ante foolishness to make the time go faster.

Joey the Kike isn't the absolute last person I'd pick to spend a morning with, but he's just next door. Back in the Ohs, when he was still just a kid, Joey did a stint in Afghanistan and lost three fingers off his left hand and more than a few of his marbles. He still checks his shoes for scorpions. And most of us, we trust that whatever you hear coming out of his mouth is pure and unadulterated baloney. It's not that he lies, or even exaggerates to make something more interesting. It's more like he's a bottomless well of bullshit, and every conversation with Joey is another tour through the byways of his shattered psyche. For years, we've been waiting for the bastard to get yanked off the street and sent away to his own padded rumpus room at Norristown, where he can while away the days trading his crapola with other guys stuck on that same ever-tilting mental plane of existence. Still, I'll be the first to admit he's ace on the job, and nobody ever has to clean up after Joey the Kike.

He lights a cigarette and takes off his left shoe, and his sock, too, because you never can tell where a scorpion might turn up.

"You didn't open the case?" he asks, banging the heel of his shoe against the edge of a shipping crate.

"Hell no, I didn't open the case. You think we'd be having this delightful conversation today if I'd delivered a violated parcel to the Czech? Or anybody else, for that matter. For pity's sake, Joey."

"You ain't sleeping," he says, not a question, just a statement of the obvious.

"I'm getting very good at lying awake," I reply. "Anyway, what's that got to do with anything?"

"Sleep deprivation makes people paranoid," he says, and bangs his loafer against the crate two or three more times. But if he manages to dislodge any scorpions, they're of the invisible brand. "Makes you prone to erratic behavior."

"Joey, please put your damn shoe back on."

"Hey, dude, you want to hear about the Trenton drop or not?" he asks, turning his sock wrong-side out for the second time. Ash falls from the cigarette dangling at the corner of his mouth.

I don't answer the question. Instead, I pick up my phone and stare at the screen, like I can will the thing to ring. All I really want right now is to get on with whatever inconvenience and unpleasantness the day holds in store, because Joey's a lot easier to take when confined spaces and the odor of raw pork fat aren't involved.

Not that he needs my permission to keep going. Not that my saying no, I *don't* want to hear about the Trenton drop, is going to put an end to it.

"Well," he says, lowering his voice like he's about to spill a state secret, "what we saw when Tony Palamara opened that briefcase – and keep in mind, it was me *and* Jack on that job, so I've got backup if you need that sort of thing – what we saw was five or six of these silver vials. I'm not sure Tony realized we got a look inside or not, and, actually, it wasn't much more than a peek. It's not like either of us was *trying* to see inside. But, yeah, that's what we saw, these silver vials lined up neat as houses, each one maybe sixty or seventy milliliters, and they all had a piece of yellow tape or a yellow sticker on them. Jack, he thinks it was some sort of high-tech, next-gen explosive, maybe something you have to mix with something else to get the big bangola, right?"

And I stare at him for a few seconds, and he stares back at me, that one green-and-black argyle sock drooping from his hand like some giant's idea of a novelty prophylactic. Whatever he sees in my face, it can't be good, not if his expression is any indication. He takes the cigarette out of his mouth and balances it on the edge of the shipping crate.

"Joey, were the vials silver, or was the silver what was inside of the vials?"

And I can tell right away it hasn't occurred to him to wonder which. Why the hell would it? He asks me what difference it makes, sounding confused and suspicious and wary all at the same time.

"So you couldn't tell?"

"Like I said, it wasn't much more than a peek. Then Tony Palamara shut the case again. But if I had to speculate, if this was a wager and there was money on the line? Was that the situation, I'd probably say the silver stuff was inside the vials."

"If you had to speculate?" I ask him, and Joey the Kike bobs his head and turns his sock right-side out again.

"What difference does it make?" he wants to know. "I haven't even gotten around to the interesting part of the story yet."

And then, before I can ask him what the interesting part might be, my phone rings, and its dispatch, and I stand there and listen while the dog barks. Straightforward janitorial work, because some asshole decided to use a shotgun when a 9mm would have sufficed. Nothing I haven't had to deal with a dozen times or more. I tell the dog we're on our way, and then I tell Joey it's his balls on the cutting board if we're late because he can't keep his shoes and socks on his goddamn feet.

05.

Some nights, mostly in the summer, Eli and me, we climb the rickety fire escape onto the roof to try to see the stars. There are a couple of injection-molded plastic lawn chairs up there, left behind by a former tenant, someone who moved out years before I moved into the building. We sit in those chairs that have come all the way from some East Asian factory shithole in Hong Kong or Taiwan, and we drink beer and smoke weed and stare up at the night spread out above Philly, trying to see anything at all. Mostly, it's a white-orange sky-glow haze, the opaque murk of photo-pollution, and I suspect we imagine far more stars than we actually see. I tell him that some night or another we'll drive way the hell out to the middle of nowhere, someplace where the sky is still mostly dark. He humors me, but Eli is a city kid, born and bred, and I think his idea of a pastoral landscape is Marconi Plaza. We might sit there and wax poetic about planets and nebulas and shit, but I have a feeling that if he ever found himself standing beneath the real deal, with all those twinkling pinpricks scattered overhead and maybe a full moon to boot, it'd probably freak him right the fuck on out.

One night he said to me, "Maybe this is preferable," and I had to ask what he meant.

"I just mean, maybe it's better this way, not being able to see the sky. Maybe, all this light, it's sort of like camouflage."

I squinted back at Eli through a cloud of fresh ganja smoke, and when he reached for the pipe I passed it to him.

"I have no idea what you're talking about," I told him, and Eli shrugged and took a big hit of the 990 Master Kush I get from a grower whose well aware how much time I've spent in Amsterdam, so she knows better than to sell me dirt grass. Eli exhaled and passed the pipe back to me.

"Maybe I don't mean anything at all," he said and gave me half a smile. "Maybe I'm just stoned and tired and talking out my ass."

I think that was the same night we might have seen a falling star, though Eli was of the opinion it wasn't anything but a pile of space junk burning up as it tumbled back to earth.

06.

I've been handling the consequences of other people's half-assed *mokroye delo* since I was sixteen going on forty-five. So, yeah, takes an awfully bad scene to get me to so much as flinch, which is not to say I *enjoy* the shit. Truth of it, nothing pisses me off worse or quicker than some bastard spinning off the rails, running around with that first-person shooter mentality that, more often than not, turns a simple, straight-up hit into a bloodbath. And that is precisely the brand of unnecessary sangre pageantry that me and Joey the Kike have just spent the last three hours mopping up. What's left of the recently deceased, along with a bin of crimson rags and sponges and the latex gloves and coveralls we wore, is stowed snuggly in the trunk of the car. Another ten minutes, it won't be our problem anymore, soon as we make the scheduled meet and greet with one of Madam Adrianne's garbage men.

So, it's hardly business as usual that Joey's behind the wheel because my hands won't stop shaking enough that I can drive. They won't stop shaking long enough for me to even light a cigarette.

"You really aren't gonna tell me what it was happened back there?" he asks for, I don't know, the hundredth time in the last thirty or forty minutes. I glance at my watch, then the speedometer, making sure we're not late and he's not speeding. At least I have that much presence of mind left to me.

"Never yet known you to be the squeamish type with wet work," he says and stops for a red light.

Most of the snow from Tuesday night has melted, but there are still plenty of off-white scabs hiding in the shadows, and there's also the filthy mix of ice and sand and schmutz heaped at either side of the street. There are people out there shivering at a bus stop, people rushing along the icy sidewalk, a homeless guy huddled in the doorway of an abandoned office building. Every last bit of that tableau is as ordinary as it gets, the humdrum day-to-day of the ineptly named City of Brotherly Love, and that ought to help, but it doesn't. All of it comes across as window dressing, meticulously crafted misdirection meant to keep me from getting a good look at what's really going down.

"Dude, seriously, you're starting to give me the heebie-jeebies," Joey says.

"Why don't you just concentrate on getting us where we're going," I tell him. "See if you can do that, all right? Cause it's about the only thing in the world you have to worry about right now."

"We're not gonna be late," says Joey the Kike. "At this rate, we might be fucking early, but we sure as hell ain't gonna be late."

I keep my mouth shut. Out there, a thin woman with a purse Doberman on a pink rhinestone leash walks past. She's wearing galoshes and a pink wool coat that only comes down to her knees. At the bus stop, tucked safe inside that translucent half-shell, a man lays down a newspaper and answers his phone. The homeless guy scratches at his beard and talks to himself. Then the traffic light turns green, and we're moving again.

This is the day that I saw silver for the third time. But no way in hell I'm going to tell Joey that.

Just like the first time, sitting on the train as it barreled towards Camden and my tryst with the Czech, I felt my ears pop, and then there was the same brief dizziness, followed by the commingled reek of ammonia, ozone, and burnt sugar. Me and Joey, we'd just found the room with the body, some poor son of a bitch who'd taken both barrels of a Remington in the face. Who knows what he'd done, or if he'd done anything at all. Could have been over money or dope or maybe someone just wanted him out of the way. I don't let myself think too much about that sort of thing. Better not to even think of the body as *someone*. Better to treat it the way a stock boy handles a messy cleanup on aisle five after someone's shopping cart has careened into a towering display of spaghetti sauce.

"Sometimes," said Joey, "I wish I'd gone to college. What about you, man? Ever long for another line of work? Something that *don't* involve scraping brains off the linoleum after a throw-down."

But me, I was too busy simply trying to breathe to remind him that I *had* gone to college, too busy trying not to gag to partake in witty repartee. The dizziness had come and gone, but that acrid stench was forcing its way past my nostrils, scalding my sinuses and the back of my throat. And I knew that Joey didn't smell it, not so much as a whiff, and that his ears hadn't popped, and that he'd not shared that fleeting moment of vertigo. He stood there, glaring at me, his expression equal parts confusion and annoyance. Finally, he shook his head and stepped over the dead guy's legs.

"Jesus and Mary, we've both seen way worse than this," he said, and right then, that's when I caught the dull sparkle on the floor. The lower jaw was still in one piece, mostly, so for half a second or so I pretended I was only seeing the glint of fluorescent lighting off a filling or a crown. But then the silvery puddle, no larger than a dime, moved. It stood out very starkly against all that blood, against the soup of brain and muscle tissue punctuated by countless shards of human skull. It flowed a few inches before encountering a jellied lump of cerebellum, and then I watched as it slowly extended…what? What the fuck would you call what I saw? A *pseudopod*? Yeah, sure. I watched as it extended a pseudopod and began crawling *over* the obstacle in its path. That's when I turned away, and when I looked back, it wasn't there anymore.

Joey curses and honks the horn. I don't know why. I don't ask him. I don't care. I'm still staring out the passenger side window at this brilliant winter day that wants or needs me to believe it's all nothing more or less than another round of the same old same old. I'm thinking about the woman on the Speedline and about the scuffed toe of the Czech's shoe, about whatever Eli saw at the noodle shop and the silver vials Joey and Jack got a peep at when Tony Palamara opened the case they'd delivered to him. I'm drawing lines and making correlations, parsing best I can, dot-to-fucking-dot, right? Nothing it takes a genius to see, even if I've no idea whatsoever what it all adds up to in the end. I blink, and the sun sparks brutally off distant blue-black towers of mirrored glass. Joey hits the horn again, broadcasting his displeasure for all Girard Avenue to hear, and I shut my eyes.

07.

And it's a night or two later that I have the dream. That I have the dream for the first time.

I've never given much thought to nightmares. Sure, I rack up more than my fair share. I wake up sweating and the sheets soaked, Eli awake, too, and asking if I'm okay. But what would you fucking expect? That's how it goes when your life is a never ending game of Stepin Fetchit and "Mistress may I have another," when you exist in the everlasting umbrage of Madam Adrianne's Grand Guignol of vice and crime and profit. No one lives this life and expects to sleep well – leastways, no one with walking-around sense. That's why white-coated bastards in pharmaceutical labs had to go and invent Zolpidem and so many other merciful soporifics, so the bad guys could get a little more shut eye every now and again.

This is not my recollection of that first time. Hell, this is not my recollection of *any* single instance of the dream. It has a hundred subtle and not-so-subtle permutations, but always it stays the same. It wears a hundred gaudy masks to half conceal an immutable underlying face. So, take this as the amalgam or composite that it is. Take this as a rough approximation. Be smart, and take this with a goddamn grain of salt.

Let's say it starts with me and Eli in our plastic lawn chairs, sitting on the roof, gazing heavenward, like either one of us has half a snowball's chance at salvation. Sure. This is as good a place to begin as any other. There we sit, holding hands, scrounging mean comfort in one another's company – only, this time, some human agency or force of nature has intervened and swept back all that orange sky-glow. The stars are spread out overhead like an astronomer's banquet, and neither of us can look away. You see pictures like that online, sure, but you don't look up and expect to behold the dazzling entrails of the Milky Way draped above your head. You don't live your whole life in the over-illuminated filth of cities and ever expect to glimpse all those stars arching pretty as you please across the celestial hemisphere.

We sit there, content and amazed, and I want to tell Eli those aren't stars. It's only fireworks on the Fourth of July or the moment the clock strikes the New Year. But he's too busy naming constellations to hear me. How Eli would know a constellation from throbbing gristle is beyond me. But there he sits, reciting them for my edification.

"That's Sagittarius," he says. "Right there, between Ophiuchus and Capricornus. The centaur, between the serpent in the west and the goat in the east." And he tells me that more extrasolar planets have been discovered in Sagittarius than in any other constellation. "*That's* why we should keep a close watch on it."

And I realize then, whiz-bang, presto, abracadabra, that the stars are wheeling overhead, exchanging positions in some crazy cosmic square dance, and Eli, *he* sees it too, and he laughs. I've never heard Eli laugh like this before, not while I was awake. It's the laughter of a child. It's a laughter filled with delight. There's innocence in a laugh like this.

And maybe, after that, I'm not on the roof anymore. Maybe, after that, I'm sitting in a crowded bar down on Locust Street. I know the place, but I can never remember its name, not in the dream. Nothing to write home about, one way or the other. Neither classy enough nor sleazy enough to be especially memorable. Just fags and dykes wall to fucking wall and lousy, ancient disco blaring through unseen speakers. There's a pint bottle of Wild Turkey sitting on the bar in front of me, and an empty shot glass. Someone's holding a gun to the back of my head. And, yeah, I *know* the feeling of having a gun to my head, because it happened this one time on a run to Atlantic City that went almost bad as bad can be. I also know that it's Joey the Kike holding the pistol, seeing as how there's a dead scorpion the color of pus lying right there on the bar beside the bottle of bourbon.

"This ain't the way it ought to be," he says, and I'm surprised I can hear his voice over the shitty music and all those queers trying to talk *over* the shitty music.

"Then how about we find some other way to work it out," I say, sounding lame as any asshole ever tried to talk his way out of a slug to the brain. "How about you sit down here next to me and we have a drink and make sure there are no more creepy crawlies in your shoes."

"I shouldn't be seen in a place like this," he says, and I hear him pull the hammer back. "People talk, they see you hanging round a place like this."

"People do fucking talk," I agree. With my left index finger, I flick the dead scorpion off the bar. No one seems to notice. For that matter, no one seems to notice he's got a gun to my head. I say, "Maybe you should bounce before some hard-nosed bastard takes a notion to make you his bitch, yeah? You ever taken it up the ass, Joey?"

"You're such a smart guy," Joey replies, "you're still gonna be passing woof tickets when you're six-feet under, ain't you? Expect you'll manage to smack talk your way out of Hell, given half a chance."

"Well, you know me, Joey. Never let 'em see you sweat. *Vini, vedi, vici* and all that *hùnzhàng*."

And I'm sitting there waiting to die, when the music stops, and all eyes turn towards the rear of the bar. I look, too, though Joey's still got his 9mm parked on my scalp. A baby spot with a green gel is playing across a tiny stage, and there's Eli with a microphone. I'd think he was actual, factual fish if I didn't know better, that's how good Eli looks in a black evening gown and pumps and a wig that makes me think of Isabella Rossellini playing Dorothy Vallens in *Blue Velvet*. The din of voices is only a murmur now, only a gentle whisper of expectation as we all wait to see which way the wind's about to blow.

"Damn, she's hot," Joey says.

"Fuckin' A, she's hot," I tell him. "You should be so goddamn lucky to get a piece of ass like that one day."

He tells me to keep quiet, zip it and toss the key, that he wants to hear, but it's not *me* he wants to hear. So I make like a good boy and oblige. After all, I want to hear this nightingale, too. And then Eli begins to sing, a cappella and in Spanish, and everyone goes hushed as midnight after Judgment Day. His voice is his voice, not some dream impersonation, and I wonder why I never knew Eli could sing.

Bueno, ahora, pagar la atención

Sólo en caso de que no había oído…

And I'm still right there in the bar, but I'm somewhere else, as well. I'm walking in a desert somewhere, like something out of an old Wild and Woolly West flick, and the sun beats down on me from a sky so blue it's almost white. There are mountains far, far away, a jagged line against the horizon, and I wonder if that's where I'm trying to get to. If there's something in the mountains that I need to see. The playa stretches out all around me, a lifeless plain of alkali flats and desiccation cracks. Maybe this was a lake or inland sea, long, long ago. Maybe the water still comes back, from time to time. Sweat runs into my eyes, and I squint against the sting.

On the little stage, Eli sings in Spanish, and I sit on my barstool with the barrel of Joey's gun prodding my skull. I wish the shot glass weren't empty, 'cause the baking desert sun has me thirsty as a motherfucker. I keep my eyes on Eli, and I hear the parching salt wind whipping across the flats, and I hear that song in a language that I can only half understand.

Basta con mirar hacia el cielo

Y gracias al Gobierno por la nieve

Y cantar la baja hacia abajo…

"What's she sayin'?" Joey the Kike wants to know, and I ask him which part of me looks Mexican.

In the desert, I stop walking and peer up at the sun. High above me, there are contrails. And I know that's what Eli's singing about – those vaporous wakes – even if I have no idea why.

"It's a dream," I tell Joey the Kike, growing impatient with the gun. "Specifically, it's *my* dream. I come here all the time, and I don't remember ever inviting you."

The playa crunches loudly beneath my feet.

Tony Palamara opens a briefcase, and I see half a dozen silver vials marked with yellow tape.

A woman on a train wipes at her nose, and my ears pop.

Eli is no longer singing in Spanish, though I don't recall the transition. No one says a word. They're all much too busy watching him make love to the resonant phallus of his microphone.

Trying to make it rain.

So when you're out there in that blizzard,
Shivering in the cold,
Just look up to the sky…

I kneel on that plain and dig my fingers into the scorched saline crust. I crush the sandy dirt in my hand, and the wind sweeps it away. And that's when I notice what looks like a kid's spinning top – only big around as a tractor-trailer's wheel – lying on the ground maybe twenty yards ahead of me. A tattered drogue parachute is attached to the enormous top by a tangled skein of nylon kernmantle cord. The wind ruffles wildly through the chute, and I notice the skid marks leading from the spinning top that isn't a spinning top, trailing away into the distance.

And sing the low-down experimental cloud-seeding
Who-needs-'em-baby? Silver-iodide blues…

I stand, and look back the way I've come. In the dream, I guess I've come from the south, walking north. So, looking south, the desert seems to run on forever, with no unobtainable mountainous El Dorado to upset the monotony. There's only the sky above, crisscrossed with contrails, and the yellow-brown playa below, the line drawn between them sharp as a paper cut. There's not even the mirage shimmer of heat I'd have expected, but, of course, this desert is only required to obey the dictates of my unconscious mind, not any laws of physical science. I stand staring at the horizon for a moment, and then resume my northwards march. I know now I'm not trying to reach the mountains. No one reaches those mountains, not no way, not no how, right? I'm only trying to go as far as the kid's top that's not a top and its rippling nylon parachute. I understand that now, and I tell Joey to either pull the trigger or put his piece away. I don't have time for reindeer games tonight. And if I did, I still wouldn't be looking for action from the likes of him.

I stare at the bar, and the pus-colored scorpion's returned. This time, I don't bother to make it go away. I do wonder if dead scorpions can still kill a guy. *Was you ever bit by a dead bee?*

All those people in the bar have begun applauding, and Eli takes a bow and sets his mike back into its stand.

"What you saw," Joey sneers, "I got as much right to know as you. We were both slopping about in that stiff's innards, and if something was wrong with him, I deserve to know. You got no place keepin' it from me."

"I didn't see anything," I tell him, wishing it were the truth. "Now, are you going to shoot me or put away the roscoe and make nice?"

"Making you nervous?" asks Joey,

"Not really, but the potential for injury is pissing me off righteously."

I reach the top that's not a top, and now I'm almost certain it's actually some sort of return capsule from a space probe. One side is scorched black, so I suppose that must be the heat shield. I stand three or four feet back, and I never, in any version of the dream, have touched the thing. It's maybe five feet in diameter, maybe a little less. I'm wondering how long its been out here, and where it might have traveled before hurtling back to earth, and why no retrieval team's come along to fetch it. I wonder if it's even a NASA probe, or maybe, instead, a chunk of foreign hardware that strayed from its target area. Either way, no one leaves shit like this laying around in the goddamn desert. I know *that* much.

"Yeah, you know it all," Joey says, and jabs me a little harder with the muzzle of his gun. "You must be the original Doctor Einstein, and me, I'm just some schmuck can't be trusted with the time of day."

Catch a falling star an' put it in your pocket...

And on the rooftop, Eli tells me, "The star at the centaur's knee is Alpha Sagittarii, or Rukbat, which means 'knee' in Arabic. Rukbat is a blue class B star, one hundred and eighteen light years away. It's twice as hot as the sun and forty times brighter."

"You been holding out on me, *chica*. Here I thought you were nothing but good looks and grace, and then you get all Wikipedia on me."

Eli laughs, and the crowded, noisy bar on Locust Street dissolves like fog, and the desert fades to half a memory. Joey the Kike and his pea-shooter, the dead scorpion and the bottle of Wild Turkey, every bit of it merely the echo of an echo now. I'm standing at the doorway of our bathroom, the tiny bathroom in mine and Eli's place in Chinatown. Regardless which rendition of the dream we're talking about, sooner or later they *all* end here. I'm standing in the open door of the bathroom, and Eli's in the old claw-foot tub. The air is thick with steam and condensation drips in crystal beads from the mirror on the medicine cabinet. Even the floor, that mosaic of white hexagonal tiles, is slick. I'm barefoot, and the ceramic feels slick beneath my feet. I swear and ask Eli if he thinks he got the water hot enough, and he asks me about the briefcase I delivered to the Czech. It doesn't even occur to me to ask how the hell he knows about the delivery.

"What about we don't talk shop just this once," I say, as though it's something we make a habit of doing. "And how about we most especially don't linger on the subject of the fucking Czech?"

"Hey, *you* brought it up, lover, not me," Joey says, returning the soap to the scallop-shaped soap dish. His hand leaves behind a smear of silver on the sudsy bar. I stare at it, trying hard to recall something important that's teetering right there on the tip end of my tongue.

For love may come an' tap you on the shoulder, some starless night...

"Make yourself useful and hand me a towel," he says. "Long as you're standing there, I mean."

I reach into the linen closet for a bath towel, and when I turn back to pass it to Eli, he's standing, the water lapping about his lower calves. Only it's not water anymore. It's something that looks like mercury, and it flows quickly up his legs, his hips, his ass, and drips like cum from the end of his dick. Eli either isn't aware of what's going on, or he doesn't care. I hand him the towel as the silver reaches his smooth, hairless chest and begins to makes its way down both his arms.

"Anyway," he says, "we can talk about it or we can not talk about it. Either way's fine by me. So long as you don't start fooling yourself into thinking *your* hands are clean. I don't want to hear about how you were only following orders, you know?"

It's easy to forget them without tryin', with just a pocketful of starlight.

My ears haven't popped, and there's been no dizziness, but, all the same, the bathroom is redolent with those caustic triplets, ammonia and ozone, and, more subtly, sugar sizzling away to a black carbon scum. The silver has reached Eli's throat, and rushes up over his chin, finding its way into his mouth and nostrils. A moment more, and he stands staring back at me with eyes like polished ball bearings.

"You and your gangster buddies, you get it in your heads you're only blameless errand boys," Eli says, and his voice has become smooth and shiny as what the silver has made of his flesh. "You think ignorance is some kind of virtue, and none of the evil shit you do for your taskmasters is ever coming back to haunt you."

I don't argue with him, no matter whether Eli (or the sterling apparition standing where Eli stood a few moments before) is right or wrong or someplace in between. I could disagree, sure, but I don't. I'm reasonably fucking confident it no longer makes any difference. The towel falls to the floor, fluttering like a drogue parachute in a desert gale, and Eli steps out of the tub, spreading silver in his wake.

© LOCKE 2013

Slouching Towards the House of Glass Coffins

Graze on my lips, and if those hills are dry, Stray lower where the pleasant fountains lie.

William Shakespeare,
"Venus and Adonis" (1592–1593)

1.

Alieka Ferenczi has been walking for seven days, ever since the roller she'd bought back in Annapolis salted and sputtered its final sorrowful sput. She'd known the mole's conversion coils were half a step from fried when she bought it off a scrapyard at the edge of the city by the sea. But she was almost at her last wad now, having already paid so much to the datswap jig for cords that would lead her across the Lunae to the walls of the Yellow House – or *might* get her there, if he'd been that solo honest jig in ever one thou. The sand and dust swirls around her, various-sized dervishes to testify to how BrantCorp and AOWT's had gone so toto hit and miss on Barsoom. Sure, there were the shallow seas stretching from Chryse north to the pole, and the southern sea, and, here and there, patches of scrubland – cactus, josh trees, verde and ironwood, yukka, shitty little paradisio's for snakes and lizards and the occasional rodent, but not much else. Alieka had always heard about how ace things had gone at far off Lake Hellas, with its drip-dense rainforgets and those silver cities rising from the shore like spirals bound for Heaven – Ausonia, New Moscow, Cañas, Tugaske, Kyoto Neo – three quarters of the planet's population crushed into the lake's eastern shore, and no newcomers welcome. Fuck all to the rest assward, right? Damn so, damn so.

These were among Alieka Ferenczi's bitter, weary thoughts as she dragged herself across wastes under the sky so bright with stars. Now and again, she'd stop and pick out the dot that was Earth. All sorta tales what went on homeworld, and they were most ghost tales for children and workers, House all happy and content out on the ring, sure. Talk about war and famine and tox oceans. Why, we're better off than them leftbacks, them shite-rat also-rans, ain't we just? Shi and she dy jarroo, lay your glimmers down if we're wrong on that. These were among the jumble of her thoughts while the winds roaring down from the western highlands beat and whipped at her traveler's fraying swaddle. She kept a hand on her leather cap lesten it sail off her scalp, and she pulled the layers of insul tighter about herself. She only walked at night, so here were the wastes at their coldest, but better than the sun. Better be gnawed at by Old Man Aeolusk than have her brains nuked by Old Lady Sol, eh?

There was a light from the stars and light from Phobos rising in the west. She often ruminated on Phobos. Her da, whom she'd never met, had died in the phyllo mines up there. Lock breach, said her ma, and the entire shaft had gone spitter and kaputsky, said her ma. Not a dram of atmo, not nuff grav to house a cow tin from floating off. "He's up there," had said her ma. "You recall that, Alieka, when you gaze at the west moon. Still up there, goin' round, round Barso. And watchin' out for you."

Never did believe that, and she tried not to ponder at his frozen corpse orbiting the planet for all those centuries to come.

Alieka managed to climb up one side of a dune, and managed not to take a tumble coming down the windward slope, so she decided that worthed her a sit at the base, just enough time for a stingy sip from her jug. Only a stingy, though, because out here on the Lunae, not even hardly enough humidity for a dew spread. Not dry as dry can get, but damno dry, betcha. Even with the purdah shielding her nose and mouth, her throat and lungs felt crisp as crack, and her lips bloody. Her sinuses ached.

May be I won't make it to the Yellow House, she thought. *Could be best, that turn, eh?* And Alieka thought how good it would feel to lie down on the sand and never get up again. Let blazing Nair's eye find her without the scant shade of the sheltie folded up in her knap, let the sand bury her, and let the scorpions and asps have their way. Tired as this, it was easy to forget why she'd ever started this fool's parade across the rusty wastes where not even the sappers and sourdoughs dared to tread.

"Muirgheal," she whispered. "Bring back Muirgheal from the Maafa. That's why, you withered cunny. You house your eyes and your mind on her. Ain't no sleep surrender, or you're something worse than the worst coward."

Not that anyone had ever come back once snatched by the Maafa. The slaver caravans tripped back and forth across the plains, and no one much argued when they set their sights on your daughter or son. Oh, there were a few had tried, put up barricades and taken up arms and all that happy crap. Right. But the Maafa were keen to any wait out, and sooner or later took their wares. You say any different, there were enough burnt settles to testify to having gone to the trouble, having been that much the imbecile. But, the long and short, Maafa bitch snatched up Muirgheal from her bed, and no matter what anyone else heard going on, 'cause no one right says no, leave her be, sidewinder eeshobee, and be on about. They took her, and she was ghosted, like never had she been. Excepting for Alieka, who'd had it stone for that pretty-pretty since they were in study together in low sector. But Alieka never had found the requisite, and so sure by now Muirgheal didn't even spare a reminisce her way. And yet, and yet, and still, here was daft Alieka Ferenczi pilgrim on the waste and marching, what?, right up to the Yellow's gates and saying "Let me in, and turn her back." Or what? Have you even thought that far ahead?

The sappers have a phrase for what happens to the human faculties out on the woestenij, and that phrase is *gone vergessenen cranio*. Or just gone, gone, gone. Same on either, and what it means is that the wanderer loses track of her or his intent, and, bereft of purpose, might turn feral or suicide on the red sands, the Kyzyl-Kum, or, luck shines down, poor soul might find its way home again or to some other home of men. But mad as Easter in Rishabha, Ramadan at Xmas. Oh, she dy jarroo, betcha flat.

Alieka bows her head, driving back the dust between her ears to uncover the memories of the one kilo canister tucked in her knap, the explosives, cush and hyped HNB, which took a hefty chunk of her savings *before* the meet with the datswap. *Here to there, old girl*, and if *here* was the bomb, then *there* was making a hole in the House big enough confusion might aft ensue she'd have time to find Muirgheal and beat a hasty get-shy before the Maafa fucks knew what had swatted them. "You don't forget that again," she whispered to the desert night, and might be the wind blowing down from the Tharsis listened and took note. But she doubted it. Alieka promised herself another five minutes rest, and then she go on about her southerly way. Just another four and one, ja, ja, shì. Safe than sore, though, so she pulls the prox rod from her knap, unfolds it, and sticks it into the sand. When she switches it on, it hums like bees.

2.

Here we are now, in the *then* of *now*, past and present and future always leapfrogging, and all cohabitating in the same instance, anyhow. But on this day, four solis before that night at the foot of that tall, tall dune out on the freezing plateau of the Lunae Palus, *this* day, Alieka Ferenczi is at the shop, just like any other Jovis afternoon. She's goggles down, grinding valves smooth enough the hydro farms won't put the boot to her boss, which means he won't put the boot to her. Five hundred ingots down, five hundred more to go before the whistle blows go home, because the boss sure ain't gonna spring for over. The shop noise is a scream to put the season of storms to shame, those perihelion sirens screeching down alleyways and street, and howling over rooftops. But these are not the thoughts Alieka Ferenczi is thinking on that four days ago now, if only because the earphones dampen the racket to the dullest whine of its true self.

She's thinking, instead, of the tix she's lucked into for the evening's match, right down front, her and her ma will be able to hear the whack, whack of the sticks against the leather balls. But then the siren sounds, the repeating triple bleats to warn all low sector of a Maafa sighting within the borders of Annapolis. Not that business as usual stops. She doesn't shut off the bonnet grind. The lane helmer doesn't pop round to end the shift and call it a day and send them safely home, send them to be sure family and friends are accounted, and, besides, all Alieka has is her ma and an elderly hound, and neither is on the Maafa's shopping list. They go for the young and the pretties. So, let the others worry, and let the militia do it's job while she does hers.

And it's only later, over their quick dinner before the match, that ma tells her how the slavers grabbed five before the law drove them away, and one of those, wouldn't you know, says she, was an old schoolmate of yours, Alieka, that sweet girl Muirgheal who always made such fine grades and wore sky-blue ribbons in her silver-grey hair. Alieka, though she'd not thought on Muirgheal Hemingtrust for years, hardly noticed the game, the goals, her ma so jubilant when home sector won, the cries of the fans, the press of the crowd, the smell of hot crisps and bags of fresh roasted chapulines. She only had room in her head for Muirgheal, whom she'd once loved, first crush and never a love thereaft. Too plain, too gruff to win a wife, and no eye for men. Muirgheal hauled away by the Maafa, chained in one of their bamboo wagons and rattling across the sands to her torture and eventual death behind the basalt walls of the Yellow House.

That night she dreamt of Muirgheal, and of all the rumored tribulations and harrows doled within those halls, how the Maafa butchers saw about their work such as no one went quickly. And before sun up she wrote a letter to her ma, packed her knap, and set about town gathering that which she imagined she would need, visiting ill-rep kiosks up west sector, spending for the tram because time was of the essence. The Maafa moved fast on gyped-up, seven-tread rollers, and might easy be fifty kilos in any direction by the now of then. It was mid-morning before she left Southgate, and too soon left the pave for southeast and the Lunae and the reputed location of the Yellow House. She knew she was pressing the mini past its castaway limits. But time was of the essence. Time was slipping by sure as the dust devils and the few birds wheeling overhead.

What you after, Alieka? Something you ain't ever had, something wants no part of you? Half forgot dream of a dream of a dream? Kiddish wishbegones? What you think you're gonna find, you find anything at all?

There was supposed to be a well at Pompeii, but the settlement had vapped since last she'd heard. The plains herders had moved on, as herders do. A dry, dry set of months, worse than usual, and the crater was cracker dry. The stones laid round the rim of the well had fallen over in the wind, and the bore had filled with dust in however many days since. She'd have to watch the level of her jug, and hope for better in the Maja. She'd have to keep the thirst in the back of her mind, lest it lead her to despair or lead to try for home again.

What you after, dirty factory prole? Cognations that slice of quim gonna have anything but plain and simple gratitude even should you get yourself in and get herself out, which you ain't gonna do, anyway? You think eve a half that you've gone soft long ago, eh? She dy jarroo, betcha nothing and get nothing back.

"I don't know," she said aloud, jostling along, astride the roller. She said these self-assurances to herself, but aloud, as the roller topping dunes and rushing down the other side, rattling kidneys as the vehicle bounced and lurched when rocky terrain was come upon. She only thought the bad thoughts, so she had to speak the good ones, even if her voice was lost in clack, clatter, roar of the conversion coils and the last-legger engine.

You after a few wadda for hauling this girl home again, home again, jiggity quick? Maybe a hero's tumble you get lucky and make it back? And you won't, 'cause you and luck ain't no kinda intimates. You, Alieka Ferenczi, gonna get no better off them Maafa fucks but maybe a slug in the gut, a cattle bolt to the skull, 'cause how they ain't about to waste the tribulations on a slag like you.

"Mysterious ways, his wonder to perform," she mutters. "Ain't that what the liturgicals say? So, I might be that mysterious way, I might, and this might be a wonder to perform, might not?"

Not even a believer, and look at you burbling holy muck.

"I believed once," she replies, talking back at herself and thinking of the news of her da dead in a Phobos blowout. That might have been what took away her faith, but it might have been half a hundred other things. "And since that's fact, I might well find divine again, might'n I not?"

And this now of then, this moment passed, but not passed then, is when the roller growled, and sparks came showing off the coils, and Alieka only just managed to throttle back and avoid a tump down a gully. She sat on the dead roller a long time, watching diminutive twin Diemos rising above the western horizon, one night past full, but still hardly brighter than Earth or Venus. She sat and thought on the walk, and on water, and on the canister of HNB in the roller's side basket. It would fit easy in her knap, not much weight at all. She sat ten or fifteen minutes, thinking on all the ways a woman can find her death in the arms of Kyzyl-Kum, as the Turkics named the wastelands. And then she took what would fit into the knap, checked the straps on her boots, and started the slog towards the fabled but all too factual Yellow House of the Maafa.

3.

She thinks, distantly, through a dumb obscuring haze of thirst and muscles stripped down to copper threads, a mouth full of ferric dust and the ferric taste of blood, not even a tear left in her, so long since a decent sip of water. She thinks, distantly, of how a *sound* mind would pause to gape at all this bahà, for no matter the scratch and scrab of the worst of the wind-raw Lunae scape is not out beyond the reach of the hand of beauty. Alieka Ferenczi, who, since birth and across all her days, has never left the smothersome abbrayshio sanctuary of Annapolis. The sun is up, but she has not stopped walking. *I am at the edge,* she thinks. *Few more steps, moments, and here I go gatherin' vergessenen cranio and never gonna strike the prize, just gonna lay me down to sleep and Mama Red will rock me off to sweet blivie. I won't need wet in the blivie black.*

She squints at the lat-long tracker on her belt, and soft blue characters glow 12.5N, 58.3W, which has got to be too far east and not near enough south, way up at the northern wind of the Maja (the terraforms promised a river here, flowing down to the Chryse wide; there's another failure). She shakes it once, a tad hard to read with the sun shining down, shakes it to see whether the box is reading wrong, because humanity will never be shed of the notion that violence convinces tech to get its shit together. It doesn't change, and so Alieka accepts the reading. She accepts she's strayed, and she'll never have the time, the strength, the will to change course now. There was meager water and food before dawn. She came across a poor excuse for a cienega in the hour before dawn. There wasn't a savior pool, but there were cacti, and she pierced her hands all over good sawing off the top of a prickle pear with her knife, and now her palms and fingers sting and ache. They'll be infected soon enough, sure, but at least there were damp and bites of that green meat. Her throat's and stomach's forgotten about that by now, and she can't have any idea why she didn't cram a few of the cladodes into her bulging knap. Junk in there she could have tossed away to make room for so precious a commodity, but rarely do the dying bother to think straight.

Alieka Ferenczi mulls over 12.5N, 58.3W, and wonders if it doesn't matter, because maybe the datswap had no damn idea of what he spoke. Maybe he only made something up there and on the spot to get her wad. Then she starts waltzing again, onwards south, even if there's no meaning in the movement, in the one foot in front of the other. It's something to do, and she's not yet (though she does not fathom why) ready to knock, knock, knock'a death's front door.

She could have kept up with the time by the arc of the sun across the sky, or by the lat-long, but where's the point, she was thinking when one is walking from nowhere to nowhere else and it can only end one way. Where's the minding clocks?

And it is while thinking this thought she sees the high mustard walls of the Yellow House, and stares a long time, because maybe it's only a mirage, cruel in its persuasiveness. This means she has to decide to follow this which might be nothing but a lie, or sit down now and pass over tricks of heat shimmer and exhaustion and sun-shuttered eyes. Moment of truth, she dy jarroo, now or not ever, fold or raise, sure. But here's the bright memory of Muirgheal, too luxe by far to ever even give the likes of oily handed Alieka two shits and a howdy you do. Here is she. Teener wants and formative urges to lift up those heavy boots and set them back again.

Maybe there's not a pork's whit of honor it what I do, thinks Alieka. *Maybe only my cunny leadin' my head, but what of it, sure. If the out's the same, then why the why. Ain't that in the gospel somewheres?*

And she thought of the canister of hyped hexanitro riding on her shoulders, and she tries to reckon the distance between her and the mustard adobe. *Can't be more than a mile,* she assures herself, though it turns out to be more like four. But she stumbles, often falling, often on her knees, through poison scrub and wadi, once almost steps on a rattler might have been as big around as her arms, coiled and rat-tat-tat, and why it didn't strike she's never going to know. But she makes it, and the walls are higher than anyone she's ever heard hold forth of subject have ever claimed. There are char-skinned, forever burned black, brown, gold-skinned men and women perched atop the caliche, armed with spears and crossbows and sonics and punch guns. There are iron gates half as tall as the enceinte, so rusty Alieka wonders how the wind hasn't whisked them away to palus. The Maafa guards don't do anything she expected. They don't open fire. They call out profanities and warnings in their glottal creole, which she only just, and just barely, understands every thirdish word.

Why am I not dead? she thinks, as an auto clicks loud enough to make her stumble back a step or two, and the gates swing inwards. *Might be, hell takes them what come looking after it, might be, sure, and why had nobody thought of this? Because. We had our expects, didn't we. We thought we knew the beasts, all on what they raid snatch, but maybe that's bein' picky in the market stalls after so much risk and troubles.*

The men and women on the wall shout some more, and something whizzes loudly, then there's a bolt, *thunk*, protruding from the ground at her feet. She shades her eyes and stares up at them. She points at herself, and they shout again, all in harmony it seems to her addled brain. So, knowing not else what they could mean (plus, all those only third words to help), or if they've understood her, Alieka steps through the gates that lead to the Yellow House itself, and they bang closed behind her. *When children dream of Sheol, the gates sound like that. Just like,* she thinks, then wishes that she hadn't.

There are more guards, dressed more raggedy than her by far, to escort her to tall lancet doors as rusty as the gate. None of them touch her, and this surprises Alieka as much as anything yet has. The house is not the shade of yellow that she always imagined it would be. Whenever she chanced to think on the color of the house, she saw it so bright it almost hurt to see, a bright shade of yellow that stood out stark against the brick-red plain. Maybe it *was* that color, to start with, the yellow of fields of sunflowers or rapa. Maybe the dust and sand have scoured it *this* color, over the many decades since it was built. Or maybe whatever transpires on inside, maybe *that's* what took away the bright. She goes along, because what else would she do? She lets them drive to and then through that gigantic doorway. And if the gate closing was the sound of the gates of Sheol banging shut, the clanging of those doors are simply beyond the terrors dreamt up by dull women of Alieka's sorry sort.

Inside, the Yellow House is not yellow. It might be no color at all, or it might be those walls, archways, ceilings, and stairwells are all black. She tries not the think on it overly much. In all directions – not so unlike the palus – it seems to go on forever. Why had she not expected that? Why had she underestimated its vastness? Well, why had she seen it the yellow of a rippling field of rapa flowers? *If we have not seen, we do not know, 'cept rumors, what the mind may conjure, and pictures, and nobody's got no pics of the Yellow House.* But, sure, on goes the halls forever, or so seems, and she is led without ever once their hands upon shoulders, arms, back, and without the prodding of spears or gun muzzles. Perhaps this is of her compliance, and perhaps it's not.

Somewhere in this place is Muirgheal, or whatever they've left of her, or made of her. Alieka does her best not to dwell on that. She wonders what's to be done with her instead, as that's far less disturbing a set of possibilities. She silently chortles to herself for ever having reckoned the one kilo canister of HNB would be enough to bring down this sprawling rack. Maybe twenty kilos might have turned the trick. Maybe all the trumpets of the army of Joshua on that day he felled Jericho. But the one is enough for a suicide, and enough to take a few of these shits with her.

They lead her to a round room with a fire pit at its center, and above the fire pit is a hole, a chimney drawing the smoke, which must lead up to the sky, the world outside. There's something turning on a spit above the fire, and to her starved self it looks as good as any pig or chicken ever yet has. But it was human once, a man or a woman, though now it's impossible to be sure which. Her mouth waters, and she curses herself to already have sunk half so low as a Maafa cannibal.

In the round room, across the fire and its grisly, broiling fare, is a dais of basalt, and on the dais is a basalt throne. A man sits there, all skin and bones and raggedy as the rest and as raggedy muff as Alieka.

"What did you come here to find?" the man asks, and it shocks her that he speaks Anglo as well as any school teacher or party member, after hearing only the creole from his pack. "Someone lost, and perhaps you have a mind we stole them away? Or are you here for something else, hoping we might take you in? Or just to satisfy a deadly curiousity that's haunted you so, so long." The man's head is shaved, or he's bald. His skin is a maze of tattoos, and maybe they mean something, something she could puzzle if she had the lux.

"Why am I not dead?" she asks him. Her voice is raw, and it hurts to speak.

"Someone bring her water," the man says, and someone does. She is careful to drink slowly, lest she vomits it all right back up again, shi, shi. She wipes her wet lips on the back of her hand, and her hand comes back bloody. She also glances down at the lat-long tracker: 21.3N, 79.1W, and that doesn't seem right at all, not after the last time she checked.

"Are you hungry, Alieka Ferenczi?" the man on the dais asks, not unkindly. She doesn't ask how he knows her name, because black witches, the lot.

She glances at the thing on the spit, fat dripping to sizzle in the coals, crispy skin, and split open here and there to reveal…

"No," she says. "I had a snake this morning."

"A snake?" he asks, skeptically.

"A rattler," she replies.

"Resourceful of you. So, I ask my questions the second time, and know my patience is not unendlich, as your people would say."

My people. My people. His people.

It's almost impossible not to drool at the odor rising from the spit above the fire pit, so, now, now, whose people has she become? Does the desert work magic, and transform Annapolis words into Maafa.

"May I sit down?" she asks.

"You may do ever as you wish."

She very near thanks him, but thinks better just in time. It's too perverse a gesture to consider. He spies at her with orange eyes, and she can't recall if the others had orange eyes, but – having sat on the hard-packed dirt floor – Alieka doesn't look up to spy back at.

"I am here to find a girl," she says, hardly above a whisper. "Her name be Muirgheal Hemingtrust, and she lived in Annapolis, and once wore blue ribbons in her hair."

"¿Es usted su madre?" the orange-eyed man asks.

Is he making fun? No. That's not the timbre of his wringer.

"No."

"So, your sister?"

"No." Alicka raises her head.

"Then, she *must* be your sheba, shi?"

Only in your wettest, caboodled dreams, factory.

"No," Alieka tells the man. "Even though I wish that were so."

He smiles, revealing teeth filed to razor-sharp triangles. "Good answer, Alieka Ferenczi. I dislikes to the clatter of falsehoods upon my ears. So, you came so far to…take her home, yes?"

"Yes."

The man frowns, and Alieka lowers her gaze, so she only has to see the glow of the fire on the dirt playing across her filthy rags.

"You must know, no one comes into the Halls of the Maafa, who is not themselves Maafa, and goes back out again, yes?"

"Those are the yarns," she answers him.

"But you came, anyway. Though no one ever does this."

She only nods.

"A gallant, yonggan slit, are you. For that, a ward, it may come. For such a yonggan kite, a gift. This is what I think. Though you may not leave, and though you may not have what you came to retrieve, I *will* grant you view to her, eh? So long as you wish to see, at that." There's a surprised rumble of voices from the guards surrounding her.

"If that's the best," she says, wanting a mouth of that roasting thing.

The man is silent a while, then he says, "That's the best, plus."

"Shi," says she, knowing not what else to say. "No fair, then, my askin' more."

"And when you've wearied of my gift, Alieka Ferenczi, praps be you think again on whether to be of the Maafa and learn the Elegy of Pain, shi? Now, with my blesses, yonggan. Go."

She doesn't see him wave his left hand at her guards, but they haul Alieka to her feet, first time their hands upon her. They lift her from the floor and lead her away from the sweet en'fast turning on the spit. Down more black (or colorless) walls and stairs, and then another door creaks open, and inside there is light that is not firelight. Inside the chamber beyond the creaking doors is genny light, fluoro maybe, but sure electrics of one sort of another. She steps inside, a ring of glass tubes, each set into the wall. The chamber is very big, and there might be thirty tubes, all told. At the center, an inner ring of what might be control panels, not so unalike those the bosses run, switches, dials, toggles, pads, and such. She does not yet look directly at the tubes, no more than glance. They are tall, though, and big round as the boles of the sobba trees growing in the middle park back homecity. One of the guards is talking, and she can understand the woman just enough to know she is being told Alicka is to stay here as long as she wishes, and that the door will not be locked, so she may leave when she is ready. And, she thinks, not to dare lay hands on the make-and-breaks. Then they leave her, and the door shuts, and she is alone with the tubes.

In my glass coffin, I am waitin'
In my glass coffin, I am waitin'
In my glass coffin, I am waitin'...

Stray lines clattering through her head. *Isn't that some old Earth song?* she thinks. Some folk ballad old when her grandmother's mother was born.

Let fall your dress
I'll pay to part
Open this mouth wide, eat your heart.

She walks the circuit of the room, does Alieka Ferenczi, and seeing the contents of each tube, those trapped within and unable to die, she is driven on towards the next. And, at finally, she arrives before that tube imprisoning the woman who was once, the now of then, a girl with sky-blue modal ribbons tied in her steel-grey hair. The woman, and what is inside the tube with her. Alieka knows those bugs, and knows what they do to a body, and that the death they bring will take many, many years. But already they've done with Muirgheal's eyes and ears, which might be a mercy and might be worse than all damnations. Alieka sits on the floor (plastic, instead of dirt or stone), and she watches the remnants of the stolen, the one whom she loves who's never loved her back again. It occurs to her that the Maafa didn't take her knap, and the HNB might not drop down the Yellow House, but it would, she guesses, be plenty more than needed to vapor this circle of Hell, she dy jarroo. Alieka takes out the canister and hugs it to her chest. She says prayers to St. Anthony of Padua, as would, maybe, her ma. Her ma says St. Anthony of Padua is patron of the lost and forsaken. Alieka prays, and she thinks of the HNB, and she thinks, too, of that thing on the spit, and the offer that the man with the orange eyes made.

Tidal Forces

Charlotte says, "That's just it, Em. There wasn't any pain. I didn't feel anything much at all." She sips her coffee and stares out the kitchen window, squinting at the bright Monday morning sunlight. The sun melts like butter across her face. It catches in the strands of her brown hair, like a late summer afternoon tangling itself in dead cornstalks. It deepens the lines around her eyes and at the corners of her mouth. She takes another sip of coffee, then sets her cup down on the table. I've never once seen her use a saucer.

And the next minute seems to last longer than it ought to last, longer than the mere sum of the sixty seconds that compose it, the way time stretches out to fill in awkward pauses. She smiles for me, and so I smile back. I don't want to smile, but isn't that what you do? The person you love is frightened, but she smiles anyway. So you have to smile back, despite your own fear. I tell myself it isn't so much an act of reciprocation as an acknowledgement. I could be more honest with myself and say I only smiled back out of guilt.

"I *wish* it had hurt," she says, finally, on the other side of all that long, long moment. I don't have to ask what she means, though *I* wish that I did. *I* wish I didn't already know. She says the same words over again, but more quietly than before, and there's a subtle shift in emphasis. "I wish it *had* hurt."

I apologize and say I shouldn't have brought it up again, and she shrugs.

"No, don't be sorry, Em. Don't let's be sorry for anything."

I'm stacking days, building a house of cards made from nothing but days. Monday is the Ace of Hearts. Saturday is the Four of Spades. Wednesday is the Seven of Clubs. Thursday night is, I suspect, the Seven of Diamonds, and it might be heavy enough to bring the whole precarious thing tumbling down around my ears. I would spend an entire hour watching cards fall, because time would stretch, the same way it stretches out to fill in awkward pauses, the way time is stretched thin in that thundering moment of a car crash. Or at the edges of a wound.

If it's Monday morning, I can lean across the breakfast table and kiss her, as if nothing has happened. And if we're lucky, that might be the moment that endures almost indefinitely. I can kiss her, taste her, savor her, drawing the moment out like a card drawn from a deck. But no, now it's Thursday night, instead of Monday morning. There's something playing on the television in the bedroom, but the sound is turned all the way down, so that whatever the something may be proceeds like a silent movie filmed in color and without intertitles. A movie for lip readers. There's no other light but the light from the television. She's lying next to me, almost undressed, asking me questions about the book I don't think I'm ever going to be able to finish. I understand she's not asking them because she needs to know the answers, which is the only reason I haven't tried to change the subject.

"The Age of Exploration was already long over with," I say. "For all intents and purposes, it ended early in the Seventeenth Century. Everything after that – reaching the north and south poles, for instance – is only a series of footnotes. There were no great blank spaces left for men to fill in. No more 'Here be monsters.'"

She's lying on top of the sheets. It's the middle of July and too hot for anything more than sheets. Clean white sheets and underwear. In the glow from the television, Charlotte looks less pale and less fragile than she would if the bedside lamp were on, and I'm grateful for the illusion. I want to stop talking, because it all sounds absurd, pedantic, all these unfinished, half-formed ideas that add up to nothing much at all. I want to stop talking and just lie here beside her.

"So writers made up stories about lost worlds," she says, having heard all this before and pretty much knowing it by heart. "But those made-up worlds weren't really *lost.* They just weren't *found* yet. They'd not yet been imagined."

"That's the point" I reply. "The value of those stories rests in their insistence that blank spaces still do exist on the map. They *have* to exist, even if it's necessary to twist and distort the map to make room for them. All those overlooked islands, inaccessible plateaus in South American jungles, the sunken continents and the entrances to a hollow earth, they were important psychological buffers against progress and certainty. It's no coincidence that they're usually places where time has stood still, to one degree or another."

"But not really so much time," she says, "as the processes of evolution, which require time."

"See? You understand this stuff better than I do," and I tell her she should write the book. I'm only half joking. That's something else Charlotte knows. I lay my hand on her exposed belly, just below the navel, and she flinches and pulls away.

"Don't do that," she says.

"All right. I won't. I wasn't thinking." I *was* thinking, but it's easier if I tell her that I wasn't.

Monday morning. Thursday night. This day or that. My own private house of cards, held together by nothing more substantial than balance and friction. And the loops I'd rather make than admit to the present. Connecting dot-to-dot, from here to there, from there to here. Here being half an hour before dawn on a Saturday, the sky growing lighter by slow degrees. Here, where I'm on my knees, and Charlotte is standing naked in front of me. Here, now, when the perfectly round hole above her left hip and below her ribcage has grown from a pinprick to the size of the saucers she never uses for her coffee cups.

"I don't think it will hurt," she tells me. And I can't see any point in asking whether she means, *I don't think it will hurt me,* or *I don't think it will hurt you.*

"Now?" I ask her, and she says, "No. Not yet. Wait."

So, handed that reprieve, I withdraw again to the relative safety of the Ace of Hearts – or Monday morning, call it what you will. In my mind's eye, I run back to the kitchen washed in warm yellow sunlight. Charlotte is telling me about the time, when she was ten years old, that she was shot with a BB gun, her brother's Red Ryder BB gun.

"It wasn't an accident," she's telling me. "He meant to do it. I still have the scar from where my mother had to dig the BB out of my ankle with tweezers and a sewing needle. It's very small, but it's a scar all the same."

"Is that what it felt like, like being hit with a BB?"

"No," she says, shaking her head and gazing down into her coffee cup. "It didn't. But when I think about the two things, it seems like there's a link between them, all these years apart. Like, somehow, this thing was an echo of the day he shot me with the BB gun."

"A meaningful coincidence," I suggest. "A sort of synchronicity."

"Maybe," Charlotte says. "But maybe not." She looks out the window again. From the kitchen, you can see the three oaks and her flower bed and the land running down to the rocks and the churning sea. "It's been an awfully long time since I read Jung. My memory's rusty. And, anyway, maybe it's not a coincidence. It could be something else. Just an echo."

"I don't understand, Charlotte. I really don't think I know what you mean."

"Never mind," she says, not taking her eyes off the window. "Whatever I do or don't mean, it isn't important."

The warm yellow light from the sun, the colorless light from a color television. A purplish sky fading towards the light of false dawn. The complete absence of light from the hole punched into her body by something that wasn't a BB. Something that also wasn't a shadow.

"What scares me most," she says (and I could draw *this* particular card from anywhere in the deck), "is that it didn't come back out the other side. So, it must still be lodged in there, *in* me."

I was watching when she was hit. I saw when she fell. I'm coming to that.

"Writers made up stories about *lost* worlds" she says again, after she's flinched, after I've pulled my hand back from the brink. "They did it because we were afraid of having found all there *was* to find. Accurate maps became more disturbing, at least unconsciously, than the idea of sailing off the edge of a flat world."

"I don't want to talk about the book."

"Maybe that's why you can't finish it."

"Maybe you don't know what you're talking about."

"Probably," she says, without the least bit of anger or impatience in her voice.

I roll over, turning my back on Charlotte and the silent television. Turning my back on what cannot be heard and doesn't want to be acknowledged. The sheets are damp with sweat, and there's the stink of ozone that's not *quite* the stink of ozone. The acrid smell that always follows her now, wherever she goes. No. That isn't true. The smell doesn't follow her, it comes *from* her. She *radiates* the stink that is almost, but not quite, the stink of ozone.

"Does *Alice's Adventures in Wonderland* count?" she asks me, even though I've said I don't want to talk about the goddamned book. I'm sure that she heard me, and I don't answer her.

Better not to linger too long on Thursday night.

Better if I return, instead, to Monday morning. Only Monday morning. Which I have carelessly, randomly, designated here as the Ace of Hearts, and hearts are cups, so Monday morning is the Ace of Cups. In four days more, Charlotte will ask me about Alice, and though I won't respond to the question (at least not aloud), I *will* recall that Lewis Carroll considered the *Queen* of Hearts – who rules over the Ace and is also the Queen of Cups – I will recollect that Lewis Carroll considered her the embodiment of a certain type of passion. That passion, he said, which is ungovernable, but which exists as an aimless, unseeing, furious thing. And he said, also, that the Queen of Cups, the Queen of Hearts, is not to be confused with the *Red* Queen, whom he named another brand of passion altogether.

Monday morning in the kitchen.

"My brother always claimed he was shooting at a blue jay and missed. He said he was aiming for the bird, and hit me. He said the sun was in his eyes."

"Did he make a habit of shooting songbirds?"

"Birds and squirrels," she says. "Once he shot a neighbor's cat, right between the eyes." And Charlotte presses the tip of an index finger to the spot between her brows. "The cat had to be taken to a vet to get the BB out, and my mom had to pay the bill. Of course, he said he wasn't shooting at the cat. He was shooting at a sparrow and missed."

"What a little bastard," I say.

"He was just a kid, only a year older than I was. Kids don't mean to be cruel, Em, they just are sometimes. From our perspectives, they appear cruel. They exist outside the boundaries of adult conceits of morality. Anyway, after the cat, my dad took the BB gun away from him. So, after that, he always kind of hated cats."

But here I am neglecting Wednesday, overlooking Wednesday, even though I went to the trouble of drawing a card for it. And it occurs to me now I didn't even draw one for Tuesday. Or Friday, for that matter. It occurs to me that I'm becoming lost in this ungainly metaphor, that the tail is wagging the dog. But Wednesday was of consequence. More so than was Thursday night, with its mute TV and the Seven of Diamonds and Charlotte shying away from my touch.

The Seven of Clubs. Wednesday, or the Seven of Pentacles, seen another way round. Charlotte, wrapped in her bathrobe, comes downstairs after taking a hot shower, and she finds me reading Kip Thorne's *Black Holes and Time Warps,* the book lying lewdly open in my lap. I quickly close it, feeling like I'm a teenager again, and my mother's just barged into my room to find me masturbating to the *Hustler* centerfold. Yes, your daughter is a lesbian, and yes, your girlfriend is reading quantum theory behind your back.

Charlotte stares at me awhile, staring silently, and then she stares at the thick volume lying on the coffee table, *Principles of Physical Cosmology.* She sits down on the floor, not far from the sofa. Her hair is dripping, spattering the hardwood.

"I don't believe you're going to find anything in there," she says, meaning the books.

"I just thought..." I begin, but let the sentence die unfinished, because I'm not at all sure *what* I was thinking. Only that I've always turned to books for solace.

And here, on the afternoon of the Seven of Pentacles, this Wednesday weighted with those seven visionary chalices, she tells me what happened in the shower. How she stood in the steaming spray watching the water rolling down her breasts and *across* her stomach and *up* her buttocks before falling into the hole in her side. Not in defiance of gravity, but in perfect accord with gravity. She hardly speaks above a whisper. I sit quietly listening, wishing that I could suppose she'd only lost her mind. Recourse to wishful thinking, the seven visionary chalices of the Seven of Pentacles, of the Seven of Clubs, or Wednesday. Running away to hide in the comfort of insanity, or the authority of books, or the delusion of lost worlds.

"I'm sorry, but what the fuck do I say to that?" I ask her, and she laughs. It's a terrible sound, that laugh, a harrowing, forsaken sound. And then she stops laughing, and I feel relief spill over me, because now she's crying, instead. There's shame at the relief, of course, but even the shame is welcome. I couldn't have stood that terrible laughter much longer. I go to her and put my arms around her and hold her, as if holding her will make it all better. The sun's almost down by the time she finally stops crying.

I have a quote from Albert Einstein, from sometime in 1912, which I found in the book by Kip Thorne, the book Charlotte caught me reading on Wednesday: "Henceforth, space by itself, and time by itself, are doomed to fade away into mere shadows, and only a kind of union of the two will preserve an independent reality."

Space, time, shadows.

As I've said, I was watching when she was hit. I saw when she fell. That was Saturday last, two days before the yellow morning in the kitchen, and not to be confused with the *next* Saturday which is the Four of Spades. I was sitting on the porch, and had been watching two noisy grey-white gulls wheeling far up against the blue summer sky. Charlotte had been working in her garden, pulling weeds. She called out to me, and I looked away from the birds. She was pointing towards the ocean, and at first I wasn't sure what it was she wanted me to see. I stared at the breakers shattering themselves against the granite boulders, and past that, to the horizon where the water was busy with its all but eternal task of shouldering the burden of the heavens. I was about to tell her that I didn't see anything. This wasn't true, of course. I just didn't see anything out of the ordinary, nothing special, nothing that ought not occupy that time and that space.

I saw nothing to give me pause.

But then I did.

Space, time, shadows.

I'll call it a shadow, because I'm at a loss for any more appropriate word. It was spread out like a shadow rushing across the waves, though, at first, I thought I was seeing something dark moving *beneath* the waves. A very big fish, perhaps. Possibly a large shark or a small whale. We've seen whales in the bay before. Or it might have been caused by a cloud passing in front of the sun, though there were no clouds that day. The truth is I knew it was none of these things. I can sit here all night long, composing a list of what it *wasn't*, and I'll never come any nearer to what it might have been.

"Emily," she shouted. "Do you *see* it?" And I called back that I did. Having noticed it, it was impossible *not* to see that grimy, indefinite smear sliding swiftly towards the shore. In a few seconds more, I realized, it would reach the boulders, and if it wasn't something beneath the water, the rocks wouldn't stop it. Part of my mind still insisted it was only a shadow, a freakish trick of the light, a mirage. Nothing substantial, certainly nothing malign, nothing that could do us any mischief or injury. No need to be alarmed, and yet I don't ever remember being as afraid as I was then. I couldn't move, but I yelled for Charlotte to run. I don't think she heard me. Or if she heard me, she was also too mesmerized by the sight of the thing to move.

I was safe, there on the porch. It came no nearer to me than ten or twenty yards. But Charlotte, standing alone at the garden gate, was well within its circumference. It swept over her, and she screamed, and fell to the ground. It swept over her, and then was gone, vanishing into the tangle of green briars and poison ivy and wind-stunted evergreens behind our house. I stood there, smelling something that almost smelled like ozone. And maybe it's an awful cliché to put to paper, but my mind *reeled*. My heart raced, and my mind reeled. For a fraction of an instant I was seized by something that was neither déjà vu nor vertigo, and I thought I might vomit.

But the sensation passed, like the shadow had, or the shadow of a shadow, and I dashed down the steps and across the grass to the place where Charlotte sat stunned among the clover and the dandelions. Her clothes and skin looked as though they'd been misted with the thinnest sheen of...what? Oil? No, no, no, not oil at all. But it's the closest I can come to describing that sticky brownish iridescence clinging to her dress and her face, her arms and the pickets of the garden fence and to every single blade of grass.

"It knocked me down," she said, sounding more amazed than hurt or frightened. Her eyes were filled with startled disbelief. "It wasn't *anything*, Em. It wasn't anything at all, but it knocked me right off my feet."

"Are you hurt?" I asked, and she shook her head.

I didn't ask her anything else, and she didn't say anything more. I helped her up and inside the house. I got her clothes off and led her into the downstairs shower. But the oily residue that the shadow had left behind had already begun to *evaporate* – and again, that's not the right word, but it's the best I can manage – before we began trying to scrub it away with soap and scalding clean water. By the next morning, there would be no sign of the stuff anywhere, inside the house or out of doors. Not so much as a stain.

"It knocked me down. It was just a shadow, but it knocked me down." I can't recall how many times she must have said that. She repeated it over and over again, as though repetition would render it less implausible, less inherently ludicrous. "A shadow knocked me down, Em. A shadow knocked me down."

But it wasn't until we were in the bedroom, and she was dressing, that I noticed the red welt above her left hip, just below her ribs. It almost looked like an insect bite, except the center was...well, when I bent down and examined it closely, I saw there *was* no center. There was only a hole. As I've said, a pinprick, but a hole all the same. There wasn't so much as a drop of blood, and she swore to me that it didn't hurt, that she was fine, and it was nothing to get excited about. She went to the medicine cabinet and found a Band-Aid to cover the welt. And I didn't see it again until the next day, which as yet has no playing card, the Sunday before the warm yellow Monday morning in the kitchen.

I'll call that Sunday by the Two of Spades.

It rains on the Two of Spades. It rains cats and dogs all the damn day long. I spend the afternoon sitting in my study, parked there in front of my computer, trying to find the end to Chapter Nine of the book I can't seem to finish. The rain beats at the windows, all rhythm and no melody. I write a line, then delete it. One step forward, two steps back. Zeno's "Achilles and the Tortoise" paradox played out at my keyboard – "That which is in locomotion must arrive at the halfway stage before it arrives at the goal," and each halfway stage has it's own halfway stage, *ad infinitum.* These are the sorts of rationalizations that comfort me as I only pretend to be working. This is the *true* reward of my twelve years of college, these erudite excuses for not getting the job done. In the days to come, I will set the same apologetics and exculpations to work on the problem of how a shadow can possibly knock a woman down, and how a hole can be explained away as no more than a wound.

Sometime after seven o'clock, Charlotte raps on the door to ask me how it's going, and what I'd like for dinner. I haven't got a ready answer for either question, and she comes in and sits down on the futon near my desk. She has to move a stack of books to make a place to sit. We talk about the weather, which she tells me is supposed to improve after sunset, that the meteorologists are saying Monday will be sunny and hot. We talk about the book – my exploration of the phenomenon of the literary *Terrae Anachronismorum,* from 1714 and Simon Tyson de Paton's *Voyages et Adventures de Jacques Massed* to 1918 and Edgar Rice Burroughs's *Out of Time's Abyss* (and beyond; see Aristotle on Zeno, above). I close Microsoft Word, accepting that nothing more will be written until at least tomorrow.

"I took off the Band-Aid," she says, reminding me of what I've spent the day trying to forget.

"When you fell, you probably jabbed yourself on a stick or something," I tell her, which doesn't explain *why* she fell, but seeks to dismiss the result of the fall.

"I don't think it was a stick."

"Well, whatever it was, you hardly got more than a scratch."

And that's when she asks me to look. I would have said no, if saying no were an option.

She stands and pulls up her T-shirt, just on the left side, and points at the hole, though there's no way I could ever miss it. On the rainy Two of Spades, hardly twenty-four hours after Charlotte was knocked off her feet by a shadow, it's already grown to the diameter of dime. I've never seen anything so black in all my life, a black so complete I'm almost certain I would go blind if I stared into it too long. I don't say these things. I don't remember what I say, so maybe I say nothing at all. At first, I think the skin at the edges of the hole is puckered, drawn tight like the skin at the edges of a scab. Then I see that's not the case at all. The skin around the periphery of the hole in her flesh is *moving*, rotating, swirling about that preposterous and undeniable blackness.

"I'm scared," she whispers. "I mean, I'm *really* fucking scared, Emily."

I start to touch the wound, and she stops me. She grabs hold of my hand and stops me.

"Don't," she says, and so I don't.

"You *know* that it can't be what it looks like," I tell her, and I think maybe I even laugh.

"Em, I don't know anything at all."

"You damn well know *that* much, Charlotte. It's some sort of infection, that's all, and – "

She releases my hand, only to cover my mouth before I can finish. Three fingers to still my lips, and she asks me if we can go upstairs, if I'll please make love to her.

"Right now, that's all I want," she says. "In all the world, there's nothing I want more."

I almost make her promise that she'll see our doctor the next day, but already some part of me has admitted to myself this is nothing a physician can diagnose or treat. We have moved out beyond medicine. We have been pushed out into these nether regions by the shadow of a shadow. I have stared directly into that hole, and already I understand it's not merely a hole in Charlotte's skin, but a hole in the cosmos. I could parade her before any number of physicians and physicists, psychologists and priests, and not a one would have the means to seal that breach. In fact, I suspect they would deny the evidence, even if it meant denying all their science and technology and faith. There are things worse than blank spaces on maps. There are moments when certitude becomes the greatest enemy of sanity. Denial becomes an antidote.

Unlike those other days and those other cards, I haven't chosen the Two of Spades at random. I've chosen it because on Thursday she asks me if Alice counts. And I have begun to assume that everything counts, just as everything is claimed by that infinitely small, infinitely dense point beyond the event horizon.

"Would you tell me, please," said Alice, a little timidly, "why you are painting those roses?"

Five and Seven said nothing, but looked at Two. Two began, in a low voice, "Why, the fact is, you see, Miss, this here ought to have been a red *rose-tree, and we put a white one in by mistake..."*

On that rainy Sunday, that Two of Spades with an incriminating red brush concealed behind its back, I do as she asks. I cannot do otherwise. I bed her. I fuck her. I am tender and violent by turns, as is she. On that stormy evening, that Two of Pentacles, that Two of *Coins* (a dime, in this case), we both futilely turn to sex looking for surcease from dread. We try to go *back* to our lives before she fell, and this is not so very different from all those "lost worlds" I've belabored in my unfinished manuscript: Maple White Land, Caprona, Skull Island, Symzonia, Pellucidar, the Mines of King Solomon. In our bed, we struggle to fashion a refuge from the present, populated by the reassuring, dependable past. And I am talking in circles within circles within circles, spiraling inward or out, it doesn't matter which.

I am arriving, very soon now, at the end of it, at the Saturday night – or more precisely, just before dawn on the Saturday morning – when the story I am writing here ends. And begins. I've taken too long to get to the point, if I assume the validity of a linear narrative. If I assume any one moment can take precedence over any other or assume the generally assumed (but unproven) inequity of relevance.

A large rose-tree stood near the entrance of the garden; the roses growing on it were white, but there were three gardeners at it, busily painting them red.

We are as intimate in those moments as two women can be, when one is forbidden to touch a dime-sized hole in the other's body. At some point, after dark, the rain stops falling, and we lie naked and still, listening to owls and whippoorwills beyond the bedroom walls.

On Wednesday, she comes downstairs and catches me reading the dry pornography of mathematics and relativity. Wednesday is the Seven of Clubs. She tells me there's nothing to be found in those books, nothing that will change what has happened, what may happen.

She says, "I don't know what will be left of me when it's done. I don't even know if I'll be enough to satisfy it, or if it will just keep getting bigger and bigger and bigger. I think it might be insatiable."

On Monday morning, she sips her coffee. We talk about eleven-year-old boys and BB guns.

But here, at last, it is shortly before sunup on a Saturday. Saturday, the Four of Spades. It's been an hour since Charlotte woke screaming, and I've sat and listened while she tried to make sense of the nightmare. The hole in her side is as wide as a softball (and, were this more obviously a comedy, I would list the objects that, by accident, have fallen into it the last few days). Besides the not-quite-ozone smell, there's now a faint but constant whistling sound, which is air being pulled into the hole. In the dream, she tells me, she knew exactly what was on the other side of the hole, but then she forgot most of it as soon as she awoke. In the dream, she says, she wasn't afraid, and that we were sitting out on the porch watching the sea while she explained it all to me. We were drinking Cokes, she said, and it was hot, and the air smelled like dog roses.

"You know I don't like Coke," I say.

"In the dream you did."

She says we were sitting on the porch, and that awful shadow came across the sea again, only this time it didn't frighten her. This time I saw it first and pointed it out to her, and we watched together as it moved rapidly towards the shore. This time, when it swept over the garden, she wasn't standing there to be knocked down.

"But you said you saw what was on the other side."

"That was later on. And I would tell you what I saw, if I could remember. But there was the sound of pipes, or a flute," she says. "I can recall that much of it, and I knew, in the dream, that the hole runs all the way to the middle, to the very center."

"The very center of what?" I ask, and she looks at me like she thinks I'm intentionally being slow-witted.

"The center of everything that ever was and is and ever will be, Em. The *center*. Only, somehow the center is both empty and filled with…" She trails off and stares at the floor.

"Filled with what?"

"I can't *say*. I don't *know*. But whatever it is, it's been there since before there was time. It's been there alone since before the universe was born."

I look up, catching our reflections in the mirror on the dressing table across the room. We're sitting on the edge of the bed, both of us naked, and I look a decade older than I am. Charlotte, though, she looks *so* young, younger than when we met. Never mind that yawning black mouth in her abdomen. In the half light before dawn, she seems to shine, a preface to the coming day, and I'm reminded of what I read about Hawking radiation and the quasar jet streams that escape some singularities. But this isn't the place or time for theories and equations. Here, there are only the two of us, and morning coming on, and what Charlotte can and cannot remember about her dream.

"Eons ago," she says, "it lost its mind. Though I don't think it ever really *had* a mind, not like a human mind. But still, it went insane, from the knowledge of what it is and what it can't ever stop being."

"You said you'd forgotten what was on the other side."

"I have. Almost all of it. This is *nothing.* If I went on a trip to Antarctica and came back and all I could tell you about my trip was that it had been very white, Antarctica, that would be like what I'm telling you now about the dream."

The Four of Spades. The Four of Swords, which cartomancers read as stillness, peace, withdrawal, the act of turning sight back upon itself. They say nothing of the attendant perils of introspection or the damnation that would be visited upon an intelligence that could never look *away.*

"It's blind," she says. "It's blind, and insane, and the music from the pipes never ends. Though, they aren't really pipes."

This is when I ask her to stand up, and she only stares at me a moment or two before doing as I've asked. This is when I kneel in front of her, and I'm dimly aware that I'm kneeling before the inadvertent avatar of a god, or God, or a pantheon, or something so immeasurably ancient and pervasive that it may as well be divine. Divine or infernal; there's really no difference, I think.

"What are you doing?" she wants to know.

"I'm losing you," I reply, "that's what I'm doing. Somewhere, some*when*, I've *already* lost you. And that means I have nothing *left* to lose."

Charlotte takes a quick step back from me, retreating towards the bedroom door, and I'm wondering if she runs, will I chase her? Having made this decision, to what lengths will I go to see it through? Would I force her? Would it be rape?

"I know what you're going to do," she says. "Only you're *not* going to do it, because I won't let you."

"You're being devoured."

"It was a dream, Em. It was only a stupid, crazy dream, and I'm not even sure what I actually remember and what I'm just making up."

"Please," I say, "please let me try." And I watch as whatever resolve she might have had breaks apart. She wants as badly as I do to hope, even though we both know there's no hope left. I watch that hideous black gyre above her hip, below her left breast. She takes two steps back towards me.

"I don't think it will hurt," she tells me. And I can't see any point in asking whether she means, *I don't think it will hurt me,* or *I don't think it will hurt you.* "I don't think there will be any pain."

"I can't see how it possibly matters anymore," I tell her. I don't say anything else. With my right hand, I reach into the hole, and my arm vanishes almost up to my shoulder. There's cold beyond any comprehension of cold. I glance up, and she's watching me. I think she's going to scream, but she doesn't. Her lips part, but she doesn't scream. I feel my arm being tugged so violently I'm sure that it's about to be torn from its socket, the humerus ripped from the glenoid fossa of the scapula, cartilage and ligaments snapped, the subclavian artery severed before I tumble back to the floor and bleed to death. I'm almost certain that's what will happen, and I grit my teeth against that impending amputation.

"I can't feel you," Charlotte whispers. "You're inside me now, but I can't feel you anywhere."

Then.

The hole is closing. We both watch as that clockwise spiral stops spinning, then begins to turn widdershins. My freezing hand clutches at the void, my fingers straining for any purchase. Something's changed; I understand that perfectly well. Out of desperation, I've chanced upon some remedy, entirely by instinct or luck, the solution to an insoluble puzzle. I also understand that I need to pull my arm back out again, before the edges of the hole reach my bicep. I imagine the collapsing rim of curved spacetime slicing cleanly through sinew and bone, and then I imagine myself fused at the shoulder to that point just above Charlotte's hip. Horror vies with cartoon absurdities in an instant that seems so swollen it could accommodate an age.

Charlotte's hands are on my shoulders, gripping me tightly, pushing me away, shoving me as hard as she's able. She's saying something, too, words I can't quite hear over the roar at the edges of that cataract created by the implosion of the quantum foam.

Oh, Kitty, how nice it would be if we could only get through into Looking-glass House! I'm sure it's got oh! such beautiful things in it! Let's pretend there's a way of getting through into it, somehow, Kitty. Let's pretend the glass has got all soft as gauze, so that we can get through…

I'm watching a shadow race across the sea.

Warm sun fills the kitchen.

I draw another card.

Charlotte is only ten years old, and a BB fired by her brother strikes her ankle. Twenty-three years later, she falls at the edge of our flower garden.

Time. Space. Shadows. Gravity and velocity. Past, present, and future. All smeared, every distinction lost, and nothing remaining that can possibly be quantified.

I shut my eyes and feel her hands on my shoulders.

And across the space within her, as my arm bridges countless light years, something brushes against my hand. Something wet, and soft, something indescribably abhorrent. Charlotte pushed me, and I was falling backwards, and now I'm not. It has seized my hand in its own – or wrapped some celestial tendril about my wrist – and for a single heartbeat it holds on before letting go.

...whatever it is, it's been there since before there was time. It's been there alone since before the universe was born.

There's pain when my head hits the bedroom floor. There's pain and stars and twittering birds. I taste blood and realize that I've bitten my lip. I open my eyes, and Charlotte's bending over me. I think there are galaxies trapped within her eyes. I glance down at that spot above her left hip, and the skin is smooth and whole. She's starting to cry, and that makes it harder to see the constellations in her eyes. I move my fingers, surprised that my arm and hand are both still there.

"I'm sorry," I say, even if I'm not sure what I'm apologizing for.

"No," she says, "don't be sorry, Em. Don't let's be sorry for anything. Not now. Not ever again."

The Sea Troll's Daughter

1.

It had been three days since the stranger returned to Invergó, there on the muddy shores of the milky blue-green bay where the glacier met the sea. Bruised and bleeding, she'd walked out of the freezing water. Much of her armor and clothing were torn or altogether missing, but she still had her spear and her dagger, and claimed to have slain the demon troll that had for so long plagued the people of the tiny village.

Yet, she returned to them with no *proof* of this mighty deed, except her word and her wounds. Many were quick to point out that the former could be lies, and that she could have come by the latter in any number of ways that did not actually involve killing the troll, or anything else, for that matter. She might have been foolhardy and wandered up onto the wide splay of the glacier, then taken a bad tumble on the ice. It might have happened just that way. Or she might have only slain a bear, or a wild boar or auroch, or a walrus, having mistook one of these beasts for the demon. Some even suggested it may have been an honest mistake, for bears and walrus, and even boars and aurochs, can be quite fearsome when angered, and if encountered unexpectedly in the night, may have easily been confused with the troll.

Others among the villagers were much less gracious, such as the blacksmith and his one-eyed wife, who went so far as to suggest the stranger's injuries may have been self inflicted. She had bludgeoned and battered herself, they argued, so that she might claim the reward, then flee the village before the creature showed itself again, exposing her deceit. This stranger from the south, they said, thought them all feebleminded. She intended to take their gold and leave them that much poorer and still troubled by the troll.

The elders of Invergó spoke with the stranger, and they relayed these concerns, even as her wounds were being cleaned and dressed. They'd arrived at a solution, by which the matter might be settled. And it seemed fair enough, at least to them.

"Merely deliver unto us the body," they told the stranger. "Show us this irrefutable testament to your handiwork, and we will happily see that you are compensated with all that has been promised to whomsoever slays the troll. All the monies and horses and mammoth hides, for ours was not an idle offer. We would not have the world thinking we are liars, but neither would we have it thinking we can be beguiled by make-believe heroics."

But, she replied, the corpse had been snatched away from her by a treacherous current. She'd searched the murky depths, all to no avail, and had been forced to return to the village empty handed, with nothing but the scars of a lengthy and terrible battle to attest to her victory over the monster.

The elders remained unconvinced, repeated their demand, and left the stranger to puzzle over her dilemma.

So, penniless and deemed either a fool or a charlatan, she sat in the moldering, broken-down hovel that passed for Invergó's one tavern, bandaged and staring forlornly into a smoky sod fire. She stayed drunk on whatever mead or barley wine the curious villagers might offer to loosen her tongue, so that she'd repeat the tale of how she'd purportedly bested the demon. They came and listened and bought her drinks, almost as though they believed her story, though it was plain none among them did.

"The fiend wasn't hard to find," the stranger muttered, thoroughly dispirited, looking from the fire to her half-empty cup to the doubtful faces of her audience. "There's a sort of reef, far down at the very bottom of the bay. The troll made his home there, in a hall fashioned from the bones of great whales and other such leviathans. How did I learn this?" she asked, and when no one ventured a guess, she continued, more dispirited than before.

"Well, after dark, I lay in wait along the shore, and there I spied your monster making off with a ewe and a lamb, one tucked under each arm, and so I trailed him into the water. He was bold, and took no notice of me, and so I swam down, down, down through the tangling blades of kelp and the ruins of sunken trees and the masts of ships that have foundered – "

"Now, exactly how did you hold your breath so long?" one of the men asked, raising a skeptical eyebrow.

"Also, how did you not succumb to the chill?" asked a woman with a fat goose in her lap. "The water is so dreadfully cold, and especially – "

"Might it be that someone here knows this tale *better* than I?" the stranger growled, and when no one admitted they did, she continued. "Now, as *I* was saying, the troll kept close to the bottom of the bay, in a hall made all of bones, and it was here that he retired with the ewe and the lamb he'd slaughtered and dragged into the water. I drew my weapon," and here she quickly slipped her dagger from its sheath for effect. The iron blade glinted dully in the firelight. Startled, the goose began honking and flapping her wings.

"I *still* don't see how you possibly held your breath so long as that," the man said, raising his voice to be heard above the noise of the frightened goose. "Not to mention the darkness. How did you see anything at all down there, it being night and the bay being so silty?"

The stranger shook her head and sighed in disgust, her face half hidden by the tangled black tresses that covered her head and hung down almost to the tavern's dirt floor. She returned the dagger to its sheath and informed the lot of them they'd hear not another word from her if they persisted with all these questions and interruptions. She also raised up her cup, and the woman with the goose nodded to the barmaid, indicating a refill was in order.

"I *found* the troll there inside its lair," the stranger continued, "feasting on the entrails and viscera of the slaughtered sheep. Inside, the walls of its lair *glowed*, and they glowed rather *brightly*, I might add, casting a ghostly phantom light all across the bottom of the bay."

"Awfully bloody convenient, that," the woman with the goose frowned, as the barmaid refilled the stranger's cup.

"*Sometimes*, the Fates, they do us a favorable turn," the stranger said, and took an especially long swallow of barley wine. She belched, then went on. "I watched the troll, I did, for a moment or two, hoping to discern any weak spots it might have in its scaly, knobby hide. That's when it espied me, and straightaway the fiend released its dinner and rushed towards me, baring a mouth filled with fangs longer even than the tusks of a bull walrus."

"Long as that?" asked the woman with the goose, stroking the bird's head.

"Longer, maybe," the stranger told her. "Of a sudden, it was upon me, all fins and claws, and there was hardly time to fix every detail in my memory. As I said, it *rushed* me, and bore me down upon the muddy belly of that accursed hall with all its weight. I thought it might crush me, stave in my skull and chest, and soon mine would count among the jumble of bleached skeletons littering that floor. There were plenty enough human bones, I *do* recall that much. Its talons sundered my armor, and sliced my flesh, and soon my blood was mingling with that of the stolen ewe and lamb. I almost despaired, then and there, and I'll admit that much freely and suffer no shame in the admission."

"Still," the woman with the goose persisted, "awfully damned convenient, all that light."

The stranger sighed and stared sullenly into the fire.

And for the people of Invergó, and also for the stranger who claimed to have done them such a service, this was the way those three days and those three nights passed. The curious came to the tavern to hear the tale, and most of them went away just as skeptical as they'd arrived. The stranger only slept when the drink overcame her, and then she sprawled on a filthy mat at one side of the hearth; at least no one saw fit to begrudge her that small luxury.

But then, late on the morning of the fourth day, the troll's mangled corpse fetched up on the tide, not far distant from the village. A clam digger and his three sons had been working the mudflats where the narrow aquamarine bay meets the open sea, and they were the ones who discovered the creature's remains. Before midday, a group had been dispatched by the village constabulary to retrieve the body and haul it across the marshes, delivering it to Invergó, where all could see and judge for themselves. Seven strong men were required to hoist the carcass onto a litter (usually reserved for transporting strips of blubber and the like), which was drawn across the mire and through the rushes by a team of six oxen. Most of the afternoon was required to cross hardly a single league. The mud was deep and the going slow, and the animals strained in their harnesses, foam flecking their lips and nostrils. One of the cattle perished from exhaustion not long after the putrefying load was finally dragged through the village gates and dumped unceremoniously upon the flagstones in the common square.

Before this day, none among them had been afforded more than the briefest, fleeting glimpse of the sea devil. And now, every man, woman, and child who'd heard the news of the recovered corpse crowded about, able to peer and gawk and prod the dead thing to their hearts' content. The mob seethed with awe and morbid curiosity, apprehension and disbelief. For their pleasure, the enormous head was raised up and an anvil slid underneath its broken jaw, and, also, a fishing gaff was inserted into the dripping mouth, that all could look upon those protruding fangs, which did, indeed, put to shame the tusks of many a bull walrus.

However, it was almost twilight before anyone thought to rouse the stranger, who was still lying unconscious on her mat in the tavern, sleeping off the proceeds of the previous evening's storytelling. She'd been dreaming of her home, which was very far to the south, beyond the raw black mountains and the glaciers, the fjords and the snow. In the dream, she'd been sitting at the edge of a wide green pool, shaded by willow boughs from the heat of the noonday sun, watching the pretty women who came to bathe there. Half a bucket of soapy, lukewarm seawater was required to wake her from this reverie, and the stranger spat and sputtered and cursed the man who'd doused her (he'd drawn the short straw). She was ready to reach for her spear when someone hastily explained that a clam digger had come across the troll's body on the mudflats, and so the people of Invergó were now quite a bit more inclined than before to accept her tale.

"That means I'll get the reward and can be shed of this sorry one-whore piss hole of a town?" she asked. The barmaid explained how the decision was still up to the elders, but that the scales *did* seem to have tipped somewhat in her favor.

And so, with help from the barmaid and the cook, the still half-drunken stranger was led from the shadows and into what passed for bright daylight, there on the gloomy streets of Invergó. Soon, she was pushing her way roughly through the mumbling throng of bodies that had gathered about the slain sea troll, and when she saw the fruits of her battle – when she saw that everyone *else* had seen them – she smiled broadly and spat directly in the monster's face.

"Do you doubt me *still*?" she called out, and managed to climb onto the creature's back, slipping off only once before she gained secure footing on its shoulders. "Will you continue to ridicule me as a liar, when the evidence is right here before your own eyes?"

"Well, it *might* conceivably have died some other way," a peat cutter said without looking at the stranger.

"Perhaps," suggested a cooper, "it swam too near the glacier, and was struck by a chunk of calving ice."

The stranger glared furiously and whirled about to face the elders, who were gathered together near the troll's webbed feet. "Do you truly mean to *cheat* me of the bounty?" she demanded. "Why, you ungrateful, two-faced gaggle of sheep fuckers," she began, then almost slipped off the cadaver again.

"Now, now," one of the elders said, holding up a hand in a gesture meant to calm the stranger. "There will, of course, be an inquest. Certainly. But, be assured, my fine woman, it is only a matter of formality, you understand. I'm sure not one here among us doubts, even for a moment, it was *your* blade returned this vile, contemptible spirit to the nether pits that spawned it."

For a few tense seconds, the stranger stared warily back at the elder, for she'd never liked men, and especially not men who used many words when only a few would suffice. She then looked out over the restless crowd, silently daring anyone present to contradict him. And, when no one did, she once again turned her gaze down to the corpse, laid out below her feet.

"I cut its throat, from ear to ear," the stranger said, though she was not entirely sure the troll *had* ears. "I gouged out the left eye, and I expect you'll come across the tip end of my blade lodged somewhere in the gore. I am Malmury, daughter of my Lord Gwrtheyrn the Undefeated, and before the eyes of the gods do I so claim this as *my* kill, and I know that even *they* would not gainsay this rightful averment."

And with that, the stranger, whom they at last knew was named Malmury, slid clumsily off the monster's back, her boots and breeches now stained with blood and the various excrescences leaking from the troll. She returned immediately to the tavern, as the salty evening air had made her quite thirsty. When she'd gone, the men and women and children of Invergó went back to examining the corpse, though a disquiet and guilty sort of solemnity had settled over them, and what was said was generally spoken in whispers. Overhead, a chorus of hungry gulls and ravens cawed and greedily surveyed the troll's shattered body.

"Malmury," the cooper murmured to the clam digger who'd found the corpse (and so was, himself, enjoying some small degree of celebrity). "A *fine* name, that. And the daughter of a lord, even. Never questioned her story in the least. No, not me."

"Nor I," whispered the peat cutter, leaning in a little closer for a better look at the creature's warty hide. "Can't imagine where she'd have gotten the notion any of us distrusted her."

Torches were lit and set up round about the troll, and much of the crowd lingered far into the night, though a few found their way back to the tavern to listen to Malmury's tale a third or fourth time, for it had grown considerably more interesting, now that it seemed to be true. A local alchemist and astrologer, rarely seen by the other inhabitants of Invergó, arrived and was permitted to take samples of the monsters flesh and saliva. It was he who located the point of the stranger's broken dagger, embedded firmly in the troll's sternum, and the artifact was duly handed over to the constabulary. A young boy in the alchemist's service made highly detailed sketches from numerous angles, and labeled anatomical features as the old man had taught him. By midnight, it became necessary to post a sentry to prevent fisherman and urchins slicing off souvenirs. But only half an hour later, a fishwife was found with a horn cut from the sea troll's cheek hidden in her bustle, and a second sentry was posted.

In the tavern, Malmury, daughter of Lord Gwrtheyrn, managed to regale her audience with increasingly fabulous variations of her battle with the demon. But no one much seemed to mind the embellishments, or that, partway through the tenth retelling of the night, it was revealed that the troll had summoned a gigantic, fire-breathing worm from the ooze that carpeted the floor of the bay, and which Malmury also claimed to have dispatched in short order.

"Sure," she said, wiping at her lips with the hem of the barmaid's skirt. "And now, there's something *else* for your clam diggers to turn up, sooner or later."

By dawn, the stench wafting from the common was becoming unbearable, and a daunting array of dogs and cats had begun to gather round about the edges of the square, attracted by the odor, which promised a fine carrion feast. The cries of the gulls and the ravens had become a cacophony, as though all the heavens had sprouted feathers and sharp, pecking beaks and were descending upon the village. The harbormaster, two physicians, and a cadre of minor civil servants were becoming concerned about the assorted noxious fluids seeping from the rapidly decomposing carcass. This poisonous concoction spilled between the cobbles and had begun to fill gutters and strangle drains as it flowed downhill, towards both the waterfront and the village well. Though there was some talk of removing the source of the taint from the village, it was decided, rather, that a low bulwark or levee of dried peat would be stacked around the corpse.

And, true, this appeared to solve the problem of seepage, for the time being, the peat acting both as a dam and serving to absorb much of the rot. But it did nothing whatsoever to deter the cats and dogs milling about the square, or the raucous cloud of birds that had begun to swoop in, snatching mouthfuls of flesh, before they could be chased away by the two sentries, who shouted at them and brandished brooms and long wooden poles.

Inside the smoky warmth of the tavern – which, by the way, was known as the Cod's Demise, though no sign had ever born that title – Malmury knew nothing of the trouble and worry her trophy was causing in the square, or the talk of having the troll hauled back into the marshes. But neither was she any longer precisely carefree, despite her drunkenness. Even as the sun was rising over the village and peat was being stacked about the corpse, a stooped and toothless old crone of a woman had entered the Cod's Demise. All those who'd been enjoying the tale's new wrinkle of a fire-breathing worm turned towards her. Not a few of them uttered prayers and clutched tightly to the fetishes they carried against the evil eye and all manner of sorcery and malevolent spirits. The crone stood near the doorway, and she leveled a long, crooked finger at Malmury.

"Her," she said ominously, in a voice that was not unlike low tide swishing about rocks and rubbery heaps of bladder rack. "She is the stranger? The one who has murdered the troll who for so long called the bay his home?"

There was a brief silence, as eyes drifted from the crone to Malmury, who was blinking and peering through a haze of alcohol and smoke, trying to get a better view of the frail, hunched woman.

"That I am," Malmury said at last, confused by this latest arrival and the way the people of Invergó appeared to fear her. Malmury tried to stand, then thought better of it and stayed in her seat by the hearth, where there was less chance of tipping over.

"Then she's the one I've come to see," said the crone, who seemed less like a living, breathing woman, and more like something assembled from bundles of twigs and scraps of leather, sloppily held together with twine, rope, and sinew. She leaned on a gnarled cane, though it was difficult to be sure if the cane were wood or bone, or some skillful amalgam of the two. "She's the interloper who has doomed this village and all those who dwell here."

Malmury, confused and growing angry, rubbed at her eyes, starting to think this was surely nothing more than an unpleasant dream, born of too much drink and the boiled mutton and cabbage she'd eaten for dinner.

"How *dare* you stand there and speak to me this way?" she barked back at the crone, trying hard not to slur as she spoke. "Aren't I the one who, only five days ago, *delivered* this place from the depredations of that demon? Am I not the one who risked her *life* in the icy brine of the bay to keep these people safe?"

"*Oh*, she thinks much of herself," the crone cackled, slowly bobbing her head, as though in time to some music nobody else could hear. "Yes, she thinks herself gallant and brave and favored by the gods of *her* land. And who can say? Maybe she is. But she should know, this is *not* her land, and we have our *own* gods. And it is one of *their* children she has slain."

Malmury sat up as straight as she could manage, which wasn't very straight at all, and, with her sloshing cup, jabbed fiercely at the old woman.

Barley wine spilled out and spattered across the toes of Malmury's boots and the hard-packed dirt floor.

"Hag," she snarled, "how dare you address me as though I'm not even present. If you have some quarrel with me, then let's hear it spoken. Else, scuttle away and bother this good house no more."

"This good *house*?" the crone asked, feigning dismay as she peered into the gloom, her stooped countenance framed by the morning light coming in through the opened door. "Beg pardon. I thought possibly I'd wandered into a rather ambitious privy hole, but that the swine had found it first."

Malmury dropped her cup and drew her chipped dagger, which she brandished menacingly at the crone. "You *will* leave now, and without another insult passing across those withered lips, or we shall be presenting *you* to the swine for their breakfast."

At this, the barmaid, a fair woman with blondish hair, bent close to Malmury and whispered in her ear, "Worse yet than the blasted troll, this one. Be cautious, my lady."

Malmury looked away from the crone, and, for a long moment, stared, instead, at the barmaid. Malmury had the distinct sensation that she was missing some crucial bit of wisdom or history that would serve to make sense of the foul old woman's intrusion and the villagers' reactions to her. Without turning from the barmaid, Malmury furrowed her brow and again pointed at the crone with her dagger.

"This slattern?" she asked, almost laughing. "This shriveled harridan not even the most miserable of harpies would claim? I'm to *fear* her?"

"No," the crone said, coming nearer now. The crowd parted to grant her passage, one or two among them stumbling in their haste to avoid the witch. "*You* need not fear *me*, Malmury Trollbane. Not this day. But, you *would* do well to find some ounce of sobriety and fear the consequences of your actions."

"She's insane," Malmury sneered, than spat at the space of damp floor between herself and the crone. "Someone show her a mercy, and find the hag a root cellar to haunt."

The old woman stopped and stared down at the glob of spittle, then raised her head, flared her nostrils, and fixed Malmury in her gaze.

"There was a balance here, Trollbane, an equity, decreed when my great grandmothers were still infants swaddled in their cribs. The debt paid for a grave injustice born of the arrogance of men. A tithe, if you will, and if it cost these people a few souls now and again, or thinned their bleating flocks, it also kept them safe from that greater wrath, which watches us always from the Sea at the Top of the World. But this selfsame balance have *you* undone, and, foolishly, they name you a hero for that deed. For their damnation and their doom."

Malmury cursed, spat again, and tried then to rise from her chair, but was held back by her own inebriation and by the barmaid's firm hand upon her shoulder.

The crone coughed and added a portion of her own jaundiced spittle to the floor of the tavern. "They will *tell* you, Trollbane, though the tales be less than half remembered among this misbegotten legion of cowards and imbeciles. You *ask* them, they will tell you what has not yet been spoken, what was never freely uttered for fear no hero would have accepted their blood money. Do not think *me* the villain in this ballad they are spinning around you."

"You would do well to *leave*, witch," answered Malmury, her voice grown low and throaty, as threatful as breakers before a storm tide or the grumble of a chained hound. "They might fear you, but I do not, and I'm in an ill temper to suffer your threats and intimations."

"Very well," the old woman replied, and she bowed her head to Malmury, though it was clear to all that the crone's gesture carried not one whit of respect. "So be it. But you *ask* them, Trollbane. You ask after the *cause* of the troll's coming, and you ask after his daughter, too."

And with that, she raised her cane, and the fumy air about her appeared to shimmer and fold back upon itself. There was a strong smell, like the scent of brimstone and of smoldering sage, and a sound, as well. Later, Malmury would not be able to decide if it was more akin to a distant thunderclap, or the crackle of burning logs. And, with that, the old woman vanished, and her spit sizzled loudly upon the floor.

"Then she *is* a sorceress," Malmury said, sliding the dagger back into its sheath.

"After a fashion," the barmaid told her, and slowly removed her grip upon Malmury's shoulder. "She's the last priestess of the Old Ways, and still pays tribute to those beings who came before the gods. I've heard her called Grímhildr, and also Gunna, though none among us recall her right name. She is powerful, and treacherous, but know that she has also done great *good* for Invergó and all the people along the coast. When there was plague, she dispelled the sickness – "

"What did she *mean*, to ask after the coming of the troll and its daughter?"

"These are not questions I would answer," the barmaid replied, and turned suddenly away. "You must take them to the elders. They can tell you these things."

Malmury nodded and sipped from her cup, her eyes wandering about the tavern, which she saw was now emptying out into the morning-drenched street. The crone's warnings had left them in no mood for tales of monsters, and had ruined their appetite for the stranger's endless boasting and bluster. No matter, Malmury thought. They'd be back come nightfall, and she was weary, besides, and needed sleep. There was now a cot waiting for her upstairs, in the loft above the kitchen, a proper bed complete with mattress and pillows stuffed with the down of geese, even a white bearskin blanket to guard against the frigid air that blew in through the cracks in the walls. She considered going before the council of elders, after she was rested and only hung over, and pressing them for answers to the crone's questions. But Malmury's head was beginning to ache, and she only entertained the proposition in passing. Already, the appearance of the old woman and what she'd said was beginning to seem less like something that had actually happened, and Malmury wondered, dimly, if she was having trouble discerning where the truth ended and her own generous embroidery of the truth began. Perhaps she'd invented the hag, feeling the tale needed an appropriate epilogue, and then, in her drunkenness, forgotten that she'd invented her.

Soon, the barmaid – whose name was Dóta – returned to lead Malmury up the narrow, creaking stairs to her small room and the cot, and Malmury forgot about sea trolls and witches and even the gold she had coming. For Dóta was a comely girl, and free with her favors, and the stranger's sex mattered little to her.

2.

The daughter of the sea troll lived among the jagged, windswept highlands that loomed above the milky blue-green bay and the village of Invergó. Here had she dwelt for almost three generations, as men reckoned the passing of time, and here did she imagine she would live until the long span of her days was at last exhausted.

Her cave lay deep within the earth, where once had been only solid basalt. But over incalculable eons, the glacier that swept down from the mountains, inching between high volcanic cliffs as it carved a wide path to the sea, had worked its way beneath the bare and stony flesh of the land. A ceaseless trickle of meltwater had carried the bedrock away, grain by igneous grain, down to the bay, as the perpetual cycle of freeze and thaw had split and shattered the stone. In time (and then, as now, the world had nothing but time), the smallest of breaches had become cracks, cracks became fissures, and intersecting labyrinths of fissures collapsed to form a cavern. And so, in this way, had the struggle between mountain and ice prepared for her a home, and she dwelt there, alone, almost beyond the memory of the village and its inhabitants, which she despised and feared and avoided when at all possible.

However, she had not always lived in the cave, nor unattended. Her mother, a child of man, had died while birthing the sea troll's daughter, and, afterwards, she'd been taken in by the widowed conjurer who would, so many years later, seek out and confront a stranger named Malmury who'd come up from the southern kingdoms. When the people of Invergó had looked upon the infant, what they'd seen was enough to guess at its parentage. And they would have put the mother to death, then and there, for her congress with the fiend, had she not been dead already. And surely, likewise, would they have murdered the baby, had the old woman not seen fit to intervene. The villagers had always feared the crone, but also they'd had cause to seek her out in times of hardship and calamity. So it gave them pause, once she'd made it known that the infant was in her care, and this knowledge stayed their hand, for a while.

In the tumbledown remains of a stone cottage, at the edge of the mudflats, the crone had raised the infant until the child was old enough to care for herself. And until even the old woman's infamy, and the prospect of losing her favors, was no longer enough to protect the sea troll's daughter from the villagers. Though more human than not, she had the creature's blood in her veins. In the eyes of some, this made her a greater abomination than her father.

Finally, rumors had spread that the girl was a danger to them all, and, after an especially harsh winter, many become convinced that she could make herself into an ocean mist and pass easily through windowpanes. In this way, it was claimed, had she begun feeding on the blood of men and women while they slept. Soon, a much-prized milking cow had been found with her udder mutilated, and the farmer had been forced to put the beast out of her misery. The very next day, the elders of Invergó had sent a warning to the crone, that their tolerance of the half breed was at an end, and she was to be remanded to the constable forthwith.

But the old woman had planned against this day. She'd discovered the cave high above the bay, and she'd taught the sea troll's daughter to find auk eggs and mushrooms and to hunt the goats and such other wild things as lived among the peaks and ravines bordering the glacier. The girl was bright, and had learned to make clothing and boots from the hides of her kills, and also had been taught herb lore, and much else that would be needed to survive on her own in that forbidding, barren place.

Late one night in the summer of her fourteenth year, she'd fled Invergó, and made her way to the cave. Only one man had ever been foolish enough to go looking for her, and his body was found pinned to an iceberg floating in the bay, his own sword driven through his chest to the hilt. After that, they left her alone, and soon the daughter of the sea troll was little more than legend, and a tale to frighten children. She began to believe, and to hope, that she would never again have cause to journey down the slopes to the village.

But then, as the stranger Malmury, senseless with drink, slept in the arms of a barmaid, the crone came to the sea troll's daughter in her dreams, as the old woman had done many times before.

"Your father has been slain," she said, not bothering to temper the words. "His corpse lies desecrated and rotting in the village square, where all can come and gloat and admire the mischief of the one who killed him."

The sea troll's daughter, whom the crone had named Sæhildr, for the ocean, had been dreaming of stalking elk and a shaggy herd of mammoth across a meadow. But the crone's voice had startled her prey, and the dream animals had all fled across the tundra.

The sea troll's daughter rolled over onto her back, stared up at the grizzled face of the old woman, and asked, "Should this bring me sorrow? Should I have tears, to receive such tidings? If so, I must admit it doesn't, and I don't. Never have I seen the face of my father, not with my waking eyes, and never has he spoken unto me, nor sought me out. I was nothing more to him than a curious consequence of his indiscretions."

"You and he lived always in different worlds," the old woman replied, but the one she called Sæhildr had turned back over onto her belly and was staring forlornly at the place where the elk and mammoth had been grazing, only a few moments before.

"It is none of my concern," the sea troll's daughter sighed, thinking she should wake soon, that then the old woman could no longer plague her thoughts. Besides, she was hungry, and she'd killed a bear only the day before.

"Sæhildr," the crone said, "I've not come expecting you to grieve, for too well do I know your mettle. I've come with a warning, as the one who slew your father may yet come seeking you."

The sea troll's daughter smiled, baring her teeth that effortlessly cracked bone that she might reach the rich marrow inside. With the hooked claws of a thumb and forefinger, she plucked the yellow blossom from an arctic poppy, and held it to her wide nostrils.

"Old mother, knowing my mettle, you should know that I am not afraid of men," she whispered, then she let the flower fall back to the ground.

"The one who slew your father was not a man, but a woman, the likes of which I've never seen," the crone replied. "She is a warrior, of noble birth, from the lands south of the mountains. She came to collect the bounty placed upon the troll's head. Sæhildr, this one is strong, and I fear for you."

In the dream, low clouds the color of steel raced by overhead, fat with snow, and the sea troll's daughter lay among the flowers of the meadow and thought about the father she'd never met. Her short tail twitched from side to side, like the tail of a lazy, contented cat, and she decapitated another poppy.

"You believe this warrior will hunt *me* now?" she asked the crone.

"What I think, Sæhildr, is that the men of Invergó have no intention of honoring their agreement to pay this woman her reward. Rather, I believe they will entice her with even greater riches, if only she will stalk and destroy the bastard daughter of their dispatched foe. The woman is greedy, and prideful, and I hold that she will hunt you, yes."

"Then let her come to me, old mother," the sea troll's daughter said. "There is little enough sport to be had in these hills. Let her come into the mountains and face me."

The old woman sighed and began to break apart on the wind, like sea foam before a wave. "She's not a fool," the crone said. "A braggart, yes, and a liar, but by her own strength and wits did she undo your father. I'd not see the same fate befall you, Sæhildr. She will lay a trap."

"Oh, I know something of traps," the troll's daughter replied, and then the dream ended. She opened her black eyes and lay awake in her freezing den, deep within the mountains. Not far from the nest of pelts that was her bed, a lantern she'd fashioned from walrus bone and blubber burned unsteadily, casting tall, writhing shadows across the basalt walls. The sea troll's daughter lay very still, watching the flame, and praying to all the beings who'd come before the gods of men that the battle with her father's killer would not be over too quickly.

3.

As it happened, however, the elders of Invergó were far too preoccupied with other matters to busy themselves trying to conceive of schemes by which they might cheat Malmury of her bounty. With each passing hour, the clam-digger's grisly trophy became increasingly putrid, and the decision not to remove it from the village's common square had set in motion a chain of events that would prove far more disastrous to the village than the *living* troll ever could have been. Moreover, Malmury was entirely too distracted by her own intoxication and with the pleasures visited upon her by the barmaid, Dóta, to even recollect she had the reward coming. So, while there can be hardly any doubt that the old crone who lived at the edge of the mudflats was, in fact, both wise and clever, she had little cause to fear for Sæhildr's immediate well being.

The troll's corpse, hauled so triumphantly from the marsh, had begun to swell in the mid-day sun, distending magnificently as the gases of decomposition built up inside its innards. Meanwhile, the flock of gulls and ravens had been joined by countless numbers of fish crows and kittiwakes, a constantly shifting, swooping, shrieking cloud that, at last, succeeded in chasing off the two sentries who'd been charged with the task of protecting the carcass from scavengers. And, no longer dissuaded by the men and their jabbing sticks, the cats and dogs that had skulked all night about the edges of the common grew bold and joined in the banquet (though the cats proved more interested in seizing unwary birds than in the sour flesh of the troll). A terrific swarm of biting flies arrived only a short time later, and there were ants, as well, and voracious beetles the size of a grown man's thumb. Crabs and less savory things made their way up from the beach. An order was posted that the citizens of Invergó should retreat to their homes and bolt all doors and windows until such time as the pandemonium could be resolved.

There was, briefly, talk of towing the body back to the salt marshes from whence it had come. But this proposal was soon dismissed as impractical and hazardous. Even if a determined crew of men dragging a litter or wagon, and armed with the requisite hooks and cables, the block and tackle, could fight their way through the seething, foraging mass of birds, cats, dogs, insects, and crustaceans, it seemed very unlikely that the corpse retained enough integrity that it could now be moved in a single piece. And just the thought of intentionally breaking it apart, tearing it open and thereby releasing whatever foul brew festered within, was enough to inspire the elders to seek some alternate route of ridding the village of the corruption and all its attendant chaos. To make matters worse, the peat levee that had been hastily stacked around the carcass suddenly failed partway through the day, disgorging all the oily fluid that had built up behind it. There was now talk of pestilence, and a second order was posted, advising the villagers that all water from the pumps was no longer potable, and that the bay, too, appeared to have been contaminated. The fish market was closed, and incoming ships forbidden to offload any of the day's catch.

And then, when the elders thought matters were surely at their worst, the alchemist's young apprentice arrived bearing a sheaf of equations and ascertainments based upon the samples taken from the carcass. In their chambers, the old men flipped through these pages for some considerable time, no one wanting to be the first to admit he didn't actually understand what he was reading. Finally, the apprentice cleared his throat, which caused them to look up at him.

"It's simple, really," the boy said. "You see, the various humors of the troll's peculiar composition have been demonstrated to undergo a predictable variance during the process of putrefaction."

The elders stared back at him, seeming no less confused by his words than by the spidery handwriting on the pages spread out before them.

"To put it more plainly," the boy said, "the creature's blood is becoming volatile. Flammable. Given significant enough concentrations, which must certainly exist by now, even explosive."

Almost in unison, the faces of the elders of Invergó went pale. One of them immediately stood and ordered the boy to fetch his master forthwith, but was duly informed that the alchemist had already fled the village. He'd packed a mule and left by the winding, narrow path that led west into the wilderness. He hoped, the apprentice told them, to observe for posterity the grandeur of the inevitable conflagration, but from a safe distance.

At once, a proclamation went out that all flames were to be extinguished, all hearths and forges and ovens, every candle and lantern, in

Invergó. Not so much as a tinderbox or pipe must be left smoldering anywhere, so dire was the threat to life and property. However, most of the men dispatched to see that this proclamation was enforced, instead fled into the marshes, or towards the foothills, or across the milky blue-green bay to the far shore, which was reckoned to be sufficiently remote that sanctuary could be found there. The calls that rang through the streets of the village were not so much "Douse the fires," or "Mind your stray embers," as "Flee for your lives, the troll's going to explode."

In their cot, in the small but cozy space above the Cod's Demise, Malmury and Dóta had been dozing. But the commotion from outside, both the wild ruckus from the feeding scavengers and the panic that was now sweeping through the village, woke them. Malmury cursed and groped about for the jug of fine apple brandy on the floor, which Dóta had pilfered from the larder. Dóta lay listening to the uproar, and, being sober, began to sense that something, somewhere, somehow had gone terribly wrong, and that they might now be in very grave danger.

Dóta handed the brandy to Malmury, who took a long pull from the jug and squinted at the barmaid.

"They have no intention of paying you," Dóta said flatly, buttoning her blouse. "We've known it all along. All of us. Everyone who lives in Invergó."

Malmury blinked and rubbed at her eyes, not quite able to make sense of what she was hearing. She had another swallow from the jug, hoping the strong liquor might clear her ears.

"It was a dreadful thing we did," Dóta admitted. "I know that now. You're brave, and risked much, and – "

"I'll *beat* it out of them," Malmury muttered.

"That might have worked," Dóta said softly, nodding her head. "Only, they don't have it. The elders, I mean. In all Invergó's coffers, there's not even a quarter what they offered."

Beyond the walls of the tavern, there was a terrific crash, then, and, soon thereafter, the sound of women screaming.

"Malmury, listen to me. You stay here, and have the last of the brandy. I'll be back very soon."

"I'll beat it out of them," Malmury declared again, though this time with slightly less conviction.

"Yes," Dóta told her. "I'm sure you will do just that. Only now, wait here. I'll return as quickly as I can."

"Bastards," Malmury sneered. "Bastards and ingrates."

"You finish the brandy," Dóta said, pointing at the jug clutched in Malmury's hands. "It's excellent brandy, and very expensive. Maybe not the same as gold, but..." and then the barmaid trailed off, seeing that Malmury had passed out again. Dóta dressed and hurried downstairs, leaving the stranger, who no longer seemed quite so strange, alone and naked, sprawled and snoring loudly on the cot.

In the street outside the Cod's Demise, the barmaid was greeted by a scene of utter chaos. The reek from the rotting troll, only palpable in the tavern, was now overwhelming, and she covered her mouth and tried not to gag. Men, women, and children rushed to and fro, many burdened with bundles of valuables or food, some on horseback, others trying to drive herds of pigs or sheep through the crowd. And, yet, rising above it all, was the deafening clamor of that horde of sea birds and dogs and cats squabbling amongst themselves for a share of the troll. Off towards the docks, someone was clanging the huge bronze bell reserved for naught but the direst of catastrophes. Dóta shrank back against the tavern wall, recalling the crone's warnings and admonitions, expecting to see, any moment now, the titanic form of one of those beings who came before the gods, towering over the rooftops, striding towards her through the village.

Just then, a tinker, who frequently spent his evenings and his earnings in the tavern, stopped and seized the barmaid by both shoulders, gazing directly into her eyes.

"You must *run*!" he implored. "Now, this very minute, you must get away from this place!"

"But why?" Dóta responded, trying to show as little of her terror as possible, trying to behave the way she imagined a woman like Malmury might behave. "What has happened?"

"It *burns*," the tinker said, and before she could ask him *what* burned, he released her and vanished into the mob. But, as if in answer to that unasked question, there came a muffled crack, and then a boom that shook the very street beneath her boots. A roiling mass of charcoal-colored smoke shot through with glowing red-orange cinders billowed up from the direction of the livery, and Dóta turned and dashed back into the Cod's Demise.

Another explosion followed, and another, and by the time she reached the cot upstairs, dust was sifting down from the rafters of the tavern, and the roofing timbers had begun to creak alarmingly. Malmury was still asleep, oblivious to whatever cataclysm was befalling Invergó. The barmaid grabbed the bearskin blanket and wrapped it about Malmury's shoulders, then slapped her several times, hard, until the woman's eyelids fluttered partway open.

"*Stop that,*" she glowered, seeming now more like an indignant girl child than the warrior who'd swum to the bottom of the bay and slain their sea troll.

"We have to *go,*" Dóta said, almost shouting to be understood above the racket. "It's not *safe* here anymore, Malmury. We have to get out of Invergó."

"But I've done *killed* the poor, sorry wretch," Malmury mumbled, shivering and pulling the bearskin tighter about her. "Have you lot gone and found another?"

"Truthfully," Dóta replied, "I do not *know* what fresh devilry this is, only that we can't stay here. There is fire, and a roar like naval cannonade."

"I was sleeping," Malmury said petulantly. I was dreaming of – "

The barmaid slapped her again, harder, and this time Malmury seized her wrist and glared blearily back at Dóta. "I *told* you not to do that."

"Aye, and I told *you* to get up off your fat ass and get moving." There was another explosion then, nearer than any of the others, and both women felt the floorboards shift and tilt below them. Malmury nodded, some dim comprehension wriggling its way through the brandy and wine.

"My horse is in the stable," she said. "I cannot leave without my horse. She was given me by my father."

Dóta shook her head, straining to help Malmury to her feet. "I'm sorry," she said. "It's too late. The stables are all ablaze." Then neither of them said anything more, and the barmaid led the stranger down the swaying stairs and through the tavern and out into the burning village.

4.

From a rocky crag high above Invergó, the sea troll's daughter watched as the town burned. Even at this distance and altitude, the earth shuddered with the force of each successive detonation. Loose stones were shaken free of the talus and rolled away down the steep slope. The sky was sooty with smoke, and beneath the pall, everything glowed from the hellish light of the flames.

And, too, she watched the progress of those who'd managed to escape the fire. Most fled westward, across the mudflats, but some had filled the hulls of doggers and dories and ventured out into the bay. She'd seen one of the little boats lurch to starboard and capsize, and was surprised at how many of those it spilled into the icy cove reached the other shore. But of all these refugees, only two had headed south, into the hills, choosing the treacherous pass that led up towards the glacier and the basalt mountains that flanked it. The daughter of the sea troll watched their progress with an especial fascination. One of them appeared to be unconscious and was slung across the back of a mule, and the other, a woman with hair the color of the sun, held tight to the mule's reins and urged it forward. With every new explosion, the animal bucked and brayed and struggled against her; once or twice, they almost went over the edge, all three of them. By the time they gained the wider ledge where Sæhildr crouched, the sun was setting and nothing much remained intact of Invergó, nothing that hadn't been touched by the devouring fire.

The sun-haired woman lashed the reigns securely to a boulder, then sat down in the rubble. She was trembling, and it was clear she'd not had time to dress with an eye towards the cold breath of the mountains. There was a heavy belt cinched about her waist, and from it hung a sheathed dagger. The sea troll's daughter noted the blade, then turned her attention to the mule and its burden. She could see now that the person slung over the animal's back was also a woman, unconscious and partially covered with a moth-eaten bearskin. Her long black hair hung down almost to the muddy ground.

Invisible from her hiding place in the scree, Sæhildr asked, "Is the bitch dead, your companion?"

Without raising her head, the sun-haired woman replied. "Now, why would I have bothered to drag a dead woman all the way up here?"

"Perhaps she is dear to you," the daughter of the sea troll replied. "It may be you did not wish to see her corpse go to ash with the others."

"She's *not* a corpse," the woman said. "Not yet, anyway." And as if to corroborate the claim, the body draped across the mule farted loudly and then muttered a few unintelligible words.

"Your sister?" the daughter of the sea troll asked, and when the sun-haired woman told her no, Sæhildr said, "She seems far too young to be your mother."

"She's not my mother. She's…a friend. More than that, she's a hero."

The sea troll's daughter licked at her lips, then glanced back to the inferno by the bay. "A hero," she said, almost too softly to be heard.

"Well, that's the way it started," the sun-haired woman said, her teeth chattering so badly she was having trouble speaking. "She came here from a kingdom beyond the mountains, and, single handedly, she slew the fiend that haunted the bay. But – "

" – then the fire came," Sæhildr said, and, with that, she stood, revealing herself to the woman. "My *father's* fire, the wrath of the Old Ones, unleashed by the blade there on your hip."

The woman stared at the sea troll's daughter, her eyes filling with wonder and fear and confusion, with panic. Her mouth opened, as though she meant to say something or to scream, but she uttered not a sound. Her hand drifted towards the dagger's hilt.

"*That*, my lady, would be a very poor idea," Sæhildr said calmly. Taller by a head than even the tallest of tall men, she stood looking down at the shivering woman, and her skin glinted oddly in the half light. "Why do you think I mean you harm?"

"You," the woman stammered. "You're the troll's whelp. I have heard the tales. The old witch is your mother."

Sæhildr made an ugly, derisive noise that was partly a laugh. "Is *that* how they tell it these days, that Gunna is my mother?"

The sun-haired woman only nodded once and stared at the rocks.

"*My* mother is dead," the troll's daughter said, moving nearer, causing the mule to bray and tug at its reigns. "And now, it seems, my father has joined her."

"I cannot let you harm her," the woman said, risking a quick sidewise glance at Sæhildr. The daughter of the sea troll laughed again, and dipped her head, almost seeming to bow. The distant firelight reflected off the small curved horns on either side of her head, hardly more than nubs and mostly hidden by her thick hair, and shone off the scales dappling her cheekbones and brow, as well.

"What you *mean* to say, is that you would have to *try* to prevent me from harming her."

"Yes," the sun-haired woman replied, and now she glanced nervously towards the mule and her unconscious companion.

"If, of course, I *intended* her harm."

"Are you saying that you don't?" the woman asked. "That you do not desire vengeance for your father's death?"

Sæhildr licked her lips again, then stepped past the seated woman to stand above the mule. The animal rolled its eyes, neighed horribly, and kicked at the air, almost dislodging its load. But then the sea troll's daughter gently laid a hand on its rump, and immediately the beast grew calm and silent once more. Sæhildr leaned forward and grasped the unconscious woman's chin, lifting it, wishing to know the face of the one who'd defeated the brute who'd raped her mother and made of his daughter so shunned and misshapen a thing.

"This one is drunk," Sæhildr said, sniffing the air.

"Very much so," the sun-haired woman replied.

"A *drunkard* slew the troll?"

"She was sober that day. I think."

Sæhildr snorted and said, "Know that there was no bond but blood between my father and I. Hence, what need have I to seek vengeance upon his executioner? Though, I will confess, I'd hoped she might bring me some measure of sport. But even that seems unlikely in her current state." She released the sleeping woman's jaw, letting it bump roughly against the mule's ribs, and stood upright again. "No, I think you need not fear for your lover's life. Not this day. Besides, hasn't the utter destruction of your village counted as a more appropriate reprisal?"

The sun-haired woman blinked, and said, "Why do you say that, that she's my lover?"

"Liquor is not the only stink on her," answered the sea troll's daughter. "Now, *deny* the truth of this, my lady, and I may yet grow angry."

The woman from doomed Invergó didn't reply, but only sighed and continued staring into the gravel at her feet.

"This one is practically naked," Sæhildr said. "And you're not much better. You'll freeze, the both of you, before morning."

"There was no time to find proper clothes," the woman protested, and the wind shifted then, bringing with it the cloying reek of the burning village.

"Not very much farther along this path, you'll come to a small cave," the sea troll's daughter said. "I will find you there, tonight, and bring what furs and provisions I can spare. Enough, perhaps, that you may yet have some slim chance of making your way through the mountains."

"I don't understand," Dóta said, exhausted and near tears, and when the troll's daughter made no response, the barmaid discovered that she and the mule and Malmury were alone on the mountain ledge. She'd not heard the demon take its leave, so maybe the stories were true, and it could become a fog and float away whenever it so pleased. Dóta sat a moment longer, watching the raging fire spread out far below them. And then she got to her feet, took up the mule's reins, and began searching for the shelter that the troll's daughter had promised her she would discover. She did not spare a thought for the people of Invergó, not for her lost family, and not even for the kindly old man who'd owned the Cod's Demise and had taken her in off the streets when she was hardly more than a babe. They were the past, and the past would keep neither her nor Malmury alive.

Twice, she lost her way among the boulders, and by the time Dóta stumbled upon the cave, a heavy snow had begun to fall, large wet flakes spiraling down from the darkness. But it was warm inside, out of the howling wind. And, what's more, she found bundles of wolf and bear pelts, seal skins and mammoth hide, some sewn together into sturdy garments. And there was salted meat, a few potatoes, and a freshly killed rabbit spitted and roasting above a small cooking fire. She would never again set eyes on the sea troll's daughter, but in the long days ahead, as Dóta and the stranger named Malmury made their way through blizzards and across fields of ice, she would often sense someone nearby, watching over them. Or only watching.

Random Thoughts Before a Fatal Crash

15/7/98

No one here seems to mind very much that my French is atrocious. I begin to suspect it isn't true, what everyone says about how Parisians sneer at and disdain and show contempt for Americans who mangle their language. Or I've been lucky. Or. Or, I don't know. From my window, there's an excellent view of Le Cimetière du Montparnasse, which I read in a guidebook was once Le Cimetière du Sud. All those white-stone monumented narrow houses, and the low conical tower, as if the dead need a lighthouse or castle keep or what have you. I read, too, stone from nearby quarries was heaped here into a spoil pile, and in the Seventeenth Century the area, before it was a boneyard, become known as Mount Parnasse: *Tho' their music here be mortal need the singer greatly care? Other songs for other worlds! the fire within him would not falter...* The stone, that rubble pile of yore before the coming of *Le Cimetière du Montparnasse*, I believe to be hewn from out limestone beds sixty, seventy-five feet down below our feet. Stone that was seafloor ooze in Tertiary ages (?). The underground quarries are still there, below the feet in France. I've spent days walking between the rows. Days and days and days. We cannot walk there after dark, not in the summer, which is a shame, and perhaps some odd desecration. In my little black book, I write the names of the moldering interred (but there are yet many whom I have not visited). These I have: Baudelaire, Carrière, de Maupassant, Robert Desnos, Beckett, cherished St. Sartre and Simone de Beauvoir, Man Ray. At Sartre Satyr Saint's grave I leave tokens: coins, stones, a battered first-edition of *L'âge de raison* I scrounged from 37 rue de la Bûcherie, Shakespeare and Company. A bouquet of flowers for Mlle. de Beauvoir I stole from Queen Kiki de Montparnasse, and I think she'll never miss the bundle of wilted roses and bracken.

The old woman who lives across the hall asked if I find inspiration here. She knows enough English that we can converse in her broken English and not my broken French. She has false teeth and once was a singer. She takes pity on me, so I show her canvases I can't finish. She brings bread and cheese sometimes, and I share wine. *Je partage mon vin*. I believe that's not too far off the mark. We talk books and art and politics. We talk. I talk and she is kind enough to listen. Her hair is akin to wild grey moss, and she sometimes forgets to wear her teeth. Her eyes are the eyes of a young girl, and the color of agate. She says her name is Dorothée Lefbèvre, though I suspect she's lying. Cannot say why. It hardly matters what she calls herself. Says she was born in 1917, and talks about the wars. I asked her, twice, to sit for me; each time she blushed and declined. We talk of aqueducts and crypts below churches. She doesn't shy at morbidity. Perhaps we'll make great friends, Dorothée Lefbèvre and I.

In the mirror where I shave, my skin has looked better. It all catches up with me, though I thought that would be later rather than sooner. All men must think that, yes? Delusions of immortality. Something of the sort. Wrinkles and grey hair. Teeth not what once they were, nor as numerous; eyes dim and bloodshot the way you know they'll never be clear again.

Today I sit and stare at the canvas, the bird-headed demon gazing down upon all the world, gazing down in derision and indifference, doing the both simultaneously. I mix paint, and it dries before I commit a single brushstroke. I hate this one. I loathe it, but it will mean a check. Hence, I will trudge on to the muddy end. I sometimes fall asleep in my chair before the easel, which I never used to do. Or cannot recall having done. I should be out walking the streets, not sleeping in a chair before a ruined canvas. I've seen precious little of the precious city.

I hear rumors of *cataphiles*, men and women who explore the ancient abscesses, sewers, *les ossuaires*, the galleries of forgotten Twelfth-Century quarries (*carrières*), subterranean lakes, and on and on. I should not be sitting here with this acrylic dead-end. There is nothing here to learn. I swear again I would cease these paintings if I had that option. I swear again they eat at my mind and soul and body, pick me apart like ravens, and I would have nothing more of them. Idiots talk of muses and inspiration, naïve words from lips of starry-eyed fools who see romance where there is little more than monotony and humiliation. When I am interviewed, I ought to say these things, but I never do; my agent holds his thumb across my throat, pressing down on my tongue. Buyers like to believe the artist labors in the joy of creation, not in despair. Not always wanting out, and ever willing to seek new manners of egress. They – the buyers – should sit dozing in my hard chair, prostrate in sleep before this hideous abortion of a painting, the ibis-crowned monster plucked from…from…I do not know where, but here it is all the same, isn't it. I ought to set it aside, at least for a few days, if only to spite the market and my agent and the galleries back in the States or London.

I should be in the museums – Musée national d'art moderne, Muséum national d'Histoire naturelle, Musée d'Art Moderne de la Ville de Paris, id est. I should leave the city and take the train to Gévaudan (now, of course, Lozère. Haute-Loire), as I planned. It may be that Dorothée would accompany me, if I paid her fare. I did ask if she knows the story of *La Bête du Gévaudan*; she did, she does. She was surprisingly well versed in the tales. Or I was surprised at her knowledge, and the one thing might not equate to the other. She has traveled the Margeride. In her youth. In some facet of her youth, all those many decades past. I will ask her perhaps. Or I will stare down this painting. In truth, *je m'en fou*, as she would say. I should seek out the deep-delving troglodytic cataphiles and ask them to lead me down to all the private Hades. I should find the tomb of Henri Fantin-Latour and leave dead flowers (*fleurs mortes*?). I should seek out a street where pretty boys sell themselves and lose myself in flesh, theirs and mine.

17/7/98

Found him down on la Rue Saint-Denis (a/k/a rue des Saints Innocents et grant chaussée de Monsieur, Sellerie de Paris, rue de Franciade, et al) that First Century Roman slash of paving now so clogged with whores, male *and* female, though the latter holds so little interest for me these days. He, who spoke not a word of English – I do not count the stray *yes* and *no* and various profanities and brand names, no, those I do not count at all – and I think he was surprised that I wanted more than a quick blow in an alleyway. I brought him back to the flat, and fucked him good and proper, then paid him extra to pose for me.

There's a heap of him still on the floor, a heap of charcoal approximation of that pinched face and lean ass and eyes that were proud despite their sorry lot. But I found him, and little more matters. He had a name, of course. Still does, unless a name thief is lose in the Quartier Saint-Germain l'Auxerrois, some beast that slinks the blacktop and storefronts in search of the praenomen and cognomen of boy whores. He might have been sixteen, seventeen, but no older. Had he been, I'd not have paid so much. I'd not have paid at all, but continued in my search. He called himself Gautier. I bent him over my bed and splayed open his ass for my starving cock. He made no sound at all. None. No complaint from my *tapin* (isn't that the current slang?), not like those whining boys in Munich and, also, yes, that one especial *trækkerdreng* in Copenhagen. In whose mouth I stuffed an overripe pear rather than bear the noises he made.

Gautier left before dawn. I said I would try to find him again sometime, one night or the next. He shrugged and left me alone.

Left me here with my stinking sins, taking sins away and leaving me with my greater damnations, these hideous paints and brushes, all fire and brimstone and cold wastes and yes, yes, *das Fegefeuer*. I haven't slept. I've had too many cups of coffee to drive back the sleep, which is the coiled hive of dreams and almost nothing more. Not rest, and that's for fucking sure. No rest now in more years than I have fingers. Coffee, though, and nicotine, amphetamines, tiny ampoules of ammonia for desperate moments. How can I not be blessed with simple insomnia?

18/7/98

The stars above cathedrals are shameless things, no less wicked than the leering, tongue-lolling gargoyles crouched by the vicious architects of Notre Dame de Paris and the Cathedral Saint-Etienne de Meaux. Only, those distant bodies in roiling rotation are so infinitely more truthful than the horrors of the Galerie des Chimères, dream gallery, nightmare palisade of godly lies and sacred intimidations. Stars have no need of intimidation, which makes them mightier than all the godheads nightmared by mere humanity. You, Monsignor Shitwit, you paint me a demon so voracious as a red giant or Sol, or a Tetragrammaton to match the electron-degenerate matter of a white dwarf, and then, *then* we'll talk of hells and heavens. I lay on my back in a forest flanking the Seine, though that must have been so very long ago: mammoth- and lion-haunted forests (though neither of these did I glimpse, for I am afforded no such mild phantasmagoria). I lay in the dew-damp grass, and the stars whirled above me, weaving celestial labyrinths with no beginnings and no endings, mazes no one enters or escapes

– *des labyrinthes sans sorties, des labyrinthes sans entrées*, so designated in my dictionary-shredded mockery. I'd have looked away, but that thought never once occurred to my sleeping mind.

Van Gogh never saw a sky like that, not in the deepest folds of his epileptic, absinthe-fueled anti-reveries. Nor Kupka, nor, nor, nor Munch with all his Madonna and spermatozoa. The Dome of Heaven whirled above me, condemning kaleidoscope that knows my every transgression because it looks on every night and, in daylight, passes notes with the perfidious sun. Back here we come to stars. Plenty of gods et goddesses are stars: Helios, Hyperion, Ra, the seven Vedic Adityas. The dome wheeled above me without wings, though I feared those absent wings that would beat with no earthly thunder in the vacuum. Beating, they would be soundless as the dead.

The sky is black-blue indigo white adamantine alabaster blackest of all blacks. Blazing bright and yet absolutely, irredeemably tenebrous.

There is terrible *purpose* in the wheel.

This I saw, with sleeping eyes wide, and no man nor woman may gainsay these observations, not without showing themselves liars, and ignorant liars at that. I lay there forever, until she said my name, and I turned to the pale naked girl on the grass not too far away. Her knees pulled up beneath her chin, hiding sex and breasts from view, modesty or habit or retreat from the chilly night air. I didn't need to ask her name; I've known all her names almost all my life. "Not wise to stare so long," she said, and smiled, showing all those teeth of hers packed in like sardine pegs on enamel and ripping incisor/canine/premolar ferocity. "Were I you, I'd look away."

I told her I already had looked away, to see her, instead.

"You stare too long at everything no sane man ought ever glimpse for a moment."

"You never have thought me a sane man."

"I never have," she agreed.

So there she sat, in the lotus folds of all her names, but let's be content with the one – *Le Petit Chaperon Rouge.* No, never mind. One will never ever do her. Addend Little Red Cap, then. And Riding Hood. *Und Rotkäppchen.* Goldenhood. Saint Margaret of Antioch. Spin them all about her as the sky spins, for now unsighted, above the Seine and the land before the coming of Paris.

"You'll not go to Gévaudan," she said with great finality.

"Why?"

"There's nothing left there for you to see, Albert. They slew her long ago. Cartel cut down *La Bête* twice a hundred and fifteen years ago. Her bones went to dust in Versailles.

I know she's confusing, conflating, two versions of the tale, that in which the beast is slain by François Antoine and that other, in which she was slain by Jean Chastel. It was Antoine sent the corpse to the Court of Louis XV, not Chastel. I don't correct her. Never have I corrected the girl, nude but for her woolen crimson and her wet black nose. She talks on while the sky wheels above the countryside: Jean Chastel's great red mastiff, maybe the beast's sire, maybe Chastel dressing the misbegotten hybrid in an armored boar skin and setting it upon peasants to slake his own perverse inclinations.

I listen, as always I listen when she speaks. Mostly, she wants to be certain I don't make the trip to Gévaudan, not even if Dorothée accompanies me.

I go back to watching that maelstrom sky, because I have guessed it's one of the missing elements in the unfinished painting. It has more to teach me than the red-capped bitch. It teaches me a labyrinth is not a place where one becomes disoriented and lost. It is a place into which one is born and may never escape.

The sun is setting when I wake.

19/7/98

The morning post brought an envelope from Manhattan, from that cunt shitbird fuck Larry fucking Tannahill. I'd have thought ending his salary would have ended his attentions. No. He sends a clipping, which I attach here (fuck knows why, that too), though the business with the film is well and truly over and done. He tore it from a magazine somewhere. It was not scissor-clipped, but torn:

Excerpt from "L'homme qui a assassiné Arthur Rackham: Une entrevue avec Albert Perrault," published in *L'Oeil* (Avril 1989, No. 452), by J. S. Molyneux (translated from the original French by J. S. Molyneux):

L'Oeil: The "Little Red Riding Hood" sequence, for example? It was not what you had envisioned?

Perrault: No, it was not. It was so completely outlandish, because the director *wanted* a crude, outlandish film. He would look at my sketches and paintings, the sculptures I did with Rob Bottin, and say, "Yes, yes, that's a good place to start, but see, we can take it so much farther." And that poor actress. **XXXXX XXXXXXXXX**, I think that was her name. She had worked on something very similar with Neil Jordan, and so **XXXXXXX** insisted upon her, though I thought she was somewhat too old for the role. Six hours in makeup for this scene, and I think it was four consecutive days she had to go through that, because they couldn't get a take **XXXXXXX** was happy with.

L'Oeil: I've seen your sketches, and, in those, the wolf's penis doesn't look like a sea cucumber.

Perrault: Of course, it doesn't. Because that was not *my* design. That was something that Bottin and his crew were asked to do, all their creation. But it is a perfect example of how outrageous **XXXXXXX** wanted this film to be, how he kept missing the mark because he wouldn't follow the work they were paying me to do. I'd wanted the "Riding Hood" sequence to be so much simpler, more eloquent, let the audience's *imagination* do more work, instead of relying heavily on prosthetics. But, no, **XXXXXXX** would have none of it, and it made him angry that I would not agree that his way was better.

L'Oeil: So you felt the sequence was a failure?

Perrault: Everything they shot was a failure. I was trying to speak to the dark forest of womanhood, and the liminal spaces between virginity and a girl's first sexual experience. But what they wanted was a freak show. By the time we were filming those scenes, I only wanted it to be over. I'd stopped arguing. By then, see, some of us were hearing that the financiers back in the States were not happy with what they were seeing, the rushes, and I was beginning to suspect we wouldn't get much farther. We'd done some footage for the mermaid scenes, on Stage A, and **XXXXXXX**'s plan had been to shoot "Riding Hood" and the mermaid scene at the same time, back-to-back, but it was a logistical nightmare, and the set for the latter was so much more complicated. It was the sea cave, where the mermaid goes to find the old hag, but **XXXXXXX** was convinced the cave should look more like the inside of a monster, a sea monster's skeleton in which the hag had taken up residence. We did a lot of work on that, but it was simply impossible on his budget. I am still amazed that filming went on as long as it did, and that there was so little, in the end, to show for all that time.

L'Oeil: It's true you have not spoken to **XXXXXXX** since?

Perrault: Absolutely true. It is true, also, that I will never speak with him again. I heard some talk about the studio trying to bring in another director to revive the project, but no one ever called me, and I was relieved.

I was drunk, and only half recall granting that interview or speaking those words. I'll open no more letters from Tannahill, but instead mark them "return to sender" or burn them. And it was Tannahill, that Scots fuck, crossed out, **X**ed out, the names, not me. I hardly give two shits who knows the particular facts of the matter.

22/7/98

Yesterday, I met a woman who said she knows a few of those *cataphiles* I mentioned. Said, too, that she'd gone down herself, into the belly of this rotten old cityscape. Nothing she did regularly, only a time or three to sate her curiosity. She told me of a chamber they've – the cataphiles, urban spelunkers – named the Beach. The earthen walls of the Beach are colorfully adorned after the style of Hokusai. Specifically, with a copycat mural of Hokusai's *The Great Wave off Kanagawa*. She talked of quarries down there where the intelligentsia hold secret court, and of abandoned subway tunnels. She offered to introduce me to a man who would take me down, and I declined. Is that my cowardice rearing it's brutal countenance? Or am I simply not in the mood for stumbling about in the dark with only an oil lantern or carbide headlamp to shine the way? I've wandered plenty other catacombs and low-ceilinged ossuaries, have I not? My feet and hands have been soiled with that dust enough times that I'll retract the question of bravery.

24/7/98

Made a meager but sufficient dinner of cold chicken, radishes, and baby carrots tonight for Dorothée and myself. Talked some about the cataphiles, and she thought anyone who'd prowl about the underbelly of Paris quite the fucking fool. I wanted to begin a conversation about dreams, but didn't. She asked questions about the unfinished painting, and I toasted that murky folly and joked it might be named *Last Drink Bird Head*. She laughed, but I think only out of a sense she ought to be polite to her host. Dorothée is the sort of woman who has no taste for self-deprecation. Ah, well. She pressed, so I showed her the two paintings I finished in Ireland and have not yet sent back to NYC to the Agent: *Leda* and *Clever Cinders*. I took them out from beneath my sagging bed, unrolled the canvases on the floor so she might politely ooh and ah, though they felt more like obligatory oohs and ahs to me. She claimed to like the former better than the latter. I tried to give it to her, but she'd have nothing of it. Mark my word, it's hard to give away your demons.

(Admission to no one but myself: The subject of this painting occurred to me shortly after viewing an exhibit of photographs from the caves of Lascaux, near the village of Montignac. The cavern walls are famously adorn'd with Paleolithic graffiti, in the main large and extinct animals and the Cro-Magnon's who hunted them. Discovered September 12, 1940, one of the images portrays a bird-headed hunter being struck down by a bison. Archaeologists have assumed the bird-headed man to be raven-headed [or at least crow-headed], "because of their [crows *et* ravens] mysterious yet conspicuous association with death." It seems a spurious conclusion to me, a jumping to an unwarranted and ill-supported conclusion, shamanic and totemic assumptions – and I will not say the man painted on the cave wall more than seventeen thousand years ago has the head of a raven, nor that of any other corvid. Only the head of a bird.)

When Dorothée had gone back to her rooms, I cleaned the dishes and found myself at a loss, not wanting to pick up the palette and brushes. Last of all wanting to do *that*. Instead, went out in search again for the boy, uncomplaining Gautier, but walking three times up and down la Rue Saint-Denis, Avenue of Whores, I caught no sight of him, was afforded not so much as a fleeting glimpse, as if he saw and then avoided me. I was discouraged, yes, but no less hungry. I paid a transvestite, in Gautier's stead. They could not have been less alike, sheheit and my missing Gautier. Sheheit (*travesti*, or is that in the *lingua italiana*?) wore proper clothes for a French street whore, and all perverse and sick of myself and angry and wishing to humiliate my own hubris, and rewarded the whore with a generous handful of *franc lourd* for letting me blow herhimit, which, said the being of fluid gender, was not usually on the menu. On my knees, I was where I should have been, the cock in my mouth, then my mouth filled up with cum and swallowing every drop, licking the swollen, pulsing phallus clean. Then I took the ass, supposing my mortification of the spirit had earned me a more genuine concupiscence. I took the ass with my dick and my tongue and two fingers, and sheheit expelled all the sounds you'd expect from a transvestite bitch bastard who prowls the streets like a solitary jackal in wolf's clothing seeking out a scrap of carrion not unlike myself.

I am alone again now. If Dorothée notes the comings and goings of my whores at all hours of the night and in the early morning, she never comments on them. She's too discrete for such prying or violations of privacy.

Oh, almost forgot. The transvestite left something behind. I keep it as a souvenir. It must have slipped from a red-taloned hand. A narrow silver band graven on the outer side with tiny flowers, and inside with a single skull. I can assign it, no doubt, a hundred meanings. I ought send it to a writerly acquaintance, because surely there's a story in that ring. But no, I think I'll hoard it for my own. I'll place it in the cedar box I bought in Shannon.

25-26/7/98

The moon tonight…no matter. No matter of the moon, as I finally pulled the tattered curtains shut and gave it no more thought than I give it now in this moment.

I sat down to write one thing, but my pen was out of ink, and while I scrounged about for a fresh cartridge, another thing distracted me. That most recent envelope from Tannahill. Which set me thinking about the day we met not too far from Inverness. He was living in a flat on High Street above a florist. I was only in Scotland for two weeks, but couldn't resist the lure of the Loch's peaty waters. Cannot ever resist the siren song of legends, be they derived from kelpies or surviving plesiosaurs or trapped seals or hoaxes. I was parked at a lookout on the A82 above Urquhart Castle. He stopped, and struck up a conversation, forcing me to lower my binoculars. I do not, as a rule, talk with strangers, but there was about Tannahill an infectious (good choice of adjective) this or that, and we stood together an hour in the chilling wind. He talked to me about the crumbling medieval edifice of Urquhart, how no one knows for sure when it was built, but surely no later than the Thirteenth Century. And that diggings and radiocarbon dates from the grounds go back to the Fourth and Sixth centuries, so something here fortified since at least as far back as that. He'd not even mentioned the "monster," which I found odd, not ribbing a tourist when a tourist deserves a ribbing. Me, I'd not have passed up the opportunity.

He told me how the Nazi's flew sorties over the lake, and also, in greater detail, of how a Wellington bomber, *R is for Robert*, bound for Heligoland, ran into nasty weather on the New Year's Eve of 1940. At eight thousand feet, the plane met with a snowstorm above the Monadhliath Hills, and somewhere over Foyers the starboard engine failed. Sputsputsputtersput. The pilot ordered six trainees to bail, and more I don't recall. Deaths. Men fly, men die. The plane was ditched in Ness, and sank, and lay on a slimy bed of silt at sixty meters down for thirty-six years, I think, until one September it was hauled back up to the light of day. Also, Tannahill told me of a woman who swam the breadth of the Loch at the age of sixteen, and that's more than eighteen hours in frigid waters. I have this memory and a head for numbers, though it never serves me profitably. I recall dates and figures that are at best, trivial. He talked of six-foot eels, but nothing more monstrous. We watched a peregrine falcon soar above the black expanse, and he asked me back to accompany him for a pint or two or three, and I went.

We fucked the first time that night, and when I returned to the States, I thought I'd never see the man again, which was fine enough by me. I was busy arranging a show, not *that* show, but that *other* show, and had no time for any persistant love affair. But he came on his own, unbidden, six months later, and tracked me to Los Angeles. I managed not to start hating him for several months, which is almost a record. I told him to leave, but he remained persistently peripheral, and still does so.

Fuck all. Now I need a new nib. I'm not even sure I have one.

26/7/98

Another letter (with clippings, etc.) from Tannahill, and I should not even have opened it. But I did, because what I don't know is worse than what I do. More of the same, and I think this is becoming seriously fucking sadistic on his part (and masochistic on mine, not tossing them unopened into the wastepaper basket right off):

From *Film Threat*'s "Top Ten 50 Lost Films of All Time" (posted to filmthreat.com, 7 January, 1997): #41 *Albert Perrault's Court of the Sidhe* (1987):

"Believed to have never progressed beyond the early stages of production, the film would have presented various pornographic re-imaginings of classic fairy tales, including 'Little Red Riding Hood,' 'The Little Mermaid,' and 'Beauty and the Beast.' Despite occasional, unsubstantiated rumors of one or more test reels circulating among collectors, there is little evidence that any part of this film has survived."

EXCEPT:

1. THE THREE REELS IN MY SAFE
2. WHATEVER IT WAS, IT WASN'T PORNOGRAPHY
3. LA BELLE ET LA BÊTE WAS NEVER PART OF THE PROJECT
4. I PERSONALLY HAVE NO KNOWLEDGE OF REELS IN POSSESSION OF "COLLECTORS"

~ and, something I wrote four years ago ~

"It rained the whole first two weeks we were out at Shepperton. It rained, the cold rain of an English summer, and there were all manner of electrical problems, and insurance troubles, and we had two of the actors walk out on us. I kept wondering, to myself, 'Where is all the goddamn money for this coming from?' Mostly, I was working closely with our makeup effects man, Rob Bottin, who had impressed me, first with *The Howling*, then *The Thing*, for John Carpenter, then *Legend*, the Ridley Scott film. I cannot recall who directed *The Howling*, but it wasn't a very good film, so I do not suppose that matters. The makeup was grueling, I know, and by the end of that second week, almost all the actors were ready to walk out on us, I think, though only two actually did quit.

"We got in one more week before the backers pulled the plug on the project and the money dried up. But by then, I was sick of the whole mess, anyway, and glad for it to end. I could see, already, from the dailies, that it wasn't what I'd hoped for or intended, not the movie that **XXXXXXX** promised me we were making. It was too graphic, and there was too much shown, too much shown that should only have been *suggested*. The emphasis on atmosphere and mood that I had been promised was being sacrificed for more blatantly prurient imagery. No one has ever yet called me a prudish man, I think, so it's not like that. I was not offended by the explicitness, but disappointed by it. Almost all of the pre-production artwork I did for the film, it belonged to the studio or the director, whichever, and was taken away to the rotten bowels of Hollywood, and I nevermore saw it again."

That was written for *Cinefex*, but the article was never published; the threat of lawsuits intervened. Which made no difference to me. I'm calling T. tonight and asking him to stop this shit, the clippings. I have work to do and no need of goddamn ghosts of stillborn undertakings. No time for the head games he mistakes for flirtation.

27/7/98

I've never been in a wood as dark as this wood. Black Forest, maybe, *Schwarzwald*, but that part is likely not of any relevance beyond…beyond, beyond. I ought be out on the rue, searching for Gautier or make-do she-males and not writing down nightmares. I ought to be fucking painting. Fucking. Painting. I'm going to finish that ogre, whether it concludes in a mess or otherwise. I have all these things to be doing that trump any need to write down bad dreams. So, hah, I write down bad dreams. Hah. Ring around the rosies, pop goes the weasel, and make the impatient waiters wait impatiently a little longer.

I've never been in a wood as dark as this wood.

I stumble among the pines and hoary oaks, fat toads and sleek hares and overhead is owl and crow song. I pick my way over and between the weave of this living Arthur Rackham tableau vivant. The air has a cinnamon tang of fiddleheads and the heady musk of decaying forest-floor detritus; leafy strata underfoot, tunneled by moles and earthworms, inhuman and untamed cataphiles. There is no path, so I cannot have *strayed* from any path. There is a labyrinth I think, and it does not begin and it does not end. I look up, but limbs hide away the writhing, star-scabbed sky. I push aside briers and hawthorn, and I see the wolf and I see the girl who sat beside me at the Seine, girl who's come to me down all my life. Here is only a fiction I'm going to hammer together from fading dreamstuff, and it's gonna make do or damn me, fuck, I don't vex myself with accuracy. I'm only tracing, rubbing charcoal at best, and will settle for indefinite, happily or not happily. Makes no difference.

I have never been in a wood this dark. I push aside the underbrush:

The wolf *thing* stands in a thicket of ferns and mushrooms, beneath the mossy boughs of unthinkably ancient trees, and it licks at its short muzzle. The actress kneeling before it is one of the two who walked off the set. Her makeup is almost as elaborate as the wolf's. The red cape has been made an integral *part* of her, something like folds of crimson skin hanging from her head and shoulders and spine, drooping from her arms like the membranes of a bat's wings. Latex or silicone prosthetics, I know that, sure, but the makeup is unnerving, and I feel faintly nauseous. The wolf thing looks down, running clawed fingers along the girl's fleshy crimson cowl, which seems to have been coated with some substance so as to resemble the slimy, glistening skin of a salamander. Hydroxypropyl cellulose, perhaps, or, more likely, methyl cellulose. The symbolism is obvious, I think, ham-fistedly fucking *too* obvious, this "red riding hood" grown into a sort of hypertrophied virginal hymen, as yet unbroken and all but smothering the girl.

"I'm bringing her bread and cream," she whispers. I lean forward, all the better to hear her. All the better to hear words I wrote, but never meant for me.

The "wolf," its scruffy, short pelt matted with leaves and burrs, it asks her, "Do you follow the Road of Needles, or the Road of Pins?"

"The Road of Pins," the girl replies. "Most assuredly, I'll take the Road of Pins."

"Well, then. I suppose I'll take the Road of Needles, and we'll see who gets there first," the wolf says.

The forest becomes…maybe a city street…something that isn't a forest. Did I ever write, anywhere, about the night I held a loaded pistol to his head while I fucked him? That bastard Tannahill, I mean. Did I ever tell *me* that. I hold so much back from myself, buried deep in mnemonic graves here in my own mental Le Cimetière du Montparnasse, but devoid of headstones. They rise though, sometimes.

28/7/98 THREE MARGUERITES

Walking in the cemetery yesterday, a Tuesday, I met a woman who recognized me (which is a thing that almost never happens) and who claimed to be a werewolf. I was out searching for the grave of Marie Dorval (1798-1849), an actress rumored to have been a lesbian lover of George Sands. I didn't find the grave, but, as I said, found this woman who claimed to be a werewolf. Or to have been a werewolf. Or that she was and wasn't, in some inconstant lunar cycle beyond my comprehension. To be sure, mad. Or I assume madness. Presumptuous cunt that I am, I assume. But she had an air of madness about her; wouldn't any woman, though, who was also, on occasion, a wolfish creature? More audacious still, she claimed a role in the slaughters at Gévaudan, to have been one among the several who came to infamy and to be known as La Bête Anthropophage du Gévaudan. Didn't point out this would have meant her to be quite advanced in years, a minimum of, say, let us say 248 years old, if she were, let us say maybe 14 when the depredations commenced. So, tatterdemalion and unwashed though she certainly was, my skepticism is not, I think, unwarranted. She looked, to my eyes, no older than thirty, but who knows the magick of lycanthropes?

Her name, she told me, was Marguerite. She gave me (like young Gautier) no surname. I asked for none. The French name daisies Marguerite. *Chrysanthemum frutescens*, start of summer into middle of autumn, long blooming and susceptible to infestation by thrips. Surely they grow in the Margeride Mountains, but that hardly even counts as circumstantial, unless she was playing a very allusive game. Who knows the sporting whims of lycanthropes?

She told me her name was Marguerite. She was a slender woman, slender nigh unto emaciated. I almost said so and wanted to buy her a meal. In the end, I didn't offer, fickle cunt that I am. She wore boots too large, a leather coat too large on her kite-frame bones, some manner of a frock beneath, torn stockings. Her head, all a matted mop of hair, was auburn. Most striking though, the eyes in the pinched and pale face: the left was brilliant green, the right an equally brilliant blue. Emerald and sapphire eyes set into that single skull. Single *et* singular. Her English was quite good, and I shall here do my best to reconstitute our conversation, though I readily confess I'd been drinking – only wine, but still. In fact, I had a bottle with me, a cheap merlot, and I shared it with the woman whose eyes were beautifully "afflicted" with what ophthalmologists or whatever call *heterochromia iridium* (a/k/a *heterochromia iridis*):

"Yes," she said. "I was there. I'll not take all the credit, though. There were others."

I asked her to name her particular victims between 1764 and 1767, and she smiled a sly kind of smile and took a pull off the merlot. "Unless you've forgotten their names, or never knew them," I added.

"I've not forgotten, and I know them," she replied. "Well, not all their names, but all their faces. That first young girl at Les Hubacs, she was mine. We drew lots, at the start. And later, the bold girl, Marie Jeanne Valet – *la Pucelle* – who fought back with only a spear fashioned from a spindle. She was also mine, and such bravery in her, I let her carry the day. A statue was raised to *la Pucelle* back in '59. I gave the child immortality. And six-year-old Marguerite Lèbre, she was one of mine, and I borrowed her name. I meant to be bold, so there were witnesses that day, as attested to by the Curate Gibergue at la Pauze…"

She went on. I'll not put it all down.

I cannot say I was even half convinced, as these are facts found anywhere one knows to look (*La Bête du Gévaudan*, M. Moreau-Bellecroix; Paris. 1945 and *La Bête du Gévaudan*. Felix Buffièr in 1994, and, for that matter, *La Bête du Gévaudan in Auvergne*. Fabre, Abbé François. Saint Flour. 1901 and Paris 1930.) The sculpture at Place des Cordeliers, Marvejols, (where, notably, La Bête was never even seen) by Emmanuel Auricoste, that's a goddamn tourist attraction. I was tempted to tempt her back to my bed, to bed my raggedy *loup faux*, my self-proclaimed *fantôme de la bête* (?). She'd not have accepted the invitation, and me in no mood for rejection. Also, why set out to spoil Dorothée's conviction or image of me as an exclusive and inveterate buggerer of the male sex?

"You are a lonely man," Marguerite said.

"And how is that?"

"You smell very much of a lonely man, and I have read interviews."

"There are worse fates."

"*Mais oui. Naturellement.* But, one wonders, is it from choice, necessity, or…" and she trailed off and picked at a weed.

"Some men – and woman – are unsuited to anything else," I told her.

"You know this?"

"I believe this. And it's not such a burden. I get more work done without the distractions of constant companions."

I asked where she lived, and, at first, she seemed reluctant to discharge an answer. She smiled and gazed up at the bright summer sky above Le Cimetière du Montparnasse. Then she told me she had a room not far from La Rotonde. A lie concocted then and there, I'd say, her needing an answer at the ready.

And then, echoing almost my dream – my sky-tortured nightmaring red cap – Marguerite said, sternly, solemnly *and* sternly, "Be lonely, then, if it suits you. But do not go to Gévaudan. Maybe there's nothing left there to see. Maybe there are old ghosts in the forests, and maybe they're still hungry. Stay here in Paris, Monsieur Perrault."

I made her no promise, one way or the other, and shortly after we parted, all polite *au revoir* and take cares and perhaps our paths will cross again. I think they won't. To be sure, I'll not seek her out, green- and blue-eyed liar that she is, apparently.

I almost decided not to mentioned her red-felt cloche, which might last have been fashionable in 1933. Then I undecided, so there it is. I'll make of it what I will. Or what I won't. Be done with this.

29/7/98

THIS

Oh, you greedy gormandiser,
What a pity you weren't wiser.
Mr. Wolf, so false and sly,
In the river now you lie!

THIS

Vous m'amusez toujours. Jamais je m'en irai chez-nous, J'ai trop grand peur des loups. (Voyageur Songs; French-Canadian, ca. 1830; collected by Edward Ermatinger)

ALSO

Since I'm making lais, Bisclavret
Is one I don't want to forget.
In Breton, "Bisclavret's" the name;
"Garwolf" in Norman means the same.
Long ago you heard the tale told –
And it used to happen, in days of old –
Quite a few men became garwolves,
And set up housekeeping in the woods.
A garwolf is a savage beast,

While the fury's on it, at least:
Eats men, wreaks evil, does no good,
Living and roaming in the deep wood.
BISCLAVRET (excerpt)
Marie de France, translated Judith P. Shoaf © 1996

AND

I left out this, this, this…snippet. In my recounting of meeting goodly fucked weary plaguing-me nigh unto Perdition and back Mr. Peter Tannahill that day at the tumbledown lochside ruins near Drumnadrochit. An accidental omission, though it might well seem anything but and otherwise. At some point, he brought up Boleskine House, and that way did his conversation turn. Near to the village of Foyers, a mansion built in the late Eighteenth Century by a man named Archibald Fraser. And then, he told how Aleister Crowley, *bête noir*, that other Loch Ness Monster, came to and purchased Boleskine House in 1899. Crowley, usual flair and all, styled himself Laird of Boleskine and Abertarff. And maybe he did unspeakable rituals in those chambers above the all-but-bottomless lake. Maybe the "Abramelin Operation" out of something known as *The Book of the Sacred Magic of Abramelin the Mage.* It all reeks to me to high fucking heavens of apocrypha and hype. But let's us just say yes, this transpired. Crowley sought a higher self in this incantation, but Tannahill said how, no, instead was conjured what Crowley named "the Abramelin devils" and much mischief, as of the antics of poltergeists – darker, but reminiscent – ensued.

"Those Led Zeppelin wankers," said Tannahill, "That Yank Jimmy Page fellow, a right Crowley devotee, he owned the dump for a time."

&

There can be no denyin' that the wind'll shake 'em down
And the flat world's flyin'. There's a new plague on the land

&

Still so dark all over Europe
And the rainbow rises here
In the western sky

SO

IN CONCLUSION

I see a pattern here, or I see no pattern at all. A pattern exists, or no pattern is here. Too much to drink, so little sleep, and a woman with eyes that are green and blue, and I cannot find my *beau garçon* – Gautier.

30/7/98

I sit on my stool before the easel. My hands are stained, acrylic stained, bleeding in reverse, and I sit on my stool and rage at this haunting, this abomination jokingly [Christ]ened *Last Drink Bird Head* a few days back. Now I know it wasn't a joke, even if and though all the various connotations the title may summon allude me. Just as I am *eluded* by its completion. It's a stillbirth, or placental afterbirth expulsion, postpartum blood only in countless avocado gangrenous black-greens instead of crimson and meat shades. All an avocado standing on a hill, also an avocado hill, roiling labyrinth sky, no in and no out, and HIM, whoever HIM might be. HIM. Ibis-crown'd dæmon from a dream I can't recall to lord over this fucking canvas. I know HIM, I know HIS name, but I will not speak it here. I dab camel's hair to napthol crimson and there you motherfucker, you deal with that hanging in your squirming goddamn sky. There. One dab or two or a third, but all a single body slumped in that worm welkin vault. Stürmischer Himmel don't know why there's no sun up in the sky but my red damn'd splotch or even if that *is* Himmel.

Go to the kitchen drawer for a paring knife, and be a slasher.

Precedent the First: 15 June 1985, the young man who slashed crotch and then splashed concentrated sulphuric acid across Rembrandt's *Danaë*, and there was little chance for restoration.

Precedent the Second: Munch's *The Scream*, vandalized with a felt-tip marker. And too, too true, the scrawl, "Could only have been painted by a madman."

Precedent the Third: 10 March 1914 and Mary Richardson's meat-cleaver savagery against Diego Velázquez's *Rokeby Venus*. Seven slashes. Slashes seven. She said later, "Because the way men visitors gaped at it all day long."

Precedent the Fourth: Repeated attacks against Rembrandt's *Night Watch* (1642).

Precedent the Fifth: Twice decapitated, "The Little Mermaid" in the harbor of Copenhagen. 24 April 1964, "sawn off and stolen by politically oriented artists of the Situationist movement, amongst them Jørgen Nash." Then, only five (or six?) months ago, 28/1/98, decapitation again, perpetrators returned the head, but were never apprehended.

Too many examples, and these only those of which I am aware.

BUT

Precedent the Sixth (and most Relevant to the Case at Hand): Claude Monet, April 1903, an exhibition of his work, and this time it was the artist himself who entered and took blade and paintbrush spatters *to his own work.*

This is all fair fucking warning, you Thoth-headed avatar fuck of my undoing perched there on your too-ripe avocado hill. I am *your* god, and not around that Other way. I have knives. I can part delicately curved beak from cranium, jaws from quadrate, skull from almost human shoulders, etcetera. You do well to remember that, afterbirth.

31/7/98

Bad night last night. Faithful Dorothée came round to find me hung over and puking sick. No lasting damage done, to myself or the execrable (or excremenitious painting).

1/8/98

"Things are entirely what they appear to be and *behind them*…there is nothing."

1938, Sartre, *La Nausée*

1/8/98

It may be a dream. Hardly matters. I meant to write *this* hours ago, but scuttled off to Sartre, instead, being lowly, loathsome coward that I am. Being coward. Hiding in history and words not of my own devising. Words not even wholly suitable, but pilfered stolen appropriated *pirated* nonetheless. Privateering as avoidance. I meant, instead, to write this what might have been dream and this what might have been waking, or this WHAT might have been liminal space straddling the two mythic kingdoms, SLEEP and AWAKE. I walked la Rue Saint-Denis, so crowded with prostitutes and those paying supplicants seeking out the ministrations and sordid deliverances of their services, but so many, so many, walking la Rue Saint-Denis was to thread a needle. I cannot prove I wasn't actually there. I can't prove I wasn't. My head choked, eyes choked with memories of bright lurid brothel signage: Club 128, "Sex Center" Projection Video, Top Sexy, Sexy Center, generic Peep Show. Video 121, generic Sex Shop; *La rue Saint-Denis est surtout constituée de sex shops*, yes and fine and true, but almost or no signs that were not in fucking English. Oh, but half times half a memory of stopping to purchase a pear at a fruit stand called *la Palais du Fruit*. Make of that what you goddamn will and pardon my murdered *Français*. In my head, the recollections are of cobblestones sticky with cum, gutters running silver-white with cum. This cannot be actual. Delusion or dreaming delusion. Faces all around like carnival masks, that painted and bright and plastic. *Those* faces, but also others of an entirely different breed. Filthy waifs and gaunt women with tarry blobs for eyes, jaundiced walking skeletons lurking in back of neon and cheap, sleazy glitz. The lure of an anglerfish comes to mind, or the tongue of a snapping turtle. Fakeout. I am asking everywhere after lost Gautier, whom I have come to believe stole something of me away when he left my studio. Same as the transvestite left the ring. My cock so hard I barely can even walk, but the thought of hands and knees in the semen-wallow gutter, no way, no way. Hands on me, hands of every comprehendible gender, and at first my polite refusals, and then I was shouting for them not to touch me, because I felt the microbes slithering from skin to skin, transepidermal, them unto me, and it might be, though I, not bathe ever again, (*what?*) but infection so deep I'll be bones in the semen by dawn. Do not fucking touch me. Only show me the way to Gautier. You must know him, that face and shyness, and if I'd had a photograph I would have shown them all. See? *This*, this here, right here, is the very man or the boy child I am seeking. And I did find him. That's the miracle of it. The loaves and fishes, manna from the sky, pillar of fire (Exodus 13:21-22; Exodus 14:24; Nehemiah 9:19, & etc.), bleeding statues, falling frogs, stigmata, Fátima (13 October 1917), miracles of modern goddamn medicine. He was standing in an alley near the intersection with rue de la Cossonnerie (a street, supposedly, with a far more savory character). It struck me in no way a surprise to see him on his knees, blowing a fellow with a wolf's head, which soon after my arrival became, instead, the head of an ibis. I was even less surprised when the man sprouted wings and flew away into the streetlight-tainted nighttime sky. Gautier stood up, wiped his mouth, and tucked his thirty pieces of silver into a front pocket of his tight, tight jeans. Don't think I don't know I was meant to see each act in its turn and interpret their meanings for precisely what they were. "Miss me?" he asked (though, didn't he *not* speak English?), and I shrugged and stepped into the alleyway, glancing first over my shoulder at the way I'd come. I wanted no followers. I wanted to be certain a line hadn't formed, impatient for the boy whore's favors. There was nothing back there but the neon and throng. Relief. How often do I ever feel relief these days? But in that moment I *did* feel relief, and I turned back to Gautier. "Do you think I missed you?" I replied, tit for tat, and he raised his eyebrows and spat into a pile of wet cardboard boxes. "I dreamed of your painting," he said, oh so very softly he said that, and by then I was sweating, and if I'd not been, that would have done the trick. "I dreamed you finished it, and then gave it to me. I dreamed I sold it to an American for a great deal of money." And I said, "You have good dreams," and he said, "Sometimes I do. Sometimes I don't. What about you, *peintre*. What are your dreams? Does an incubus come and crouch on your chest when you sleep?" I saw, then, that as we'd been speaking, his eyebrows had grown so that they met in the middle, and it occurred to me a contagion had been passed from the wolf/ibis-headed john. If I cut fair Gautier, would I find a second skin turned inside out? If I cut him, would I find fur? There was plenty of space in even that narrow, stinking alley for a trial, an inquisition, and, quick as thieves, I weighed the wants of my cock against my interest in the Truth, and, too, the fact that I could have both. But the contagion might be catching, might it not? Did I wish to join Gautier in this lycanthropy of the soul? Why, if I chose that route, I could go to Gévaudan, after all. I could pick up where Marguerite and her unnamed compatriots had left off more than two hundred years before, yes? "Can't stand here all night," Gautier said, and he said it with a haughty, impatient air that made up my mind then and there. I drew the paring knife from my belt and, stepping quickly towards him, moving fast and leaving only inches to spare, drove the blade into his chest to the hilt. He didn't scream, so all the better. I twisted the blade, as I've seen done in action flicks. His blood spilled so warmly it was almost hot over my right hand, near to steaming, and I considered the possibility all over again. Maybe I'd be numbered among the infected, despite my sloppy caution. I looked into his eyes, and he looked into mine. I twisted the blade again, and he only looked a little disappointed before slumping to the ground at my feet. His descent was in no especial way different from the position he'd have assumed were I then a paying customer and not an executioner. "Does he know my name?" I asked the dying boy. He answered, words death rattling from his slight and violated chest, "All our names are known to him, Sir. 'I am thy writing palette, O Thoth, and I have brought unto thee thine ink-jar. I am not of those who work iniquity in their secret places; let not evil happen unto me.' Thought you were Monsieur Myth Savvy. Thought you'd know that for sure." For good measure, I kicked him, and turned to walk away in the same instant I became quite convinced I'd never drawn the paring knife. I stood with my back to the living Gautier, and he was saying that he was available, if I was interested. Why would I have sought him out, were I not interested. It was a nasty trick (adianoeta noted and no pun intended), turning the tables on me like that. Dying at my feet and condemning me with the taint of wolf and ibis blood, then my having never even pulled the knife, much less plunged it into his jaded heart. "Will you come home with me," I asked, but he inquired, "Do you have a home, Monsieur?" So I put the question to him a second time. "If you have the cost of my company," he said. Which is to say, he said no. And I recalled the Hag of Montparnasse: "You smell very much of a lonely man…" I stared at a flashing sign promising LIVE GIRLS (supposing the dead ones are unpopular or in short supply), and eventually I said to him, "Not what I had in mind, Gautier." Car horn. Beat for emphasis. Sharp intake of breath. "You know I'm your money's worth." And I replied, "No. Wait here, and I'm sure you will attract the attention of some other pantheon. A forgotten god or goddess will come along, sooner or later." He said not another word, and I left him standing there. I'll never go looking again. A black dog followed me almost all the way back to the flat, though I took a taxi. I glimpsed it now and then. It wore many faces. *Many gods and many voices.*

3/8/98

Found, today, pinned to the door of my flat (unsigned; provenance unknown; we shall not think on that):

Mater luporum, mater moeniorum, stella montana, ora pro nobis. Virgo arborum, virgo vastitatis, umbra corniculans, ora pro nobis. Regina mutatum, regina siderum, ficus aeterna, ora pro nobis. Domina omnium nocte dieque errantium, nunc et in hora mortis nostrae, ora pro nobis.

Which I translate as:

Mother of wolves, mother of walls, star of the mountains, pray for us. Virgin of trees, virgin of desert, horned moon's shadow, pray for us. Queen of changes, queen of constellations, eternal fig-tree, pray for us. Mistress of all who by night and day wander, now and at the hour of our death, pray for us.

The piece was titled "The Magdalene of Gérandan."

4/8/98

This morning I read in *Le Monde* of the death of a young male prostitute in an alley off rue Saint-Denis. He was stabbed repeatedly in the throat and face. His genitals were missing. The paper didn't give his name.

The painting is finished.

I put in a call to Manhattan.

Dear Tannahill,

So, I am going to Gévaudan, it seems, to the granite bosom of the Margerides. I cannot say what I will find there, or what shall find me. The bronze statue of a girl fending off a simultaneously wolf- and lion-like creature with a spindle. *La forêt de la bête*, a wood darker than any wood I've ever seen, outside a soundstage. And I'll see other things. I've told Dorothée, and she seemed genuinely disappointed that I'll soon be gone, and that I don't expect to return to this residence.

I reminded her this was never meant to be permanent. "Just passing through. Only a place to finish a painting."

"Ah, well," she said. "The countryside is beautiful this time of year. The pastures will all be bright with marguerites. Promise you'll send me...*un carte postale, oui*?

"Of course. Of course, I will."

Mailing these pages off to you, Tannahill; make of them what you will. I'm done with them, as I am done with you. I've rented a motorcycle, and I've only one stop to make before departing Paris. I want this city behind me, no matter what lies out before me. Go now. You're free to leave. Turn the page.

Albert Perrault
5 August 1998
19 rue Fauvet

Excerpt from Baillargeon, Gautier. *Gilded Thomas Art Review* (Vol. 31, No. 7, Fall 2006; Minneapolis, MN):

"...certainly, far stranger things have been suggested regarding both his life and his works. And given the particulars of his short career, his involvement in the occult, and his penchant for cryptic affectations, it does not seem – to this author – so outlandish to ascribe to Albert Perrault a morbid sort of prescience or to believe that his presentation of *Last Drink Bird Head* upon the eve of his fatal motorcycle accident on the rue Cuvier was a carefully orchestrated move, designed to preserve his mystique *ad finem*. Indeed, it almost seems outlandish to believe otherwise."

As to the painting itself (currently on loan to the Musée National d'Art Moderne), *Last Drink Bird Head* is one of Perrault's largest and most thematically oblique canvases. After his disappointing experiments with sculpture and multi-media, it harks back to the paintings that heralded his ascent almost a decade ago. Here we have, once again, his 'retro-expressionist-impressionist' vision and also a clear return to his earlier obsession with mythology.

A lone figure stands on a barren hilltop, silhouetted against a writhing night sky. However, this sky does not writhe with stars or moonlight, as in Van Gogh's *Starry Night*, but rather here the very *fabric* of the sky writhes. The canvas itself seems to convulse. The blackness of a firmament which might well reflect Perrault's conception of an antipathetic cosmos, and might also be read as the projection of the painting's central figure and, by extension, the artist's own psyche. There is but a single red dab of light in all that black, contorted sky (recalling his earlier *Fecunda ratis*), and it seems more like a baleful eye than any ordinary celestial body. The distinctive shape and thickness of the brushstrokes have rendered this sky a violent thing, and I have found that it's difficult not to view the brushstrokes as the corridors of a sort of madman's maze, leading round and round and, ultimately, nowhere at all.

And if the sky of *Last Drink Bird Head* could be said to form a labyrinth, then the figure dominating the foreground might fairly be construed as its inevitable 'minotaur' – that is, a malformed chimera trapped forever within its looping confines. The figure has previously been described by one prominent reviewer as representing the falcon-headed Egyptian sky god Horus (or Nekheny). Yet it seems clear to me that Perrault's 'Bird Head' avatar cannot accurately be described as 'falcon-headed.' Rather, the profile presented – a small skull and long, slender, decurved bill – is more strongly reminiscent of an ibis. This, then, brings to mind a different Egyptian deity entirely – Thoth, scribe of the gods and intermediator between forces of good and evil."

©Locke 2013

The Ape's Wife

Neither yet awake nor quite asleep, she pauses in her dreaming to listen to the distant sounds of the jungle approaching twilight. They are each balanced now between one world and another – she between sleep and waking, and the jungle between day and night. Dreaming, she is once again the woman she was before she came to the island, the starving woman on that *other* island, that faraway island that was not warm and green, but had come to seem to her always cold and grey, stinking of dirty snow and the exhaust of automobiles and buses. She stands outside a lunch room on Mulberry Street, her empty belly rumbling as she watches other people eat. The evening begins to fill up with the raucous screams of nocturnal birds and flying reptiles and a gentle tropical wind rustling through the leaves of banana and banyan trees, through cycads and ferns grown as tall or taller than the brick and steel and concrete canyon that surrounds her.

She leans forward, and her breath fogs the lunch room's plate-glass window, but none of those faces turn to stare back at her. They are all too occupied with their meals, these swells with their forks and knives and china platters buried under mounds of scrambled eggs or roast beef on toast or mashed potatoes and gravy. They raise china cups of hot black coffee to their lips and pretend she isn't there. This winter night is too filled with starving, tattered women on the bum. There is not time to notice them all, so better to notice none of them, better not to allow the sight of real hunger to spoil your appetite. A little farther down the street there is a Greek who sells apples and oranges and pears from a little sidewalk stand, and she wonders how long before he catches her stealing, him or someone else. She has never been a particularly lucky girl.

Somewhere close by, a parrot shrieks and another parrot answers it, and finally she turns away from the people and the tiled walls of the lunch room and opens her eyes; the Manhattan street vanishes in a slushy, disorienting flurry and takes the cold with it. She is still hungry, but for a while she is content to lie in her carefully woven nest of rattan, bamboo, and ebony branches, blinking away the last shreds of sleep and gazing deeply into the rising mists and gathering dusk. She has made her home high atop a weathered promontory, this charcoal peak of lava rock and tephra a vestige of the island's fiery origins. It is for this summit's unusual shape – not so unlike a human skull – that white men named the place. And it is here that she last saw the giant ape, before it left her to pursue the moving-picture man and Captain Englehorn, the first mate and the rest of the crew of the *Venture*, left her alone to get itself killed and hauled away in the rusty hold of that evil-smelling ship.

At least, that is one version of the story she tells herself to explain why the beast never returned for her. It may not be the truth. Perhaps the ape died somewhere in the swampy jungle spread out below the mountain, somewhere along the meandering river leading down to the sea. She has learned that there is no end of ways to die on the island, and that nothing alive is so fierce or so cunning as to be entirely immune to those countless perils. The ape's hide was riddled with bullets, and it might simply have succumbed to its wounds and bled to death. Time and again, she has imagined this, the ape only halfway back to the wall but growing suddenly too weak to continue the chase, and perhaps it stopped, surrendering to pain and exhaustion, and sat down in a glade somewhere below the cliffs, resting against the bole of an enormous tree. Maybe it sat there, peering through a break in the perpetual mist and the forest canopy, gazing forlornly back up at the skull-shaped mountain. It would have been a terrible, lonely death, but not so terrible an end as the beast might have met had it managed to gain the ancient aboriginal gates and the sandy peninsula beyond.

She has, on occasion, imagined another outcome, one in which the enraged god-thing overtook the men from the steamer, either in the jungle or somewhere out beyond the wall, in the village or on the beachhead. And though the ape was killed by their gunshots and gas bombs (for surely he would have returned, otherwise), first they died screaming, every last mother's son of them. She has taken some grim satisfaction in this fantasy, on days when she has had need of grim satisfaction. But she knows it isn't true, if only because she watched with her own eyes the *Venture* sailing away from the place where it had anchored out past the reefs, the smoke from its single stack drawing an ashen smudge across the blue morning sky. They escaped, at least enough of them to pilot the ship, and left her for dead or good as dead.

She stretches and sits up in her nest, watching the sun as it sinks slowly into the shimmering, flat monotony of the Indian Ocean, the dying day setting the western horizon on fire. She stands, and the red-orange light paints her naked skin the color of clay. Her stomach growls again, and she thinks of her small hoard of fruit and nuts, dried fish and a couple of turtle eggs she found the day before, all wrapped up safe in banana leaves and hidden in amongst the stones and brambles. Here, she need only fear nightmares of hunger and never hunger itself. There is the faint, rotten smell of sulfur emanating from the cavern that forms the skull's left eye socket, as the mountain's malodorous breath wafts up from bubbling hot springs deep within the grotto. She has long since grown accustomed to the stench and has found that the treacherous maze of bubbling lakes and mud helps to protect her from many of the island's predators. For this reason, more than any other, more even than the sentimentality that she no longer denies, she chose these steep volcanic cliffs for her eyrie.

Stepping from her bed, the stones warm against the thickly calloused soles of her feet, she remembers a bit of melody, a ghostly snatch of lyrics that has followed her up from the dream of the city and the woman she will never be again. She closes her eyes, shutting out the jungle noises for just a moment, and listens to the faint crackle of a half-forgotten radio broadcast.

Once I built a tower up to the sun,
Brick and rivet and lime.
Once I built a tower,
Now it's done.
Brother, can you spare a dime?

And when she opens her eyes again, the sun is almost gone, just a blazing sliver remaining now above the sea. She sighs and reminds herself that there is no percentage in recalling the clutter and racket of that lost world. Not now. Not here. Night is coming on, sweeping in fast and mean on leathery pterodactyl wings and the wings of flying foxes and the wings of *ur*-birds, and like so many of the island's inhabitants, she puts all else from her mind and rises to meet it. The island has made of her a night thing, has stripped her of old diurnal ways. Better to sleep through the stifling equatorial days than to lie awake through the equally stifling nights; better the company of the sun for her uneasy dreams than the moon's cool, seductive glow and her terror of what might be watching hungrily from the cover of darkness.

When she has eaten, she sits awhile near the cliff's edge, contemplating what month this might be, what month in which year. It is a futile, but harmless, pastime. At first, she scratched marks on stone to keep track of the passing time, but after only a few hundred marks she forgot one day, and then another, and when she finally remembered again, she found she was uncertain how many days had come and gone during her forgetfulness. It was then that she came to understood the futility of counting days in this place – indeed, the futility of the very concept of time. She has thought often that the island must be time's primordial orphan, a castaway, not unlike herself, stranded in some nether or lower region, this sweltering antediluvian limbo where there is only the rising and setting of the sun, the phases of the moon, the long rainy season which is hardly less hot or less brutal than the longer dry. Maybe the men who built the wall long ago were a race of sorcerers, and in their arrogance they committed a grave transgression against time, some unspeakable contravention of the sanctity of months and hours. And so Khronos cast this place back down into the gulf of Chaos, and now it is damned to exist forever apart from the tick-tock, calendar-page blessings of Aeon.

Sure, she still recalls a few hazy scraps of Greek mythology, and Roman, too, this farmer's only daughter who always got good marks and waited until school was done before leaving the cornfields of Indiana to go east to seek her fortune in New York and New Jersey. All her girlhood dreams of the stage, the silver screen, and her name on theater marquees, but by the time she reached Fort Lee, most of the studios were relocating west to California, following the promise of a more hospitable, more profitable climate. Black Tuesday had left its stain upon the country, and she never found more than extra work at the few remaining studios, happy just to play anonymous faces in crowd scenes and the like, and finally she could not even find that. Finally, she was fit only for the squalor of bread lines and mission soup kitchens and flop houses, until the night she met a man who promised to make her a star, who, chasing dreams of his own, dragged her halfway round the world and then abandoned her here in this serpent-haunted and time-forsaken wilderness. The irony is not lost on her. Seeking fame and adoration, she has found, instead, what might well be the ultimate obscurity.

Below her, some creature suddenly cries out in pain from the forest tangle clinging to the slopes of the mountain, and she squints into the darkness. She knows that hers are only one of a hundred – or a thousand – pairs of eyes that have stopped to see, to try and catch a glimpse of whatever bloody panoply is being played out among the vines and undergrowth, and that this is only one of the innumerable slaughters to come before sunrise. Something screams and so all eyes turn to see, for every thing that creeps or crawls, flits or slithers upon the island will fall prey, one day or another. And she is no exception.

One day, perhaps, the island itself will fall, not so unlike the dissatisfied angels in Milton or in Blake.

Ann Darrow opens her eyes, having nodded off again, and she is once more only a civilized woman not yet grown old, but no longer young. One who has been taken away from the world and touched, then returned and set adrift in the sooty gulches and avenues and asphalt ravines of this modern, electric city. But that was such a long time ago, before the war that proved the Great War was not so very great after all, that it was not the war to end all wars. Japan has been burned with the fire of two tiny manufactured suns. Europe lies in ruins, and already the fighting has begun again and young men are dying in Korea. History is a steamroller. History is a litany of war.

She sits alone in the Natural History Museum off Central Park, a bench all to herself in the alcove where the giant ape's broken skeleton was mounted for public exhibition after the creature tumbled from the top of the Empire State, plummeting more than twelve hundred feet to the frozen streets below. There is an informative placard (white letters on black) declaring it *Brontopithecus singularis* Osborn (1934), the only known specimen, now believed extinct. *So there*, she thinks. Denham and his men dragged it from the not-quite-impenetrable sanctuary of its jungle and hauled it back to Broadway; they chained it and murdered it and, in that final act of desecration, they *named* it. The enigma was dissected and quantified, given its rightful place in the grand analytic scheme, in the Latinized order of things, and that's one less blank spot to cause the mapmakers and zoologists to scratch their heads. Now, Carl Denham's monster is no threat at all, only another harmless, impressive heap of bones shellacked and wired together in this stately, static mausoleum. And hardly anyone remembers or comes to look upon these bleached remains. The world is a steamroller. The Eighth Wonder of the World was old news twenty years ago, and now it is only a chapter in some dusty textbook devoted to anthropological curiosities.

He was the king and the god of the world he knew, but now he comes to civilization, merely a captive, a show to gratify your curiosity. Curiosity killed the cat, and it slew the ape, as well, and that December night hundreds died for the price of a theater ticket, the fatal price of *their* curiosity and Carl Denham's hubris. By dawn, the passion play was done, and the king and god of Skull Island lay crucified by biplanes, by the pilots and trigger-happy Navy men borne aloft in Curtis Helldivers armed with .50 caliber machine guns. A tiered Golgotha skyscraper, one-hundred-and-two stories of steel and glass and concrete, a dizzying Art-Deco Calvary, and no chance of resurrection save what the museum's anatomists and taxidermists might in time effect.

Ann Darrow closes her eyes, because she can only ever bear to look at the bones for just so long and no longer. Henry Fairfield Osborn, the museum's former president, had wanted to name it after *her*, in her *honour* – *Brontopithecus darrowii,* "Darrow's thunder ape" – but she'd threatened a lawsuit against him *and* his museum, and so he'd christened the species *singularis*, instead. She'd played her Judas role, delivering the jungle god to Manhattan's Roman holiday, and wasn't that enough? Must she also have her name forever nailed up there with the poor beast's corpse? Maybe she deserved as much or far worse, but Osborn's "honour" was poetic justice she managed to evade.

There are voices now, a mother and her little girl, so Ann knows that she's no longer alone in the alcove. She keeps her eyes tightly shut, wishing she could shut her ears as well and not hear the things that are being said.

"Why did they kill him?" asks the little girl.

"It was a very dangerous animal," her mother replies sensibly. "It got loose and hurt people. I was just a child then, about your age."

"They could have put it in a zoo," the girl protests. "They didn't have to kill it."

"I don't think a zoo would ever have been safe. It broke free and hurt a lot of innocent people."

"But there aren't any more monkeys like it."

"There are still plenty of gorillas in Africa," the mother replies.

"Not that big," says the little girl. "Not as big as an elephant."

"No," the mother agrees. "Not as big as an elephant. But then we hardly need gorillas as big as elephants, now do we?"

Ann clenches her jaws, grinding her teeth together, biting her tongue (so to speak), and gripping the edge of the bench with nails chewed down to the quick.

They'll leave soon, she reminds herself. *They always do, get bored and move along after only a minute or so. It won't be much longer.*

"What does *that* part say?" the child asks, so her mother reads to her from the text printed on the placard.

"Well, it says, 'Kong was not a true gorilla, but a close cousin, and belongs in the Superfamily Hominoidea with gorillas, chimpanzees, orangutans, gibbons, and human beings. His exceptional size might have evolved in response to his island isolation.'"

"What's a *super* family?"

"I don't really know, dear."

"What's a gibbon?"

"Another sort of monkey, I suppose."

"But we don't believe in evolution, do we?"

"No, we don't."

"So God made Kong, just like he made us?"

"Yes, honey. God made Kong."

And then there's a pause, and Ann holds her breath, wishing she were still dozing, still lost in her terrible dreams, because this waking world is so much more terrible.

"I want to see the *Tyrannosaurus* again," says the little girl, "and the *Triceratops*, too." Her mother says okay, there's just enough time to see the dinosaurs again before we have to meet your Daddy, and Ann sits still and listens to their footsteps on the polished marble floor, growing fainter and fainter until silence has at last been restored to the alcove. But now the sterile, drab museum smells are gone, supplanted by the various rank odors of the apartment Jack rented for the both of them before he shipped out on a merchant steamer, the *Polyphemus*, bound for the Azores and then Lisbon and the Mediterranean. He never made it much farther than São Miguel, because the steamer was torpedoed by a Nazi U-boat and went down with all hands onboard. Ann opens her eyes, and the strange dream of the museum and the ape's skeleton has already begun to fade. It isn't morning yet, and the lamp beside the bed washes the tiny room with yellow-white light that makes her eyes ache.

She sits up, pushing the sheets away, exposing the ratty grey mattress underneath. The bedclothes are damp with her sweat and with radiator steam, and she reaches for the half-empty gin bottle there beside the lamp. The booze used to keep the dreams at bay, but these last few months, since she got the telegram informing her that Jack Driscoll was drowned and given up for dead and she would never be seeing him again, the nightmares have seemed hardly the least bit intimidated by alcohol. She squints at the clock, way over on the chifforobe, and sees that it's not yet even four a.m. Still hours until sunrise, hours until the bitter comfort of winter sunlight through the bedroom curtains. She tips the bottle to her lips, and the liquor tastes like turpentine and regret and everything she's lost in the last three years. Better she would have never been anything more than a starving woman stealing apples and oranges and bread to try to stay alive, better she would have never stepped foot on the *Venture*. Better she would have died in the green hell of that uncharted island. She can easily imagine a thousand ways it might have gone better, all grim, but better than *this* drunken half-life. She does not torture herself with fairy-tale fantasies of happy endings that never were and never will be. There's enough pain in the world without that luxury.

She takes another swallow from the bottle, then reminds herself that it has to last until morning and sets it back down on the table. But morning seems at least as far away as that night on the island, as far away as the carcass of the sailor she married. Often, she dreams of him, mangled by shrapnel and gnawed by the barbed teeth of deep-sea fish, burned alive and rotted beyond recognition, tangled in the wreckage and ropes and cables of a ship somewhere at the bottom of the Atlantic Ocean. He peers out at her with eyes that are no longer eyes at all, but only empty sockets where eels and spiny albino crabs nestle. She usually wakes screaming from those dreams, wakes to the bastard next door pounding on the wall with the heel of a shoe or just his bare fist and shouting how he's gonna call the cops if she can't keep it down. He has a job and has to sleep, and he can't have some goddamn rummy broad half the bay over or gone crazy with the DTs keeping him awake. The old Italian cunt who runs this dump, she says she's tired of hearing the complaints, and either the hollering stops or Ann will have to find another place to flop. She tries not to think about how she'll have to leave soon, anyway. She had a little money stashed in the lining of her coat, from all the interviews she gave the papers and magazines and the newsreel people, but now it's almost gone. Soon, she'll be back out on the bum, sleeping in mission beds or worse places, whoring for the sauce and as few bites of food as she can possibly get by on. Another month, at most, and isn't that what they mean by coming full circle?

She lies down again, trying not to smell herself or the pillowcase or the sheets, thinking about bright July sun falling warm between green leaves. And soon, she drifts off once more, listening to the rumble of a garbage truck down on Canal Street, the rattle of its engine and the squeal of its breaks not so very different from the primeval grunts and cries that filled the torrid air of the ape's profane cathedral.

And perhaps now she is lying safe and drunk in a squalid Bowery tenement and only dreaming away the sorry dregs of her life, and it's not the freezing morning when Jack led her from the skyscraper's spire down to the bedlam of Fifth Avenue. Maybe these are nothing more than an alcoholic's fevered recollections, and she is not being bundled in wool blankets and shielded from reporters and photographers and the sight of the ape's shattered body.

"It's over," says Jack, and she wants to believe that's true, by all the saints in Heaven and all the sinners in Hell, wherever and whenever she is, she wants to believe that it is finally and irrevocably over. There is not one moment to be relived, not ever again, because it has *ended*, and she is rescued, like Beauty somehow delivered from the clutching paws of the Beast. But there is so much commotion, the chatter of confused and frightened bystanders, the triumphant, confident cheers and shouting of soldiers and policemen, and she's begging Jack to get her out of it, away from it. It *must* be real, all of it, real and here and now, because she has never been so horribly cold in her dreams. She shivers and stares up at the narrow slice of sky visible between the buildings. The summit of that tallest of all tall towers is already washed with dawn, but down here on the street, it may as well still be midnight.

Life is just a bowl of cherries.
Don't take it serious; it's too mysterious.
At eight each morning I have got a date,
To take my plunge 'round the Empire State.
You'll admit it's not the berries,
In a building that's so tall...

"It's over," Jack assures her for the tenth or twentieth or fiftieth time. "They got him. The airplanes got him, Ann. He can't hurt you, not anymore."

And she's trying to remember through the clamor of voices and machines and the popping of flash bulbs – *Did he hurt me? Is that what happened?* – when the crowd divides like the holy winds of Jehovah parting the waters for Moses, and for the first time she can see what's left of the ape. She screams, and they all *think* she's screaming in terror at the sight of a monster. They do not know the truth, and maybe she does not yet know herself and it will be weeks or months before she fully comprehends why she is standing there screaming, unable to look away from the impossible, immense mound of black fur and jutting white bone and the dark rivulets of blood leaking sluggishly from the dead and vanquished thing.

"Don't," Jack says, and he covers her eyes. "It's nothing you need to see."

So she does *not* see, shutting her bright blue eyes and all the eyes of her soul, the eyes without and those other eyes within. Shutting *herself*, slamming closed doors and windows of perception, and how could she have known that she was locking in more than she was locking out. *Don't look at it*, he said, much too late, and these images are burned forever into her lidless, unsleeping mind's eye.

A sable hill from which red torrents flow.

Ann kneels in clay and mud the colour of a slaughterhouse floor, all the shades of shit and blood and gore, and dips her fingertips into the stream. She has performed this simple act of prostration times beyond counting, and it no longer holds for her any revulsion. She comes here from her nest high in the smoldering ruins of Manhattan and places her hand inside the wound, like St. Thomas fondling the pierced side of Christ. She comes down to remember, because there is an unpardonable sin in forgetting such a forfeiture. In this deep canyon molded not by geologic upheaval and erosion but by the tireless, automatic industry of man, she bows her head before the black hill. God sleeps there below the hill, and one day he will awaken from his slumber, for all those in the city are not faithless. Some still remember and follow the buckled blacktop paths, weaving their determined pilgrims' way along decaying thoroughfares and between twisted girders and the tumbledown heaps of burnt-out rubble. The city was cast down when God fell from his throne (or was pushed, as some have dared to whisper), and his fall broke apart the ribs of the world and sundered even the progression of one day unto the next so that time must now spill backwards to fill in the chasm. Ann leans forward, sinking her hand in up to the wrist, and the steaming crimson stream begins to clot and scab where it touches her skin.

Above her, the black hill seems to shudder, to shift almost imperceptibly in its sleep.

She has thought repeatedly of drowning herself in the stream, has wondered what it would be like to submerge in those veins and be carried along through silent veils of silt and ruby-tinted light. She might dissolve and be no more than another bit of flotsam, unburdened by bitter memory and self-knowledge and these rituals to keep a comatose god alive. She would open her mouth wide, and as the air rushed from her lungs and across her mouth, she would fill herself with His blood. She has even entertained the notion that such a sacrifice would be enough to wake the black sleeper, and as the waters that are not waters carried her away, the god beast might stir. As she melted, He would open His eyes and shake Himself free of the holdfasts of that tarmac and cement and sewer-pipe grave. It *could* be that simple. In her waking dreams, she has learned there is incalculable magic in sacrifice.

Ann withdraws her hand from the stream, and blood drips from her fingers, rejoining the whole as it flows away north and east towards the noxious lake that has formed where once lay the carefully landscaped and sculpted conceits of Mr. Olmsted and Mr. Vaux's Central Park. She will not wipe her hand clean as would some infidel, but rather permit the blood to dry to a claret crust upon her skin, for she has already committed blasphemy enough for three lifetimes. The shuddering black hill is still again, and a vinegar wind blows through the tall grass on either side of the stream.

And then Ann realizes that she's being watched from the gaping brick maw that was a jeweler's window long ago. The frame is still rimmed round about with jagged crystal teeth waiting to snap shut on unwary dreamers, waiting to shred and pierce, starved for diamonds and sapphires and emeralds, but more than ready to accept mere meat. In dusty shafts of sunlight, Ann can see the form of a young girl gazing out at her.

"What do you want?" Ann calls to her, and a moment or two later, the girl replies.

"You have become a goddess," she says, moving a little nearer the broken shop window so that Ann might have a better look at her. "But even a goddess cannot dream forever. I have come a long way and through many perils to speak with you, Golden Mother, and I did not expect to find you sleeping and hiding in the lies told by dreams."

"I'm not hiding," Ann replies very softly, so softly she thinks surely the girl will not have heard.

"Forgive me, Golden Mother, but you are. You are seeking refuge in guilt that is not your guilt."

"I am not your mother," Ann tells her. "I have never been anyone's mother."

A branch whips around and catches her in the face, a leaf's razor edge to draw a nasty cut across her forehead. But the pain slices cleanly through exhaustion and shock and brings her suddenly back to herself, back to *this* night and *this* moment, their mad, headlong dash from the river to the gate. The Cyclopean wall rises up before them, towering above the tree tops. There cannot now be more than a hundred yards remaining between them and the safety of the gate, but the ape is so very close behind. A fire-eyed demon who refuses to be so easily cheated of his prize by mere mortal men. The jungle cringes around them, flinching at the cacophony of Kong's approach, and even the air seems to draw back from that typhoon of muscle and fury, his angry roars and thunderous footfalls to divide all creation. Her right hand is gripped tightly in Jack's left, and he's all but dragging her forward. Ann can no longer feel her bare feet, which have been bruised and gouged and torn, and it is a miracle she can still run at all. Now, she can make out the dim silhouettes of men standing atop the wall, white men with guns and guttering torches, and, for a moment, she allows herself to hope.

"You are needed, Golden Mother," the girl says, and then she steps through the open mouth of the shop window. The blistering sun shimmers off her smooth, dark skin. "You are needed *here* and *now*," she says. "That night and every way that it might have gone, but did not, are passed forever beyond your reach."

"You don't *see* what I can see," Ann tells the girl, hearing the desperation and resentment in her own voice.

And what she sees is the wall and that last barrier of banyan figs and tree ferns. What she sees is the open gate and the way out of this nightmare, the road home.

"Only dreams," the girl says, not unkindly, and she takes a step nearer the red stream. "Only the phantoms of things that have never happened and never will."

"No," says Ann, and she shakes her head. "We *made* it to the gate. Jack and I both, together. We ran and we ran and we ran, and the ape was right there on top of us all the way, so close that I could smell his breath. But we didn't look back, not even once. We *ran*, and, in the end, we made it to the gate."

"No, Golden Mother. It did not happen that way."

One of the sailors on the wall is shouting a warning now, and at first, Ann believes it's only because he can see Kong behind them. But then something huge lunges from the underbrush, all scales and knobby scutes, scrabbling talons and the blue-green iridescent flash of eyes fashioned for night hunting. The high, sharp quills sprouting from the creature's backbone clatter one against the other like bony castanets, and it snatches Jack Driscoll in its saurian jaws and drags him screaming into the reedy shadows. On the wall, someone shouts, and she hears the staccato report of rifle fire.

The brown girl stands on the far side of the stream flowing along Fifth Avenue, the tall grass murmuring about her knees. "You have become lost in All-At-Once time, and you must find your way back from the Everywhen. I can help."

"I do not *need* your help," Ann snarls. "You keep away from me, you goddamn, filthy heathen."

Beneath the vast, star-specked Indonesian sky, Ann Darrow stands alone. Jack is gone, taken by some unnamable abomination, and in another second the ape will be upon her. This is when she realizes that she's bleeding, a dark bloom unfolding from her right breast, staining the gossamer rags that are all that remain of her dress and underclothes. She doesn't yet feel the sting of the bullet, a single shot gone wild, intended for Jack's attacker, but finding her, instead. *I do not blame you*, she thinks, slowly collapsing, going down onto her knees in the thick carpet of moss and ferns. *It was an accident, and I do not blame anyone.*

"That is a lie," the girl says from the other side of the red stream. "You *do* blame them, Golden Mother, and you blame yourself, most of all."

Ann stares up at the dilapidated skyline of a city as lost in time as she, and the Vault of Heaven turns above them like a dime-store kaleidoscope.

Once I built a railroad, I made it run, made it race against time. Once I built a railroad; now it's done. Brother, can you spare a dime? Once I built a tower, up to the sun, brick, and rivet, and lime; Once I built a tower, now it's done. Brother, can you spare a dime?

"When does this end?" she asks, asking the girl or herself or no one at all. "*Where* does it end?"

"Take my hand," the girl replies and reaches out to Ann, a bridge spanning the rill and time and spanning all these endless possibilities. "Take my hand and come back over. Just step across and stand with me."

"No," Ann hears herself say, though it isn't at all what she *wanted* to say or what she *meant* to say. "No, I can't do that. I'm sorry."

And the air around her reeks of hay and sawdust, human filth and beer and cigarette smoke, and the sideshow barker is howling his line of ballyhoo to all the rubes who've paid their two-bits to get a seat under the tent. All the yokels and hayseeds who have come to point and whisper and laugh and gawk at the figure cowering inside the cage.

"Them bars there, they are solid carbon *steel*, mind you," the barker informs them. "Manufactured special for us by the same Pittsburgh firm that supplies prison bars to Alcatraz. Ain't nothing else known to man strong enough to contain *her*, and if not for those iron bars, well…rest assured, my good people, we have not in the *least* exaggerated the threat she poses to life and limb, in the absence of such precautions."

Inside the cage, Ann squats in a corner, staring out at all the faces staring in. Only she has not been Ann Darrow in years – just ask the barker or the garish canvas flaps rattling in the chilly breeze of an Indiana autumn evening. She is the Ape Woman of Sumatra, captured at great personal risk by intrepid explorers and hauled out into the incandescent light of the Twentieth Century. She is naked, except for the moth-eaten scraps of buffalo and bear pelts they have given her to wear. Every inch of exposed skin is smeared with dirt and offal and whatever other filth has accumulated in her cage since it was last mucked out. Her snarled and matted hair hangs in her face, and there's nothing the least bit human in the guttural serenade of growls and hoots and yaps that escapes her lips.

The barker slams his walking cane against the iron bars, and she throws her head back and howls. A woman in the front row faints and has to be carried outside.

"She was the queen and the goddess of the strange world she knew," bellows the barker, "but now she comes to civilization, merely a captive, a show to gratify your curiosity. Learned men at colleges – forsaking the words of the Good Book – proclaim that we are *all* descended from monkeys. And, I'll tell you, seeing *this* wretched bitch, I am *almost* tempted to believe them, and also to suspect that in dark and far-flung corners of the globe there exist to this day beings *still* more simian than human, lower even than your ordinary niggers, hottentots, negritos, and lowly African pygmies."

Ann Darrow stands on the muddy bank of the red stream, and the girl from the ruined and vine-draped jewelry shop holds out her hand, the brown-skinned girl who has somehow found her way into the most secret, tortured recesses of Ann's consciousness.

"The world is still here," the girl says, "only waiting for you to return."

"I have heard another tale of her origin," the barker confides. "But I must *warn* you, it is not fit for the faint of heart or the ears of decent Christian women."

There is a long pause, while two or three of the women rise from their folding chairs and hurriedly leave the tent. The barker tugs at his pink suspenders and grins an enormous, satisfied grin, then glances into the cage.

"As I was saying," he continues, "there is *another* story. The Chinaman who sold me this pitiful oddity of human *de*volution said that its mother was born of French aristocracy, the lone survivor of a calamitous shipwreck, cast ashore on black volcanic sands. There, in the hideous misery and perdition of that Sumatran wilderness, the poor woman was *defiled* by some lustful species of jungle imp, though whether it were chimp or baboon I cannot say."

There is a collective gasp from the men and women inside the tent, and the barker rattles the bars again, eliciting another irate howl from its occupant.

"And here before you is the foul *spawn* of that unnatural union of anthropoid and womankind. The aged Celestial confided to me that the mother expired shortly after giving birth, God rest her immortal soul. Her death was a mercy, I should think, as she would have lived always in shame and horror at having borne into the world this shameful, misbegotten progeny."

"Take my hand," the girl says, reaching into the iron cage. "You do not have to stay here. Take my hand, Golden Mother, and I will help you find the path."

There below the hairy black tumulus, the great slumbering titan belching forth the headwaters of all the earth's rivers, Ann Darrow takes a single hesitant step into the red stream. *This is the most perilous part of the journey,* she thinks, reaching to accept the girl's outstretched hand. *It wants me, this torrent, and if I am not careful, it will pull me down and drown me for my trespasses.*

"It's only a little ways more," the girl tells her and smiles. "Just step across to me."

The barker raps his silver-handled walking cane sharply against the bars of the cage, so that Ann remembers where she is and when, and doing so, forgets herself again. For the benefit of all those licentious, ogling eyes, all those slack jaws that have paid precious quarters to be shocked and titillated, she bites the head off a live hen, and when she has eaten her fill of the bird, she spreads her thighs and masturbates for the delight of her audience with filthy, bloodstained fingers.

Elsewhen, she takes another step towards the girl, and the softly gurgling stream wraps itself greedily about her calves. Her feet sink deeply into the slimy bottom, and the sinuous, clammy bodies of conger eels and salamanders wriggle between her ankles and twine themselves about her legs. She cannot reach the girl, and the opposite bank may as well be a thousand miles away.

In a smoke-filled screening room, Ann Darrow sits beside Carl Denham while the footage he shot on the island almost a year ago flickers across the screen at twenty-four frames per second. They are not alone, the room half-filled with low-level studio men from RKO and Paramount and Universal and a couple of would-be financiers lured here by the Hollywood rumor mill. Ann watches the images revealed in grainy shades of grey, in overexposed whites and underexposed smudges of black.

"What exactly are we supposed to be looking at?" someone asks, impatiently.

"We shot this stuff from the top of the wall, once Englehorn's men had managed to frighten away all the goddamn tar babies. Just wait. It's coming."

"Denham, we've already been sitting here half an hour. This shit's pretty underwhelming, you ask me. You're better off sticking to the safari pictures."

"It's *coming*," Denham insists and chomps anxiously at the stem of his pipe.

And Ann knows he's right, that it's coming, because this is not the first time she's seen the footage. Up there on the screen, the eye of the camera looks out over the jungle canopy, and it always reminds her of Gustave Doré's visions of Eden from her mother's copy of *Paradise Lost*, or the illustrations of lush Pre-Adamite landscapes from a geology book she once perused in the New York Public Library.

"Honestly, Mr. Denham," the man from RKO sighs. "I've got a meeting in twenty minutes – "

"*There*," Denham says, pointing at the screen. "There it is. Right fucking *there*. Do you see it?"

And the studio men and the would-be financiers fall silent as the beast's head and shoulders emerge from the tangle of vines and orchid-encrusted branches and wide palm fronds. It stops and turns its mammoth head towards the camera, glaring hatefully up at the wall and directly into the smoke-filled room, across a million years and nine thousand miles. There is a dreadful, unexpected intelligence in those dark eyes as the creature tries to comprehend the purpose of the weird, pale men and their hand-crank contraption perched there on the wall above it. Its lips fold back, baring gigantic canines, eyeteeth longer than a grown man's hand, and there is a low, rumbling sound, then a screeching sort of yell, before the thing the natives called *Kong* turns and vanishes back into the forest.

"Great god," the Universal man whispers.

"Yes, gentlemen," says Denham, sounding very pleased with himself and no longer the least bit anxious, certain that he has them all right where he wants them. "That's just *exactly* what those tar babies think. They worship it and offer up human sacrifices. Why, they wanted Ann here. Offered us six of their women so she could become the *bride* of Kong. And *there's* our story, gentlemen."

"Great god," the Universal man says again, louder than before.

"But an expedition like this costs money," Denham tells them, getting down to brass tacks as the reel ends and the lights come up. "I mean to make a picture the whole damn *world's* gonna pay to see, and I can't do that without committed backers."

"Excuse me," Ann says, rising from her seat, feeling sick and dizzy and wanting to be away from these men and all their talk of profit and spectacle, wanting to drive the sight of the ape from her mind, once and for all.

"I'm fine, really," she tells them. "I just need some fresh air."

On the far side of the stream, the brown girl urges her forward; no more than twenty feet left to go and Ann will have reached the other side.

"You're waking up," the girl says. "You're almost there. Give me your hand."

I'm only going over Jordan

I'm only going over home...

And the moments flash and glimmer as the dream breaks apart around her, and the barker rattles the iron bars of a stinking cage, and her empty stomach rumbles as she watches men and women bending over their plates in a lunch room, and she sits on a bench in an alcove on the third floor of the American Museum of Natural History. Crossing the red stream, Ann Darrow hemorrhages time and possibility, all these seconds and hours and days vomited forth like a bellyful of tainted meals. She shuts her eyes and takes another step, sinking even deeper in the mud, the blood risen now as high as her waist. Here is the morning they brought her down from the Empire State Building, and the morning she wakes in her nest on Skull Mountain, and the night she watched Jack Driscoll devoured well within sight of the archaic gates. Here's the Bowery tenement, and here the screening room, and here a fallen Manhattan, crumbling and lost in the storm-tossed gulf of eons, set adrift no differently than she has set herself adrift. Every moment, all at once, each as real as every other; never mind the contradictions; each moment damned and equally inevitable, all following from a stolen apple and the man who paid the Greek a dollar to look the other way.

The world is a steamroller.

Once I built a railroad; now it's done.

She stands alone in the seaward lee of the great wall and knows that its gates have been forever shut against her *and* all the daughters of men yet to come. This hallowed, living wall of human bone and sinew erected to protect what scrap of Paradise lies inside, not the dissolute, iniquitous world of men sprawling beyond its borders. Winged Cherubim stand guard on either side, and in their leonine forepaws they grasp flaming swords forged in unknown furnaces before the coming of the World, fiery brands that reach all the way to the sky and about which spin the hearts of newborn hurricanes. The molten eyes of the Cherubim watch her every move, and their indifferent minds know her every secret thought, these dispassionate servants of the vengeful god of her father and her mother. Neither tears nor all her words will ever wring mercy from these sentinels, for they know precisely what she is, and they know her crimes.

I am she who cries out,
and I am cast forth upon the face of the earth.

The starving, ragged woman who stole an apple. Starving in body and in mind, starving in spirit, if so base a thing as she can be said to possess a soul. Starving, and ragged in all ways.

I am the members of my mother.
I am the barren one
and many are her sons.
I am she whose wedding is great,
and I have not taken a husband.

And as is the way of all exiles, she cannot kill hope that her exile will one day end. Even the withering gaze of the Cherubim cannot kill that hope, and so hope is the cruelest reward.

Brother, can you spare a dime?

"Take my hand," the girl says, and Ann Darrow feels herself grown weightless and buoyed from that foul brook, hauled free of the morass of her own nightmares and regret onto a clean shore of verdant mosses and zoysiagrass, bamboo and reeds, and the girl leans down and kisses her gently on the forehead. The girl smells like sweat and nutmeg and the pungent yellow pigment dabbed across her cheeks. The girl is salvation.

"You have come *home* to us, Golden Mother," she says, and there are tears in her eyes.

"You don't see," Ann whispers, the words slipping out across her tongue and teeth and lips like her own ghost's death rattle. If the jungle air were not so still and heavy, not so turgid with the smells of living and dying, decay and birth and conception, she's sure it would lift her as easily as it might a stray feather and carry her away. She lies very still, her head cradled in the girl's lap, and the stream flowing past them is only water and the random detritus of any forest stream.

"The world blinds those who cannot close their eyes," the girl tells her. "You were not always a god and have come here from some outer, dissolute world, so it may be you were never taught how to travel that path and not become lost in All-At-Once time."

Ann Darrow digs her fingers into the soft, damp earth, driving them into the loam of the jungle floor, holding on and still expecting *this* scene to shift, to unfurl, to send her tumbling pell-mell and head over heels into some other *now*, some other *where*.

And sometime later, when she's strong enough to stand again, and the sickening vertiginous sensation of fluidity has at last begun to ebb, the girl helps Ann to her feet, and together they follow the narrow dirt trail leading back up this long ravine to the temple. Like Ann, the girl is naked save a leather breechcloth tied about her waist. They walk together beneath the sagging boughs of trees that must have been old before Ann's great-great grandmothers were born, and here and there is ample evidence of the civilization that ruled the island in some murky, immemorial past – glimpses of great stone idols worn away by time and rain and the humid air, disintegrating walls and archways leaning at such precarious angles Ann cannot fathom why they have not yet succumbed to gravity. Crumbling bas-reliefs depicting the loathsome gods and demons and the bizarre reptilian denizens of this place. As they draw nearer to the temple, the ruins become somewhat more intact, though even here the splayed roots of the trees are slowly forcing the masonry apart. The roots put Ann in mind of the tentacles of gargantuan octopuses or cuttlefish, and that is how she envisions the spirit of the jungles and marshes fanning out around this ridge – grey tentacles advancing inch by inch, year by year, inexorably reclaiming what has been theirs all along.

As she and the girl begin to climb the steep, crooked steps leading up from the deep ravine – stones smoothed by untold generations of footsteps – Ann stops to catch her breath and asks the brown girl how she knew where to look, how it was she found her at the stream. But the girl only stares at her, confused and uncomprehending, and then she frowns and shakes her head and says something in the native tongue. In Anne's long years on the island, since the *Venture* deserted her and sailed away with what remained of the dead ape, she has never learned more than a few words of that language, and she has never tried to teach this girl, nor any of her people, English. The girl looks back the way they've come; she presses the fingers of her left hand against her breast, above her heart, then uses the same hand to motion towards Ann.

Life is just a bowl of cherries.

Don't take it serious; it's too mysterious.

By sunset, Ann has taken her place on the rough-hewn throne carved from beds of coral limestone thrust up from the seafloor in the throes of the island's cataclysmic genesis. As night begins to gather once again, torches are lit, and the people come bearing sweet-smelling baskets of flowers and fruit, fish and the roasted flesh of gulls and rats and crocodiles. They lay multicolored garlands and strings of pearls at her feet, a necklace of ankylosaur teeth, rodent claws, and monkey vertebrae, and she is only the Golden Mother once again. They bow and genuflect, and the tropical night rings out with joyous songs she cannot understand. The men and woman decorate their bodies with yellow paint in an effort to emulate Ann's blonde hair, and a sort of pantomime is acted out for her benefit, as it is once every month, on the night of the new moon. She does not *need* to understand their words to grasp its meaning – the coming of the *Venture* from somewhere far away, Ann offered up as the bride of a god, her marriage and the death of Kong, and the obligatory ascent of the Golden Mother from a hellish underworld to preside in his stead. She who steals a god's heart must herself become a god.

The end of one myth and the beginning of another, the turning of a page. *I am not lost,* Ann thinks. *I am right here, right now – here and now where, surely, I must belong,* and she watches the glowing bonfire embers rising up to meet the dark sky. She knows she will see that terrible black hill again, the hill that is not a hill and its fetid crimson river, but she knows, too, that there will always be a road back from her dreams, from that All-At-Once tapestry of possibility and penitence. In her dreams, she will be lost and wander those treacherous, deceitful paths of Might-Have-Been, and always she will wake and find herself once more.

Notes

"The Steam Dancer (1896)" ~ I strongly suspect this is the most reprinted of the recent crop of "steampunk" stories. Fortunately, I'm extremely fond of it. "The Steam Dancer (1896)" originally appeared in the June 2007 (#19) issue of my monthly e-zine, *Sirenia Digest*, and has since been reprinted in *Subterranean: Tales of Dark Fantasy* (2008), *Steampunk Reloaded* (2010), *The Mammoth Book of Steampunk* (2012), and *Lightspeed Magazine* (2012) where it can be found as in both prose *and* audio format. Frankly, I think this story deserved a Nebula. Or a Hugo. Either one. Probably not both, though; I'm not greedy. It was written in June 2007.

"The Maltese Unicorn" ~ Here's a story that began as a joke. Ellen Datlow had invited me to write a story for *Supernatural Noir*, an anthology of, well, supernatural noir. I'm a huge fan of noir – film and prose – but had a lot of trouble coming up with a story I wanted to write. In my blog (5/6/10), I wrote, "Last night, trying to sleep, thinking about potential stories, the title 'The Maltese Unicorn' popped into my head. Gagh. No, I will *not* be writing a story called 'The Maltese Unicorn.' I wanted to punch myself in the face just for *thinking* of it." But then, the next day, the title lingered, and a plot involving a dildo carved from a unicorn's horn began to take shape. I sheepishly pitched it to Ellen. She said, "Go for it!" So, I did. The homages to Dashiell Hammett and Raymond Chandler are, of course, obvious. The story was written in May and June of 2010.

"One Tree Hill (The World As Cataclysm)" ~ This is the newest of the stories included in this collection, written in July 2012 for Issue #80 of *Sirenia Digest*. It has a sort of quiet wrongness – weirdness – about it that I'm almost always striving for, but rarely achieve.

"The Collier's Venus (1898)" - Few short stories have given me as much trouble as this one did. I'm pretty sure it actually did not *want* to be written. But it was, in October and November 2008, for Ellen Datlow's *Naked City* anthology. It's one of five stories I've set in the fictional frontier town of Cherry Creek, Colorado. I wanted the title to be "The Automatic Mastodon," but the story, it had other plans.

"Galápagos" - Jonathan Strahan asked me to write a story for *Eclipse Three*, but I can't recall much about this story's genesis. I do, however, recall the title had originally been intended for a different story entirely, and that "Galápagos" was a bitch to get started. It earned a place on the Honor List for the 2009 James Tiptree, Jr. Award, for its exploration of gender, and of that I am very, very proud.

"Tall Bodies" - Another story from *Sirenia Digest* #80, and like "One Tree Hill," this one went right where I wanted it to go. The feat of capturing the inexplicable and knowing that it must *remain* inexplicable, or there was no point in writing the damned thing. I suspect this story was, at least in part, inspired by Richard A. Kirk's beautiful, disarming endpapers to mine and Poppy Z. Brite's 2001 collaboration, *Wrong Things*.

"As Red As Red" - Written in March and April of 2009, for Ellen Datlow and Nick Mamatas' *Haunted Legends* anthology, it was inspired in part by a couple of miserably cold, slushy days in Newport. And, too, by pretty much everything that inspired *The Red Tree*, which I'd finished the previous October. In a sense, "As Red As Red" is a sideways footnote to the novel, exploring a few bits of Rhode Island folklore that didn't make the final cut. But it also presages some of the major themes of *The Drowning Girl: A Memoir*, and so acts as a sort of bridge between those two novels. The story was nominated for the Shirley Jackson Award.

"Hydraguros" - This story originally appeared in *Sirenia Digest* #50 (January 2010), and was then reprinted in *Subterranean: Tales of Dark Fantasy 2*. It's a prime example of the sort of science fiction story that I most enjoy writing. I'm not sure what to call it, though. Near future neo-noir? David Bowie's *Outside* (1995) first led me to discovering this voice, this approach, which I have also employed in tales like "In View of

Nothing" and "A Season of Broken Dolls." Two years on, "Hydraguros" remains a personal favorite.

"Slouching Towards the House of Glass Coffins" ~ And here's another sort of science fiction entirely. This story was written in August 2011, for *Sirenia Digest* #69. I keep going back to Mars. This story bears the mark of my frustration with the way that almost all science fiction ignores the reality of linguistic evolution, largely, I suspect because working out and employing the results of such phenomena as unidirectional short-term drift and cyclic long-term drift is simply to much trouble. Add to that my suspicion that most readers don't want to have to work that hard, and, unfortunately, the end product is a lopsided undertaking. Writers imagine radically new technologies and cultures, but ignore that most fundamental aspect of story: the language by which it is conveyed. With "Slouching Towards the House of Glass Coffins," I only begin to superficially address the problem; I've done so to much greater degrees in some of my (not surprisingly) more obscure sf. Also, I should probably mention this story shares quite a bit in common with an earlier piece, "Bradbury Weather."

"Tidal Forces" ~ Another story that first appeared in *Sirenia Digest* (#55). It was later reprinted in Jonathan Strahan's *Eclipse Four.* I wanted to write something about individual dissolution, something about a personal apocalypse, and about intimacy and the lengths that may be necessary to save the ones we love. It's an odd tale, as mine go, in that it has, I think, a "happy ending." Also, only after finishing "Tidal Forces" did I realize that I'd already written almost the exact story twice before: "Sanderlings" (2010) and "The Bone's Prayer" (2009). It was an eerie realization. Regardless, I finally got it right with "Tidal Forces," which was written in June 2010, and was chosen for Jonathan Strahan's *The Best Science Fiction and Fantasy of the Year Volume Six* (Jonathan really liked this story!).

"The Sea Troll's Daughter" ~ I was approached by Lou Anders and Jonathan Strahan to write a sword and sorcery story, which was a thing I'd never even attempted. After a bit of dithering, a sort of feminist retelling of *Beowulf* occurred to me (I very rarely consider my stories to have any sort of sociopolitical slant, so this one is also unusual in that respect). The original title was "Wormchild," though I discarded that almost immediately. Written in June and July of 2009, it first appeared in *Swords and Dark Magic: The New Sword and Sorcery* (2010), and was later reprinted in *The Sword and Sorcery Anthology* (2012). Truthfully, this is a story that I believe deserved a lot more attention than it received. Yeah, I do say so myself. And, while I'm at it, "The Sea Troll's Daughter" should have at least been *nominated* for a World Fantasy Award.

"Random Thoughts Before a Fatal Crash" ~ Anyone familiar with my work should also be familiar with one of my recurring characters, a fairy-tale obsessed artist named Albert Perrault, who first appeared in "The Road of Pins," written way back in 2001. Though the story included his death, he subsequently played a crucial role in several stories, culminating with his pivotal part in my novel *The Drowning Girl: A Memoir* (2012). The narrator concludes with a section labeled "Back Pages" (thank you, Bob Dylan), and though "Random Notes Before a Fatal Crash" was written in March and April 2011 for *Sirenia Digest* #64, and subsequently reprinted in *Subterranean Magazine* (Spring 2012), I got it in my head that this rather long piece belonged in "Back Pages." Peter Straub quickly and firmly pointed out that it didn't, and it was removed from the manuscript before publication. Thank you again, Peter, for stopping me from breaking the book. Also, "The Magdalene of Gévaudan" was written by Sonya Taaffe, and is the only part of "Random Notes Before a Fatal Crash" that *was* included in *The Drowning Girl: A Memoir*. The title *Last Drink Bird Heard*, blame Jeff VanderMeer for that.

"The Ape's Wife" ~ This story was written in April 2007 for *Clarkesworld Magazine,* and was voted "readers' favorite" for that year. It was also chosen for Stephen Jones' *The Mammoth Book of Best New Horror (Volume 19).* As with "Emptiness Spoke Eloquent" and "From Cabinet 34, Drawn 6" before it, "The Ape's Wife" is the result of my occasional desire to play around with how stories might have ended in some alternate universe or another. *King Kong* was one of the many things that, as a child, fostered my love of paleontology, and it was wonderful repaying that debt.

Black Helicopters (included only with the limited edition) ~ Having just finished the only genuinely wretched novel of my career (title tactfully withheld), I needed to write something I would love, something that would allow me to sink back into the dense and slippery language that is natural to me. That and a nonlinear narrative. A nonlinear narrative that preserved the *in*explicable, instead of making it *ex*plicable. That said, *Black Helicopters* doesn't feel finished. I suspect I could easily expand it to 50,000 words. However, this would be an unfurling of events (earlier and later events) within story that remain currently unspoken, not the elucidation of that which has been written. I can't help believe it should be a short novel, not a novella. There's too much of it still rattling about my head.

Acknowledgements

My thanks to the editors who solicited and bought the tales that first appeared in anthologies and magazines, and to the editors who published reprints; to the many subscribers to *Sirenia Digest*, for they keep the lights on (literally *and* metaphorically); to William K. Schafer of Subterranean Press, who not only published this collection, but who suggested its title (and insisted I write *Black Helicopters*) and is an amazingly patient man; to Vincent Locke for his illustrations and Vincent Chong for his cover; to Kyle Cassidy for the author's photo; to Merrilee Heifetz and Sarah Nagel at Writers House, saviors, the both of them; to Sonya Taaffe for "The Magdalene of Gévaudan"; to Denise Davis of Brown University for French translation on *Black Helicopters* (8); to Lee Moyer; and to my partner, Kathryn A. Pollnac, who hasn't yet murdered me in my sleep, though I certainly have it coming.

Author's Biography

Caitlín R. Kiernan is the author of several novels, including *The Red Tree* (nominated for the Shirley Jackson and World Fantasy awards) and, most recently, *The Drowning Girl: A Memoir* (winner of the Bram Stoker and James Tiptree, Jr. awards, nominated for the Nebula, British Fantasy, Mythopoeic, Locus, Shirley Jackson, and World Fantasy awards). Her tales of the weird, fantastic, and macabre have been collected in several volumes, including *Tales of Pain and Wonder*; *From Weird and Distant Shores*; *To Charles Fort, With Love; Alabaster*; *A is for Alien*; *The Ammonite Violin & Others; Confessions of a Five-Chambered Heart*; and *Two Worlds and In Between: The Best of Caitlín R. Kiernan (Volume One).* Her early erotica has been collected in two volumes: *Frog Toes and Tentacles* and *Tales from the Woeful Platypus*. From 1996 to 2001, she scripted *The Dreaming* for DC/Vertigo, and has recently returned to graphic novels with her critically acclaimed series, *Alabaster* (Dark Horse Comics). Trained as a vertebrate paleontologist, her research has appeared in the *Journal of Vertebrate Paleontology*, *Journal of Paleontology*, *The Mosasaur*, and the *International Bulletin of Zoological Nomenclature.* She lives in Providence, Rhode Island with her partner Kathryn and two Siamese cats.

About the Font

This book was set in Garamond, a typeface named after the French punch-cutter Claude Garamond (c. 1480–1561). Garamond has been chosen here for its ability to convey a sense of fluidity and consistency. It has been chosen by the author because this typeface is among the most legible and readable old-style serif print typefaces. In terms of ink usage, Garamond is also considered to be one of the most eco-friendly major fonts.